THE CHROMATIC COURT

Edited by Peter Rawlik

Illustrated by Johannes Chazot

Featuring designs by Sophie Iles

18THWALL

THE CHROMATIC COURT
An 18thWall Productions book published by
arrangement with Peter Rawlik
verba mea in minibus
desiderium meum
Cover and illustrations by Johannes Chazot
Jacket Design by Elisgraphics
Design by Sophie Iles
Line-edited by Stephanie Perisić

ISBN-13: 978-1-946033-10-9
ISBN-10: 1-946033-10-3

Table of Contents

THE COLOR OF THINGS

Peter Rawlik

For better or worse, there has grown up around Hastur an entire sub-mythos linking him to Robert W. Chambers' King in Yellow. What Howard Phillips Lovecraft intended with those lines—those tantalizing unspecific lines—that he wrote in *The Whisperer in Darkness*:

> *I found myself faced by names and terms that I had heard elsewhere in the most hideous of connections— Yuggoth, Great Cthulhu, Tsathoggua, Yog-Sothoth, R'Lyeh, Nyarlathotep, Azathoth, Hastur, Yian, Leng, the Lake of Hali, Bethmoora, the Yellow Sign, L'mur-Kathulos, Bran and the Magnum Innominandum—and was drawn back through nameless aeons and inconceivable dimensions to worlds of elder, outer entity at which the crazed author of the Necronomicon had only guessed in the vaguest way.... There is a whole secret cult of evil men (a man of your mystical erudition will understand me when I link them with Hastur and the Yellow Sign) devoted to the purpose of tracking them down and injuring them on behalf of the*

monstrous powers from other dimensions.

In my opinion it was likely just another in a long line of literary jests, inserting nods to Robert E. Howard, Clark Ashton Smith, Ambrose Bierce and Robert W. Chambers, nothing more. Yet, from that simple association August Derleth and others set about comingling the mythos of Hastur with that of the King in Yellow and setting the two on a path of inter-tradition cosmic miscegenation that eventually resulted in the conflation of the two entities. Though there are those who consider themselves purists, and demand a Hastur-free King in Yellow (particularly my colleague Joseph Pulver), for most Cthulhu Mythos enthusiasts, the King in Yellow has become an avatar of Hastur.

There are a myriad of authors who have dabbled in the melding of the two entities, and many examples can be found in the anthologies such as Lin Carter's *The Spawn of Cthulhu*, Robert M. Price's *The Hastur Cycle*, and Peter Worthy's *Rehearsals for Oblivion*. I myself played into this in my homage to Frank Herbert's *Dune*, "In the Hall of the Yellow King," found in Silvia Moreno-Garcia's *Future Lovecraft* and later as part of my chronicle *The Peaslee Papers*. If I had left it at that perhaps nothing else would have come of it, but somehow, somewhen the idea struck me that if Hastur could have a color-based avatar, why couldn't the other cosmic entities of the mythos? It wasn't that much of a leap. Nyarlathotep already bore the epithet of the Black Man, and Rlim Shaikorath was the White Worm. Certain associations seemed obvious. The tipping point came when Brian M. Sammons asked me to provide a story for his Western-themed horror anthology *The Edge of Sundown*. My mind immediately went to gambling, and I saw the back room of a saloon with a table in the center and things, inhuman things, playing cards, but it was a wholly unfamiliar game, and the stakes were the universe itself. As a joke I based the rules for the Game of Mao (a nod to Arthur Machen) on Mau Mau and the colored card game Uno, both of which are card-shedding games and the latter of which is a favorite of my children. My one conceit in my story, "Drake Takes a Hand," is that the colored cards are linked to various mythos entities, and for the first time The Sepia Prince, an avatar of Cthulhu, appears. I should have left it at that, but I didn't. The Sepia Prince appears again in my story "The Sepia Prints" in Glynn Owen Barrass' anthology *In the Court of the Yellow King,*; this time he is a character excised from a production of The ing in Yellow play, but who still lingers in the basements of the Paris Opera House. This story also went on to form one of the chapters of my novel *Reanimatrix*, which was heavily influenced by Otto Preminger's *Laura*, David Lynch's *Twin Peaks*, and the first season of HBO's *True Detective* (amongst other things).

Things should have died there, but the idea still lingered—lurked in the ether—and one day I received a note from my colleague Micah Harris whom I knew from his work in the *Tales of the Shadowmen* anthologies (Black Coat Press), and his Cthulhu Mythos linked *The Eldritch Adventures of Becky Sharpe*. Would I be interested in doing an anthology based around the color-linked avatars? It was an interesting proposal, and one that I had to mull over for a week or so. I had edited *Legacy of the Reanimator* (with Brian M. Sammons) but that had been invitation only, I hadn't done an open call anthology before. I hemmed and hawed for a few days, but finally agreed. We would ask people to pick a color, a mythos entity and an art form and meld them all together into something that would both entertain and frighten, expanding on the color mythos, building what could only be described as *The Chromatic Court*. How bad could the open call possibly be? It was worse than I had imagined, but buried within the seemingly hundreds of submissions that bore no relation at all to our wants appeared stories that got exactly what we were looking for. Some from friends, some from familiar names, some from people I had never heard from before, but were suddenly pleased to have discovered.

Christine Morgan gave us a haunting tale of the countryside and the power of scent, while Joe Pulver presents a minor member of the court whose skill at manipulation and inspiration just might make you love her, or drive you mad. Paul StJohn Mackintosh gives us a tale of what one can see hidden in the architecture all around us, and what it might mean. Rick Lai has produced a mad melding of fiction, truths and half-truths that dwell in the Paris streets that somehow melds perfectly into Jon Black's "The Green Muse." John Linwood Grant takes us to the horror of the Great War in "The Songs of the Burning Men," which juxtaposes with Glynn Owen Barrass' rather amusing but still chilling "Curse of the White Inferno." Simon Bucher-Jones gives us his short but powerful "The Blues of the Endless Sky" which could only ever be followed by Micah Harris' "Tatterdemalion in Grey." David Bernard lightens the tone with the playful "The Frieze of Helmsley Ainsworth" (which reminds me of a *Night Gallery* episode) but Logan Noble drags us back into the deep forest of despair with "The Matron of the Wood." The entire collection is topped off by MaTT Loughlin's "The Duke of Rust" which took one of the more obscure members of the mythos and did something truly terrifying.

I welcome you to the Chromatic Court and if you find your visit enjoyable I hope that you shall return. There are other stories—good stories—that limitations forced us to leave out. But I want you to see them, they need to be seen, they are waiting, wanting to be seen. The court is waiting, its members lurking in the wings, fawning at the throne, calling your name. Can you hear them?

They can hear you.

When Lavender is
in Bloom

Christine Morgan

"It is a bad place for a stranger," the old man told me. "You'd better take a guide."

I turned to look at him. He sat frail and wizened in a wheelchair, wearing a soft heather-colored sweater. A crocheted blanket lay over his lap, suede slippers protruding from beneath its edge. How he had gotten up here to this cliffside viewpoint was, at first, beyond me. Then I saw, not far away, one of the many care-complexes clustered along the outskirts of the town, and supposed he must have wheeled his way over from there.

"I shall not lose myself," I replied, or hoped I did, in my careful guidebook French. The local dialect was different from the Rosetta Stone crash-course I'd undertaken before this trip, and I went about in perpetual fear of inadvertently insulting someone.

His smile was the saddest I'd ever seen, the sigh accompanying it a wistful breath of eternities. "That's what I said, so long ago. That's what I said. And of course I did lose myself. I lost myself and it was wonderful. I would have stayed lost there forever. You're American, aren't you?"

"Yes." I knew of fellow travelers who preferred pretending otherwise, claiming to be from Canada to escape the not-altogether-undeserved reputation, but I sensed no accusation in his query.

He nodded. "So was I, once."

A moment passed, a waiting pause that seemed to hang like a held breath between us.

"Once?" I asked, when it seemed an encouraging nudge was somehow expected.

"When I was young," he said. "Young, like you. American, like you. Though, when I set out for my day's ramble through the moors, I went with a gun upon my shoulder, thinking perhaps to hunt."

I held up my botanical collection kit. "I only hunt with this."

"Good. That's good. Quieter. More peaceful. Though there is something to be said for the older ways, as well. When hunting was as much art as sport."

Below us, where the steep switchbacked path I meant soon to descend met the sprawling denseness of hilly green grass and bracken I also meant soon to traverse, a brown hare bounded from the underbrush in long leaps as if to prove his point. A breeze wafted up to us, cool and sweetly fragrant, laden with the clean scents of nature. It stirred wisps of hair against my neck, long strands escaped from both braid and hiker's cap.

The old man looked me over, and I braced for the usual admonitions, as if every woman traveling abroad alone was sure to end up in some Eli Roth torture dungeon. Instead, he smiled again with his sad smile, and said, "Beautiful, and cruel."

"I beg your pardon?"

"The moors. Beautiful and cruel, like a woman. They are enchanted, you know. I used to go back often. As often as I could. Always searching...always hoping...that *this* would be the time, each time, and I would find my way again...my heart bade me try and try, even as my mind already accepted the truth. Had I not seen the stone? The shrine? Had I not read the words inscribed upon it? Oh, but fate is also beautiful and cruel, and history inexorable."

"I don't understand," I said.

He went on as if I hadn't spoken. "The past was set; I had been and gone and played my part. I left her. I did not wish to. I would have stayed. But fate, so cruel, so beautiful, had other plans. No matter how I retraced my steps, how long I wandered, how far I explored…no matter how many nights I spent sleeping there beneath the sky…and sometimes I would hear the whirr of wings, the cry of a hawk or hound, and such joy would leap within me…"

His voice trailed off into a quaver, even as tears trailed from the creased corners of his eyes.

"Monsieur…" I'd taken a half-step toward him, reaching out as if to place a hand upon his shoulder, moved by his evident grief despite my lack of understanding. Before I could complete the gesture, his own hand shot up and seized mine. His grip was tremulous, but surprisingly strong.

"I had seen the stone, the shrine," he repeated. "She died for love of me. She pined, she languished. Perhaps she believed I had abandoned her. I was torn from her, cruelly torn, and there would be no returning. I could not change the past."

Uncomfortable, if not quite alarmed, I tried gently to free myself. He held firm. His eyes met mine, and through their veil of tears they were sharp and bright.

"After a while," he said, "I stopped. I stopped trying. After years had gone by. So many years. She loved a *young* man, you see. A healthy one, and handsome. Not some ancient relic in a chair. What use would I be to her now, even if I did find my way?"

Someone came hurrying toward us, a bustling gingerish fellow with a broad and freckled face. He wore the kind of smock-top and pants I associated with hospital scrubs, in a shade somewhere between mint and moss. Various antiseptic smells—liquid sanitizer, bleach, iodine—hung around him in a cloud, and the fact he'd attempted to counter these with liberal applications of body spray and aftershave did not help the situation.

"Philip, Philip!" he chided in the sort of tone one would use with a wayward child. "Whatever are you doing out here? My apologies, mam'selle! Did he frighten you?"

"Of course not," I said. "We were merely talking."

The old man, Philip, had released my hand. His momentary vigor, the strength of his grip and the bright sharpness of his eyes, dulled. He sagged in his wheelchair, looking even frailer and more diminished. His gaze drifted off forlornly across the vast expanse of moors.

I was struck by a sudden, unfamiliar, almost overpowering urge to kneel and embrace him. To tell him that, yes, I knew what it was to yearn for what was lost, for history and bittersweet nostalgia.

Was that not why I'd come on this trip? To attempt, in my own fashion, to recapture bygone eras? To return to simpler times, reclaim the cleaner and purer essences of an earlier age? For personal reasons as well as for business, though my personal reasons might have been deemed less than acceptable in other than these tolerant, enlightened, more modern days.

The fellow in moss-mint scrubs came closer, further assailing me with an intensifying melange of chemicals. No doubt, he thought his grooming regimen would make a favorable impression on the ladies, be they nurses or doctors or visiting relatives of patients. Or, as was the current case, a chance-met vacationer such as myself. His grin broadened. Little did he know, of course, that such particular pursuit was an effort in futility to begin with, and his pungent choice of product only made matters worse. My nose wrinkled.

I noted, by contrast and in passing, that his charge smelled mainly of unscented soap and a pleasant blend of breakfast teas, underlain with a faint hint of some medicinal ointment.

"It was a snake," Philip said. "A serpent, a venomous viper. It struck me. It would have bitten her as well, but I flung her away."

"Don't mind him." The orderly fussed around, adjusting the crocheted lap-blanket draped over the old man's legs. "He's no harm at all. Just wandered off, as they do sometimes. You see how it is."

Oh, I saw how it was, and found it disturbing, even offensive. The patronizing manner, the tut-tutting, the talking over and around, the conspiratorial tone almost like a wink. How tragic, the elderly, how pitiable in their decaying bodies, with their eroding mental states. While we, we two, *we* possessed vigor and vitality. *We* counted. *We* mattered.

"Jeanne," Philip sighed, still gazing as if into a distance of years as well as miles. "My dear Jeanne."

"It has been nice meeting you," I said to him directly. "But I must be on my way, if I'm to be back before dark."

He blinked, drew a breath, met my eyes. "If you meet her, tell her I never meant to leave. I never meant to hurt her or cause her any distress."

"Philip," chided the orderly. "Enough of that. You'll upset this pretty—"

I leveled him a cool look, then bent and touched the old man's bony wrist. "I will. If I meet her, I will tell her."

His other hand covered mine, warm, and patted. "Thank you."

"Mam'selle, you should not encourage him." The orderly's tone had changed, become huffy and brusque. Disapproving. How dare I. "Come along, Philip. Let's get you home."

Lingering a moment, I watched him wheel the chair away. He pushed it with purposeful strides toward the care-complex. Philip sat placidly, letting himself be rolled, head hanging. It still seemed I felt the warmth of his hand on mine, and my heart went out to him.

Then I adjusted the straps of my small day-pack, slung my botanical kit over my shoulder, snapped my folding titanium hiking stick to full extension, and faced the switchbacked cliff-path. I inhaled deeply of the fragrance-laden air. Earthy. Natural and clean.

I smelled wildflowers and budding blossoms, and…lavender? It seemed too early for lavender; my itinerary

13

included Provence in July, when it would be at the height of the season.

Yet, I did catch whiffs of it now, lovely and teasing on the breeze.

The moors spread and stretched and sprawled toward the horizon. From here, they appeared to be low green hills and shadowed valleys, dotted with boulders. A deception, I knew; once down among them, those hills and valleys would be ridges and ravines, the boulders great rearing granite outcrops. The grass would be not parklike lawn but deep and untamed meadow. Bracken and brambles would knot among the yellow gorse and supple reeds. Springs would well from damp earth or trickle from cleft stones, feeding into streams and meandering creeklets just as likely to vanish as to lead toward the sea.

Beautiful and cruel, Philip had said. Beautiful and cruel, like a woman.

Like his Jeanne?

He had not sounded, when he spoke of her, as if she'd been the cruel one. Nor had he. Only fate, also cruel and beautiful, bringing lovers together only to tear them apart.

I could not see, from this high vantage point, the soft blue-purple dustings of lavender in profusion, but as I drew another deep breath, I took in the scent stronger than ever. An early-blooming variety, perhaps. Something classic, but fresh and new.

It might be just what I needed. To my family, this trip was an indulgence, a graduation gift, a chance for me to sate my youthful wanderlust before settling in as a productive member of our business empire. They would have me in board rooms and executive offices, wearing smart designer skirt-suits and take-no-prisoners heels.

Whereas I, I had other plans. I wanted to create. To launch my own line, my own brand. To take the company in a different, back-to-basics direction.

We were perfumers. We had been perfumers as long as our genealogy could be traced, through Colonial times and the Renaissance. Possibly as far as the Black Death; my ancestors could have been selling pockets full of posies to ward off the stench of plague.

Posies…rosewater and rosehips…dried citrus peel…cedar shavings…cloves…lavender and mint and lemongrass…myrrh and cassia…pine…herbs, oils, extracts, and spices…violet and jasmine…ambergris and musk.

The way it used to be done. When someone's choice of perfume might be highly individualized, even custom-crafted to complement and enhance their own pheromones. Before chemistry took over, synthetics, mass production.

Nowadays, it was less about the actual scent and more about price, prestige, packaging. The more expensive, the better. Perfumes with names meant to evoke sex and wealth and power, without giving any indication what they might smell like…because that didn't matter. What mattered was cut crystal bottles and gold inlay, celebrity endorsements, exclusive boutiques.

Elements like cedar, rosehips, orange peel and lavender were widely considered elderly hallmarks these days, old-fashioned stuff. Potpourri dishes and sachets for the underwear drawer. Musty-dusty floral phantoms, the ghosts of corsages pressed and forgotten for decades between diary pages. Associated with antimacassars, delicate collections of teacups and saucers, spinsters, widows, grandmothers and great-aunts.

Well, not *my* grandmothers and great-aunts, that much was for certain. *My* grandmothers and great-aunts were jet-setters, society queens, fashion plates. Impeccable and perfect. Devout disciples of Our Lady of Perpetual Botox. Birthdays were marked with poison-sweet passive-aggressive gift certificates to salons or spas or clinics. They had been cougars before 'cougar' was a thing, *femmes fatale*, man-eaters.

And here I was, in sturdy boots and trousers, setting off across the trackless moors. Not touring Paris or Monte Carlo or Venice. Staying at village inns instead of posh hotels.

"You'd better take a guide," Philip had told me.

"I shall not lose myself," I'd said.

I certainly did not intend to. I had GPS on my phone, but was sensible enough to realize cell reception couldn't be guaranteed, so I also had a proper compass and maps tucked into my day-pack. I had water bottles, energy bars, a lightweight space-age thermal tarpaulin, matches. I was prepared.

As I'd surmised, the terrain did prove far more rugged than it had appeared from above. What I'd taken for low shrubs turned out to be stands of brush and bramble sometimes as high as my head. Birds flitted here and there. More hares bounded away at my approach. Once, a hawk dived, stunning in its deadly majesty.

The elusive scent of lavender continued to tease and tantalize, leading me onward. I glimpsed many varieties of wildflower, some unfamiliar to me. I took pictures with my phone and gathered samples with my collection kit. The sun hung as if in timeless suspension in a silvery-clear arching span of sky.

"You'd better take a guide," he'd said.

To which I, with all the confidence of youth, had replied I would not lose myself.

Imagine therefore my chagrin when I paused for a rest and a snack, and looked around to realize I had no idea where I was. A not-unpleasant ache of exertion in my legs suggested I'd been hiking quite some time indeed, though that hardly seemed possible when the sun had barely...

Wait.

When had the sun dropped so close to setting? When had the sky gone from silver-clear to a soft and dusky purple-blue, the very shade of lavender in bloom?

I checked my phone. It confirmed the lateness of the hour, as well as my suspicions about reliable cell reception.

Had I really gone and lost myself after all?

A warm flush having nothing to do with exercise suffused my cheeks. I clambered to the highest vantage point I could find, peering for landmarks. The cliffs I'd descended were no longer in view. I saw no lights, no houses, no signs of habitation whatsoever.

Consulting my maps and compass, I made what I determined to be the most likely guess and struck out at a purposeful pace. I already knew the chances of reaching my snug room at the inn before dark were remote, and was both bracing for and resigning myself to a night spent roughing it.

The lavender twilight glowed vibrant, shedding a strange iridescence over a fine evening mist now rising from the moor. Pools and creeklets glimmered. It was beautiful…

"Beautiful, and cruel," Philip's voice seemed to whisper. "Like a woman."

The lovely scent of lavender seemed more prevalent as well. I wondered if it was an illusion in my mind, brought on by the sky's dramatic hue, or if I were about to stumble into full fields of it after all. With a farmstead where I might shelter for the night, the guest of humble country folk who would offer to share homemade bread and rustic stew, and provide me a cot where I'd sleep bundled safe under a quilt.

Instead, I found tumbled blocks of masonry and crumbling curves of wall. It was some sort of structure, a ruin overgrown with moss and ivy. A little church, perhaps, or the remains of an old keep.

Or *un petit chateau.*

The words came unbidden to my mind. I shrugged them away, thinking at the very least the ruins would be a place to make my camp. By the fading purple light, with hawks observing keenly from the treetops, I set about collecting fallen branches. A patch of bare flagstone in what must have been a courtyard would do as a place to build a fire, if I decided I needed one.

As I went about this task, I glimpsed another piece of stonework some distance from the outer wall. I used the flashlight app on my phone to make my way over to it, curious, and found it to be a monument.

Again, I seemed to more hear than simply recall the anguished voice of Philip. "I had seen the stone, the shrine…she died for love of me…Jeanne, my dear Jeanne…"

I read the inscription. I brushed my fingertips over the carved letters and numbers. My skin prickled with gooseflesh for a moment, and then I thought I understood.

He had come here, as a young man, to the moors. He'd found this very spot, this very stone with a name the same as his own upon it. But, rather than recognize it as mere uncanny coincidence, he had fabricated a tragic fancy, dreamed up a romance of doomed love. It had taken hold of him and held tight ever since.

The poor man. My heart went out to him again. Old and frail, wheelchair-bound, locked in his dementia, forever in love with his imagination of someone who'd died centuries ago.

How beautiful...and, yes, how cruel.

Like a woman.

Like the sculpture of a woman also marking this monument. Perhaps she was meant to be an angel or a saint, or perhaps the Virgin Mary. But there was little angelic or saintly, little holy or beatific, in her timeworn expression.

Beautiful, and cruel. Avaricious. Cold.

Other letters, done by some later and far less skilled hand, had been crudely chipped into the stone below her visage.

Y-D-H-R, they appeared to be.

They troubled me for no good reason. I thought of the I-N-R-I often seen on images of Christ, and supposed it must mean something similar, but had never encountered this particular example before.

With my phone, I took a picture of the monument with its carvings and inscriptions. The quick bright pop from the flash made the cruel-beautiful features seem to twitch, seem to twist for a brief instant into a malevolent leer.

Gooseflesh raced across my skin again. I shivered.

Don't blink, I thought, and wished I hadn't.

Suddenly, I no longer wanted to camp here for the night. It felt wrong. A trespass, a transgression, a mistake. I did not belong in the shadowed ruins of this *Chateau d'Ys.* I could make camp elsewhere.

Away from this desolate, sorrowing place. Away from that stone shrine with its merciless goddess.

I went with little regard for direction, simply hiked at a good clip until the encroaching dusk made my footsteps too precarious. Then, aided again by the flashlight app, I found a dry-looking hollow. I did without a fire, just wrapping myself in the crinkly silver space-age tarpaulin.

My sleep, when it came, was thin and fitful. Every rustle startled me wide-eyed in the darkness. Instead of the dense fog I expected, stars pierced white as diamonds in a dome of crystalline black.

At some point, I must have fallen into a deeper doze, because I woke from it to find dew dampening my clothes. The sky was lavender again, but this time in pale pastel, like a swath of fine silk edged with cloudy lace and gold filigree.

I sat up, feeling more refreshed and rested than I had any right to. I wasn't even stiff from a full day of hiking followed by a night curled on the ground. Tiny birds flitted from twig to twig, bees bumbled among the flowers, and the morning air smelled sweet.

As I stretched and rubbed my eyes, I heard an excited yipping. Next I knew, I had a lapful of dog, all cornsilk fluff and exuberance, whole-hindquarters wagging, with a determination to lick every inch of my face.

"Hello!" I sputtered, helpless not to laugh. "Hello there, aren't you a friendly one?"

The dog yipped again, presumably in agreement. I found that silly, because I'd unthinkingly spoken in English...and then found it sillier I should worry, when this was a dog. As I raised my hands to fend off its furiously diligent pink tongue, I noticed that my new friend sported a fancy velvet collar, from which hung some sort of engraved tag. But, with all the energetic wiggling, I only caught a glimpse of a peculiar symbol.

Then a melodic, girlish voice called out. "Hastur! Hastur, my little pup, where have you gone?" She, however, *did* speak French, with a quaintly pretty accent.

Hastur barked, cavorting around me as I got to my feet. The owner of the melodic voice and I saw each other at the same moment, and we both gasped. She, no doubt, because she had not expected to find some stranger in the moors…and me, because…well, because 'quaintly pretty' described far more than just her accent. It described everything about her, from the style of her dress to her smooth-as-cream complexion, even the beribboned bonnet and gauzy parasol.

My age or a little younger, she looked as if she'd stepped entire from the pages of a Jane Austen novel. And here I was, rumpled and dew-dampened, having slept in my clothes, my braid a fraying rope-twist of wisps and straggles.

"Oh!" she said, pressing a hand to her bosom. "How you have surprised me!"

"I'm sorry." My guidebook French sounded clumsier than ever. "I became lost. I spent the night."

"How dreadful! You must come to the house. We will see you fed and cared for."

"I'd hate to be a bother—"

"Pff." She dismissed my demurral with a flick of the same hand she'd pressed to her bosom. "It would be no bother. It would be a pleasure. We do not often have guests. Please. Do come to the house."

As if I could refuse? "Thank you," I said.

I gathered my belongings as she summoned Hastur to her side. The dog went with prompt obedience. I noticed her glancing quizzically at various items—my cell phone, the thermal tarpaulin, the folding titanium hiking stick—but she said nothing about them.

We introduced ourselves as we set out walking, Hastur running through the grass ahead of us, stirring up and chasing butterflies.

"American," said the young lady, tilting her pretty head to one side. "I have never before met an American."

I half-expected her to tell me her name was Jeanne, but it proved instead to be Renaea.

"Renaea," I repeated.

"Yes." She ducked her face with a shy smile, but not before I saw charming dimples and a delicate blush. "Renaea de Lavande."

"Lavender? As in the plant, or the color?"

Her laugh was music. "Oh, both; they are the same. And the scent. Lavender is in all three things the definition of itself. What else could make such claim?"

"Orange?" I suggested.

"The fruit, yes, and the color…but orange itself is not a scent."

"Rose, then," I said.

Again came the musical laugh. "Ah, but think, if you say the color, it means a shade of pink, while if you say the flower, well, are not roses found in a variety of colors? At the house, we have them in red and white and yellow besides."

"You have gardens?"

"Many gardens. And many gardeners to tend them. My family have been, for long years, growers of exquisite blooms."

"So I see," I said, the words spilling from my lips before I could recall them, my tone far too warm, far too intimate.

The dimples and delicate blush made a reappearance. Had I been lost already, here upon the moors? That was nothing compared to how lost my heart was now, and all the more so when she folded her slim fingers through mine.

"Gardens," she went on, "in the French and the English style. And hot-houses for rare orchids brought from afar."

We walked, hands linked as if it was the most natural thing in all the world. It *felt* like the most natural thing in all the world. I knew it likely meant nothing, was likely a simple gesture of innocent affection on her part, yet felt like so very much more.

We walked, and she talked, and I listened and nodded. The sky cleared to blue, and the sun shone pale gold. A grey hare sprang from the underbrush and Hastur gave chase, but was no hound to the hunt, and came trotting back to us as the hare escaped.

"…but, most of all, most prized, are our lavender fields."

21

And the breeze brought the strengthening fragrance, sweet and lovely, so that when we topped a rise and a valley opened welcoming before us, I thought I'd be ready for the sight I beheld.

I was not ready.

It was breathtaking, a lush and luxurious expanse, sure to put even the vaunted fields of Provence to shame. Low hills rolled light green and purple, the plants not laid out in tidy rows but permitted their unfettered freedom. They were fluffy puffballs at this distance, cloudy fragrant powder puffs, feathery and soft, rippling in the breeze like the fronds of anemones swaying to an unseen oceanic current.

Rising from the middle of it, an island in this lavender sea, was the house Renaea had mentioned. And, again, I was not ready. I'd been thinking cottage, something fairytale and Disney-esque, or a little Tudor-style construction of dark beams and whitewashed walls.

But, no, it was a proper country house, a modest manor in the old tradition, with carriage house and outbuildings, a round crushed-gravel drive with fishpond at the center…and the gardens.

Oh, the gardens! Also as Renaea had mentioned, in the French and English style, but far grander than my imagination had led me to expect. On one side of the manor, the grounds were Versailles in miniature, manicured hedges and trees trimmed to careful shapes, flawless lawns, geometric designs, pools and fountains, marble benches. On the other, it was Stratford-on-Avon, tall grasses brimming with aster and sweet verbena, lilies, columbine, daisies, peonies, and primrose in a full rainbow of colors.

"This is where you live?" I asked, my senses drinking it all in.

"I was born here, as was my mother, and her mother before her," said Renaea.

"How large is your family?"

"Not so very large these days. My parents are often away, touring some court or other. They are very in demand, you see, as floral arrangers for events. You do know, I'm sure, there is a language in flowers, a secret language. Each has its meaning. Each sends its message. A bouquet is a poem; I have seen sonnets in vases. What they present, my parents, are symphonies fit for queens and princes."

"You don't mean you're here alone."

"Oh, no, not alone. There is Pelagie, the housekeeper, who was my nurse when I was a child. There are the gardeners, of course, and a groom and cook, and servants."

"How very *Downton Abbey*," I remarked, observing the absence of any power lines, telephone poles, satellite dishes, or similar indications of modern conveniences.

"I plead pardon?"

"Nothing. It's magnificent."

"It is true, though, that although not alone, it can at times be lonely. I am so very glad to have met you. You must stay a while."

"I'd like that," I said with earnestness. "But I'm not really dressed for a visit. I only went out for a day-hike."

"For which trouble you spent a night cold upon the moors!" Renaea squeezed my hand. "Come and refresh yourself. We will find you something suitable to wear. You must be faint with thirst and hunger as well."

She led me through the meandering fields of lavender. The scent was blissful heaven. Each plant seemed the picture of perfect health, in full bloom despite the earliness of the season. So, too, were all the flowers in the gardens. All in bloom, all at their peak and in their prime, all at this same time of the year.

Which shouldn't have been the case. Which was, really, quite botanically impossible.

I started to say as much to Renaea, but thought better of it.

The same proved true, I soon saw, for the fruit trees. Here were plump cherries rich and ripe as garnets, and pale pink cherry blossoms, sharing the same boughs…plums and apricots likewise…

We reached a willow-shaded lane that brought us to the gravel drive. From here, the hills of lavender went on as if forever. Gardeners worked among them, men wearing

23

homespun and suspenders, silent men who nodded deference to us as we passed by.

Many more questions clamored in my mind. But, again, I thought better of voicing them. I let myself be ushered into the stately house. I let myself be turned over to the housekeeper, Pelagie, a stout and efficient woman with a cap of neat grey curls. Maids were summoned. Clothes were sent for. I was shown to a guest room that surpassed in every way the quaint little inn where I'd booked lodging.

Fortunately, the lack of modern conveniences did not extend to running water. A hot bath later—infused with lavender, of course—I felt my night outdoors melting away. I donned the clothes that had been left for me, similarly old-fashioned to what Renaea wore, unfamiliar yet surprisingly comfortable. The dress was goldenrod overlain with ivory lace, the shoes were genuine kidskin, and I was able with some effort to twist my hair up into a loose and vaguely Regency-looking bun.

Now I, too, looked as if I'd stepped from the pages of a Jane Austen novel. My grandmothers and great-aunts would have, one and all, pinched the facelifted bridges of their noses to ward off a despairing tension headache at the very idea. But I liked it.

So did Renaea, when I joined her in the morning room where a late breakfast had been set out. She sprang up with a delighted cry, rushed to me, and clasped both my hands in hers.

"How lovely you are!" she exclaimed. "That color suits you so!"

Hastur sniffed and wagged approval, then sat pertly at our feet plying us with cute head-tilts and soulful doggy eyes as we ate. Neither of us could resist sharing with him morsels of buttered croissant, thin-sliced ham, and cheese. We sipped tea with lavender honey, nibbled berries with clotted cream, and talked.

She told me more of the secret language of flowers and floral arranging. Romances, even entire courtships, could be carried out with barely an uttered word, clandestine messages of passion exchanged with the untutored oblivious left none the wiser. I told her about my travels, my family, our business as perfumers. I told her how I'd come on this trip with the hopes of rediscovering the old ways, the lost arts.

After our meal, we strolled the gardens. We went once again hand-in-hand, still as if this were the most natural thing in the world. Renaea pointed out to me various buds and blossoms and their meanings. I wondered if it was just my wishful imaginings that she should particularly indicate those she said were for desperate passion, and forbidden desire.

Some ways from the house, we reached a white gazebo that had until then somehow missed my notice. Yet, here it was, quaint and charming amid the lavender, overlooking a duckpond where lilypads floated. We sat side by side upon a wicker lounge, hands clasped, while Hastur gamboled in the grass.

Then I asked her, perhaps foolishly, about the Chateau d'Ys.

"Oh, *that* place," she said. "Have you been there? Was it haunted?"

"I was there, yes," I said. "As for haunted, I can't say...*is* it?"

"If anywhere is, it should be. Such a sad story. Pelagie told me. She once claimed she worked there, in her youth. Jokingly, of course. Not even Pelagie is so ancient!"

She laughed, and I laughed with her, recalling the date inscribed upon the weathered stone marker I'd seen, there at the ruins. A date centuries removed from my own time...

Quickly, I banished that line of thought.

"Besides," Renaea continued, "she has also told me of the Green Wolf, and the Black Goat, the Widow of the Woods, and the Maskless King, and I know such tales cannot be true. Still, truth or fancy, d'Ys is indeed sorrowful."

"A sad story," I echoed. "How so?"

"Jeanne d'Ys was he last lady of the castle," said Renaea. "Well, a girl, like us; she was barely twenty when she died. They say she...they say she met a stranger upon the moors, and...and fell in love. He was from very far away. Very, very far. But they had only a day or two together, before he disappeared."

"What happened to him?"

"No one knows for certain. One version of the story has it that he gave his life saving hers, another that her relatives had him murdered. Or that he seduced and abandoned her, and broke her heart. I do not like to believe the last one. I believe he loved her, too, but fate was cruel."

"Beautiful and cruel," I said.

"Pardon?"

I shook my head. "So, he just vanished? Without a trace, no body left behind, never seen or heard from again?"

"Such is the story." Renaea paused, her gaze shifting away from me to watch Hastur capering at the duckpond's bank. When she spoke again, her tone was hushed and faltering. "Do...do you think it's possible?"

"For someone to disappear?"

"No...to...to meet someone upon the moors, a stranger...and fall in love?"

My breath caught. My pulse fluttered. Did she mean...could she...

There was nothing else to do but turn to her, gently lift her chin, and kiss her. For a frightening instant, she seemed frozen, rigid with shock. She would draw back, horrified. She would slap me. With eyes and voice gone cold, she would demand I go, and never venture here again. Unnatural, she'd call me. Sick, even depraved.

Renaea gave no such dreaded, dreadful reaction. After that initial startled instant, she swayed toward me as if melting. Her lips parted with tender sweetness. We kissed, there on the wicker lounge. We embraced and held each other in the gazebo's shade. Lavender's cool fragrance wafted all around us. Words were no longer needed. We said them anyway, in wondering sighs and murmurs.

Somehow, the afternoon went by almost before we knew it. We kissed once more, and Renaea touched her soft palm to my cheek.

"But will it end the same for us?" she asked. "Will you disappear, and leave me?"

"No!" I cried, covering her hand with mine to hold it there. "No, I want to stay. I never want to leave you, not for a single day, not even for an hour. I want to be here with you, always."

Hadn't Philip said much the same, to his dear Jeanne?

I believed him now. Not dementia, not some madness of the moors, a chance coincidence of names carved into stone. It was true. It was real.

This place *was* enchanted; it had me in its spell. My former life was meaningless. Everything I'd searched for was to be found here. Here among the lavender, among the gardens. I would learn the language of flowers, the art of their arranging. I would craft sonnets and symphonies for my beloved Renaea, and I would make perfumes such as the world had never seen, and we would be happy here, happy here forever.

Together, no longer hand-in-hand but fondly arm-in-arm, we made our way back to the stately country house. Hastur ran ahead of us, yipping, the gold-inlaid ornament on his collar twinkling in the late day's sun.

"We must wash and dress for dinner," Renaea told me as we stepped through the great front door and ascended the curving stair. "After, I will show you the conservatory."

"I look forward to it," I said. A quick glance around preceded a quicker kiss, and then we parted ways for our separate rooms.

When I reached mine, I found other garments laid out and waiting. A silk dress like shimmering twilight, a shoulder-wrap of silvery lace, dainty slippers. They fit as if tailored to my measure. I brushed out my hair and fashioned it into an elegant chignon. The vanity table had been supplied with a small selection of cosmetics, which I also made use of.

There also, in the room, were my old clothes. Cleaned and folded, piled neatly on a chair. How ugly they seemed! How awful, coarse, and crude! I never wanted to wear them again. Never wanted to *see* them, would have been just as glad to watch them burn. My boots were there as well, the clumsy clunky things, set on a mat below the chair. My day-pack hung on the chair's back, and even that looked foreign, almost alien, to my eyes.

My folding titanium hiking stick...my cell phone, its screen a blank and glassy strangeness...the maps and compass...water bottles, energy bars...they did not belong here. They should not be here. Why would I need energy bars when I'd be going down to dinner? As for the cell phone...

Force of habit nonetheless made me pick it up and switch it on. The battery still had life—I had the charger in a side pocket of the day-pack, for all the use it'd be—but no bars, no service. The icons might as well have been hieroglyphs. I barely cared or remembered what most of them meant. On a whim, though, I snapped a selfie.

The bright pop of the flash reminded me anew of the previous picture I'd taken, at the monument shrine near the ruined Chateau d'Ys. That cruel and beautiful graven image, goddess or angel or saint, the fleeting impression of stone features twitching, the cold and malevolent leer.

I put the phone away, feeling oddly guilty for my technological transgression. I daubed attar of lavender at the pulse-points of throat and wrist, and went downstairs.

Renaea met me, a vision in softest chiffon. Her hair had been upswept and adorned with flowers. A corsage graced her breast. I knew, even from the few lessons she'd already taught me, that they had been chosen to speak, in their silent language, of love.

We dined. On precisely what, I barely attended. Each course was delicious, exquisite; that much was undeniable. Some light broth flavored with herbs and crumbled petals...some sort of small fowl, Cornish hen perhaps, roasted stuffed with rosehips and served in a sweet rose-wine sauce...crisp salads, seasoned vegetables...an array of fruit pastries...but what I feasted on most, what both sated and stirred my appetites, was the company of my dearest Renaea.

After, as promised, she did show me the conservatory. How I had missed seeing it from outside of the house, I couldn't guess. It was a large round room of latticework and glass panes, sloped ceiling rising to a point high overhead. By day, in the sunshine, I'm sure it dazzled with color and light. Here, now, at this hour, it was whisper and shadow, a velvety hush of darkness faintly illuminated by filtered moon-rays and stars.

All around us were potted plants and raised planters, trellises embroidered with climbing vines, feathery fronds, sleeping buds tucked tight, night-blooms unfurling to release their heady fragrances. I recognized several as exotic species and rare varieties, imported from Africa and South America, the tropics, the Orient—however politically incorrect the term might be in my own day and age.

As we moved among them, again arm-in-arm, Renaea in her own hushed whispers identified those unfamiliar to me. Here were the twinned *camilla* and *cassilda*, here in a mosaic basin of water a cluster of lilies from Lake Hali, and here—

I stopped. We had come nearly to the center of the conservatory, where a pedestal rose from sprays of leafy greenery. Atop it, where a sundial might have been, was the sculpture of a feminine figure, a robed woman.

The style and artistry were different, the stone neither timeworn nor weathered, but her face…her features…

"What is it?" inquired Renaea, stopping as well. She followed my glance, and smiled. "Ah, you've found *La Perennielle.*"

"Who?"

"Our lavender lady, patroness saint to my family."

The figure's arms were crossed at her chest in the manner of Egyptian statues, though in her hands she held not ankhs or staves but bundles of flowering stalks. Even depicted in stone, I could tell that, yes, they were sprigs of lavender.

But her face was, I was sure of it, the same as I'd seen on the monument at d'Ys. Beautiful, and cruel. Regal, but avaricious and cold. Ready to twitch at a flash into a malevolent leer.

"Pelagie says she represents the eternal renewal," Renaea went on, "reinventing herself in incarnation after incarnation, constantly reborn."

I leaned closer, pushing aside the dry, brittle curls of dead leaves collected at the statue's base. The flat disk of the pedestal upon which it stood was worked into floral patterns and spirals, but directly at the robed woman's feet was a scroll like something from medieval heraldry, bearing the letters Y-D-H-R in ornate calligraphy.

"...that rebirth demands sacrifi—" Renaea was saying, when the tiniest flicker of movement just above her head caught my eye.

A teardrop-shape darker than the conservatory's whispering shadows...a fine pearly-pale filament extending up from it. Even as I realized with a chill what it was—a spider, a glossy black spider, descending its line—it alit upon one of the flowers Renaea wore in her hair.

She must have seen my look of horror, pausing in mid-word to ask what was the matter.

"Do not move!" I told her.

The spider scurried down the side of her neck, a loathsome black inkblot against her smooth, pale, perfect skin. It bore a mark on its back; not a scarlet hourglass or white fiddle, it was blue-purple in color, like a budding lavender bract.

Its legs must have tickled, because she reached involuntarily as if to brush it away despite my warning. I seized her wrist, staying her, while my other hand shot out. I snatched up the spider in my fist, felt it writhing and squirming, felt a sharp sting of pain before I crushed it.

The venom's effects were immediate.

I staggered, gasping for breath, a terrible icy numbness rushing through my body. Renaea clutched at me. I heard her calling my name...calling for help...screaming for Pelagie and the servants...I heard her sobbing, begging me not to leave her, telling me I'd promised to stay, that she would surely die without me.

My fingertips caressed her cheek. She was weeping. I wanted to reassure her, wanted to say so very much.

But I fell, and it seemed I kept falling, falling and falling away into an eternity of forever.

30

When I returned to myself, it was as if from a tremendous distance.

And to a tremendous despair.

Without even opening my eyes, I knew.

I knew from the astringent, antiseptic, chemical smells. I knew from the squeak of soft-soled shoes on tile and the metallic rattle-roll of carts. From the tight stickiness of tape holding an IV needle in place, the machine-laundered texture of the thin cotton gown, the upper part of the bed tilted up…oh yes, I knew.

The bed would have rails, and a curtain on a track. Perhaps there'd be cards propped on a windowsill, perhaps shop-bought flower arrangements shouting gibberish. A television would be on but muted, tuned to news or soccer, closed-captioning scrolling in French. The walls would be painted some shade meant to be soothing.

Tears beaded my lashes, spilled from beneath closed lids to trickle freely down my face.

How had it played out? Missing tourist, search parties? A chance discovery by fellow hikers? Had I been unconscious when they found me? Had I been raving, a madwoman on the moors? What might I have told them? What might I have said?

Not that it mattered. Not that I cared.

So what if everyone thought me insane? So what if my family pressed for competency hearings and committal?

Let them medicate me. Let them lock me up in some room with soft walls. Let them talk to me in that *tone*, that patronizing doctor-nurse-orderly tone, as if to a dim-witted child. Let them hook me up with electroshock, if they wanted.

So what?

I had lost my beloved Renaea. I'd never be able to get back to her again, not if I spent a lifetime looking. Even if I found the same place, the country house would be long gone by now, its gardens and lavender fields overgrown, its dear young mistress…

The tears spilled faster. My chest ached. My body shook from the effort of holding in a tempest of shrieking, wailing grief.

Y-D-R-H. *La Perennielle.* Rebirth demanded sacrifice.

If the door to my room had been left discreetly ajar, the faint creak of hinges and a draft of moving air informed me it had been pushed wider, someone coming in. With tears streaming, body shaking, fists clenched, there'd be no way to feign having been asleep.

I braced myself for squeaky-sole nurse-shoes footsteps, and for that *tone*...some chirpy-sweet variation on "well, look who's awake" or condescending "and how are we feeling today?"

Instead, I heard a slow trundling as of rubber-fitted wheels. And someone said, "I believe you."

I opened my eyes to see exactly the sort of room I'd expected, the paint a green somewhere between moss and mint...the same color as the scrubs the staff would wear...and the window looked out on a view of well-tended grounds, beyond which the cliffs dropped away to the moors.

Philip, in a different sweater but the same chair, with the same crocheted blanket spread over his lap, wheeled to my bedside. He offered me a box of tissues, then patted my arm.

"I believe you," he said again.

"I...I believe you, too," I managed, through sniffles and breathy hitching hiccups. I mopped my face, blew my nose. "Not that anyone else will ever believe either of us."

He smiled, not without sadness and sympathy. We sat a while together, in a silence of our shared despair. This, for all these years, had been his life. A suffering prison, torn between truth and insanity. Both equally without comfort, because, in the end, it did not matter.

I let my head fall against the pillow. My disconsolate gaze roved the room, half-unseeing, still blurred by tears. The muted television, the expected senseless cacophony in some deliver-florist's vase upon a table, a little wardrobe-closet where—

Where my day-pack hung on a hook. My day-pack, with my cell phone snugged securely in its usual side pocket.

My cell phone, with which I'd snapped a selfie after dressing for dinner.

With such a picture ... with actual proof ...

Why, then, should I suddenly feel so cold? So breathless with apprehension? So suddenly terrified?

If there *was* ...

Oh, but if there *wasn't* ...

And it seemed I heard a goddess laughing, beautiful and cruel.

LOVE AND TREACHERY

Joseph S. Pulver, Sr.

For Vincent Starrett

November.

The moon shines whitely.

There were leaves, (yellow and rust) whirling about, (lover's red) in tango, (rust and brown and tan) leapfrogging, (half not washed of green, drenched flame) colliding, (epilogue brown) undercutting, (darkling orange) solo dervishes.

The moon shines whitely. Her pale hands rebuke its cold words.

November covering autumn with nothing. Camilla stands at her window, whitely (paler than the bones of the throne of the ghoul-king), and looks upon the rows of equations gone, digests the empty that no longer reflect, or weave melody from wedded heart-strings. Plots void of kindness, absent the drums' synchronicity. The blooms she placed as mourners are done withered dry.

The moon shines whitely, brightly, yet it finds no tear upon Camilla's cheek for old lovers.

Outside, something *alone* calls.

Only a spell of wind, speaking of ownership, replies.

Knowing how hard it is to digest the empty page, she wonders if the thing is anchored to a flame curved and shaped by split.

"Yes, the currents inmost."

Her ivory teeth, barely a shade whiter than her bone-white skin, flash, as she grins.

"Lies. Insurrections."

Turning away from the window, her eye catches the chessboard. Shoeless, slipperless, bone-white feet cross the bone-white carpet to the small table it rests on.

"The white queen, tingling with life, stands. Black, struck, now sails in landless blackness."

Camilla's slender bone-white fingers remove the black king from the board.

Each thought to make me a pawn. "To hurt my heart and chain me to a drowning anchor in Frownland. They thought their poison would bind my last breath in Death's dark ink, but my destination, heart-deep, King-promised, is a full horizon, not the poet's 'skeleton dimension.'"

Beside the chessboard sits a 22 pp. quarto, *The King In Yellow A Play In Two Acts.* "White *always* moves first."

Camilla moves the quarto and sets the black king, fallen, upon it. Beneath the play rests another quarto, 8 pp. thicker than first, *The Moon Shines Whitely Upon The White Queen A Play In One Act.*

"Always."

Camilla is quick to pick up the quarto an open it. There is joy in her fingers, in her eyes. The ivory teeth her smile reveals shine brighter than the steady beam of the white moon. She seems to be floating.

Her lips part, and her tongue, singing, releases the content of the first page. "'*She will be there.* There is no weakness in the flame of the thundering Queen.'"

"This is my play to cast. Fools. They though petite held no power, thought they held the sword and thus the path to power...I am no frail wisp; I am the wolf, the avalanche that cleaves. The consequences of intrigues and follies born in Oblivion dance upon my fingertips."

I am my father's daughter.

Standing in a ray of crazy moonlight that's crashed ashore, she looks down at the scalloped tatters of her bone-white gown. Wiggles her toes.

"I am the one who stands on the moon-bleached balcony and reads the mosaic of the cloudwaves; Uhot failed, Thale failed. Aldones was unworthy of rank in the Dynasty. Denis had his chance and chose unwisely."

Her eye turns from the bone-white page and addresses the small black pawns on the chessboard. "No man shall decide where my bridal flowers shall swoon. I will never be what mere, lowly men like to think women to be, I am Queen in the towers and in the Winter Garden. It is my image that graces the halls and corridors of Carcosa—*I am not dim.* Delight is what I am—power, the light in a star, the lamp that inspires and strikes. I shall never be content to be seamstress or a cleaning lady, nor shall I be the set-dresser for some fool's play. I am the canon and the lead actor; I have created the sets and stages and written the dialogue. They will bow and call me Mother, and the song of beauty never to be hidden away and boarded up, and, as they knee and pray to the vast unknowable I hold in my hands, they will call me Titan; I control the production."

His back to his current piece, Yvain sits at the window with a glass of gin and a cigarette. He understands Camilla, waiting for the unveiling, walks the corridors.

Beyond the misty spires of the city, night's hours, as lonely as autumnal sonatas, are a fog outside the windows. Their midnight-laden manuscripts murmur at the window-panes. The cold leering moon offers no North Star or compass needle to the shoreless moments as they pass.

There is a fire in the hearth and four lanterns are lit.
Yvain's bone-white mask is on the table with his instruments.
The life-size work stands beside it.

His eyes come back from the moon.

"Camilla." Regal. Cold, when the mood comes upon her,
as the tar-black darkness between the stars. Unmasked. Her
bone-white wings flare out, ready to receive the spells of
Infinity. Her gown reveals her hair is a hood of flames that
will not be bound.

He is happy with the shape of her breasts, with her slender
hands, with each finely-wrought bone-white feather of her
expansive wings.

She will be happy.

There will be a miracle, hearts that gaze upon it will be
swept away, or there will be blood.

"The Queen will be pleased."

He believes. Hopes. Tells himself, as he has fifty times. As
he has every time he has created a new tribute to her.

But the eyes—

Ink black. Mad-black *and filled with stars*. They must be
right.

"It is a dangerous thing to dissatisfy a living goddess."

He grinds the stub of his cigarette beneath his boot heel.

"Be careful of her ego; it carries darkness…it does. Does.
Its sharpness slays." Issues with his own rise. His hands come
together and form a large fist.

He turns away. Thinks of coffee, and maybe sleep, solid
sleep, warm, devoid of toss and fret.

But the long, thick shadow of the unfinished work, a slaver
he's been bound to for four months, stains the floor his eyes
rest on. It's a hallucination and an emergency; it's beautiful,
fatal, panic takes him.

He was in an alley of death, a dimension of
metamorphoses, when she found him. Yvain; broken, sore,
bitten by every scorpion of malediction and pain. He was self-
doubt and shame seeking the exit. Camilla put her arms
around his shell and formulated her magic. She took him
home. Fed him. Washed him. Gave him wine and gin and

painted boulevards. She knew he was weak, but capable, and with will, the will of a nurturing mother without "I can't" in her vocabulary, she created him.

"You will be my Michelangelo. Every dim hall and chilled, unadorned corridor, you will transform; my countenance will glorify Carcosa. I will make you immortal."

And he did. Frescoes, portraits. Busts. Sculptures taller than a tall man.

He did.

Love her.

"Camilla."

Proved it every time he put brush to canvas. Every time his chisel revealed her beauty, her perfection.

His journey never done, this work is no less.

Staring at the shape of her breasts, at her erect nipples, the sculpture captured them perfectly. Longing…for the bed of pleasure she has never allowed him.

Camilla spent years creating him. Freeing his hands from the bricks of crude, she waited for them and him to unblur, to focus.

If he needed to be screamed at, she pitched riots.

He's seen her naked dozens of times.

She bought his clothes. Paid for his rooms and his studio; used spells and lies and deceptions to procure his women.

But she never allowed Yvain the comforts of her bed.

He's seen her naked dozens of times.

He didn't have a single memory, but of a wish, embraced in her bedroom. He never saw a sheet, not one gleaming decoration of fire.

He's seen her naked dozens of times.

Seen her in other arms. They had her, her sigh, her lips reciting undressed love.

Never his.

What should be his.

Never let him express the smile of his desire.

It tore at him.

Contoured him.

Uhot came. Puffed. Arrogant. Tall. Wide in the shoulders and chest. Dark, in league with hypocrisy. A werewolf in courtly robes. A boorish clown who told all he was a warrior, he'd slain dragons with his strikes, sent super men scurrying home; a thousand lamentations in a hundred lands testified to his feats. Restless and bored, between lovers, Camilla succumbed to his overtures. Months passed, they called it love. At the height of summer they held hands less, sat a few inches further apart, he'd toss an attempt at wit at his comrades and she, it seemed, had suddenly forgotten how to laugh or grin. A night came and Camilla found Uhot with his head between Cassilda's thighs. Camilla's black eyes filled with madness. She hissed words Death understood. The moon above trembled.

Uhot vanished.

There was good-bye.

Alar sent a fine captain, by reputation, loved and admired for his achievements, to the court in Carcosa. He plied his fine charms, wooing Camilla. Camilla, dreaming of his arms and detente, agreed with the terms in the boudoir, seemed to fly. Young Alar, three and twenty springs, laughed with Camilla, signed what needed to be signed, and the night after he spent the cold hours of a bleak September night in Camilla's warm bed, tried to negotiate another peace *in Cassilda's bed.*

Camilla's black eyes filled with madness. She hissed words Death understood. The moon above trembled.

Young Alar's head, eyeless, tongue removed, was sent back to Alar.

Thale stood centerstage, promised Camilla heart and dreams. Lied. Death's spell brushed him and the bitterblack, carrion deathbirds that circle the bitterblack towers of Carcosa, descended.

Camilla stood on the balcony overlooking Hali and the feast of the carrion deathbirds. Her lips curled. "Every *wrong* thing dies."

Denis, square-jawed, daring, arrived as savior, vowed to cure Camilla's betrayed heart. "I love you" painted in fantastic colors. They danced, sang. Whispered. He played ringmaster in Camilla's circus bed. Wanton leapt, leapfrogged—confessed and begged. The lovers played trapeze artists, erotic magicians. Their chants (claiming they could never be torn down or apart, claiming they would never traffic with autumn) and dances were many and varied, as they explored kiss and fuck. But he, too, thinking more is better, took note of Cassilda's licentious offerings, and found his way to Cassilda's bed. No off with his head this time. Camilla had him chained a tower spire. The moon came up. It cast its cold bright illuminations on Denis, cut, broken, caressed by cruel…and the bitterblack, carrion deathbirds that circle the bitterblack towers of Carcosa, descended.

Again, there was good-bye.

Aldones opened the door and brought more light into Camilla's world, was a knight of laughter and sudden joys, tender seeking supple. He animated luminous poetry, spoke of healing and grandeur, and he, as captain tingling with the expanding gestures of a star, in word and touch, lit the stage of her beautiful body with extraordinary gifts. Camilla felt love. Loved to love. Until word came to her of an old pestilence. "*Cassilda.*" Plans for the wedding met the sword; Aldones would not share the crown with Camilla, wouldn't create a legacy trumpeted through the ages. Six members of the royal guard dragged Aldones to a filthy dungeon cell; Camilla's fever burned along the blade of her knife— "Cassilda? Cassilda? With my sister?" Transplanted from vigorous being to ended, there was nothing left to embalm.

Love over. Flameless. Silent.

Silent.

Light does not come up. Does not widen and wipe out desolation.

Camilla's lovers come. Forget their tongues, or where to place their hands. Plans full of inexhaustible commit wrong place, wrong time. The good-bye days are bloody.

For three days, Camilla, who had risen from her unshared bed and donned the mask again, was in no mood to pose. She roamed from room to balcony, grumbled, arched to look out a window.

"My thoughts are drenched by blank pages. Do I blame the stars? Or the faults I find spilled from the mouths of men? Hollowness is loathsome."

Outside her high window, the bitterblack, carrion deathbirds that circle the bitterblack towers continued their slow circles, making no reply.

For three days she's been shadowed, at exactly 20 paces, by a violinist and a violist. Both strangely robed in fabrics of rainbow-colored mosaics, and masked in canary yellow masks. They repeat the same song, a skeletal reworking of Aurore d'Ardeche's *The Ebb of Reason Scène Lyrique* for Soprano, Tenor, and Octet after *The King in Yellow*, Op. 30 (1896), varying the tempo and exchanging compositional roles with each variation.

When the musicians pause, Camilla turns and instructs them to "Play one that has the air of a mysterious, darkling fog of autumnal woodwinds and slow strings, as devoid of sentimentality as the passage of night winds." "It's a haunting piece, hued in October nightshades of ennui." And they begin again, as she, wide-eyed with discovery, looks at the pair and says, "Yes. That's the one I was seeking." Or "Yes, that one…but slower."

Two paces to her left is her court's newest poet; like the others that trail Camilla, she's masked, hers is heart-red.

"You are Bori's student? He's praised you, some new entertainment you've written for my court. Why…do none of you write plays about me? I am the Queen in Carcosa; all of this…is mine. Entertain me with your new work."

Bori's student, no longer a young woman, opens her notebook and begins to read from her new play, *Traffic With Autumn.*

"Traffic With Autumn: Scene 2; Act 2
(Nearing twilight. A bitterly cold autumn. Two sisters,
daughters of the King and Lady Cassilda, the eldest,
the gazes of the court call her the saddest heart in the
world, and her licentious younger sibling, sit together
on a cast-iron loveseat in a frost-burned garden of dry
sluices and weathered trellises. They look out over a
cheerless horizon of muddy fields.)
ANDROMEDA, THE ELDER SISTER
These musicless shadows clutch my heart.
EUROPA, THE YOUNGER SISTER
Drizzle and greyness offer no courtesy to this castle.
ANDROMEDA
Have you word?
EUROPA
There are tears on this woman's story.
(She turns in her seat and looks back at the dark
windows of the castle.)
And from the day it began, intense eyes follow me.
ANDROMEDA
Intrigues, and lies, *and the poisoned curse of the*
witch, embroidered on the frayed skirt of autumn. Toil
and blood and no *who cares for me.*
EUROPA
Nightmares, quicker now. Their carriage will not
pause, they ride to drink us.
(She moves her unsandaled feet, the shorn wings of
dead black moths, covering the parched-ground,
flutter.)
If they would speak not—
ANDROMEDA
(Looks at the tattered silk that covers her legs.)

We are the slaves of repulsive monsters and spleen.
Denied the peace we pine for…by…this distance. I
have spent too much time in this cauldron.
EUROPA
(*Gravely.*)
I row…Yet, my desire to be free of this devil
unleashed, serves me not…I look in the mirror and
see, I have only myself to blame."

Camilla, without turning to the poet. "You read to me of
the daughters of the King and Lady Cassilda? Daring. You
may continue."

"Traffic With Autumn: Scene 1; Act 2
(Nearing twilight. A bitterly cold autumn. Two sisters,
the eldest, the gazes of the court call her the saddest
heart in the world, and her licentious younger sibling,
sit together on a cast-iron loveseat in a frost-burned
garden of dry sluices and weathered trellises. They
gaze out over a dour horizon of rotting fields.)
ANDROMEDA
These musicless shadows clutch my heart. *The*
goodbye…Every tremor and itch of Truth.
(*Her hands come together and hold each other, as if a*
brick wall that could protect the flesh within.)
What haunts always haunts again.
EUROPA, THE YOUNGER SISTER
For you there is no healing. Strange things continue to
bury you in woe.
ANDROMEDA
Tired is my soul. Having crawled through the
unnatural, it is withered to the bone.
EUROPA
When the light came ashore and offered the ritual of
flowers to your comely arms, you should have
accepted the comfort of its hand.
ANDROMEDA
Will you again rave on the whole night?

EUROPA
You accuse me of being the revolution?
ANDROMEDA
You were the naysayer's sword.
(*Andromeda rises and steps behind the cast iron loveseat, stands with her back to her sister.*)
EUROPA
(*Without turning to face her sister.*)
I was light…I am your mirror.
ANDROMEDA
Memory confines, reshapes our steps. All the days and nights…it is all that we can see. It destroys the art we are.
EUROPA
Your pathos could never stand The Light.
(*Andromeda turns and looks down at her sister. She has begun weeping.*)
ANDROMEDA
The Dynasty was a stake—it tried to silence my slight aria, I felt like a witch wrongly accused…The forge of its light would have burned me alive, Sister.
(*There is the great sound of dooming bells in the distance.*)
EUROPA
Its eternal knife still may."

"The eternal knife will. Do you know why? Because I demand it." Camilla turns and looks at the poet. "I take it there is more to this? Well, go on."

"*Traffic With Autumn: Scene 2; Act 1*
(*A bitterly cold spring. Two sisters, a spinster virgin and her immodest younger sibling, sit together on a peeling, cast-iron loveseat in a parched garden of dry sluices and weathered trellises crisscrossed with dead vines. They are looking out over a horizon painted by the torturer's hands.*)
ANDROMEDA, THE ELDER SISTER

The bruising wind of broken spring arrives.

EUROPA, THE YOUNGER SISTER

And with it, the quiet elegance of the tombstones beckons to those with sore autumnal hearts.

ANDROMEDA

Will your good and true knight arrive with the night fogs?

EUROPA

If he can? The rain-drenched far-away is crossed by briars…and cursed with many venoms.

ANDROMEDA

Have you been to see the fortune teller?

(A small brown bird crashes upon the dry lawn at Andromeda's feet. Its tiny throat has been torn out. There is a maddened-shriek in the darkening twilight sky above the startled sisters.)

(Europa screams. Andromeda kneels down and picks up the creature.)

ANDROMEDA

(Sotto voce.)

Her fair larks will no longer adorn the infinite.

(Europa looks into the dead black eyes of the ravaged creature and leaps from her seat. Runs toward the palace of her father. Andromeda looks down at her bare feet and the litter of dead black moths that cover the flat stepping stones; there is a dryness in her throat. She begins to weep.)

(Many lands away. Hood of a rusty old, big-block Dodge pickup. Two sisters slipping pop from glass bottles. The younger of the pair blows air into her straw, creating bubbles.)

EMMY

—dreamed I walked through his library. And get this, I was naked, not a stitch on.

ANDI

Was he there?

EMMY

Yes.

ANDI
Did he see you…*naked*?
EMMY
He sure got his eyes full. They were big, full of a
man's hungry.
ANDI
So?
EMMY
Wouldn't you just like to know?
ANDI
I'd tell you. C'mon now, I told you *my dream*.
EMMY
You should get a man. You know how they look at
you, all you got. You get one that likes it, he'll drive
you around and buy you pop and candy. Jimmy Ray
takes Becca Dunn to the movie show all the time and
he takes her to Sharp's and they sit at the counter and
have lunch; think on that the next time a man looks at
what you got. You like that Cinderella story, I know
you'd like to be a queen, be pampered and all. Lot of
women like it, and they know what they can
get…Gives you the power over them.
ANDI
Or whuped-good you pick the wrong one. You better
effect care, girl, or you'll end-up with child. Think on
what Daddy would do if he saw yore belly growin'.
EMMY
Daddy wooda lay his hands on me. Not ever.
ANDI
No, wooda have to, he'd give Mama the sign and have
her and the women do what he wanted done. You
know the power he's got. Haley's and Alar's won't
cross him. John Law neither. Better just think on that
and keep your womanly comforts to yerself.
EMMY
I believe you're just jealous that Spec Pesice's older
brother, Duane, has eyes for me. I remember when
you were upset when Donnie Lee was talkin' to me.

ANDI

Yer the one dreamin' of walkin' naked in Duane's library. Funny place to be naked.

(The next evening. Daddy sits on the porch, telling his stories. The girls like the one about the day he took Mama to the fair and saw jugglers and ate cotton candy.)

DADDY

Got dark...Eight, maybe? All the lights came on quick as a finger-snap, more lights than you girls ever saw. Red and green blazin' on the rides. Twirlin' and goin' 'round so fast you'd be shaken and dizzy in a blink...Carnival had blue ones, Mama sure liked them, and orange was everyplace your eye gazed. Had food everyplace too. Prize-winnin' pies and hand-squeezed lemonade. Hot dogs long 'nough to feed a litter of pups.

EMMY

Ice cream?

DADDY

'Nough for every kid at the fun fair to have one in each hand, and one melted all over his shirt. Weuns goin' to have to take ya'll to one...One of these days.

EMMY

When?

DADDY

Soon enough, Emmy. Maybe come summer, when it passes through 'gain.

EMMY

And did they have music for dancin'?

DADDY

Fiddles and mandolins, and a young banjo picker, powerful as Old Sam Earle's shine, put rattle in your head and get yore toes tappin'. Had the old boys and gals havin' a large time. Mama tried to get me to, but I wasn't of a mind to just then.

EMMY

What other things did you see, Daddy?

DADDY

Sights, and signs…for snake oil and rides, and 'bout
every stripe of trickster can be imagined. Said, they
had a girl in the sideshow could change into a fox,
right before yore eyes. Had this furrin-man, name of
Amazo. Said he could read your thoughts and see all
the way inta your dreams, learn'd to in someplace in
Europe where old sagas of strange goin's-on are fact.
Had this woman in a red dress come down off the
stage and pick a spectator. She handed 'im a hand-
mirror, like the one yore mama has on her night table.
Told 'im to look into the glass, look deep. Up on that
stage, Amazo stared into a twin of the mirror and went
into a state, told 'im what he saw of their life and
dreams. Was some lit right-outta there, like they was
forked by Old Scratch himself.

EMMY

Where you fearful, Daddy?

DADDY

Ever see yore Daddy tremble?

EMMY

Ain't, sir.

*(The moon has come up. It casts its cold bright
illuminations on Daddy. His hand rises from his
kneecap and he points at Emmy.)*

DADDY

Never will.

ANDI

Sounds kinda like one of them fairy-tale places in
Mama's old book.

DADDY

Fairy-tale place to one soul might be the hard truth of
yonder to 'nother…You take my meaning, girl?

ANDI

I do, Daddy.

*(Mama opens the screen door half-way, she does not
step outside. Looks at her daughters, opens the door
fully.)*

MAMA

Bedtime, girls. Tomorrow's on the wind and there's preparations that will need our hands.

EMMY

Mama, Daddy was—

MAMA

Come now.

(The girls go inside the house and Mama closes the screen door. Daddy looks up at the far, cold moon. Grins.)"

Camilla stops in the middle of the corridor: "I remember my father's grin. The dreams of tomorrow that were forgotten—Hali is filled with the vanished. Did I tell you to stop reading, woman? Go on, go on. Let us see if this spell you are weaving has something to say. "

Tense, she knows Majesty can be reckless and lose reason for no reason. Seeking composed, she exhales. The poet's tone carries more fear as she begins the next passage.

"Traffic With Autumn: Scene 1; Act 2

EUROPA

I see the Great Grey One.

ANDROMEDA

Here? Touching the night?

EUROPA

His words are worms, storms that flood my eyes.

ANDROMEDA

Do you hear the stillness of Nowhere ring?

EUROPA

His mouth speaks in a thousand languages.

(Andromeda rises and steps behind the cast iron loveseat. She slowly lifts her head and gazes out over a dour horizon of twilight-cloaked, muddy fields.)

ANDROMEDA

With morning-light, should it arrive and leave any hearts as witness, there will come further mourning.

EUROPA

(Still sitting, hands folded in her lap, on a cast-iron loveseat, looking down at her bare feet and the litter of dead moths that cover the ground.)
Every bird will die in this bitterly-cold autumn.
ANDROMEDA
The light of a poet will surely come ashore and offer comfort. This cannot be the end to heart-blood and tongues of longing.
ANDROMEDA
(Placing her hand, simmered in madness and tears, on her sister's shoulder.)
I want blue and open doors, not arrowheads. Do you hear me?
EUROPA
In a thousand languages, he whispers to me, every bird will die.
ANDROMEDA
(As if she's been bitten by fire, as if she can shield her heart from arrowheads, her hand flies from her sister's shoulder to her breast.)
No bouquet of harmony. Bones…and rain again.
EUROPA
Everywhere: His greyness…
(It begins to drizzle.)
and rain."

Camilla, her words slow and even though they clutch an inferno: "Every bird will die. Deceitful songs. Lies and false whispers."

The poet does not pause as Camilla speaks.

"THE PHANTOM OF TRUTH: itwas. twosisters. inaroom. ahideawayforcreatureswhocannotsleep. oneinblackandred. oneinwhiteandwhiteandwhite. facetofacepastandevertogether. bothhavetheirshoesoff. tworealitieslivinginonereality. botharethinking. rememberingitwas. sufferingtheovenoftime. dreamingitcouldhavebeen. shoutingnosliently.

51

bothareedgy. nervousdestined—
eventhemoonspeaksofit. dontrusteachother.
(asitwasthen. itisagain.) "no." "no."
darkbrowneyeswatchtheshadowappear. movecloser.
(asitwasthen. itisagain.)
doesoftbrowneyeswatchtheshadowappear.
movecloser. closer. (asitwasthen. itisagain.) "no."
"no." theterriblestrangerstretchingthehours.
hereyesonhispath. hereyesonhisfeathers. closer.
thesongofhismeasurelesscloakreeksoffaroffplaces.
(asitwasthen.) slaveswoken. (itisagain.) "no." "no."
faroffplacesemptyplacesrainingtakingrouteandmidstan
dtakingbreath.
itis.now.curtainsopenwidethemoonafraidtospeak.(agai
n.)twosisters.outsidethehideawayroomfleeingtearshini
ngontheirback.tworealitieslivinginonereality.facetofac
epastofwretchedshapesanddryinggraveandevertogethe
r.facetofacewithlastthingsruinedtruthdryteacupsnearho
me.thedancingshadowoftheterriblestranger.(fromcolda
far.)closercloser.twosisters.(thedebrisofgreedandthepai
ntofcloakedlies.)whocannotsleep.oneinragsofblackand
red.oneinaweatheredfleetofwhiteandwhiteandwhite.he
reyesonhispath."nosun."hereyesonhisfeathers."nolight
."memoriesbludge.teethareshown.ontheloomofyearnin
gtwosisterssickoffatespulsingcompassaresilenced.note
ars.(thestarschangenot.)nolaments.(theblacknessbetwe
enthestarsuffersnotheyhavegone.)nograves.wholetheir
shellsarehungonabarrentree.crowsandravensbloom."

"Waiting for lovers. Crying. Crowned with weeds, broken
by impious acts…blind." Camilla shutters. "Why must they
always be blind?" A moment later. "I think this will be
presented to my court."

Bone-white mask to heart-red mask. "Why did you read
the scenes out of order? What sense is there in that?"

"My Queen, my play is a work in progress. I have yet to
decide on the order of a few scenes and my feelings on

presentation change with each reading. I did not mean to offend or—"

"Time, and what it brings and takes, changes. It will not be locked into simple understandable patterns. Yes. That, I have experienced. Too many times. Too many."

Camilla leans in, removes her bone-white mask, whispers. "You, too, have endured love, yes? I see it in you. The spells. The screams. The *disgust*. Wind and waves; we mourn and no explanation arrives. Madness and memory and sleepless nights…What of tenderness *that lasts*?"

Camilla drops her mask on the floor of bone-white tile and, as if a wispy phantom set in motion by unseen currents, drifts away.

The bone-white moon shines whitely in Yvain's cold studio. Gin (more than half the bottle) to help defeat weakness and an endless chain of cigarettes, each lit from the tip of the burning one in his hand.

Dreams crying in the shadows.

The chisel has not moved.

For an hour he's looked at her shoeless, slipperless, bone-white feet. His rough hand tenderly caressing her bone-white hand, Yvain wedded his heart-strings to the cascade of sensual congress he feels for her.

"Camilla." His sigh would be musical were it not broken by no exquisite return.

She will be here soon. To pose. Perfect her shape, all she sprays into the room. Perfect her comforts, were she to grant them.

Pale perfection in a pool where the moon shines whitely. He'll bite his tongue, hold back his yearning fingers, and stare, covet; he, taxed, will be a cage, a well of felt. And Camilla will stand there, ripe, gripping all he is.

"Struck. And she does not even see. Those eyes. Blind, to me, to what I have to give." Gulp of gin. "Camilla, you sit, alone, upon a throne of bones; I could be the king of your heart. Our angels and demons would play, sing. Cast the shadows away." Staring at the shape of her breasts, at her erect nipples, the sculpture captured them perfectly. Longing for the bed of pleasure she has never imagined. "We could be soft and borderless; a furnace."

Drains the glass of gin.

Pours. Gulps. "In my arms your bridal flowers would bloom."

Fucked them all; like some cheap clinging whore. And they fucked you with treachery. Spread your thighs and took them in your mouth. Let them blacken your soul.

"Boris?"

"Your Majesty."

"You wear despair."

"A long night. The coffin chill. Too much drink. The faraway was too near."

"Yes, the shreds and tatters, from time to time the madness lights my hours with storms, too. It's the curse of romantic blood, isn't it?"

"Yes, Your Majesty, the desire."

"Pick up your chisel and sweep away the gloom."

Camilla steps into a pool of bone-white moonlight. Resumes a pose she's become used to, laughs at something she does not share.

He's drowning in the sight of her, wanting, needing, to take her, to contour.

She should be mine. Her lips should tell me she is. Her lips—

the tip of a tongue licking the corner of a mouth. the mouth parting an invitation. breath melted to breath. warmth becomes heat. tongue sighing on its partner. partner's yes pressing, opening please. she inhales, her heart skips. he inhales and grows stiffer. below she's as wet as her tongue (and no finger has yet to touch her), wants to be wetter, wants his tongue's warmth to open her. warmth as dream warmth as

54

living warmth glowing wet easy carrying tongues to crazy
crazy is forever is the lyrist the vortex the obsession recruiting
plenty loosening up a trick with juicy. lipstick offers keys and
his urges addiction accepts the horizon and the performance.
drinks bathes groans. she wants her cunt full of his humping.
wants to squeeze it mumbles moisture as commentary. lips
apart. one inch. ready for speed. ready to uncork heat bounce
on the intoxication the sensitive soft mound of a bottom lip
rubbing the declared more of his upper lip. more more more
all and no stop. tongues come together again and breath as
one the wet tango, outgrowths of neverstop, spiral, her on top
him around (sliding back) till above. the tip of a finger on her
lower lip, she opens, wants it inside, she licks it sucks it
dreams…eeltongues opening fleshmouths to hang stars, seas
of affection—outgrowths of neverstop, on faces creating new
entangled. tongues snowing flowers that will not be wasted.
his mouth on her eyes. and again softer. burning calendars on
her eyelids. his mouth on her neck all its tender colors
hunting. his mouth on her neck burning calendars below her
chin. the gates of her dreamscentedocean are open begging—

Behind her. His lips one inch from her perfect bone-white
shoulder.

Magnetized. Leans in. Presses his lips to her bone-white
shoulder.

She whirls. Her petite hand a fist.

Contact.

"You presume."

Blood on his lips.

"A no one. Nothing. Unworthy."

His chisel, a riot at the end of his arm, must. Replies—
"No." Its battle-cry. There. There, south of her smooth belly.
His cheeks lined with tears. There, a torn breast. More.
Giving. Taking. His lips curled. There—*Uhot fucked her—
Alar fucker her—Thale fucked her—Denis fucked her—
Aldones fucked her*. Chisel's thunderbreath rips her cheek,
pulls down, her redlips are wider.

*Uhot fucked her—Alar fucker her—Thale fucked her—
Denis fucked her—Aldones fucked her.*

55

Chisel. *There*!

THERE!

Again and again till death.

Until there is no more.

Naked.

Hit the floor with a lifeless thud. Bone-white legs, bone-white shoulders, bone-white knees. Sprawled on the cold stone floor.

The moon shines whitely.

On his knees above perfection destroyed. Afraid to touch her.

Refusing to believe.

Her blood on his lips. On his hands.

On his chest.

Blood in his hair.

On his groin.

Weeping. Burning in the love story ruined.

Ruined. The nights, the wars she carried in her pockets. Her energy. Everything she could have been—the shape and force of her story.

His tears at her throat. On her breast. On the floor.

Hissing. No words, only felt.

Disbelief.

"No."

The chisel, sopping with cooling blood, flies across the room. Clangs. The shadows do not stir.

Hissing.

Weeping.

"No!" Cacophony. "Noooooo." The screaming blackness of threnody. "*Nooooooooooooooooo.*" Lamentation.

An hour on the floor. On his knees. Trembling. Reaching and not touching. He's looked at her shoeless, slipperless, bone-white feet. Touching. Kissed her eyes. Arranged her hair. His rough hand tenderly held her bone-white hand. The weight of his face on her bone-white breast changes the shape of what was once round soft and perfect.

The bone-white moon has gone behind clouds.

Yvain's finished the bottle of gin, killed the hard pack of cigarettes. Wrapped her cold shell in an old tarp.

Pace of a funeral procession, carries her to the shore of Hali. Pushes her into the water. She sinks below the cloudwaves.

Yvain opened the window of his tower room; two hundred feet below, there is no clearness, no peace, only darkened fate. He is into another bottle of gin; there is no forgiveness in it.

He stands, sweating drunk weeping, his bloody chisel on the floor beside the opened book. His statue of Camilla is not finished but the new play was. Over a dozen of his bloody fingerprints stain the margins. Through his tears, Boris Yvain has read and reread its final passages more than a dozen times tonight.

> "(Nearing twilight. A bitterly cold autumn. Two sisters sit together on a cast-iron loveseat in a frost-burned garden of dry sluices and weathered trellises. They look out over a cheerless horizon of greyness.)
> ANDROMEDA, THE ELDER SISTER
> She is gone.
> EUROPA, THE YOUNGER SISTER
> This castle, its court, will fall.
> ANDROMEDA
> All will dry and die in sad Carcosa.
> EUROPA
> There are tears on the woman's story.
> (She turns in her seat and looks back at the dark windows of the castle.)
> From the day it began, intrigues and lies followed her.
> ANDROMEDA

All light lost…lost. Embroidered on the frayed skirt of autumn. Toil and blood and no *who cares for me* for her.
EUROPA
A thousand years of greyness.
ANDROMEDA
Faith, and all hopes, rotted by the storm, can we endure the rain?
EUROPA
We must. We must cling to the legend.
ANDROMEDA
The Last Queen can never die. Yet, she is gone.
EUROPA
Remember what Papa said that night on the porch before Mama called us inside. 'Hali will take her, and below the cloudwaves, in the blueblack canyons of the deeps, its dreams and tonics will reanimate what cannot be undone. For a thousand years and a day, a regal swan, bone-white and shining like fish scales, a graceful swan with ink-black eyes filled with stars— its Aphrodite perfume laced with the aroma of roses and a woman's lower playground heating the air, will sail the cloudwaves. On that day, when the sky blazes with blue, when the Queen is fully repaired, she will come ashore and again sit upon the bone-white swan throne.'
ANDROMEDA
Papa never lied. He was always faithful."

Yvain stands on the ledge of the opened window of his Spartan tower room. In his right hand he holds her left hand, the last piece of her unfinished statue, the only piece he has not smashed.

Outside, circling the tower, the silent, bitterblack, carrion deathbirds, wait.

(10cc "Cry," "I'm Not In Love"; Donna Summer "I Feel Love"; Sade "Smooth Operator"; John Secada "Just Another

Day (Without You)"; Bee Gees "Fanny (Be Tender With My Love)"; Madeleine Payroux "Love And Treachery"; Joe Henry "Sold", "Stop", "Struck"; Leonard Cohen "Tower of Song"; Frank Sinatra "In The Wee Small Hours Of The Morning"; Ray LaMontagne "Jolene")

THE GREY QUEEN

Paul StJohn Mackintosh

Cassie was studying in the Mackintosh Library in the Glasgow School of Art, prepping for the third and final stage of her course, when she first saw the Sign. She knew it was the wrong time to get fixated on something new, with Spring Break just over, and her last term to get under way, but she couldn't help being captivated. There, set into the dark wood of one of the window bays, was a brass plaque she could not recall seeing before, incised with a strange trifoliate design, like a skeletal clover leaf; and it seemed to vibrate and shiver in a way that made her squint.

Cassie was naturally attracted by effects like that, which had inspired her field of study and her graduate thesis. Trompe-l'œil, forced perspective, quodlibets, and all the other illusionistic tricks that artists and architects use to create space and objects where none existed and distort form, fascinated her. She had almost opted for Painting and Printmaking, before settling on Interior Design within the School's one-year intensive Masters in Design course in Graphics,

Illustration and Photography. Her work still tended to focus on mural decoration and walls, like the reproductions of Rex Whistler's grisailles for Lady Mountbatten's boudoir now open on the reading desk in front of her, tessellating imaginary plasterwork across the table. And right there on the wall was an example that she hadn't noticed before, the work of Charles Rennie Mackintosh himself. ("There's a lot of Mackintoshes around, lassie. Take the train up to Inverness, and the place is full of them," she'd been warned when she began the course. "You'd best call him Rennie Mackintosh if you want anyone to be sure who you mean.")

She got up from her desk, stepped over to the shimmering design by the window, and probed it with hesitant fingers. Nothing changed under her fingertips: all she felt was cool metal, and yet the shape continued to shimmer beneath and between them. She wondered for a moment whether that could be an effect of the weak April sunlight, filtered through typical Glasgow overcast, and picked up a folio from the nearby desk to shade the plaque from the window. The flickering persisted without direct light. Cassie realized she'd been holding her breath, and when she let it out in a sigh, other students nearby looked up and stared at her. Blushing, she put the folio down. Still, she couldn't step away from the plaque, and she pulled out her phone and snapped off half a dozen shots of it, checking the image gallery immediately after. Light effects could be complex in that dark interior, she knew, with its wood and metal surfaces that hovered somewhere between a forest clearing and a dark reliquary, but the strange shimmer persisted on the phone screen. She fingered the Rennie Mackintosh silver necklace she wore habitually as she gazed at the images.

So inspiring were the images, Cassie decided to take them to her supervisor to ask about them. Frankly, her final term needed a kickstart to give it some central focus. Her critical reflective journal, an essential part of her coursework, bore an uncomfortable resemblance to a random scrapbook in some parts, when it was supposed to be a systematic, analytical exercise in deepening her understanding of her own aesthetic and its theoretical context. Her elective in frescography at least had a clear career goal, but she already had run into trouble in turning all her precious computer time on the School's Computer-Aided Mural packages into anything more disciplined than haphazard images on virtual walls. She'd hit a wall, she sometimes quipped to herself, in the brief lulls when her anxieties abated enough to allow that insight to resurface. Maybe Rennie Mackintosh had just signposted her way through that wall.

Without waiting, Cassie walked straight out of the Mackintosh Building's brooding red-gold facade on Renfrew Street and crossed over to the far paler and more contemporary frontage of the Reid Building, just opened to house the School of Design. The new edifice still smelt of paint and fresh plastic, and the staff were clearly not yet settled in, but she found her way through the bustle to the office of Donald Hume, Senior Lecturer and Programme Leader at the School. As it turned out, he was free, and his assistant showed her straight in.

"What can I do for you, Cassie?" he asked, springing up from behind his desk like the older, more Georgian Peter Capaldi he resembled. "What's so urgent to have got you running up to see me like this?"

"Well, I wanted to pick your brains about something I just came across in the Mackintosh Building, Professor," she admitted, doffing her bag and laying her phone down on his desk. "It looks like it might be relevant to my work, and I'd like to incorporate it into my final project, if it turns out to fit."

"A lot of Mackintosh's interior work was essentially mural rather than architectural. I'm surprised you didn't pick up on the parallel before. But let's take a look." Dr Hume pored over her phone screen, then blinked in recognition. "Ah, that's the Yellow Sign," he mused.

"The what?" Cassie hadn't heard that name before, though her supervisor seemed completely familiar with it. "What is it?"

"Oh, it's a rare motif from the 1890s, contemporary with Rennie Mackintosh's own designs for the School of Art," Dr Hume explained, tugging at his chin. "You can find it elsewhere in his work as well: in some of the ideal designs he did for houses of artists and art lovers, after he completed his work on the School of Art in 1896. Quite haunting, isn't it?"

"But it never seems to stand still," Cassie muttered. "I wonder how Rennie Mackintosh got that effect?"

"No one's quite sure," Dr Hume replied. "But critics have explained it as something like hazel eyes."

"Huh?" Cassie blinked, suddenly conscious of her own large brown eyes, and glancing involuntarily into Dr Hume's steel greys.

"Hazel eyes aren't actually an eye colour as such," he explained. "That's why they sometimes can appear to shift anywhere from green to dark brown. Their shade is a result of Rayleigh scattering, the same process that makes the sky blue, operating on an underlying substrate of melanin, and it changes according to the lighting conditions, whether the eyes are dilated, and so on."

"So you think Rennie Mackintosh came up with that design by staring into hazel eyes?" Cassie replied, trying to keep the irony out of her voice.

"Hardly," Dr Hume chuckled. "In fact, that design and that effect aren't unique to Rennie Mackintosh himself. They're associated with a cult play of his period, a fin-de-siècle drama like one of Maeterlinck's, called *The King in Yellow*. The play was suppressed almost as soon as it appeared, same as the first edition of *The 120 Days of Sodom*, but it was a popular fad for a time, like absinthe drinking or Theosophy. And although there's no documentary proof, most critics believe that Rennie Mackintosh must have read the play, and come across the Yellow Sign at the same time. Both would have been well known in Glasgow artistic circles at that date. Remember that the Glasgow Four, his little artistic coterie with Herbert MacNair and the Macdonald sisters before he married Margaret, was also known as the Spook School. Kind of suggestive, don't you think?"

"So if that sign was one of the Aesthetic symbols of the Gay Nineties, could there be any pattern books or other guides to reproducing that effect?" Cassie persisted, twiddling her silver pendant between her fingers. "You know, anything that might have been picked up by the Decadents and the Arts and Crafts Movements, then fallen out of fashion later? I mean, it's quite incredible, isn't it?"

"Rennie Mackintosh isn't exactly my field, even though he is the local hero," Dr Hume mused. "I do know that art historians have been labouring for over a century to try and account for the strangeness and mystery in some of his design schemes. If he did use any systematic symbolism, no one's satisfactorily explained it, though we do know that he was a fan of the Rosicrucians. But I tell you who you should talk to: Professor Alan Grant, Director of the Centre for the Study of Perceptual Experience. It's part of the College of Arts at the University of Glasgow, even though it's about as deeply scientific as you can get without a PhD in quantum mechanics. He and I got to talking about the Yellow Sign a couple of years back, when we did a joint show with the University on visual illusions at the Glasgow Science Fair. I'll email him and copy you in; he'll be able to tell you more."

"Thanks, Doc," Cassie beamed, and snatched up her phone. "See you in class."

"Just make sure you stay on track with this," Dr Hume chided her, as she stepped out.

Cassie left the Reid Building to walk back down the hill to her digs, under a Glasgow grey sky, that Glaswegian dourness which she so welcomed because it suited her personal style: a palette of greys, too pale for a straight Goth look. Scotland had plenty of grey days wherever you went, though, and she didn't intend to stay on in the city beyond graduation in September.

Cassie had opted for a single year in Glasgow, because she couldn't afford the two-year M.Des in Communication Design. With her career goal post-graduation so clear in mind, she hadn't seen this as a drawback—not with the bright future she envisaged in set design or interior decoration. Practice-led and process-oriented: that was what the programme outline said, and that was exactly what she needed, one of the few certainties that gave structure and direction to her chaos of a life. Besides, the money she saved by opting for one year instead of two left her able to rent a one-bedroom flat on the postgraduate floor of Blythswood House on West Regent Street, a few blocks downhill from the Mackintosh Building. Just off Sauchiehall Street, the School of Art's Garnethill campus was truly in the heart of Glasgow, but Cassie, used to the sea views of Rosyth and Queensferry, and prospects of the Firth of Forth from central Edinburgh, found the whole area oppressive.

Today, even in the short walk from campus to hall of residence, some brickies on the street corner whistled at her as she swept past in her flowing grey gown. Decades after William McIlvanney had rolled out Laidlaw, Glasgow was still as much of an open sewer of toxic masculinity as any Tartan Noir novel. Cassie struggled with an anxiety-spectrum disorder dating back to her unhappy childhood, and her grim adolescence with her crass, uncomprehending family in Fife, and she needed her safe spaces, sheltered from that kind of emotional abrasion. At least the hall of residence was fully secure, and she could even shut herself away from her fellow tenants when she needed to. The Mondrianesque bareness of its interior scheme was totally against her taste, though, with its squared-off walls and surfaces painted bright solid colours where they weren't white. She had used some of her computing time on the faculty's frescography programs to print off a slew of monochrome designs, from grisaille altar panels to funerary art, exactly tailored to the wall spaces of her apartment, so she could paper over that blankness with shades of grey.

She found a relatively friendly reception waiting for her in the common area, where the other post-grads were planning a Cinco de Mayo party, with masks scattered around them on the sofas and tables. Or not quite planning: arguing. It seemed one of them was objecting to appropriation of Mexican cultural symbols.

"Aww, clam up, ya bawbag," said another, already quaffing from an open bottle of Belhaven, even in the early afternoon. "I didnae hear anywan screamin' 'cultural appropriation' when Canaucks buy kilts in Buchanan Street, or Mel Gibson dawbs hissel in woad."

"Here, Cassie, isn't this your style?" Siobhan, one of her closest local friends, held up a grey Cinco de Mayo skull mask and waved it at her.

"The whole thing's a fake," persisted the knowledgeable, chalk-white post-grad who had started the whole cultural appropriation argument. "A Yankee relic of FDR's cultural diplomacy in the 1930s. Why, even those skulls are more about the Day of the Dead than Cinco de Mayo."

"They cannae be, look, they git Cinco de Fookin Mayo printed aw ower 'em," retaliated the Belhaven drinker. "Awa' n' shite, ya numpty. Dae ye huv tae mak such a fookin palaver tae drink some fookin tequila?"

Cassie eyed the skull masks with far more than culturally sensitive distaste: the grey, monochrome, polychrome, psychedelic designs tore at her eyes, with every sort of motif from flowers to crystals, to peace signs, to even smaller skulls, pressed into service to flesh out their designs. Their hollow eye sockets stared back. Suddenly dizzy, she put her hand to her forehead and excused herself, retreating to her room.

Safe behind closed doors, surrounded by the grey paper flats, Cassie opened her ageing laptop and Googled *The King in Yellow*. She found a short Wikipedia entry on the play. Written by an anonymous author, probably American, who may or may not have shot himself shortly after finishing it, *The King in Yellow* first appeared in 1895 in French as *Le Roi en jaune,* although the English original surfaced soon after. Authorities in France and elsewhere apparently acted in concert to suppress it, and the play had since practically disappeared. Curiously for Wikipedia, the entry had very few external links, just a couple of references to an American scholar, Robert W. Chambers, who apparently had dedicated his life to researching it, and mentioned the Yellow Sign only as a motif associated with the play, linked to optical illusions. Amazon could turn up no editions of the play either, beyond a few references to ancient out-of-print copies, with incredibly high prices offered for them. Wider searches on Google produced references to urban legends and forbidden books. Cassie speculated whether the authorities were still trying to suppress the play over a century later. Obviously, Dr Hume had been right when he used the word cult about it.

Her email dinged. Dr Hume had contacted his opposite number in the University as promised, and Professor Grant had replied with an appointment a few days hence. Cassie accepted it. Then she decided to leave the mystery of *The King in Yellow* on one side, settled down to some more mundane coursework on mural designs, but her eyes had grown tired and she kept seeing patterns when she blinked, chiefly the Yellow Sign.

The Centre for the Study of Perceptual Experience was a few hundred metres west of the Garnethill campus, on the far side of the River Kelvin and Kelvingrove Park, near another Rennie Mackintosh place of pilgrimage, the artist's house and museum. Cassie decided to walk there, not least because the stroll through the park opened up the landscape and relieved the claustrophobia she felt elsewhere among Glasgow's closely-packed terraces, however mellow their golden sandstone. And it was a balmy late April day, with the sky Rayleigh-scattering blue, warming her so pleasantly that even her dove-grey gown felt too dark and heavy for the weather for once.

Professor Grant remarked on it when they met. "Ah, I see you favour grey," he said jovially, looking her dress up and down as he clasped her hand in both of his. "You know that most mammals see the world in shades of grey? Humans and other apes are among the few that don't."

In the flesh, he turned out to be a short, stocky, square-featured, almost caricature Scot, with his golden freckles, outdoor tan, and crisply curled, close-cropped, greying fair hair. At first sight, Cassie thought immediately of dwarven, the alternate colour word for old gold, the same shade as Rennie Mackintosh's brass fittings in the Library.

"No, I didn't know that," she answered, interested despite herself. "Why is that?"

"Selective pressure," Grant replied, somewhat smugly. "The earliest mammals had to be nocturnal to compete, while they were snapping at the ankles of the dinosaurs, so they developed eyes maximized for night vision. But once the monkeys got up in the trees, surrounded by fruit, they lost the ability to synthesize their own vitamin C. Colour vision became an advantage for seeking out fruit with high concentrations of vit C."

"Well, I didn't know that," Cassie chuckled. "Thank you for helping me out with my favourite colour."

"My pleasure." Grant clapped his hands, waved her to the other office chair, and sat down behind his desk. "So, let me see what else I can help you out with."

Cassie took a printed copy of the Yellow Sign from her bag and laid it down on the desk. "I'm wondering if you could help me work out how Rennie Mackintosh got this effect, and the ideas or anything that helped him do it. I mean, you can see it, right? Even on a paper printout, it vibrates in front of your eyes."

Grant squinted at the image. "Yeah, I remember this is what me and Dr Hume were talking about. It's quite an impression, isn't it? We even did some spectral measurements on it, to see if there's something going on with light refraction that we didn't know about. But it's not a physical phenomenon. The vibration you're seeing is not in the image itself: it's in your head."

"So how's that happen?" Cassie asked.

Grant pursed his lips for a moment before replying. "We suspect the Sign is a form constant."

"A what?"

Grant sniffed disdainfully. "As a graphic arts major, I'm surprised you haven't come across them before. They were first defined by Heinrich Klüver, a German psychologist, when he was studying the effects of peyote back in the 1920s, and found that certain patterns tended to crop up again and again in the hallucinations of mescaline users. He defined four types: lattices, cobwebs, tunnels, and spirals. They turn up in other types of hallucination and altered states of consciousness as well: dreams, near-death experiences, epileptic seizures, migraines, hypnagogic states, oxygen starvation. They're believed to be a result of the way the physiology of vision is organized, especially pattern mapping from the retina to the visual cortex. Basically, they're fundamental to our deep brain structure."

"I'd sort of worked out it was probably something like that, based on other optical illusions," Cassie pointed out hesitantly. "I just wanted a steer on how he might have done it. You know, so maybe I could follow in his footsteps?"

Grant shrugged. "Trial and error? He kept pushing till he got what looked right? Or a dream vision, like Kekulé's rings?" Seeing Cassie's puzzled look, he explained: "August Kekulé, the organic chemist: he discovered the ring structure of the benzene molecule, claiming that he saw it in a day-dream of a snake seizing its own tail, like the Worm Ouroboros that early alchemists were so fond of. And, well, it could be: form constants do appear in dreams. But we reckon he had a more concrete inspiration."

"Something to do with that *King in Yellow* play, right?" Cassie picked up from him. "Dr Hume told me about that too. It's not really much of a help, though. I mean, if you read a mystery play that pretty much sunk out of sight as soon as it was published, how does that help you create an optical illusion?"

"Well, as far as we know, the first edition of *The King in Yellow* did contain a reproduction of the Yellow Sign," Grant went on. "If Rennie Mackintosh ever read a copy, of course he'd have seen that. It's kind of hard to substantiate, though, because no first edition survives outside private collections, or, would you believe, the Vatican Library's closed collection? It was on the Index of Prohibited Books. It's one of the few rare first editions that's never been reproduced in facsimile on the internet, so far as anyone can tell.

Speculation is that the unknown author of the play and his circle happened across the Yellow Sign themselves, by accident or design, because of what the play is, or what they intended it to be."

"And what is that?" Cassie asked.

"It's a mindworm. A dangerous meme virus. Like Roko's Basilisk."

"What?"

"Roko's Basilisk. It's a thought experiment, devised by some poster to a nutty transhumanist forum called LessWrong, whose handle was Roko. Here, I'll show you."

Grant took a pad and pen in his short, thick fingers, sketched something, and put the pad on the desk in front of her. He'd sketched two boxes, one, marked A, captioned "Devote your life to bringing Roko's Basilisk into being," and the other, marked B, captioned "Nothing—or Eternal Torment."

Cassie studied the sketch. "Well, that looks creepy," she mused. "So, let me guess: I have to choose Box A or Box B?"

"Not exactly: and that's the clever part." Grant sucked his pen, looking as though he'd thought up the idea himself. "It's a variant of a thought experiment originally called Newcomb's paradox. You can choose either Box B, or both boxes. In the original, Box A always contains a thousand dollars. Box B either contains nothing, or a million dollars. And the contents of Box B are chosen by an infallible entity called the Predictor—an alien, a superintelligent AI, a psychic, God, whatever—who has predicted exactly what you will choose. You know that if the Predictor predicted you'll choose Box B, then Box B will always contain the million dollars. If the Predictor predicted you'll choose both boxes, then Box B will always be empty. And the Predictor also knows you know this. Oh, and if you just flip a coin to choose, then Box B will always be empty."

Cassie shrugged, slightly irritated by Grant's stream of gnomic explanations. "So what's so clever? You always take Box B."

Grant pulled the pen out of his mouth and twirled it between his fingers. "But the Predictor already knows what you've chosen. Always. Infallibly. Its understanding of how you think is critical to the outcome of the choice, and it already chose what was in the boxes, before you even made your choice. How can it do that? Most probably, by running a simulation to see what happens. But to be infallible, it needs to simulate everything, including you: your consciousness, your awareness. So in fact, you may already be in the Matrix making the choice, not the real you at all."

"Alright, that's creepy enough." Cassie shuddered. "So what's the Basilisk part, and all this eternal suffering stuff?"

"Oh, that's an extra layer of nasty, for the *Matrix* and *Terminator* fans, and other true believers in Artificial Intelligence and the coming of our robot overlords," Grant chuckled. "Roko was one of them, and he spun his own version of Newcomb's paradox for that audience. For the LessWrong crowd, a basilisk is any information that can harm or endanger those who learn it. And Roko's Basilisk is an omniscient AI who has come into being some time in the future, and either can look back into the past to see what you're going to do, or is already running this reality as a simulation." He banged the heel of his palm on the wooden desk. "And Roko's Basilisk is offering you a choice: take both boxes, and help it to come into being, or take Box B, and it will put you in Hell for eternity. So which are you going to choose?"

Cassie chuckled as well, nervously. "But that's all bullshit, right?"

Grant shrugged again. "Maybe. But enough readers of the LessWrong forum believed it to be given nightmares—and worse. After all, the way they see it, the moment you hear, or even think about, that argument, the AI already starts holding you to account. A few apparently came close to nervous breakdowns just worrying about that. LessWrong's founder banned the discussion almost as soon as it went up, partly to spare them those nightmares, and partly to...um, avoid giving any future AI an incentive to blackmail them that way. So yes, he really believed it was a risk, or at least a possibility, too. And I don't think you need to believe in it to see that Roko's Basilisk is already doing some harm."

Cassie was more than nervous now: she was genuinely chilled. "Well, you've probably given me a few nightmares of my own," she mumbled.

"I'm sorry about that, but I did want to show you the issues about things like the Yellow Sign and *The King in Yellow*." Grant at least looked a little less smug.

"Well, if it is so, what the hell were they thinking of in the first place dreaming it up?" Cassie was now genuinely aggrieved. "I mean, was it supposed to be some kind of artistic terrorism?"

Grant stopped her. "Maybe. Scholars do believe that the original author was looking for both artistic and poetic versions of a psychological or philosophical phenomenon, like pairing a visual paradox with a verbal paradox. Think of Lewis Carroll. You don't have to be a scientist to see that all types of paradox have something in common, whether you see them or you say them. But it may not be malicious. It could just be the truth. And yes," he continued, holding up his hand before Cassie's puzzlement could grow even more glaring, "I know that does need more explanation. There's a new formal, mathematical theory of consciousness called conscious agents theory, worked out by Donald Hoffman, a professor in California, and his partners. It's been partly developed out of game theory, by testing its premises in scenario after scenario, in millions of mathematical simulations, with all kinds of different starting values. What those simulations found, time after time, was that agents whose perceptions were optimized for utility always won out over those whose senses were geared for truth. In other words, the world we perceive is like a user interface, and the more you try to push through that interface to the underlying reality, the more it degrades and becomes useless. Ultimately, the truth will kill you."

"Well, that's very nice," Cassie riposted.

"Oh, if you think that's bad, there's far worse, and more established, mental killers than that around. You want to know the Number One mindworm of them all? Existential doubt. We don't exist, we only think we do; are we really here; all that guff. That's enough to completely fuck you up, if you really think about it. Descartes created an entire philosophy trying to get away from it. The rational self-conscious mind using its own processes to chew away at itself, until there's nothing left, like the Worm Ouroboros swallowing its own tail. That one's a bugger to get away from. Och, it's even been used to explain the Glasgow effect."

"What on earth has all this to do with the Glasgow effect?" Cassie griped.

"Alienation, lassie. Poverty, bad diet and substance abuse aren't enough in themselves to account for Glasgow's appalling mortality rates: Glasgow's figures for alcoholism and obesity aren't any worse than many northern English cities. Now, some sociologists suspect those are symptoms, rather than the underlying causes, pointing to a culture of despair, where people just don't have enough faith to live. And that's just one of the worst cases of a flaw fundamental to the human condition. On average, every 40 seconds someone, somewhere in the world, has killed themselves. That's over one million suicides worldwide each year. Forget Iraq or Syria: that figure dwarfs the casualties for all the current conflicts worldwide."

"And I came here to find out more about a bloody design." Patience at last exhausted, Cassie got up, grabbing her bag. "I'm sorry, Professor, but if you don't mind, this is all turning into just a bit too much of a downer for me."

"Look, I'm sorry too." Grant did look contrite. "I just wanted to give you some idea of what's really going on with the Yellow Sign, and Mackintosh's source for it. But if you wanted some kind of how-to manual to create the same kind of effect, I'm afraid that as far as we know, there isn't one. Somehow it just knocks a hole in the wall of our inner model of reality, and that's all we can say. And frankly, I'd be careful of it, if I were you."

"Don't worry yourself, Professor," Cassie responded more calmly, moved by a sudden insight she hadn't quite articulated to herself yet. "I think you actually did help me work out what I need to do."

Grant didn't seem entirely put at ease by her response, but he shook hands with her civilly enough. Cassie felt like she'd been interviewing an expert witness in some Tartan Noir criminal investigation: an especially unsettling one. As soon as she was out of the Centre's undistinguished slab facade, she hurried down Gibson Street to cross the River Kelvin by the Eldon Street Bridge, Kelvingrove Park forgotten, anxious to get back to her room by the fastest possible route. The first thing she needed to do, she knew, was download *The King in Yellow.* She hadn't bothered to run down a copy yet, but she knew they existed, somewhere out there in distant archives in cyberspace, not exactly in plain view, but not exactly inaccessible either. She even thought of downloading it straight onto her phone, but decided she couldn't follow a playscript properly on that small screen. Once on the bridge, though, she caught sight of a figure standing by the green railing along its northern side, staring directly at her. The figure wore a grey hoodie, with the hood pulled up, even though the now-overcast weather was still balmy and warm, with what looked like bleached or greyish jeans. When she looked into its hood, though, she saw almost the same shade of grey as the cloth encircling it, with two black holes for eyes, and no mouth. If it was a balaclava or ski mask the strange grey man was wearing, she couldn't make out any details. A van slid between them, but when it had passed, she saw the figure was still staring at her exactly as before, as though its eyes had tracked her right through the sides of the van. And it seemed to be moving along the far pavement in step with her.

Glasgow brutality and Glasgow poverty were as unfamiliar to Cassie as Glasgow creativity and Glasgow savvy, and far more intimidating. She had been pleasantly surprised when she first arrived on Clydeside to find that the urban legends of Gorbals violence and No Mean City were hugely overblown, if they ever really had much substance behind them at all. They were still there in the back of her mind though, and

Grant's lecture had brought them all back. She took a firm grip on her bag, and ran down Eldon Street and Woodlands Road, until the figure was left far behind.

After that experience, it was a relief to lock her apartment door behind her, ferret out a copy of the mysterious play online, and lose herself in the world of Camilla and the Stranger, Aldones and Uoth, Hastur and the Phantom of Truth, in lost Carcosa where black stars rise and the cloud waves beat forever on the shore of the Lake of Hali. She learned of Aldebaran and the Hyades, and of the awful coming of the King, the King of rags and patches, with the mantle of hyperbolic ruffles, whose scalloped tatters must hide Yhtill forever. So absorbed did she become that she passed the May Day celebrations shut away in her room, only emerging afterwards, bedraggled and thinner, but energized by her new concentration and focus. The insight she had gained in Grant's room was substantiated now, and the enigma of the Yellow Sign was no longer opaque. Her purpose was clear.

"I want to rejig my coursework for the rest of the term," she told Dr Hume, when she came out of her fugue. "Your Professor Grant inspired me. I'm going to need some more computer time and perhaps some more contacts with the University, but I know what I want to do."

"Well, would you care to explain a little more?" Dr Hume responded, speaking slowly and carefully. "I'd be glad to know why you're embarking on such a big step."

"I want to model imaginary dimensions," she explained. "Four-dimensional spaces, even more, whatever I can. Möbius strips, Klein bottles, Boy's surface, tesseracts, hypercubes, everything. Trompe l'oeil is all about incorporating the illusion of three dimensions into two, right? I want to see what I can do about incorporating even more dimensions into 2-D images: the fourth dimension, maybe more: like mathematicians do when they try to make visual representations of those higher-dimensional forms. I mean, that's what the Sign does, right?" she faltered.

"Are you keeping up your appointments with Student Support Services?" Dr Hume asked suddenly, gazing narrowly at her.

"What's that got to do with it?" she shot back, almost angry.

"Oh, I'm just concerned that you're undertaking something very ambitious," he continued, more gently. "This is all very novel, aside from being very resource-intensive. It's likely to be taxing on anybody's mental stamina."

"So what?" she shrugged. "It's new. It's original. And I've already got through most of my course. Frescography is a coming field, only really around since the 1990s; you know that. I'll be able to find work once I graduate, pretty much whatever I do now. For the moment, all I need to do is tweak my CAM packages—with a little help from the School of Mathematics, maybe. Let me do it, Doc, and I'll be out of your hair."

With evident reluctance, Dr Hume agreed, after extracting a promise from her that she would keep up her student counselling appointments. Cassie sourced another contact from Professor Grant: a post-graduate research student of Geometry and Topology at the University, called Pringle. She met up with him, appropriately enough, in the refined, Mackintosh-designed Willow Tea Rooms on Sauchiehall Street.

"Miss de Castaigne?" he asked her tentatively, once he had worked out which table she was sitting at. "That's a funny surname, isn't it?"

Cassie had heard, and given, many explanations for the family surname over the years—a relic of the Auld Alliance between Scotland and France, descent from Protestant Huguenot refugees fleeing Louis XIV's Revocation of the Edict of Nantes, and so on. There was even a standing family joke that they were all lineal descendants of the Man in the Iron Mask. For Pringle, though, she just shrugged.

"I think I get some idea of what you're about," he continued, nervously shifting about in his chair to stare first at the reproductions of Margaret MacDonald's famous gesso panels of winsome queens and handmaidens, and then back at Cassie herself. "Big on the Mackintosh stuff, are we?"

"Well, I didn't copy those works for my dresses, but yes, you could say there's some ideas in common," she riposted, half irritated, half amused by the bony, excitable carrot-top. "Now, here are the CAD/CAM packages I'm currently using. I want to adapt those for modelling higher-dimensional spaces, and printing the results out on a large scale. Mural scale," she emphasized, glancing towards the ostentatiously Glasgow School facade of the Tea Rooms. "Can you do that for me?"

"Oh yea, I can do that stuff," Pringle chewed his lower lip with his snaggle teeth as he squinted at her list. "Higher-dimensional modelling has all kinds of applications these days, in statistics and data manipulation. I'll talk to the School of Art's IT department and work it out for ye. Just don't go blaming me if your printing goes all funny."

"Oh, and why would that be now?" She raised an eyebrow.

"This stuff has more practical uses than you might think. Engineers make conveyor belts out of Möbius strips these days: only one side, less wear, less tear. Just don't go trying to paste up wallpaper that way."

"I'll bear it in mind," she chuckled, though something about what Pringle had just said struck her with a very slight chill. Then another idea came to her.

"Look, there's some other software I'd like you to modify if you can," she whispered, leaning closer to him. "It's a bit more than you were asked to do, but it's much the same thing, okay?"

"Well, tell me," Pringle responded dubiously.

"It's the 3D modelling packages I use for stage and set design work," she explained. "Could you do the same for them too? I'd like to try some of the mural effects in there as well."

Pringle wrinkled his nose. "Well, I might be able to. But wouldn't it be the same if you just ran up the flat images in your CAM software, then fed them into your set design package?"

"I'd like to see if I can do it all in one," she wheedled. "Could you?"

"I'll try," Pringle conceded.

After the meeting, though, as she made her way back to the hall of residence down Sauchiehall Street, Cassie struggled with Pringle's insight. She wasn't the kind who could just shrug off comments on her appearance. With her figure she couldn't get away with short skirts and figure-hugging attire, she knew, gazing at the tight party dresses in a shopfront under a logo made up of just the shaded parts of letters, giving the illusion of a complete word. Yes, she had to admit, Mackintosh's and Margaret MacDonald's regal figures struck a chord with her, as did that whole lost world of delicate feminine sensitivity they evoked, the dreamlike ambiance of the royal court of Carcosa in *The King in Yellow.* To project an air of femininity with her lankier limbs, she needed those queenly dresses and long robes, relying on grey to hide her outline. She was among the one percent of the world population that actually chose grey as their favourite colour. Mackintosh must have loved it too, with his late watercolour of "The Grey Iris." Grey, she knew, was an achromatic colour, a colour without colour, which somehow seemed right for her in its absence of specific identity, and neutral capacity to mask her true form. As she contemplated the store mannequins, she noticed what looked like a pale hooded outline superimposed on them in the reflections of passers-by on the window glass. She spun round, expecting the mysterious figure in its hoodie, but no one was there.

Pringle proved good as his word on all counts, and had her up and running on the new software within a day, both on her own laptop, and on the Art School's more powerful graphics workstations. With his mathematics modules installed, modelling programs that previously worked in three dimensions could now express forms in five or six. She started to look further afield for inspiration: Fornasetti, Magritte, Arcimboldo, and above all, Escher, his captivating lithographs of illusions that distorted space, turned the eye back on itself, all executed in tones of grey. Her reflective journal started to fill with directed, meaningful content, almost all of it related to the expression of higher-dimensional manifolds in three dimensions, or even in two, pictorial representations of spaces where Euclid's parallel postulate failed. Never much of a mathematician before now, Cassie found she had an instinctive understanding of hyperbolic and elliptic geometry, that somehow subsisted in her eyes. She forgot to wash. Her long dark hair grew lank and stringy, her grey dresses frowsy and soiled. Despite her promise to Dr Hume, she started to skip her counselling appointments. She was too preoccupied trying to pin down the revelation that her new inspiration had given her, pursuing it through ever more complicated spaces, dimly shadowed in her mind and in the digital imagination of machines. She changed her laptop's wallpaper to a copy of Escher's "Relativity," with its faceless grey figures walking up and down staircases that intersected at all angles and conjoined landscapes in totally different spaces, blindly going about their tasks, eating, drinking, walking arm in arm, gazing at the impossible scene without eyes.

The only break in her days and nights of ceaseless and almost sleepless concentration came by force. Arguments laid aside, the post-grad crowd had taken over the Vic Bar for their Cinco de Mayo party. The Vic Bar, on the corner of Renfrew Street, usually appealed to Cassie for the same reason her digs did: she could make a bee-line for it from the main faculty buildings and disappear into it without too much exposure to the outside world. That evening, she would have preferred to avoid it, but Siobhan caught sight of her on her way out of the Reid Building after a heavy session on the workstations, and pulled her in by the elbow.

"Where ye bin, hen?" she asked. "Bin worrit about ye."

"Oh, just concentrating on my elective," she replied, trying to shrug off the enquiry.

"C'mon, September's months away. Ye need tae relax," Siobhan insisted, and dragged her over to the trestle table serving margaritas. It took Cassie an effort of will to stop herself projecting shapes into the wood grain. She blinked, and looked around. At least only a few people were wearing sombreros, but otherwise the whole venue was done out in full Cinco de Mayo drag, complete with technicolour skulls everywhere, and on many faces, either as masks or makeup. In an excess of good taste, a band onstage, in full Breaking Bad chic, was covering narcocorrido ballads. The art students, dressed to kill, and out of their heads on tequila, weed and pills, were loving it.

Cassie couldn't imagine how any chemical cocktail could make the phantasmagoria of stage lights, fluorescent masks, hideous greasepaint, glow sticks and deafening music any more hideous. The student body pushed and knocked against her indifferently, the brutal music beat on her eardrums. She felt an anxiety attack coming on, and started looking for the exit, shaking off Siobhan. Then, amid the jostling ponchos, wrestler leotards, human pinatas, psychobilly leathers and vamp senoritas, she saw once again the grey figure in its hood, looking completely at home, just part of the crowd, until it turned its head toward her. Once again, she saw its empty, pallid mask. She felt a sharp pain in her gut, and recalled her Buffy the Vampire Slayer lore about unearthly presences inducing PMS. The flashing, strobing stage spotlights threw swatches of colour across and into its hood, but somehow none seemed to touch the surface of its mask. She couldn't help but think of the Stranger in the play, who might or might not have been identical to the Phantom of Truth, who might or might not be the actual King. Without thinking, she turned and bolted for the door, and didn't stop running until she was back in her room.

After that, she hardly dared emerge, except to buy food or to use the workstations, feverishly plugging away at her designs. She lost track of passing time, just one more of the narrow cramped dimensions whose confines she was now transcending in her work, where she followed several timelike directions hinted at by the ultrahyperbolic equation, indeterminate, parallel, beyond mere human comprehension. She ate when she felt empty, evacuated when she felt full, ignored day and night, as though she was living by a different diurnal rhythm, one bound by twin suns. Her room filled with printouts, paper scraps, geometrical models, Möbius twists, litter whose scraps still seemed to tug at spacetime and point the way into some other void, even when she kicked a path through between desk and bathroom and bed with her soiled shoes.

Finally, without being able to consciously pinpoint why, she felt she had reached a culmination. She stopped and reviewed her files, her designs, the software that could capture the Yellow Sign and its insane brethren, the imaginary, incomprehensible, denizens of higher dimensions that would break the minds of those who dared try and comprehend them: higher orders of space where two Möbius strips could be joined together along both their edges; where a three-dimensional solid could have only one side. She walked in her imagination, and in the modelled spaces onscreen, down five-dimensional corridors lined with infinite mirrored recessions into parallel spaces filled with objects that burst the bounds of reality, black holes of the mind, sucking senses and awareness away behind some event horizon of comprehension, where they could never return to life in the light. And eventually, she arrived at the great stage, where all had their entrances and exits. Using the animation features in her set design package, she had created a complete virtual performance of *The King in Yellow*, with lay figures taking each role, following every stage direction, their featureless heads senselessly masked, their monotonous text-to-speech voices repeating every line of dialogue, in set designs all prepared for the coming of the King, reaching into higher dimensions where Carcosa's towers rose behind the moon.

She watched the play run through to its end. Then she shut down all the software and deleted every directory, every package. Using the tip of a nail file, she unscrewed the base of her laptop, found its hard drive, and levered it out. She found a black bin liner under the sink in her kitchenette, and dropped the drive into it, then gathered and wadded every paper, every printout, in the apartment and piled them on top.

On her way out of the apartment, bin liner in hand, she bumped into Siobhan, who wrinkled her nose slightly at the smell of unwashed hair and flesh, but politely ignored it.

"Have ye heard? The Reid Building's just won the AJ100 Building of the Year Award. Imagine giving that white mausoleum the prize. Still, we're going to celebrate later. Want to join?"

Cassie shrugged and excused herself, then made her way out of the hall of residence and up the hill to the campus, dropping off the bin liner in a skip along the way. The Glasgow sky was grey and pallid as ever. She slipped into the School of Design, accessed her files on the network, and deleted them too. Then she paid a visit to the art supplies store.

Crossing Renfrew Street, she made her way into the Mackintosh Building. All around, undergraduate students were making final adjustments to their end-of-year show, and in the bustle, no one noticed her slip through the throng and down the central staircase, down to a neglected corner of the basement at the west end of the building, directly under the Library.

Now she knew what the Sign was for. There was no knowing how many others Mackintosh might have hidden in the building, or what other eldritch shapes and forms he could have incorporated into the design, ready to punch a hole through the wall of human reality and let in what lay outside. That was what she had stop.

Her long flowing grey robes gave her all the concealment she needed to sneak in the canisters of spray foam. A quick Google search had turned up a case of a house in America that had spontaneously combusted, giving her her means. She positioned several clusters of cans together at the bases of wooden pillars underneath the Library, and placed the biggest bundle in front of a projector, with a wad of paper soaked in lighter fluid stuck in the middle of the canisters. Once the projector was switched on, she knew, its fierce light would set the paper aflame in seconds. The School of Art's blog had been full of accounts of the building's new fire suppression system, due to come online within days, and she knew she had to act now to be sure. She planned to trigger the projector just before she left, to set out for other Mackintosh buildings where the Sign might be hidden. But first, she found the control panel for the new sprinklers, turned off every switch she could see, traced the wires back to the nearest junction box, and pulled the fuse.

Movement flickered at the corner of her eyes. Afraid that a security guard had finally worked out her plan, she turned, ready to trip the switch on the projector and flee if she could. There, blocking her exit, was the same grey figure, hood still up, advancing on her. If she cried out, perhaps the students elsewhere in the building would hear, but already she felt enmeshed in the grey cobwebs of her own plan, hemmed in by the evidence, snared by guilt. Then she looked into his hood, and her cry froze in her throat before the Pallid Mask, as she recognized the Phantom of Truth, herald or avatar of the King. She backed away, stumbling, retreating before him, hands clutching at wall and table as he drove her back, until she tripped and fell backwards, triggering the projector as she did so. Smoke began to rise from its exhaust fan against the merciless glare on the white wall. By its radiance, she saw the black pools of eyes inside his hood as he leaned over her, starless skies, black as the black stars that rise over lost Carcosa, voids that swallowed all illumination and gave back nothing. At last she saw that the leprous, jaundiced face was naked, and wore no mask.

Glasgow Guardian, 24 May 2014:

Body Found as Mackintosh Building Fire Investigation Continues

As speculation persists over the cause of the catastrophic fire of 23 May that devastated the historic Mackintosh Building at the Glasgow School of Art, the Scottish Fire and Rescue Service have recovered a body from the ruins of the destroyed library. Emergency services explained that the body was hidden under a pile of grey ash in the basement near the source of the blaze, and only came to light after an intensive search. Foul play is not suspected. Forensic dental work and jewellery worn by the victim have identified the body as that of Castor de Castaigne, a student at the School of Art, who had been on the Glasgow Social Care and Health Services watch list for some time as a potential suicide risk during his sexual reassignment.

A spokesperson for LGBT Youth Scotland said: "This tragic death is typical of the sad toll among the transsexual community, who are desperately vulnerable, especially when rejected by friends, families, and society at large. Glasgow badly needs to devote more resources and more understanding to addressing this epidemic in our midst."

The joint investigation between Police Scotland and the Scottish Fire and Rescue Service has so far failed to establish any link between de Castaigne and the cause of the blaze.

THE MAN IN PURPLE TATTERS

Rick Lai

Introductory Note: The following is a translation of the last story from a 1737 French collection of folk tales. The translator, James Allington, mailed this sample story to various publishers in the hope of securing an advance to translate the entire book. Allington's tragic 1934 suicide prevented this project from reaching fruition.

Loyal disciples, the moment has come for my final tale, I have entertained you with marvelous accounts of the survivals of lost Shâlmali inside the Pyrennes, the loyal retainers of the mummified Pelishtim, the crimson jewel of Costranno, the disastrous Shrewsfield nuptials, the addiction of Genghir, the leprous Hunters at the Hour of Mutation, the places called Dagoth, the Chewer of Cornwall, the boneless progeny of Yin Chhaya, the nocturnal habits of the Auber clan, the culinary skills of the abbot Henricus, the lunar celebrations of Nakura, the remarkable lineage of Yogash the Nugite, and the judgment rendered by the Cadj of Bussorah. Now I shall regale you with a revelation concerning one of the most respected families in France.

Submitted for your perusal are a pair of documents. Astute scholars will notice the discrepancies between the accounts of the Black Priest's capture in the first document and *The Chronicle of Jacques Sogue*. The author of the latter work inflated the size of the force commanded by the Sieur de Trevec to a thousand men, and mistakenly portrayed Saladin as the Black Priest's patron.

The Testament of Paul Henri Balfour

Our family confessor, Father Joseph, brought the Caravan of the Shepherds to my attention. This wandering troupe of performers had been touring the Duchy of Brittany for weeks. My uncle Yves, the Sieur de Trevec, had permitted the Caravan to pitch its tents on his estates. Father Joseph had heard troubling rumors that the Caravan was engaged in witchcraft. He urged me to arrest these sorcerers and turn over them over to the Holy Church for proper punishment.

Before departing to see my uncle, I gazed at the portrait of my beloved father, Alain Balfour, the prior Baron de Korlette. When Richard the Lion-Hearted had joined the Kings' Crusade, his sister-in-law, Duchess Constance of Brittany, had permitted my father to form a company of Breton volunteers to assist in reclaiming the Holy Land. Serving as my father's chief lieutenant in this campaign was my mother's brother, the Sieur de Trevec.

"Father Joseph is an interfering fool!" proclaimed my uncle upon being informed of my mission. "The Caravan is not a nest of devil worshippers. They are Christians from Syria. They wait for the emergence of a star that foretells the Second Coming of Christ. In fact, their leader is Rustum Dadh, the Persian who served your father faithfully."

"My father's translator in the Holy Land! I shall hold a banquet in his honor!"

"Rustum is in no condition to celebrate. His face is frozen in a blank expression. He alluded to a horrible ordeal. I pressed him to say more, but he insisted that the details were for your ears only."

"Then why has he not contacted me?"

"Only Rustum can provide the answer, but I can tell you this. He asked me about the Man in Purple Tatters."

My uncle was referring to a horribly deformed individual who had interrupted a banquet at the nearby Chateau d'Ys five years ago. While the intruder was never found, a subsequent investigation revealed a troubling discovery at the nearby cemetery. The locks on my family's vault had been broken.

As I rode towards the Caravan of the Shepherds, I recalled my father's accounts of Rustum Dadh. Originally a member of the Christian community in Persia, he had fled to Palestine to escape the persecution of the Assassins. This infamous association of murderers dominated the mountains of his native land. To his dismay, the Assassins gained control of Masyaf, a city in northern Syria. The Sultan of the Saracens, Saladin, had initially sought to suppress the Assassins. One night, Saladin awoke to find a note pinned to his pillow by a poisoned dagger. Having proven their ability to slay Saladin, the Assassins successfully imposed peace terms on him. Saladin's accord with the Assassins had outraged Rustum. He offered his services as translator to the Crusaders led by my father. When King Richard withdrew his forces after signing a treaty with Saladin, Rustum remained in the Holy Land.

The Caravan of Shepherds consisted of about twenty wagons. The performers included jugglers, acrobats, puppeteers, and men on stilts. There was a single pitched tent. A sign on the right side of the entrance simply read "Astrologer of the Shepherds." On the left side was a black goat tethered to a pole. Attired in a white robe and gloves, a bald man exited the tent. Mounted on my horse, I approached him,

"Welcome, Baron de Korlette," announced the man in white.

"How do you know my name?"

"You greatly resemble your father. I knew him in the Holy Land. I am Rustum Dadh, the Astrologer of the Caravan. Please dismount and accept the hospitality of my tent."

Inside the tent were a table and two chairs. A pitcher and two wooden cups rested on the table. "Please be seated," requested Rustum. My eyes scanned the Persian's countenance. His face was expressionless. All life seemed to have been drained out of it.

"You are staring at me," interrupted Rustum. "My facial muscles are paralyzed. I am incapable of registering emotion. My malady is due to the shock of witnessing the extermination of my entire family at the hands of a powerful enemy. The Sieur de Trevec informs me that you have a wife and three children."

"True, but why mention them?"

"Because my enemy is your enemy! The monster who butchered my family threatens yours! Forgive me, son of my old friend! I vacillated over contacting you. I hoped to eradicate this horror without involving you."

Rustum reached for the pitcher. "This is consecrated milk from the goat outside. Before we discuss the death of my loved ones, join me in a toast of long life to yours."

After Rustum poured the milk, we drank together.

"You have tasted the Sacred Milk of the Great Mother!" proclaimed Rustum. "May it show you the Awesome Truth of the Ruler of All That Was."

A great weariness overtook me. My eyes closed in deep slumber. I dreamed of a door bearing the symbol of a white hand. Opening the door, I witnessed a series of scenes from the past.

A church appeared. I recognized it as the Chapel of St. Gilda on the Breton coast. Thirteen individuals entered the holy sanctuary. They all wore black robes with raised hoods, but one of the robes was adorned with a black star outlined in

90

purple. The interior of the Chapel had been desecrated. The altar was draped in black. The nearby crucifix was inverted. Three idols now resided to the left of the altar. The first was a satyr with ram-like horns, despite its clearly masculine face, it had the breasts of a woman. the second was of a wizened old man devouring a child while sitting in a throne designed from conch shell. The third was a bald man with a strikingly handsome face and the wings of a bat.

The figure in the robe with the black star took his position in front of the altar as the twelve others knelt before him. Lowering his hood, he revealed himself to be a bearded man with long black hair and bushy eyebrows. He proceeded to perform an obscene mockery of the sacred Mass. Eventually he reached the portion of his unholy ceremony that corresponded to a Sermon.

"The Black Priesthood is under assault from Duke Geoffrey," stated the man with the ebony star. His right hand reached into a small pouch tied around his waist. He pulled out the small wax effigy of a man riding a horse. "This is the image of our oppressor. The Duke is participating in the jousting tournament in Paris as I speak. The time has come for this persecutor to face the wrath of the King of the Disinherited and the Older Ones who preceded him on Earth. We have gathered here to perform the Rite of the Nodensestbat. I, the Abbé Sogue. who deserted the Church of Rome for the True Faith that began in the Tower of Semaxii, shall make the invocation.

"In the name of the Ram with a Thousand Young and its Unspeakable Consort. and their Herald, the Monarch of Yrimid, I petition the Lord of The Great Abyss to smite our accursed foe! O Thamogorgos, O Darkness that spawned the Black Goat, O Primal Master of the Sea Serpents, O Sovereign of the Night-Gaunts, we beseech you to punish Duke Geoffrey of Brittany! May the hoofs of your phantom chargers crush him as I crush his likeness!"

His hands seized the waxen effigy and quashed it into an unrecognizable pulp.

The scene shifted to a jousting tournament. A bout had just occurred. The loser had been unseated from his horse. Mounted on his steed, the winner raised his lance in triumph.

"Victory belongs to the Duke of Brittany," declared the master of ceremonies.

Led by the King of France, the crowd applauded. Suddenly the extremely loud neighing of horses interrupted the applause. Geoffrey's charger suddenly fell sideways. to the ground bearing its passenger with it. With his right leg pinned beneath his horse, Geoffrey could not escape his saddle. Blood bust forth from the rider and his steed as if they were being trampled by unseen hoofs. The spectators gasped in horror.

The images of the Duke's ghastly demise vanished. Once more I saw the interior of the Chapel of St, Gildas. The Abbé Sogue laughed. "Our prayers have been answered. The Duke is no more.''

The doors of the Chapel burst asunder. A squad of soldiers invaded the church.

When I next beheld Sogue, he was residing in a prison cell. On the other side of the bars stood a lean man with a stern face. The coat of arms decorating his chest identified him as the Marquis de Plougastel.

"Your hesitation proved fatal, Marquis," uttered Sogue. "Your soldiers may have apprehended me, but they failed to save your liege."

"The Duke's death did not inconvenience me, Black Priest," answered his captor. "His widow rewarded me generously after assuming power. The Duchess has proven to be a wise successor to her late, lamented husband. She has even empowered me to make you a generous offer. You are condemned to be burnt alive tomorrow. Would you like to avoid such a fate?"

"The Duchess would never grant me my freedom."

"True, but she ii willing to offer you a less painful death."

"What price must I pay to merit this act of clemency?"

"Reveal the name of your Master."

"He has many names. Erlik, Zukala-Koth, Ahriman, Lucifer, and Shaitan are a few noteworthy examples."

"Do not toy with me, Sogue! You know that I m referring to your superior in the Black priesthood. The Devil has corrupted someone even higher than you in the hierarchy of the Church."

"What will be the less painful death offered in exchange for my Master's name?"

"You would be given a rope and permitted to hang yourself in your cell."

"As a connoisseur of murder, I am fully aware of the possible suffering inflected by a hangman's rope. If done properly, the victim perishes from a broken neck. If done improperly, the consequence is an excruciating painful death by strangulation. Your alternative to immolation lacks appeal."

"Perhaps you have a superior form of execution."

"From my various experiences, the quickest form of death is to have your throat torn open by a night-gaunt."

"A night-gaunt? What sort instrument is that?"

"A night-gaunt is not an instrument. It is a winged demon with horns, a blank face and a barbed tail. It slays efficiently."

"I have no such creature at my disposal."

"If you lent me the chalk that you confiscated from my pouch, I could summon a night-gaunt."

"If I did that, you would command the night-gaunt to slay me, break open your cell door. and fly away to a place of sanctuary. Fortunately, you lack the means to do so."

"But my Master in the Black Priesthood possesses the chalk to invoke a night-gaunt. One of these remarkable predators entered through the window behind you moments ago."

Before the Marquis could turn around, the sharp claws of a night-gaunt sliced open his throat. The nobleman's lifeless body hit the floor. After ripping the door of Sogue's cell off its hinges, the monster's hands smashed open a large hole in the wall of the prison. Grabbing Sogue, the faceless beast flew into the night.

Carrying the Black Priest, the night-gaunt traveled across land and sea for hours. Finally, the demon reached a fortress high in the mountains. Accompanied by armored guards, a man in golden robes patiently waited in the courtyard. A golden mask bearing the countenance of a bearded man totally encased his head. Flapping its wings slowly, the night-gaunt landed in the courtyard. After gently depositing its passenger on the ground, the featureless demon returned to the sky.

"Welcome to the fortress of the Assassins in Maysaf," said the man in flawless French. 'I am Rashid ad-Din Sinan, the Old Man of the Mountains. My ally in Europe, the Master of the Black Priesthood, has successfully requested that I grant you sanctuary."

"Thank you, my Lord, how did you learn my language?"

"From a soldier captured during the Second Crusade. Inevitably there will be another such invasion. You shall prove invaluable to me when a Third Crusade erupts."

"Do any of your guards also speak French?"

"They do not. You may speak freely in front of them."

"My Master informs you that your gardens are inhabited by the most beautiful women on Earth."

"I use them to delude my followers into believing that I am a prophet of Allah. After drugging my recruits with hashish, I create the illusion that they have been temporarily transported to a glorious paradise inhabited by lovely maidens. None of them realize they are being deceived by a servant of Shaitan."

"Will I be allowed' access to these women?"

"If you wish, but I doubt that they shall satisfy you. Do you really desire a woman who personifies a false Heaven? Or would you prefer a woman who embodies the true pleasures of Hell?"

"I would indeed."

"Then I must introduce you to the Siren of Cyprus."

A man walked through a stone corridor lit by torchlight. His young and vibrant face resembled Rustum's. Next to him walked my father. I was observing events from the Third Crusade.

"Rustum, a stranger was apprehended outside Acre. I want you present during the interrogation."

My father and Rustum entered a room. Standing inside was a tall figure wearing a purple robe with a black star embroidered on the chest. The robe's hood covered the captive's face. The prisoner was guarded by Yves de Trevec and another soldier.

"The Siren of Cyprus!" shouted Rustum. "She is a witch in league with the Assassins. I glimpsed her once near their Persian stronghold on Mount Alamut. She bears the face of a decaying corpse."

"Pull back the prisoner's hood," commanded my father. Yves yanked back the hood revealing the face of a muscular man with a black beard. He looked about thirty years old. The prisoner pointed to a sack resting on a table.

"If you wish to see the Siren, Baron de Korlette, empty the bag your men confiscated."

My father untied the sack and turned it upside down A woman's severed head and a wooden box fell on the table. Lifting the head by its long black hair, Rustum scrutinized the features. The decapitated woman had large eyes, fanged teeth and moldy, corpse-like skin.

"That is the face I beheld in Persia," grimly stated Rustum.

My father directed his gaze into the steel-gray eyes of the prisoner. "Who are you?"

"Men know me as Jonathan Carter, the Witch-Finder of Rotherwood. I belong to the company of Wilfrid the Saxon. He will vouch for me."

"Sir Wilfrid went to Jaffa with King Richard," replied my father.

"Unless you act quickly," said Carter, "we will lose the opportunity to bring the Black Priest of St. Gildas to justice."

"The Black Priest!" exclaimed my father. "How could you possibly know of him?"

"From the lips of King Richard himself. He gave me the mission of slaying the Black Priest."

"If you are acting on King Richard's orders, you will be able to answer this question. Why does he desire the Black Priest's death?"

"King Richard's brother, Duke Geoffrey of Brittany, discovered a secret cabal of Satanists, the Black Priesthood, within the highest circles of the Church. Geoffrey attacked monasteries harboring the Black Priesthood. When Geoffrey was fatally trampled in a jousting tournament, Duchess Constance accused the Black Priesthood of engineering her husband's death. The Abbé Sogue was arrested for presiding over a celebration of the Black Mass at St. Gildas. Exposed as a Black Priest, Sogue was condemned to be burned alive. During his secret trial, the renegade cleric admitted invoking the Invisible Horses of Thamogorgos to murder Geoffrey. Before his sentence could be carried out, the Black Priest escaped."

"Your information tallies with the account I heard from Duchess Constance," acknowledged my father. "The whereabouts of the Black Priest have long been a mystery. How do you know Sogue is in the Holy Land?"

"Soon after King Richard conquered Acre, he received a secret message from Saladin that the Black Priest was residing with the Assassins in Masyaf," explained Carter.

"Why would Saladin do such a thing? He is our enemy!"

"But a chivalrous enemy nonetheless, Baron. Saladin hopes to negotiate a peace treaty with Richard. His revelation of Sogue's location was intended to gain Richard's trust. The King sent me on a mission to penetrate Masyaf and kill the Black Priest. To confirm the apostate's death, I was to bring Richard his head. Unfortunately, Sogue had departed Masyaf by the time I arrived. The Siren of Cyprus detected my presence, and made me a prisoner of the Assassins."

"The Assassins are not known for keeping prisoners," interjected Rustum. "Why did they spare your life?"

"They were merely postponing my execution. Despite their lip service to the veneration of Allah, the Assassins really worship Satan and the Outer Monstrosities. Those demons require human sacrifice. I was slated to be a blood offering to the Nameless One of the Dark Gateway. Have you heard of her?"

"A she-demon who once dwelt amid the ruins of Chorazin in northern Galilee," said Rustum. "It was prophesized that she would give birth to the Anti-Christ in Chorazin. In order to circumvent the prophesy, the wise King Solomon imprisoned the Nameless One in a remote corner of the world."

"Despite her absence, Chorazin remains a sacred shrine to the Nameless One," added Carter. "The Black Priest was appointed custodian of her shrine prior to my capture. Escorted by ten armed Assassins, the Siren of Cyprus was bringing me to Chorazin to be surrendered for sacrifice. Luckily, I was able to break my bonds and wrestle a sword from one of my captors. You see what happened to the Siren. The lifeless carcasses of her subordinates became a feast for the vultures."

"Liar!" accused Yves. "Do you really expect us to believe that you slew that creature and ten men all by yourself!"

The Witch-Finder's eyes became narrow slits. "If you doubt my veracity, I can always prove it in trial by combat?"

"Enough of this petty squabbling!" decreed my father. "Witch-Finder, why are you wearing the Siren's robe?"

"In order to bypass Saladin's patrols by impersonating the Siren. As part of the accords with the Assassins, the Siren of Cyprus was allowed freedom of movement throughout Saladin's territories."

"Your statement implies a possible strategy to use against the Black Priest," concluded my father. "Tell me your plan."

"Chorazin is located behind Saladin's lines. Sogue is expecting the Siren, ten guards and a captive. If you provide me men to impersonate the Siren and her escort. I could lead them to Chorazin. This subterfuge will fool Saladin's forces and allow us to kill the Black Priest."

My father nodded his head in agreement. "An excellent proposal, Witch-Finder. I shall adopt it with three modifications. First, I want the Black Priest captured alive. Although Sogue at his trial claimed to be the head of the

Black Priesthood, the true leader remains at large. Torture should force the truth out of sorcerer's mouth before a public beheading. Second, the Sieur de Treves shall lead the expedition. Third, Jonathan Carter shall remain here after coaching Rustum on how to impersonate the Siren." My father shifted his eyes towards the soldier standing next to Yves. "Hulbert Andre of Normandy shall pose as the sacrificial victim. If none of the expedition return, the information provided by Carter shall be judged to be false. Such a verdict will result in Carter being beheaded in the Black Priest's place."

"There is one more essential component, stressed Carter. Open the box."

My father raised the lid of the box that had earlier been removed from the sack. Inside was a ring, a silver key and a parchment in an unknown language. The ring bore the image of a black pentagon.

"The designated sacrifice is expected to wear this ring," underscored Carter. "Its absence would make our foes suspicious."

Andre put the ring on his finger. "If our mission succeeds, may I have the ring as a lucky keepsake?"

"Yes," replied my father.

"May I request a reward as well, Baron?" asked Carter.

"You may."

"My request is twofold. First, I want the honor of presenting the Black Priest's head to King Richard."

"Contingent on the mission's success, your request shall be granted."

"Second, the silver key and the parchment belonged to the Siren. May I have them as my own mementoes?"

"A curious request, but I will honor it."

"We have slain all your bodyguards!" shouted Yves. "And you are weaponless! Surrender, Sogue!"

My visions of the past had skipped the details of the arrival of my uncle and his allies at Chorazin. Clearly their surprise attack had decimated the Black Priest's forces. With his hands raised in the air, the Black Priest walked out of the ruins of an ancient temple.

"O Nameless One of the Black Pentagon, protect thy acolyte!"

The ring on Hulbert Andre's finger glowed. A giant black hand materialized next to one of the Crusaders. Seizing the soldier, the hand squeezed him until only a bloody smear remained on the fingers. The hand then disappeared.

Andre spotted a stone wall among the ruins of Chorazin It bore the etching of a five-pointed star surrounded by a circle. "The Pentacle of Solomon!" he exclaimed. Two black hands now materialized. Or were they more like paws? My uncle stood between them. The hands were about to crush him in a clap of death when Andre rubbed the center of the star with his ring.

Andre's ring ceased glowing. The Black Priest screamed just before toppling unconscious to the ground. The black hands vanished. Andre and my uncle ran towards the fallen sorcerer. They were soon joined by their comrades.

As the Crusader departed for Acre, I contemplated the events that unfolded. Chorazin had once been inhabited by a demon that King Solomon had imprisoned elsewhere. The sacrificial ring glowed because the Black Priest was using it to summon appendages of the demon to Chorazin, and the etched Pentacle had been made by Solomon. Rubbing the ring against the etching had closed the mystical doorway and released a magical backlash that overcame the Black Priest. Shortly after reaching these conclusions, I was shown the events which transpired in Acre.

The Black Priest stood upright against a wooden post. His arms were bent backwards with his wrists tied behind the post. His ankles were also bound to the post. Clothed only in pants, his torso was scarred with smoldering brands in the shape of an arrowhead.

Standing in front of the branded man were my father flanked by Yves and Rustum. My uncle stood next to a brazier with hot coals. He held in his hand a branding iron whose fiery tip ended in an arrowhead.

"The Sieur de Trevec has repeatedly pierced your body with arrowheads, Sogue, yet you remain recalcitrant," commented my father. "If you refuse to answer my question once more, my colleague will demonstrate his expertise with a hot iron on your face."

"Have your stooge disfigure me," uttered the defiant Black Priest. "I have nothing left to live for. You murdered the only person I truly loved, Baron."

"I find your statement perplexing. I have not slain anyone whom you could possibly have loved."

"I loved the Siren of Cyprus."

"How can you love such a hideous beast?"

"Her beauty resided in her eyes. They reflect the purest form of ecstasy. I would pay any price to feast on her eyes one final time."'

"Why do you believe your paramour to be deceased?"

"Do not toy with me, Baron. Your Persian lackey was wearing her robe when your soldiers surprised me in Chorazin. It must have been stripped from her corpse."

"Neither I nor anyone under my command has physically harmed the Siren. The robe was taken from a healthy prisoner currently residing in a nearby dungeon. If you answer my question, you shall see your lover's eyes before you die."

"Swear by the soul of your firstborn that you speak the truth!"

"I have no firstborn. I am unmarried."

"Then swear by the soul of your firstborn-to-be!"

"I, Alain Balfour, Baron de Korlette, swear by the soul of my firstborn-to-be that I speak the truth."

"Swear that your firstborn shall suffer the Doom of Nelliefer if you have deceived me!"

"I swear!"

"Then ask your question. By the Lord of the Dark Star, I shall answer it honestly."

"Who is your superior in the Black Priesthood?"

"Azédarac, the Bishop of Ximes."

"Rustum, arrange for Sogue to see the eyes of his lover," ordered my father. "Fetch the prisoner."

The Persian departed for a short interval. Rustum returned with the Witch-Finder carrying his sack.

"What trickery is this?" asked the Black Priest.

"I neglected to mention that the Siren's robe was worn by someone else," answered my father. "This is Jonathan Carter. He bears the dubious distinction of being a former prisoner of both the Siren and myself. Witch-Finder, I promised the Black Priest that he could view the eyes of his precious Siren. Please fulfill my pledge."

"Gladly," added the Witch-Finder. He yanked the Siren's head out of the bag. The Black Priest stared into her lifeless eyes.

"Jonathan Carter, you shall be condemned to an eternity of warfare!" screamed the Black Priest. "When you finally find true happiness, you shall be yanked across space and time to an exile ending in death! Sieur de Trevec, I shall return to St. Gildas—"

"Be silent, spawn of Satan!" yelled Yves. His branding iron pressed brutally into the necromancer's forehead. Even after my uncle removed his fiery instrument, the exhausted Black Priest continued to speak.

"For the violence you did to me, I will do violence to you. For the evil I suffered at your hands, I will work evil on you and your descendants. Woe to your children, Sieur de Trevec!"

"Execute the prisoner!" commanded my father.

Drawing his sword quickly from its scabbard, my uncle's arm ruthlessly struck. The Black Priest's head fell to the ground.

My father turned towards Carter. "Witch-Finder, you have your freedom. Take the traitor's head to King Richard in Jaffa. You shall have the key and parchment. Do you wish the Siren's robe as well?"

Carter shook his head. "I have no need of it, Baron."

"Then I shall keep it as a trophy symbolizing my triumph over the Black Priest. It will make an excellent bathrobe."

The execution field faded to be replaced by the image of my father and uncle in the dining room of our ancestral estate, the Chateau de Korlette.

"I gave Duchess Constance a transcript of the Black Priest's interrogation," related my father. "Since the Bishop of Ximes is outside her jurisdiction, she could do little more than inform the King of France."

"Azédarac has the reputation of being a saintly man," emphasized my uncle. "It will take more than the Black Priest's accusation to topple him."

"We shall see, but there is another matter to discuss. I refer to my pending nuptials with your sister."

"What shall you name our son?" asked my mother from her bed.

"Auguste Guillaume," proudly proclaimed my father. Fulfilling the jest made in the Holy Land, he wore the Siren's garment as his bathrobe. My father held my older brother in the cradle of his arms.

"Do you enjoy the touch of my robe?" teased my father. "Perhaps you shall wear it when you are all grown up."

Suddenly my father's eyes widened in horror. Auguste had ceased breathing.

"The accusations leveled by the Duchess of Brittany were easy to deflect." The speaker wore the vestments of a bishop. "King Philippe was easily persuaded that the charges against me were false information fashioned to divert him from exercising his territorial designs on Brittany. My stature in Ximes remains unassailable. If I were to die tomorrow, I would be canonized as St. Azédarac."

You should arrange a fitting punishment for Baron de Korlette," suggested a man with a vulpine face,

"There is no need, my dear Jehan." Azédarac handed his subordinate a scroll. "Read the Baron's written account of Sogue's execution. The Crusader's own mistakes have doomed his firstborn."

Jehan perused the document. "The Baron swore that he had not lied, but the Black Priest tricked him. 'Swear that your firstborn shall suffer the Doom of Nelliefer if you have deceived me!' A man can deceive without technically lying, and the Baron's action prove that point. What exactly is the Doom of Nelliefer?"

"Nelliefer was a Princess of Cyprus who married Pharaoh Cheops of Egypt. As punishment for murdering her husband, she was buried alive. The Baron's firstborn shall fall in a death-like trance from which he shall awaken after burial."

My father gazed down on Auguste's coffin in the family vault. "You were my little prince. You never grew into the fine young man who could wear my purple robe, but I wrapped it round your tiny body. May it serve as a blanket to keep your innocent soul warm as you begin your ascent towards Paradise."

My tearful father departed after locking the crypt, A few minutes expired before a baby's pitiful cries issued from the coffin.

A blanket of darkness stretched endlessly. Two bright beacons of light materialized in the eternal fog of night. Closer inspection revealed the beacons to be eyes.

"Feed, little one," advised the soothing female voice. "Feed om my maternal milk. You will live. You shall become a being like me.

"It is ironic that I rescued you. The Witch-Finder may have beheaded me, but the brain can survive for a brief period after decapitation. Invoking the Silver Key of Yian-Ho, I transferred my soul into the Realm of Dreams. The night-gaunts now have a new high-priestess in the Caves of Ngranek. Your possession of my cloak caused your cries to reach me in my new abode. I initially wanted to ignore you. Sending his soul into the Realm of Dreams, Azédarac of the Black Priesthood had told me of your father's role in my lover's death. My heart was filled with malice.

"Yet your cries awakened memories of my prior life as Nellifer, Queen of the Nile. I remembered my despair after being entombed alive by my husband's fanatical followers. My screams of agony were heard by Akivasha, the Vampire Princess of Stygia. She sent the Dwellers under the Tomb to rescue me. The subterranean burrowers taught me how to achieve immortality by devouring human flesh. As a consequence, I gradually transformed into an entity resembling the rotting corpses that served as my diet.

"Remembering my own torment and deliverance, I took pity on you. My materialization in the waking world is of limited duration. Once my breast milk completes your metamorphosis. I shall teach you how to forage for food. Your childhood shall seem wondrous and strange. You shall imagine this crypt to be a vast castle of which you are the sole human inhabitant. Only if you leave the confines of the crypt shall the illusion be shattered. On that day, knowledge of your true nature shall flood your thoughts.

"You will find yourself treated as an outcast by humanity. Your sole recourse will be to flee to Egypt. There exists a sanctuary underneath the Great Pyramid. It is presided over by another protégé of Akivasha."

Carrying a torch, a man with the head of a dog advanced through a series of underground tunnels. Following him is a dim figure. His image cannot be fully perceived because he is wrapped in a tattered purple robe. He must be the Man in Purple Tatters who invaded the Chateau d'Ys.

The torch bearer finally stopped before a woman with dark hair. Her face was turned sideways. She seemed to be the possessor of great beauty until her head tilted revealing the other side eaten away by worms.

"Nitokris," hissed the torchbearer.

"Nitokris," repeated the Man in Purple Tatters, ''the Queen of the Ghouls."

In imitation of the Black Priest, Rustum Dadh was bound to a post. His chest and arms were branded with arrowheads. On

104

the ground were scattered several mutilated corpses. Standing amid the carnage was the Man in Purple. His countenance was finally visible under the hood. It was a decaying face like the Siren's. Yet its features resembled my own.

The Man in Purple Tatters used a talon to remove a piece of meat that was stuck in his teeth. "Your granddaughter was an even finer delicacy than your sister. You must be wondering why I am doing all this. You probably suspect that I am avenging the death of the Black Priest. Frankly I care nothing for him. This vendetta was conducted primarily to gain expertise in destroying a man's entire family in front of him. I may need to repeat this exercise in Brittany.

"Nothing to say, Rustum? Oh, please forgive me. I forgot my removal of your tongue. There was another reason you merit my attention. You have something that I need."

I cannot describe the act of barbarity that followed, but the horror of it forced me out of my trance. When I awoke, my eyes glimpsed the Astrologer's white robe and gloves. Lying next to them was the mask cunningly made from Rustum's flesh. Raising my gaze upward, I beheld the Man in Purple Tatters.

"My apologies for lacing your milk with the Black Lotus of the Xu-Thal tribe. We have not been properly introduced. I am Auguste Guillaume Balfour, the rightful Baron de Korlette. We need to discuss the terms of your surrender, my younger brother."

The Warning of Francois Honoré Balfour
My ancestor's account of the events in 1220 ends abruptly. He did not mention the complex terms of *The Covenant of the Firstborn* signed by Paul Henri Balfour and his loathsome sibling. Auguste was secretly recognized by the Balfour family as the rightful Baron de Korlette for the remainder of

his life. My ancestor probably imagined that Auguste's lifespan was the same as a normal human being. More than five hundred year later, Auguste still lived.

In exchange for allowing my father and his heirs to be publicly recognized as the Barons de Korlette, the legitimate Baron swore to protect my family from harm. Implicit in that pledge was the threat that my family would be exterminated if it ever violated *The Covenant of the Firstborn*. Auguste would spend the majority of his time absent from the family estate. Every winter solstice, Auguste would have a private dinner alone with the nominal Baron. The two participants were permitted separate meals. Auguste would be allowed to bring his own food.

Auguste was far-seeing. *The Covenant of the Firstborn* he made allowance for my family's title and possessions being altered. Such an event actually happened. During the Mad War, the Balfours supported the French monarchy against the reigning Duke of Brittany. In recognition of my family's role in securing the French domination of Brittany, Charles VIII rewarded us in 1492 with an estate near Voyonnes in Picardy. The title Baron de Korlette was supplanted by Comte d'Erlette. By the conditions of *The Covenant of the Firstborn*, Auguste was secretly recognized as the legitimate Comte d'Erlette.

Like their baronial predecessors, the nominal Comtes kept the other Balfour family members in total ignorance of Auguste's existence. As each male heir ascended to the title, he received a locked box. Opening the box, the new holder of the family title would find a letter from the recently deceased Comte alongside *The Testament of Paul Henri Balfour* and *The Covenant of the Firstborn*.

I asked August why he imposed *The Covenant of the Firstborn* on his human relatives. His simple reply was that he felt obligated to secure his birthright. I suspect his true motivation stems from a sense of social inferiority among his fellow creatures of the night. Auguste was a Ghoul, a monster who generally satisfied his appetite for human flesh by violating graveyards. In the course of several conversations,

Auguste discussed the social order of the Ghouls. There exist various varieties of ghouls, but they fall essentially in two categories. The first belong to pre-Adamite races. The second are humans who have been transformed into hybrids by necromancy. Auguste was a hybrid. Even though some hybrids like Nitokris have risen to positions of power in the Cults of the Ghouls, hybrids were snobbishly treated as inferiors by the pre-Adamites. By dominating his human kin, Auguste was compensating for his own subservience to the pre-Adamites.

Auguste's habit was to abduct infants and eat them raw during the annual Yule feast. Stories spread throughout Brittany and subsequently Picardy of the dreaded Man in Purple Tatters, the devourer of children during the Christmas season. A myth even evolved that he was the demonic spirit of King Herod, still thirsting for the blood of the infant Jesus. Auguste initially confined his predatory instincts to the children of commoners. This arrangement was wonderfully convenient since the offspring of peasants are plentiful and easily forgotten by magistrates and constables. Regrettably, Auguste digested the daughter of my neighbor, Baron d'Oulignes, last year. The authorities at Voyonnes could not simply ignore the disappearance of a member of the nobility. An enterprising young member of the Voyonnes constabulary, Porion, traced the crime to the door of the Chateau d'Erlette. The clear threat to my family was easily negated by a substantial bribe which included a letter recommending Porion to the Lieutenant General of Louis XV's police. Porion found a convenient scapegoat in a local woodcutter. The whole matter was hushed up by the sloppily prolonged public hanging of an innocent man.

Nevertheless, Auguste had become a liability to our family. This development was quite unanticipated. Despite his eccentric appetites, Auguste had proven himself a political strategist as cunning as Cardinal Richelieu. His advice may have only been given during the annual Yule feast, but it steered the family through the pitfalls of the Hundred Years War, engineered the relocation to Picardy, prevented a potentially disastrous alliance with the Huguenots, and extricated my father unscathed from the Affair of the Poisons. As the d'Oulignes kidnapping demonstrated, Auguste was showing signs of impaired judgment. Even a Ghoul was not immune to senility. For the sake of the Balfours, Auguste had to be assassinated.

In preparation for Auguste's murder, I commissioned Johann Stiffter, the gunsmith of Prague, to construct an ingeniously concealed rifle. Since I requested that the weapon fire silver bullets, Stiffter assumed my intended quarry was a werewolf. An English client had commissioned an unusual pistol for such a purpose in the past. Since the false perception that I was a lycanthrope hunter ensured Stiffter's silence, I did not enlighten him regarding the true nature of my target.

When Auguste in his tattered garment came to our annual banquet, I began to relent in my determination to extinguish his life. He had chosen the son of a carpenter for this year's sacrificial meal. The selection was discrete as well as appropriately iconoclastic considering the season. My good intentions swiftly evaporated.

"Did you enjoy your supper, Uncle Auguste?"

"No, the quality of peasant stock in Picardy has deteriorated considerably over the last decade. Today only a plump child of the aristocracy can satisfy my palate. I had such a delicacy last year. Similar specimens shall be found for our future celebrations.'

"There is a book that I want to discuss with you, Uncle." I handed Auguste a slim volume written in English. My kinsman silently read the title page: "*Le Culte du Gouffre (The Cult of the Abyss)* by Antoine-Marie Augustin de Montmorency-les-Roches, translated from the French by John Grymlann."

"The author was a Satanist who died in the Bastille," I explained. "The book was suppressed in France, but I managed to unearth an English translation. The tome deals with the Hidden Ones of the Brazen King, a Satanic cult in Bayonne, The Hidden Ones await the coming of the Anti-Christ. The cult used the milk of a black goat in its rituals.

This reminded me of the Caravan of the Shepherds in your younger brother's account."

"Very observant, Francois. While the Caravan openly pretended to anticipate the Second Coming, they really desire fulfilment of the Chorazin prophecy regarding the Anti-Christ. The Hidden Ones and the Caravan are merely different names for the same ancient faith."

"Do you believe in the Anti-Christ, Uncle?"

"Did Azédarac believe in God? The Caravan were merely fools manipulated for my own purposes."

"Le Culte du Gouffre claims that all sorcery flows from two stars in the cosmos, Dark Yrimid and Infernal Yramid."

"A bit of an exaggeration, but they are still important sources of magical power. The sages Eibon and Carnamagos knew those two stars as Yuzh and Yamil Zacra."

"I recently had a Newtonian telescope mounted on the eastern tower overlooking the Somme. My endeavors to locate those stars in the night sky have proved fruitless. Can you pinpoint them?"

"Absolutely. I have familiarity with operating reflective telescopes. Old Jehan has such a telescope installed in his home in Ximes."

"Old Jehan! Certainly not Azédarac's former assistant!"

"The same. That reprobate is even older than me! After leaving the Bishop's service, Jehan established himself as a supplier of essential salts to the Triumvirate of the Dragon's Head. He sometimes enlists Ghouls to gather the salts or him."

"What exactly is this Triumvirate"

"That's a long story for another evening. For now, I will simply note that the Triumvirate is a trio of necromancers whose membership has changed over the centuries."

After completely picking clean the bones of the carpenter's son, Auguste followed me to the east tower. The telescope was on a circular base capable of a complete rotation of 360 degrees. The Man in Purple Tatters pointed majestically towards the moonlit sky. "Dark Yrimid is in the west." He rotated the telescope to face away from the river. His right eye looked through the eye-lens of the telescope as his hand manipulated the knob that supposedly focused the mirrors inside. He did not realize that the knob was the trigger on a rifle cunningly concealed in the telescope until the silver bullet obliterated his right eye and penetrated his brain.

The dying Auguste staggered backwards until his back ran into the tower's ramparts. Losing his balance, the monster fell off tower into the waters of the Somme. The Man in Purple Tatters was no more. His body rests at the bottom of the river.

The Covenant of the Firstborn is now ashes.

I am the true Comte d'Erlette. I preserved the accounts of Paul Henri Balfour and myself to act as a warning to my future successors. My son and the Comtes that follow him will now be provided with a box containing these two documents. The Man in Purple Tatters is dead, but our family secret must be known to his associate, the immortal Jehan. If that ageless wizard ever threatens our family, he must be made the recipient of another silver bullet.

A Final Word

I stole the preceding two documents after my fangs tore open the throat of Francois Honoré Balfour. The silver bullet lodged inside my brain is slowly killing me, but I shall survive long enough to plant the seed of retribution. Long ago I promised my brother that I would exterminate all his descendants if I was ever betrayed. Francois spawned a large brood. The luxury of time has been denied me. If I sought to slay the surviving Balfours individually before the silver bullet finalized its gift of oblivion, only a handful of them would perish. My vengeance must take another path.

Just as Francois baited his trap with a book, *Le Culte du Gouffre*, my retaliation shall be sparked by a similar work fashioned by my intellect, *Les Cultes des Goules*. Yes, my readers, the very text whose last tale is reaching the conclusion. During my final days, I have dictated all the stories contained herein to my loyal friend, Jehan, who shall arrange their publication.

I am Auguste Guillaume Balfour, Comte d'Erlette, but what are you, my readers? Do you belong to the oppressed majority in France? The Balfours view your kind as disposable fodder. Does your soul cry out in outrage? Why be devoured when you can be a devourer? Rise up! Destroy the Balfours and all families like them! Kill them all! Execute them all! I write in 1737, but these words have primed a weapon. It may take decades for my bullet to fire, but France shall eventually be covered with the blood of the Balfours and their fellow aristocrats.

When that day of reckoning arrives, I shall no longer be among the living. The silver bullet would have finally completed its mission. Jehan has already made arrangements for the delivery of my remains to the Ghouls of Nitokris. My brethren shall celebrate by eating my body and drinking my blood, but what of my soul? Shall it be feasted upon by a different kind of predator? It may be delusions caused by the projectile inside my skull, but my dreams have been filled by visions of the Siren of Cyprus. Are our minds still inked by the torn remnants of her robe? Does she intend to devour my soul? Or will she resurrect me in the Realm of Dreams? Shall I be joining her as a high priest of the night-gaunts in the Caves of Ngranek? Perhaps I shall be once more the lonely child exploring the dark corridors of an unknown castle. The time is approaching for the Man in Purple Tatters to learn the answer to the riddle of death. *Adieu.*

THE GREEN MUSE

Jon Black

"You know about the deaths?" Louis Vauxcelles asked with incongruous glee.

Squirming in his chair, Drieu Gaudin replied: "In Montmartre? The artists?" Since Drieu arrived in Paris six months ago and landed his job at *Gil Blas*, the literary newspaper's editor had displayed no interest in him. Until today, when Vauxcelles summoned Drieu into his opulently apportioned office.

Vauxcelles nodded. "Five painters dead in as many weeks. Notice I say painters, not artists," he sniffed. "Even for Montmartre, we're talking about the very worst. Cubists," the editor did not so much speak that word as seethe it. "People are whispering 'murder.' The gendarmes aren't talking. But rumors and the scandal sheets hint at outrageous things.

"We have an opportunity here. We've been forced to accept the artistic conceits of the impressionists and post-impressionists, acknowledging some of them were not talentless. Then came the indignities of the Fauves, with their childish paintings and wild colors and forms. But never has there been anything like the Cubists. They deliberately mock beauty and tradition. I believe Cubism intends to destroy art itself."

Vauxcelles paused. "I've looked through your articles, especially your art reviews. May I advance a guess that you studied painting before coming to Paris from…wherever you're from?"

"Aquitaine, yes. I studied at the École Beaux Arts in Pau and…" Drieu intended to add he still painted but Vauxcelles cut him off.

"I don't need details. I just need to know you're the one I want."

"What, exactly, do you want?" Drieu asked.

"For you to get inside the Montmartre set. I can't use my other art writers. They'd be recognized. But you're new. You're unknown. Once you're in, learn what you can about the deaths and write about it. A rash of dead Cubists? You know there's scandal behind it. But, if you need, embellish your findings. I want something so depraved it will end Cubism for good. I'll ensure your story gets onto the front page and that your future with *Gil Blas* is long and bright.

"I'm honored by the opportunity and your trust. But shouldn't Cubism be fought on artistic grounds rather than scandal surrounding dead artists? It doesn't seem right."

"The Cubists and all the small-mindedness and aesthetic brutality masquerading under the label 'avant-garde' don't play by gentlemen's rules. We can't afford to, either."

"I'm not a crime reporter. Death and tragedy, they make me uncomfortable. So ghoulish."

"Let me be clear, this is not a request. Do it. Or you're out. You're a promising young writer. But Paris has a dozen promising young writers waiting to take your place. This city swallows people like they'd never been born," Vauxcelles' smile could be mistaken for sympathy.

Drieu knew he'd been fortunate to land this position so quickly. At *Gil Blas*, Paris' top cultural journal, he wrote about art, literature, theatre, and other haute themes without the pedestrian stories with which most novice journalists had to content themselves. "Very well, how do I start?"

"Begin with the newspapers and scandal sheets. Familiarize yourself with the facts. When you're done, I've got someone to you lead into Montmartre itself."

Departing the office, Drieu took a moment to chat with Barbette, Vauxcelles' personal assistant. As she could afford a Paul Poiret dress to wear to work, he suspected she provided him other services as well. Drieu did not let that preclude some good natured flirting. Putting down the latest issue *La Figaro*, filled with coverage of the tragic fate of White Star's "unsinkable" liner, Barbette batted her eyelashes and responded in kind.

That evening, back at the 11th Arrondissement hôtel he'd occupied since coming to Paris, Drieu cleared away the remains of the chicken broth and vegetables potage he'd made. After meeting with Vauxcelles, he'd treated himself; adding some wild mushrooms bought from the country woman near his omnibus stop. He corked his leftover *vin rouge* and carefully wrapped the remaining half-baguette, setting them aside for breakfast.

After pressing his other suit, Drieu reposed at his desk. Its mottled patches of vanished lacquer exposed the bare wood underneath. Staring at his secondhand Écrie Royal typewriter and desiring to write, only restlessness came to him. Moving to a threadbare chair, he attempted to read *Le Monde* and the provincial papers his mother posted from Bordeaux. Still, restless returned.

Finally, from his desk's bottom drawer, Drieu removed the sketch. Using colored pencils, he'd made it at a gallery showing. Drieu carried it to his easel, which faced the wall in case polite company came. Rotating the easel toward him, he resumed painting his half-finished copy of Vlaminck's *Potato Pickers* recreated from the sketch. Drieu secretly admired, even envied, the Fauves' use of vivid colors to hint at that which could not be rendered directly.

Mixing viridian green on his pallet, he fleshed out the vibrant foliage which tied together *Potato Pickers'* impossibly blue sky with the riotous orange and reds of its fields. Drieu knew many people, including his editor, would not approve.

115

Drieu reached *Gil Blas* early next morning. Like any good paper, it kept an eye on the competition by subscribing to most of Paris's 80 newspapers: the conservative *La Figaro*, the socialist *La Monde*, the ponderous *Le Temps*, the trite *Le Petit Journal*, the fanatically religious and anti-Dreyfusard *Le Croix,* and even *Excelsior*, *Gil Blas'* only rival as a cultural daily.

The periodicals painted a broad outline. Five deceased artists: Karl Schroeder, a recent arrival from Zurich's coffeehouses. A brace of locals, Zacharie Jacquier and Antonin Basnard. Rudolpho Odelion from Cuernavaca, Mexico, had been a sculptor dabbling in painting. And, most recently, Valentin Accambray, a Creole from La Reunion called "Le Canari," both for his sunflower yellow hair and propensity for gossip.

Four were found in their studios. Even the authorities and respectable press acknowledged that three of them qualified as "locked room" mysteries that would interest Arsène Lupin, or his stodgier counterpart in Baker Street across the Channel. But they remained curiously reticent about the causes of death.

What Drieu needed next could not be had within the offices of a respectable periodical like *Gil Blas.* On the streets, he made his way from newsstand to newsstand snapping up issues of Paris's scandal sheets. These publications, typically printed on low-quality paper, prized graphic photos and lurid prose over typesetting, proofing, and truthfulness.

The scandal sheets suggested that the legitimate press barely scratched the surface of the outré elements in the artists' demise. Their cause of death remained undetermined. But the options were bizarre.

It could be the foul, mucus-like substance found on each body. Some victims were merely splattered, others had been drenched. The ichor was described variously as blue-green or blue-gray. The gendarmerie suspected some kind of poison. Toxicology reports proved inconclusive.

Or it might be the punctures. Tightly grouped wounds the size of fingers, as if the victims had been stabbed repeatedly by a rapier, ice pick, or some great insect's proboscis. Yet the wounds often missed the vitals.

The scandal sheets provided curious revelations about two victims. Le Canari was found outside, far from his studio. Face down, his arms and legs were splayed as if sprinting. The mysterious blue-gray sputum stained his yellow hair.

Odelion, the sculptor, had mixed all the sculpting plaster in his studio and, when he died, was frantically applying it where his walls met ceiling and floor as well as to the door jambs and window sills. Dried plaster covered his hands and clotted his hair. It was believed the sculptor had kept a dog. A glob of plaster on the floor preserved a large, canid paw print. Efforts were underway to locate the animal.

Scandal sheets and legitimate papers alike noted "expressions of fright" etched on the dead men's faces.

Research complete, the following morning Drieu again waited to meet Vauxcelles. Outside the editor's office, Drieu watched him on the phone. Someone had worked the man over good. One eye had swollen shut. A shiner the color of a spoiled oyster ringed the other. His upper lip was busted. He looked like a Chaïm Soutine portrait. Not that Drieu would have told Vauxcelles that.

"What happened to him?" Drieu whispered to Barbette.

"Cravan," she replied. "Vauxcelles wrote an anti-Cubist editorial that he took exception to."

"I thought Cravan hated Cubism too?"

"He does. Apparently he thinks Vauxcelles doesn't hate Cubism for the right reasons."

Drieu nodded. Even by Montmartre standards, Arthur Cravan was a cautionary tale: a poet and art critic with sidelines in prizefighting and pimping. It was a potent blend. A boxer-besting Cravan in the ring might be lampooned in Alexandrine verse. As Vauxcelles showed, a critic crossing him could get beaten to a bloody pulp. Though incomprehensible to outside world, it showed the seriousness with which the City of Lights took art.

Summoning Drieu into his office, the editor fixed him with a stare proclaiming, *"Not one word about how I look."*

Happy to oblige, Drieu opted for something safer. "I've read the papers."

"All of them? Even the rags?" his editor challenged.

"Enough of them," he admitted, mealy-mouthed.

"What have you learned, Monsieur 'Enough of Them?' Summarize your findings for me."

"All but one artist were found in their studios. Three were locked in. Covered by strange slime and unusual wounds, nobody really knows what killed them. Two, Le Canari and the sculptor, acted strangely before dying."

"Short. But correct in the particulars. Perhaps my faith in you was not misplaced," Vauxcelles paused. "What theories do you have?"

"Some sort of drug?" Drieu ventured.

"That occurred to me as well."

"Initially, I also considered illness. Or a kind of mass hysteria, like what Mesmer discussed. But why would illness strike only Cubists? And mass hysteria can't explain physical evidence like the wounds and goo."

Vauxcelles made a steeple with his fingers. "Your reasoning is sound. Don't dismiss other possibilities completely but, yes, I believe a drug is your best lead. You've gone as far as newspapers will take you. It's time to get your hands dirty. But you'll need a guide for Montmartre. His name is named Pepin. You will meet him tonight," Vauxcelles explained. "I've used him for years, whenever I need tidbits about what's going on in Montmartre."

"How will I know him?" Drieu inquired.

"He'll recognize you. No doubt you'll be the only clean one," Vauxcelles chortled, pleased with himself.

"Where do I meet him?"

"At the Zut, of course."

Montmartre, Paris' tallest hill, occupied its own world. The expanding metropolis swallowed the picturesque farming village of a century ago. The painters and poets came soon after, living by their inscrutable whims. After the Commune's fall, the city built the Sacré-Cœur Basilica on Montmartre's summit. A futile attempt to remind the bohemians that God, and the Third Republic, ruled here.

After struggling through Montmartre's twisting lanes, Drieu stood nervously outside the Zut. Copying a Vlaminck at home was one thing…but going into the Zut? Paris had dozens of words for establishments serving alcohol, each carrying particular connotations. *Tapis-franc* indicated a sordid dive patronized by criminals and deviants. The Zut was the worst of them, a hangout for anarchists, bohemians, cutthroats, decadents, and gangsters. Its three dimly lit, smoky rooms often earned comparison with the hells of Dante's *Inferno*: each more dangerous and debauched than the last.

In the end, memory of Vauxcelles' threat to fire him compelled Drieu through the door. A curtain of smoke and wall of noise greeted him. Voices sang, shouted, argued, and courted in a dozen languages. Bretons sung folk tunes in one corner. In another, a band scratched out tunes on violins, a viol, and an accordion as actresses, or perhaps *petits poules*, applauded raucously. Distinctive by their garb and language, two Russian Jews debated furiously; audible even above the din. Italian clowns performed, knocking other patrons out of their way. A donkey pranced among the patrons, seemingly confirming the worst tales of excess.

Many eyes fell upon Drieu. Uncharitably, it seemed. "You must be Vauxcelles' man," a voice spoke behind him. Drieu beheld a man at once short, fat, and bald. Pepin donned the pinched waistcoat of a gangster while affecting a distinctive vermillion bowler hat.

"Does my attire give me away?" Drieu asked, conscious of his own staid garb.

"It doesn't help," Pepin admitted. "But, mostly, it's that you look so damn uncomfortable. Let's get you a drink."

Drieu followed Pepin. Behind the bar, an enormous man wearing peasant clothes and a shapeless cloth cap poured drinks. His expansive beard merited a painting in its own right; full of whites, and grays, and blacks. But his childlike face beamed with kindness. As the gentle giant handed them beers, Pepin introduced him as Père Frédé, the Zut's proprietor.

Inwardly, Drieu acknowledged the Zut did not appear to be a den of thieves after all. Not a dangerous one, anyway. Still, he dared not try his luck with the second room.

Sipping their beers, Pepin explained to Drieu that Montmartre dubbed the mysterious deaths "*Vérole Verte.*" The Green Pox. Despite the strange moniker, opinions diverged regarding whether it truly resulted from a disease or, instead, some new drug. Artists from less civilized lands whispered a supernatural agency lurked behind it.

Drieu and Pepin planned. Four places where artists died were off limits. Nor would there be much to see, anyway. Paris' landlords, never renowned for sensitivity, had no doubt haphazardly cleaned the studios and rented them out again. That left Le Canari, who perished on the streets of the Pigalle neighborhood. Pepin suggested visiting and asking questions.

"At night?" Drieu asked, surprised.

"You come from elsewhere. Let me explain something. Paris is two cities, Day Paris and Night Paris. Your painter died at night. We need to talk with the creatures of Night Paris."

Finishing their drinks, Pepin attempted small talk, asking Drieu about his origins, his work at *Gil Blas*, opinions of Paris, and what he did to relax. On guard, the writer kept his responses to one or two words.

"If we're going to get anywhere and convince people to talk," Pepin said finally, "you must loosen up! You can't go around like an iced fish!" Pepin rumpled Drieu's clothes and insisted he down another beer. "At least pretend you're having fun!"

Nursing his second beer, Drieu opened a bit. Pepin proved difficult not to like. Affecting gangster's attire, he was actually a harmless petty criminal; no more crooked than half of Paris' "legitimate" businessmen.

Pepin's charmingly shady patter was interrupted by a squad of gendarmes forcing their way into the Zut. As their captain demanded patrons produce their papers, his men bared their teeth and white truncheons. Sliding from behind his bar, Père Frédé placed himself between the gendarmes and his patrons. "This is my place. Why are you here? These people just want a drink."

"Don't play games, Frédé. You know we are looking for anarchists."

"Leave us alone. There are no anarchists here."

"Even if that were true, we would be looking for criminals."

"There are no criminals here," Freddie shook his head.

"If that were true, we would be looking for foreigners without papers."

"None of those either."

"Then we would be looking for whores."

"I'm sorry, I did not see your wives come in."

Bellowing with rage, the captain slammed Frédé against the wall. His fellow gendarmes dragged the proprietor off to the local station.

Patrons passed the hat for Frédé's bail, giving whatever they could. A few sous. A franc or two, if the week had been good. Pepin explained that this scene played out often. The Zut's proprietor always protected his patrons, which included more than a few anarchists, criminals, immigrants, and *petits poules*. In turn, they all loved him for it.

As the hat neared, Pepin winked. "It looks like they've raised enough for Frédé. What say we head to Pigalle and see what we can learn of your dead Creole?"

Gaslights along Rue Andre Antoine and Rue Ravignan bathed revelers and pickpockets alike in a soft, warm glow. Up alleyways, however, darkness reigned. Drieu witnessed furtive movement along their edges. Sometimes humans, sometimes feral dogs. Predators, whether they walked on two or four legs.

Without the cleansing breezes of Montmartre's slopes, Pigalle was less salubrious. Equally impoverished but, with fewer studios and more brothels, it showcased a different facet of Paris' underbelly. Using an article about Le Canari's death from *L'Oeil de la Police*, they identified where his body had been found. Shuddering, Drieu crossed himself. The painter perished where Rue Chaptal intersected the smaller Rue d'Auseil. Even in Aquitaine, he'd heard of that legend-haunted byway.

Seeing the area in context underscored something newspaper reports and scandal sheet photos had not. Le Canari died in public view. He did not expire in some obscure corner but in a highly visible section of Rue Chaptal. Not in wan predawn hours, but in evening's full flower, when people abounded.

Drieu and Pepin sought out urchins, newspaper sellers, vendors, and the ubiquitous concierges that looked after residential buildings. In short, those likely to be on the street or watching the street when the artist perished. They told strange tales. Le Canari had walked anxiously, bottle in hand, looking like a man deep in delirium. Suddenly, he sprinted as if life itself depended on it.

Billowing, acrid fog engulfed the painter. Some said its vapors were not merely chartreuse but luminescent. Authorities proclaimed it one of the miasmas occasionally striking the habitations of Paris' lower classes. Pigalle's residents had doubts. The tendrilous vapors engulfed only the area surrounding the Creole. One moment he ran. The next, fog swallowed him. The one after that, the mists dissipated, revealing the artist dead upon the cobblestones, covered with slime.

An aged flower seller, his legs sacrificed to Napoleon III's ill-fated baiting of Prussia, proved keen of memory. "The concierge," he pointed out a nearby tenement, "screamed when it happened. Never heard a scream like it before. Not even on the battlefield at Sedan. When she came to, she repeated '*Se méfier! Chiens d'enfer!*' over and over. She's religious."

"Some people are," Drieu observed noncommittally.

"Not like her," he scoffed. "Saw the devil in every face. Demons in every corner. A misery to her tenants and a plague on their visitors. Finally, a doctor arrived and gave her two grains of opium. A mercy to her. And the rest of us. They've sent her to relatives to sooth her nerves. The neighborhood considers it good riddance."

L'Oeil de la Police reported locals had stripped Le Canari of anything of value. "Sad commentary on the neighborhood's degeneracy," it editorialized. From residents, Drieu confirmed the corpse had been looted. Better knowing who, and how, to ask, Pepin located the thief.

He gave his name as "Méquard," an alias. Pepin was a poseur. Méquard, with his slicked hair, gold earring, crooked cap, pencil moustache, and nipped waistcoat, offered the genuine article. "Yeah, I rolled him," he answered Drieu nonchalantly while playing with a butterfly knife. "What's it to you? You his brothers or something?"

"We're interested in what you found," Drieu explained. "Anything interesting?" When Méquard raised his eyebrows, Pepin forked over a wad of francs.

Méquard kept Le Canari's cash but had already fenced the valuables: a pistol, cigars, mother-of-pearl lighter, pocket watch, silver ring, St. Francis Xavier medal, and, especially, Le Canari's identity card, which could be sold to some foreigner whose papers were not in order. For a few francs more, Méquard handed over the remainders: an empty wallet, empty absinthe bottle, and a Bakelite comb.

"You kept an empty absinthe bottle?" Drieu wondered.

"Wasn't empty when I picked it up," he declared unapologetically. "It didn't break when the stiff dropped it and about half was left. My cleaning lady hasn't been around to toss it," he jested.

"You saw the body. What do you think killed him?"

"I know the *vaches*," Méquard used the criminal class's term for police, "are arguing whether it was that green shit or crazy wounds that killed him."

Drieu noted the inconsistency. "Green? The press says blue."

"When I rolled the body, it looked emerald green," Méquard announced. "It turned blue over a few hours. That's what the papers and *vaches* saw."

That could be valuable to know. And it shed light on the term *Vérole Verte,* the Green Pox. The residents of Montmartre and Pigalle, it seemed, knew more than gendarmes or journalists.

"Did that kill him? Or was it the wounds."

"Neither. I saw that poor bastard's face. I'd wager my own *mère* he died from pure terror."

Feeling eyes upon his back, Drieu turned. At Rue d'Auseil's entrance skulked a crone dressed like a *monjoline*, a streetwalker who beat the odds by living to old age while plying her trade. Black lace, such as widows wore, obscured her face. Filled with dread nothing about the poor creature justified, Drieu again crossed himself. Tugging at Pepin's sleeve, they departed with Le Canari's possessions.

Drieu slept late, rising only when sunlight streaming in through the window forced wakefulness. Reexamining the scandal sheets after last night's expedition, vigorous knocking disturbed his efforts.

"Someone claims to have business with you," his concierge said, making no attempt to conceal disdain.

Down on the street, Drieu found Pepin. "Another death has occurred," the rogue whispered under the concierge's skeptical eye. "They say it was the *Vérole Verte*." Running upstairs, Drieu donned a jacket and slipped useful items into its pockets. Rejoining Pepin, after the rogue doffed his vermillion bowler in mocking farewell to the concierge, they departed.

"Who?" Drieu inquired as they walked rapidly to Montmartre.

"Kasyanko. A Russian, from St. Petersburg. And a Cubist!"

"How did he die?"

"I don't have details. We can see for ourselves."

Onlookers loitered outside the Rue d' Orsel building where the Russian had kept his studio. The shrill-voiced concierge harangued them all to depart. Momentarily impressed by their own cleverness, Drieu and Pepin discovered they were not alone in using the tradesmen's stairs at the building's rear. They joined a smaller crowd around the doorway to Kasyanko's studio. Pushing forward, a muscular gendarme blocked then.

"*Merde*, I know him," Pepin breathed.

"Dirty?"

"Worse, clean. We can't bribe him," Pepin admitted. "Maybe we can con him, though."

"Well, Monsieur Pepin, why am I not surprised to find you here?" the Gendarme mocked. "What's your story this time?"

"Please, officer, we were supposed to see Kasyanko about buying a painting."

"I don't know much about art," he answered, "But I know when artists die their prices go through the roof. You'll have to bargain with his next of kin. Like everyone else."

Drieu handed the gendarme his press card. "I am writing a piece about Kasyanko. I understand this is inconvenient. But I am happy to note, in print, those who assist me with a story."

Beaming at the prospect of his name in print, the gendarme waved the men into the studio. Drieu grinned at Pepin. "Not every bribe says 'Banque de France' on it."

Surveying the studio, Drieu found much to take in. Detectives surrounded Kasyanko's mortal remains, covered by a white sheet stained with green-blue pus. Research had not prepared Drieu for seeing it. The substance was distinctly uncanny.

Noticing the young woman being interviewed by detectives, Drieu's heart skipped a beat. Her eyes and curled locks of deep, lustrous black contrasted with perfect alabaster skin.

"The artist's model," the gendarme whispered. "She's discovered the body. Or so she says."

Even with makeup streaked by tears, she was remarkable. Drieu strained to eavesdrop as she answered the detectives' questions in Italian-accented French.

"I know of her," Pepin commented. "She is called Cara."

Drieu scanned the rest of the studio. Near Kasyanko's easel stood a raised platform with a cloth backdrop. To its side, a paper partition allowed models privacy when changing. The tiny kitchen held a table and battered icebox.

Peering into the adjacent room, little more than a closet, Drieu found Kasyanko's bedroom. No frame or springs, only a mattress on the floor. A nightstand with basin, mirror, wardrobe of outrageous clothing, and tiny writing desk completed the furnishings. Empty bottles and half-burned candles covered every surface.

Objects d'art and intriguing junk adorned the studio. Photographs of an onion-domed city overlooking a frozen river, presumably St. Petersburg, were pinned to the wall. Empty liquor bottles, mostly absinthe, littered the floor.

Gravitating to Kasyanko's canvases, Drieu discovered a mystery. His cubist works were executed in two different styles. One was clean and crisp; rather like Léger. The other, darker and deeper, as if Braque had continued his earliest Cubist efforts. Drieu, no Cubism aficionado, still recognized it as the aesthetically and technically superior style.

A painting in that first style rested on the easel. Or mostly in the first style. A dramatic metamorphosis had occurred. Kasyanko brought to life a Cubist still-life of melon-greens, apple-reds, and beech-beiges in a matrix of triangles and quadrilaterals with proportions defying Euclid. Gazing at the canvas, the shapes momentary appeared to move and spin, making Drieu nauseous.

More vividly colored than Kasyanko's pigments, the mysterious ichor splattering the painting slowly dripped downward. Recalling Méquard's description, Drieu thought it had already grown bluer. Reaching out to touch it, he halted, thinking better of it…especially with the impression the slime inched toward him.

Even with the gendarme's good graces, only so much could be learned with the authorities present. Whispering secretively, Drieu and Pepin planned a nocturnal return. The criminal assured Drieu he could get them in. Before departing, Drieu slipped an empty absinthe bottle into his pocket.

That night, Drieu waited at the Zut. A quarter hour passed. Then a half. A full hour. Then two. No sign of Pepin. Emboldened by Père Frédé's beers, Drieu resolved to try on his own. If worse came to worse, he could always retreat and play the ingénu.

Returning to Kasyanko's building, he cursed upon finding the tradesman's entrance barred. Around front, the concierge had collapsed upon a rattan chair, snoring and occasionally kicking an empty bottle of *eau de vie*. Carefully, Drieu crept past.

Reaching the studio door, he realized his plan's flaw. Pepin, presumably, knew ways to unlock doors. Drieu did not. Maybe that was for the best. What if the gendarmes hadn't removed the body? The idea of being alone in the dark with it terrified him. Perhaps because it seemed safely futile, he tried the nob. Drieu jumped as the nob not only turned in his hand. He noted the door already stood slightly ajar.

The studio looked stranger than by daylight. The easel and objects d'art cast unnatural shadows on the walls. Noise from the bedroom startled him. As a robed figure exited, struggling under some burden, Drieu's heart threatened to leap from his mouth. Looking like a medieval frère in her cowled robe, Cara, the artist's model, clutched canvases of various sizes under her arms.

"You're robbing your dead employer?" Drieu proclaimed incredulously. He saw denial in her eyes. Recalling the two different painting styles in the studio, epiphany struck him: "They're yours, aren't they?"

"After modeling for him, I told him I painted," she whispered. "I showed him my work. He offered to be my dealer, to sell my paintings, and promote my name. I resisted. Over time, I became his lover as well as his model. He kept asking to be my dealer. Eventually, I relented.

"It never went anywhere. Someone was always coming to see my work, soon. Or somebody he would talk to, soon. Always he said 'soon, soon, soon.' I discovered the bastard had been selling my work…after painting over my signature with his. He was always jealous of my art. He couldn't stand me being more talented."

Glancing at the canvases she carried, Drieu saw the superior style he'd noted earlier.

As Cara's eyes burned with sadness and rage, her long anthracite curls swayed hypnotically. Drieu felt like Dante gazing into the face of Beatrice. A thought ruined the moment. If she spoke truthfully, it represented one hell of a motive for murder.

Even in the dimness, Cara read his eyes as surely as he had read hers. "You saw the sheet covering Kasyanko. Do you believe I could do that? Could anyone?" Her eyes grew suspicious. "What are you doing here, anyway? I saw you earlier with that snitch, Pepin."

"Writing an article about the deaths," Drieu admitted. "Wanting to learn more." He made a decision. How much it owed to his sense of justice and how much to Cara's big, dark eyes, he'd never know. "I'll help you carry your canvasses."

Fortune smiled on them as they carried her works past the snoring concierge and to Cara's hôtel without incident. Drieu's space proved palatial compared with the room Cara rented. Its window offered an unfortunate view of Eiffel's folly. Erected for the 1889 Exposition as an exemplar of French engineering, its creator suffered the delusion his eyesore would one day become a beloved Parisian landmark.

"How can I thank you?" she asked.

Drieu dared not voice the first thing coming to mind. But he noticed the late night café on the ground floor. "Buy me a café-crème?"

"Not sufficient. Let me cook for you." Cara boiled water on a hot plate, mixing in chicken stock and handfuls of tubular pasta. Setting that aside, she heated cream, olive oil, and pungent white cheese in a second pot. Chopping spinach and walnuts, she added them to the simmering mixture. Pouring her sauce over the pasta on two plates, she served them with leftover *pain français* and uncorked a bottle of *vin blanc*.

Complimenting Cara on the delicious dish, he remarked that it was different from the red-sauced pastas he'd had previously.

"It's very common in Florence, where I'm from."

That provided an opening to pry into Cara's background. She'd always wanted to paint, something her very traditional family forbade. When Cara persisted, she was disowned. Nothing left to lose, she made her way to Paris. Her story, however, grew opaque regarding certain pieces of jewelry she'd pawned to get her start in the City of Lights.

In turn, Drieu came clean about the scandal at the École Beaux Arts. It had been a woman. Not below his station, but above it. To preserve their reputations, both families suggested he depart Aquitaine. Coming to Paris, he'd serendipitously landed the *Gil Blas* position. Writing about painting, and dabbling on canvases in secrecy, he envied gifted painters like Cara. They were the true heroes of the Parisian melodrama. Writers merely provided the supporting players. Journalists and critics? A cut below that.

"Why didn't you call him out?" Drieu asked suddenly.

"What?"

"Kasyanko. Why didn't you call him out on stealing your work?"

"What if I did? Who would believe me?" Cara asked wearily. "For all the talk of 'avant-garde,' Montmartre is a boy's club. It has room for only so many Suzanne Valadons or Marie Laurencins."

"What was Kasyanko like?" Drieu shifted topics, "Toward the end?"

"Strange. Scary. He only drank and painted. I'm not even sure he slept. He obsessed over Cubism. As he painted, he'd mumble about Picasso, Braque, Gris, Léger, and the rest. Calling them idiots."

"Did he say why?"

"They didn't understand Cubism. What it was really for," she paused. "I don't know what he meant. Despite what he'd done to me, I visited every day to check on him and bring food. He grew volatile, devouring himself from the inside. He knew it, too. But, as long as artistic inspiration came, he didn't care."

"Cara, you know these people. You know their ways. I don't know what's happened to my guide. But I'd rather have you. You're one of them," while true, it hardly constituted his only reason for preferring Cara's company over Pepin's. "Be my eyes. My ears. My guide. I'll give your art a review in *Gil Blas*."

"A favorable review?"

"A very favorable review."

"Agreed."

Back home, Drieu pulled out the absinthe bottle from Kasyanko's and compared it with the one acquired off the deceased Le Canari. They matched. *Absinthe la Reine*. The Queen's Absinthe. "Queen? What queen?" Drieu wondered aloud.

While hardly a connoisseur, Drieu had never encountered the brand. It boasted of containing "exotic herbs from the distant Orient." On either side of its label was the silhouette of an elongated woman dressed in exotic garb and wearing a crown.

With his magnifying glass, Drieu poured over the scandal sheets on his table. Gazing at blurry photos of where the other artists died, he spotted another bottle of Absinthe la Reine. And possibly a second.

To discuss how to proceed, Drieu and Cara arranged to meet at the café downstairs from her room. Preparing, Drieu took extra care as he washed and shaved, then daubed *eau de cologne* on his wrists.

Over café-crèmes, Drieu asked Cara about the dead men's curious common denominator. "He always liked absinthe best," she characterized Kasyanko. "Claimed it fueled his creativity. But after discovering Absinthe la Reine, nothing else would do. He said it expanded his mind while painting. And he wasn't alone in saying such things."

They put their heads together. Many people consumed Absinthe La Reine. Plenty of artists, even. But *Vérole Verte* struck only cubists. To Vauxcelles' chagrin through, most Cubists still drew breath. Presumably, they imbibed something different. Apparently, the Green Pox required the intersection of Cubism and Absinthe la Reine. Drieu and Cara decided to investigate both angles simultaneously.

"If I wanted to understand Cubism," Drieu asked, "who would I talk to?"

"Picasso."

"I thought that's what you'd say. Where can we find him?"

"He lives at the Bateau Lavoir. I don't advise that. Better to find him where he's socializing. But that changes fast. When a place becomes trendy, Picasso and his crowd move on."

"Can you find out for me?"

"Sure. What are you going to do?"

"I'm going to look at a distillery."

Occupying a workshop from the previous century, Absinthe la Reine's distillery sat at the end of a dilapidated and deserted street. The distillery's rear picturesquely abutted the *Cimetière de Montmartre*. The situation did not encourage visitation.

The reek of burning coal filled the air mixed with aromas of pungent herbs like wormwood, anise, and others Drieu could not name. Promotional murals covered the building's exterior. Recent as the paintings must have been, they appeared weathered and peeling.

The massive sliding door at the distillery's front, wide enough for two wagons to pass abreast, stood half open. Inside, Drieu discovered a cavernous space. At its heart nested a vast coal-fueled boiler from which steam pipes arched overhead into enormous copper alembics where herbs infused the liquor while it distilled. Absinthe, still clear at this stage, poured from tapered spouts into barrels which burly laborers rolled across the floor to diluting vats. There, a second herbal infusion gave the drink its celebrated color. To Drieu, the entire process seemed more akin to alchemy than industry.

Above, catwalks allowed access to the steam pipes while providing overwatch of the room. Rather than foremen or mechanics, the occupants of these elevated walkways were lithe men wearing loose slacks and a chemise, both of solid black. Pacing along the catwalk with observant eyes, their garb and features announced the distiller had not lied when boasting familiarity with the "exotic orient."

Passing through the distilling room, Drieu received suspicious glances from shady workers. But nobody challenged his presence. In the next room, he found a hand-operated bottling and corking machine. Workers affixed the distillery's distinctive labels to full bottles before crating and stacking them, ready for distribution throughout Montmartre. On the bottling room's far side, a door opened onto a rear yard of yellowed grass. It ended at the Cimetière de Montmartre's wall, the tops of countless crosses, crucifixes, and statues visible above.

Turning, Drieu faced one of the men wearing black. He had crept upon him with absolute stealth. Drieu supposed the man was Asian, but he did not really resemble any others Drieu had encountered. An utterly alien aspect hung about him. Large, widely spaced eyes remained unmoving and unblinking. His face was impassive, absent of expression. The exposed skin on his hands and face appeared unwholesome.

As the man said nothing, Drieu grew increasingly uncomfortable. Almost against his will, he broke the silence. "I'm sorry," he stammered. "I was curious. Walking by, I saw the door open. I wanted to see what it was like…"

"You should not be here," the man said in flat but perfect French. "It is dangerous."

As Drieu's face asked in confusion, he continued. "Steam. Hot liquid. Glass. Many possibilities for accidents…unfortunate accidents. The distiller does not like…interlopers."

Seized by uneasiness, Drieu apologized several times while backing out of the distillery and onto the street. Uncomfortably close, the strange guardian followed him to the door. He remained there, unblinking eyes tracking Drieu until he was out of sight.

Before retreating from the distillery, Drieu glimpsed another figure. Tall and stately, he donned aristocratic *fin de siècle* clothing capped by a black turban such as an exotic mystic might wear. Leaning against the catwalk's railing, his gaze seemed to blaze like coals. Drieu knew the eyes were fixed upon him.

Drieu contemplated the sign showing a rabbit leaping from a saucepan. It heralded a Montmartre landmark. *Lapin Agile,* the Nimble Rabbit, was where Cara's sources claimed Picasso could be found these days. It occupied two adjoining houses on the steeply sloping Rue de Saules, painted weathered peach with green trim. Revelers drinking and singing the latest *chansons réaliste* packed the outdoor tables. Leaning against the wall, a man watched Drieu and Cara as they picked their way to the door. His Breton cloak, opera hat, and monocle made him distinctive.

At the Lapin Agile could be found everyone Montmartre celebrated…and Vauxcelles reviled. Guillaume Apollinaire, who was to poetry what Picasso was to painting, held court. Modigliani moved through the crowd, charming everybody, but with a special eye for beautiful women. Drieu and Cara saw the man they sought conversing with two Germans. Drieu marveled at how unremarkable he appeared: short and plain, with disheveled hair. Only the depth of his expression hinted at something extraordinary. Many called him art's antichrist. A few believed him its messiah. It had to be admitted that, each day, the latter view gained a few converts.

"Mr. Picasso…" Drieu interrupted more jarringly than intended. The Spaniard rounded on him, eyes proclaiming irritation. From his belt, Picasso produced a revolver and began firing into the ceiling.

Someone took Drieu's hand. He and Cara were led away by the man in the opera hat. Outside, he sat them down. "Fools," he chided in a melodic Breton accent. "One does not simply…" he made circle of his thumb and fingers, "engage Picasso. You must earn his trust. Preferably by having someone he trusts vouch for you. What do you want with him, anyway?" Max Jacob, poet, author, and Picasso's self-appointed protector, demanded.

"We want to ask him about Cubism," Cara volunteered, more smitten by Max's fame, or infamy, than Drieu. "It's about the *Vérole Verte*."

Max nodded before turning eyes on Drieu. "And what does the man from *Gil Blas* have to say?" he inquired, flashing a smile that, while arrogant, was not unkind.

"It's true. Strange as it sounds, we think there is a connection."

Expecting to be dismissed outright, it surprised Drieu when the poet demanded they show him their hands. Max read their palms, running a graceful finger over every line. Drieu thought the poet lingered rather longer over his palm than Cara's. Closer to the man, Drieu scented the sweet-sour smell of ether cloying to his clothes.

Reaching into the cloak, he produced well-worn playing cards. "I will read your cards," Max proclaimed. "If I like what I see, I will introduce you to Picasso." Shuffling, Max placed the deck on a table. "Cut," he commanded Drieu. Afterward, the poet laid out five cards in a simple *cruciforme* spread. Drieu's great-grandmother had done such things back in Aquitaine.

Turning the cards over revealed the Nine of Spades, Nine of Clubs, King of Clubs, Ten of Spades, and an inverted joker.

Max gazed wide-eyed at Drieu. "The cards say danger threatens Paris. Danger from Outside. They tell me you are the one who might stop it," he put a hand on Drieu's face, "but, beautiful boy, this will not end well for you…" Remembering he was addressing two people, his tone and demeanor changed. "I will introduce you to Picasso."

Drieu was uncertain what to make of the poet's spiritualist-sounding patter. If it got them to Picasso, he didn't really care. Cara proved more inquisitive. "If you believe the reading you gave, why are you so blasé about it?"

Max laughed. "Do you think this is the first time the Beyond has menaced the City of Lights?" Conspiratorially, he asked. "You saw the pistol Picasso fired?"

"We could hardly miss it," Drieu reminded him.

"It belonged to Alfred Jarry. His play that you know as *Ubu Roi* originally bore the title *Ubbo Roi*." Max searched their faces. "I see that means nothing to you. It was not a play per se. But its seemingly nonsensical words banished something awful, just as Ubu was thwarted. But, in the end, it killed Jarry."

True to his word, Max presented them to Picasso and the Lapin Agile's other luminaries. Drieu and Cara immersed themselves in singing, carousing, and banter. Picasso proved sullen anytime he was not the center of attention and looked green with jealousy at praise for other painters' work. Modigliani exuded constant bonhomie, broken by periodic coughing fits. Apollinaire was master of any number of topics. Max entertained them all, dancing with language the way the *Ballets Russes* danced across stage. Drieu had the time of his life. Still, he did not care for the way Cara gazed at Modigliani and Picasso.

"So," Picasso said finally, "What did you want to ask?"

"I want to know about Cubism."

The painter reacted with a most singular expression. Realizing a fish asked to explain water might look similarly, Drieu reframed his question. "Why take painting in that direction?"

"You do not understand. Most of them don't," Picasso began. "Painting is dead. At least painting as you know it. Photography killed it. But, in death, painting is free. Our quest is figuring out where it goes from here. Now we can show inner truth instead of outer reality. We can paint subjects from multiple perspectives in time, space, and meaning. By showing a subject from many directions, Cubism is like forcing a sculpture onto canvas. And painting shows us things which cannot be. The impossible will never appear on a photographic plate, but can be rendered on canvas."

When Drieu asked detailed questions, Picasso held up a hand. "I can tell you anything about Cubist painting. If you want to talk Cubist theory, ask Princet."

"Who?"

"Maurice Princet. The mathematician. He used to carouse with us. When I began Cubism, and all the others followed, he explained the math behind it. If you want theory, he's the one."

Research at *Gil Blas* revealed Maurice Princet was an actuary employed by one of the republic's top firms. It also produced a Montmartre address, surprising for a respectably bourgeois profession. Knocks at the corresponding townhouse were answered by a neatly-groomed middle-aged man who acknowledged being Maurice Princet.

"We want to ask you about Cubism," Drieu explained.

"Why? I'm no artist."

"As we hear it, you developed the theory," Cara said.

"An overstatement, my dear," he laughed politely. "I once ran with the Bateau Lavoir crowd. When Picasso, Braque, and the rest started toward Cubism, I indicated some interesting mathematics to it."

"For example?" Drieu asked.

"For one, the fourth dimension. Because Cubism represents subjects from multiple angles, it has fourth dimensional elements. There is a book, *Elementary Treatise on the Geometry of Four Dimensions*. I introduced the Cubists to it. They absorbed it to various levels. Picasso, especially, has an intuitive grasp of n-dimensional continuums. When he started sketches for *Les Demoiselles d'Avignon,* I saw he'd drawn diagrams from that book on his pad. They evolved into the figures in the painting."

Escorting his visitors to a wall-mounted slate board, Princet chalked several four dimensional diagrams. "See? They are very like Picasso's work. Or Braque's. They represent a subject from many perspectives. But, if you make the subject an observer as well, aren't you moving in multiple directions from one point? Not only in space but also time?

"The permutations are endless. Starting as the subject, if you moved inward rather than outward, theory says you would pinch yourself off from the universe. Remember, this is in time as well as space, so it would be like you never existed at all. It would look something like this," Princet said, adding another diagram to the slate.

"Do you know about the recent deaths?" Cara switched topics.

"The *Vérole Verte*? I've heard of it, yes."

"Are you familiar with the dead artists' work? Did they do anything different from other Cubists?" she continued.

"Look, I haven't been part of that scene in a long time."

"If you don't mind us asking, what happened? Why did you drop out of the Bateau Lavoir group?" Drieu wondered.

"Have you heard of Madam Derain?"

Even beyond Montmartre, the wife of the fauvist Andre Derain was celebrated as a great beauty. "Of course," Drieu responded as Cara nodded.

"Before she became Madame Derain, she was known as Madame Princet," the mathematician acknowledged. "Somehow, I lost my fondness for artists after that."

When neither of them knew how to respond, Princet broke the silence. "It's alright. I've moved on. You seem like nice young people. I'm sorry I can't give you better answers, but I have something that will help."

Rummaging through his library, Princet produced a book. "I have one copy left." He pressed into Drieu's hands a copy of *Elementary Treatise on the Geometry of Four Dimensions* by Esprit Jouffret. "I know it sounds dry," the mathematician said. "I assure you it is quite interesting."

Drieu was skeptical.

In the following days, they practically lived at the café under Cara's hôtel, taking turns reading the book and downing café-crèmes. Like Princet, Jouffret had been a mathematician and actuary. Unlike Princet, his mathematical knowledge had also served darker ends as an artillerist in the Franco-Prussian war.

Though not ponderous, the text proved extremely bizarre. Speaking of the fourth dimension, it alleged that reality, as commonly understood, encompassed only a tiny fragment of an incalculable whole. Energy and matter. Time and space. Mathematically, it claimed, they were interchangeable. Theoretically, one could move any direction along that continuum to any point.

As Princet suggested, the book's diagrams called to mind various Cubists. Notably Picasso and Braque, but also Kasyanko's final canvas.

Frustrated, Drieu and Cara felt the text hinted at things; knocking upon doors Jouffret was either unwilling or unable to open. It repeatedly referenced another work, *Science and Hypothesis,* by Henri Poincaré. They decided to follow the trail there.

Copies of *Science and Hypothesis* could be consulted at Paris' universities as well as the *Bibliothèque Nationale*. It seemed easier, however, just to beard the author, a professor and a member of the Academy of Science. Inquiring at the Academy, where Poincaré served as an officer, they discovered the scholar was on indefinite medical sabbatical.

They acquired an elite Sixth Arrondissement address for the man. The nurse answering its door explained Monsieur Poincaré suffered in the final stages of cancer of the throat and consumed frightening doses of laudanum. Excusing themselves, the nurse surprised them by insisting her patient would be glad for any company not hers and ushering them inside.

Mortality's reek spoiled the otherwise tastefully apportioned chambers. In the bedchamber, they found Poincaré, covers pulled around him. His complexion was waxen and sallow while fever and opiates dulled his gaze.

Asking him about the fourth dimension, its connection to Cubism, and other matters raised by Jouffret, Poincaré spoke with an unmistakable death rattle. His replies started off as rambling and obscure. Four-dimensional shapes. Indivisibility of space and time. Photo-electrics. Brownian motion. Gravity waves. Lorentz transformations. Hypercubes. The relatively of physical laws. Throughout his answers, he spoke of a "chaotic deterministic system" underpinning all existence.

Just as Drieu despaired of getting coherent answers, Poincaré's eyes gained a measure of clarity. "If people really understood what the new math and physics heralded," he pronounced, "Ninety-nine in a hundred would throw themselves back into the Dark Ages sans a second thought. We are no different than the primitive farmer who, seeing his flat field, concluded the Earth was also flat. Even with our greatest telescopes, we see only the tiniest sliver of reality.

"The essence of *Science and Hypothesis* is that absolute scientific truth is unattainable because no such thing exists. What we call truth is merely the convenient modeling of local reality. Lorentz realized time is not absolute. He called it 'local time,' but wouldn't take it to its logical conclusion. Why should it be restricted to time? Do we not, in fact, experience 'local reality?' Herr Einstein and I corresponded about that. Years before he called it 'relativity,' I called it 'local reality.'

"It is possible to shift from one local reality to another," Poincaré said as Drieu worried he had begun rambling again. "At the École Polytechnique, I belonged to a group, perhaps cabal would be a better word, of students who believed mathematical frontiers would be breached not with the wisdom of the future, but of the past.

"In locked rooms, by dimmed lights, we consulted authors whose perusal would have earned us expulsion: d'Abano, d'Erlette, Flamel, Al-Jabir, Paracelsus, Pythagoras. They claimed secret wisdom allowing them to pass through the gate of local reality and access the full multiverse of time and space.

"Such travel bends the mind in ways not natural. These masters required visual representations of the gates they created. Peasants called them magical symbols, though they were actually complex mathematical diagrams."

In the dust on his nightstand, between empty laudanum bottles, Poincaré traced such a figure with his finger. Not so different from diagrams in Jouffret's book. Not so different from images painted on avant-garde canvasses across Montmartre.

"The diagrams were important," he continued, "but even the greatest needed more help breaking through local reality. Usually a drug. The most potent was Liao or Lau, the green fungus. Liao came from two sources. One, the half-mythic Plateau of Leng somewhere amidst the Himalayas. The other, a long vanished island. Liao empowered an individual with the proper sigil to guide his travel to other times and other spaces."

Drieu remembered the phrase on Absinthe la Reine's label, "Exotic herbs from the distant Orient." Could Liao be among the herbs infused into the absinthe? And could it somehow be deadly in combination with an artistic movement depicting radical manifestations of space and time? Assuming such things were possible...

"How much math must one understand to do this? Could it be done accidently?" he asked Poincaré.

"Colleagues have disowned me for saying this, but math's truest insights are intuitive. I dislike overreliance on logic. An inspired artist could grasp the technique better than the École Polytechnique's headiest graduate. Still, it requires both the drug and sigil. The color helps, too. Green. Like Liao itself. Light at that wavelength softens the barriers between realities."

141

"What would happen if someone consumed Liao without intending to travel?" Cara wondered.

"Intense and unpleasant hallucinations, I expect. Followed by an even more intense and unpleasant headache the following day."

"And what if someone took Liao and created a sigil, or something like one, without understanding what they were doing?"

"They would be in the greatest danger imaginable."

"Why?"

"Jouffret references space-time's multiverse teeming with life, but also fails to follow it through to its proper conclusions. Our tiny mote of reality is inhabited. Of course only hubris would assume other parts are not inhabited as well. But only dangerous conceit would assume such life conforms to morality or benevolence as we know it.

"Throughout writings on chronologic and dimensional travel are allusions to the 'Hounds of Tindlos.' Inhabiting one of existence's most distant and alien corners, they hunt down those who stray from their local reality and punish them for the presumption. These Hounds track them across eons if necessary."

"Do you really believe such things?" Drieu demanded. "Hounds hunting down people who had left...local reality?" Even asking the question made him feel like a patient at Pitié-Salpêtrière in the midst of rambling delusions. But he also recalled the exclamations from the poor concierge who witnessed Le Canari's demise: *Chiens d'enfer!* The Hounds of Hell.

"That the multiverse swarms with inhabitants is mathematically unassailable," Poincaré began. "And too many sources attest to the Hounds to be coincidence. In an infinite multiverse, the probability of something like them existing approaches a hundred percent."

"Thank you for your time," Drieu said as they departed.

In the dim chambers of a dying genius, his fantastical notions possessed a curious power. Sounding as if they not only *could* be, but *must* be. Out among Paris' daylight and open air, the commonplace reasserted itself. Poincaré's assertions sounded laughable, even pitiable. Such things did not exist.

Still, that part of him inherited from his Aquitanian great-grandmother believed it was just possible that Absinthe la Reine's distiller had unwittingly unleashed a macabre and bizarre catastrophe upon Montmartre. And must be made to stop.

Even lacking Poincaré's mystical Laio, some ingredient of Absinthe la Reine might trigger a bizarre fatal reaction in certain people. In theory, Drieu could accept that hypothesis and bring his investigation to a close. But that would mean an end to excuses for seeing Cara. Unwilling to allow that, he resolved to keep investigating.

Drieu was pleasantly surprised when his calling card earned an invitation to dine with Absinthe la Reine's owner at the distillery that evening. Cara had already accepted a last minute modeling job from van Dongen. While the idea of her sitting for the smooth-talking Dutch giant made him uneasy, perhaps it was just as well. Departing his rooms, just to be safe, Drieu slipped his Henri revolver into his pocket.

Nearing his destination, Drieu noted the same crone he'd spotted in Rue Chaptal. She clutched a bundle of burned papers and, though widow's lace obscured her face, he had the unsettling notion she watched him. Unnerved, Drieu doubled his pace.

Arriving as the last of the distillery's workers departed, the sketchy laborers regarded Drieu as if knowing something he didn't. Quickly intercepted by one of the exotic black-robed guardians, Drieu followed him into an office suite he'd missed during his earlier visit. Jade-tinted paintings of Asia and the Himalayas adorned the walls, reminding Drieu of the work of Nicholas Roerich or Albert Maignan. On closer examination, the subject matter here ran from disquieting to damnable. An elongated female figure, like the Art Nouveau fashion plates in *Fémina* magazine or the silhouettes on the distillery's label, featured prominently. Wearing a crown, perhaps she was the eponymous La Reine? Curiously, her face always turned away from the viewer.

In an office converted into a dining room, Drieu was presented to the distiller. The figure Drieu glimpsed on the catwalk at the conclusion of his last visit proved no less striking upon a second viewing. Deep sockets cast heavy shadows over eyes radiating inner intensity. Bareheaded now, his silver and jet hair jutted to a sharp widow's peak. Exotic rings adorned his fingers. Introducing himself as Lucien, he added: "Though no longer discernable by my speech, I am a Parisian."

The distillery's guardians also acted as Lucien's servants. Upon his nod, one uncorked an absinthe bottle and filled two elegant stemmed glasses. In absinthe's immemorial ritual, he slowly trickled in chilled water, transmuting it from liquid emerald to liquid jade. Suspending sugar crystal over the glasses on a silver spoon, more water allowed sweetness to slowly seep in.

"I've heard the English sometimes set the sugar alight. Philistines," Lucian proclaimed, raising his flute and toasting his guest's health, Drieu faced a choice. Evidence argued something deadly lurked in the libation. But the deceased had all been habitués, if not outright addicts. Ignoring Poincaré's fancies, surely a single glass could do no harm.

Absinthe it was, but with subtle notes of unknown spices. He discovered flavors for which he knew no name. The sensation was not unpleasant. Indeed, finding it alluring, Drieu gained insight into the artists' infatuation.

As black-clad servants refilled the flutes, others brought food. Perhaps even more exotic than the green spirit, the succulent poultry mixed with mushrooms and bathed in ginger sauce rested atop noodles so fine they were like gossamer.

Absinthe was always heady, but la Reine proved particularly potent. Conversing, Drieu felt that his thoughts raced ahead of him, threatening to escape entirely. To quash the impression the wall paintings moved, his eyes focused on Lucien's, foggily aware that the distiller shared his backstory.

"…always yearning to wander, I went east. The wonders and horrors of the Ottoman court. The mysteries of India. After Shanghai's decadence and the terror of the Boxer Rebellion, I abandoned civilization for the mountains. Frostbitten and asphyxiating, I found my way to the Plateau of Leng, of which many whisper but few have visited. The natives, the *Hommes d'Leng* rescued me. At times, they seemed almost a separate people. But, you must understand, their civilization was already ancient when Cheops and Zoser began stacking rocks on the Giza Plateau and when Hammurabi first sought to tame humanity's savagery. But the Hommes d'Leng have much to teach us.

"I spent many years there and could have remained, had I not been determined to return to Paris with some means for making my fortune. Knowing this city possesses an unquenchable thirst and being familiar with spices unknown to the Parisian pallet, I returned and established an absinth distillery for artists, a community that values novelty and sensation. After interesting them in my world, some of the Hommes d'Leng accompanied me.

Drieu recognized the name Leng from Poincaré's ramblings. "In your time there, did you ever encounter a drug, or fungus, called Laio?"

"What do you know of Laio?" the distiller inquired.

His head swimming, Drieu found his tongue curiously loosened. He blurted out the saga of investigating the Cubists' deaths and the increasingly strange paths it led down.

"It is fortunate I invited you here. You've done well for yourself. Better than I expected. Without that red-hatted fool of guide who led you to the Russian's studio, I presumed you'd be lost. I was wrong. Not that you'll profit by it.

"You see, I know Liao's properties well. And, understanding that every painting is a gate, I anticipated its

145

interaction with art. Still, I never dared hope for something like Cubism. The combination is like hanging a haunch of meat around one's neck in the presence of wolves...or Hounds."

Preparing to flee, Drieu discovered it was too late. Behind his chair stood a pair of Hommes d' Leng. The instant he moved, each wrapped a restraining hand around one of his arms. "Do you mean to murder me?"

"I will do nothing to you," this distiller grinned.

"Your minions, then?"

"Nor them. Fortunately, our neighbors are very useful for disposing of unwanted...problems. Monsieur Gaudin, I bid you *adieu*."

His darkly-attired captors escorted Drieu out of the distillery and through its rear yard to the rusting iron gate in the cemetery wall. A sigil, similar to Poincaré's diagrams, was scrawled upon it. As one guard opened the gate, his fellow shoved Drieu through. The portal closed behind him with a worryingly final clang and Drieu found himself shut into the Cimetière de Montmartre.

In darkness, thick mists swirled across the cemetery's pathways. Tombs, monuments, and mausoleums loomed black and indistinct in the fog. The statues proved especially terrible, suggesting half-formed figures ready to leap upon him. Frost crunching under Drieu's feet and the sight of his breath testified to unseasonable cold.

He became disoriented. True, the cemetery was huge. But, certainly, Drieu should have reached an exit by now. Darkness and mist played tricks on his eyes. Some of the monuments' dates made no sense.

Stumbling upon a raised marble tomb, Drieu realized too late the statues reposing on its top were made from flesh, not stone. The creatures, shaped like mockeries of men but with features at once cadaverous and vulpine, stopped their revels and appraised him. The largest, clad in the uniform of Bonaparte's men, gnawed a femur. The others wore rotting funeral clothes…which one supplemented with a blood-encrusted vermillion bowler hat.

Ghouls. Drieu wondered how long Parisians had told tales of the cemeteries' other inhabitants and their vast undercity. No modern person believed such stories. Or, at least, admitted it.

"Lookie here, something fresh," their leader said in the peasant argot of a century ago. Eyeing Drieu hungrily, he snapped the femur between his clawed hands and sucked its marrow.

Drieu ran. Howling and meeping, the ghouls pursued. Sometimes on two legs, most often on four. Up and down rows of monuments and across the turning, twisting pathways he ran. Rounding a corner, Drieu found himself trapped in a dead end where three mausoleums intersected. With no chance of scrambling over the tall monuments before his pursuers caught up, he prepared to face them.

"I'm armed," he screamed as the ghouls turned the corner. Reaching into his pocket for the revolver, he discovered it gone. The Hommes d'Leng must have lifted it at the distillery. As the monsters bore down upon him, Drieu shut his eyes and awaited the end.

Their leader recoiled suddenly. "You reek of time," the ghoul told Drieu accusingly. "Likely as not, the Hounds will scent you," his clawed hand made an arcane gesture. "Killing you would be a mercy. But I won't chance your scent cloying to us."

With that, the ghouls scattered into the mists.

Hours later, Drieu emerged from the gates of Cimetière de Montmartre. Dead of night instantly became morning, dawns' light spreading over Paris's church spires and hôtels. Behind him, the cemetery was free of mist. Yet, if the chill dampness of his clothes didn't tell Drieu he hadn't imagined everything, the familiar vermillion bowler hat clutched in his hands did.

After encountering the ghouls, Poincaré's claims sounded less outré. As Drieu confided to Cara what transpired at the distillery and after, something in his aspect must have convinced her. She voiced not a doubt regarding his tale. Instead she agreed that, for the sake of Montmartre and its artists, the distillery must be destroyed. That task was beyond an art critic and painter. They needed an army. Fortunately, what was Paris if not an endless series of small armies?

Impressed by Zut's *esprit de corps*, without going into detail, Drieu told Père Frédé about the distillery's complicity in the *Vérole Verte* deaths and Pepin's disappearance. Banging a ladle on a copper pot to get his patrons' attention, Frédé loudly repeated the news. "Schroeder, Jaquier, Basnard, Odelion, Le Canari, Kasyanko, Pepin," Frédé called out the names of the dead, "were all part of the Zut family. Our family." He looked at Drieu, "Say 'when' and every anarchist, bravo, and criminal, here will march with you."

The following dusk, Drieu's little army assembled down the street from the distillery before advancing. Spotting the mob, the distillery workers shut and barred the sliding door. Unfazed, a gang from the Zut overturned an ash barrel, using it as a ram. A second group hopped the fence, hoping to force entrance through the rear. Two dozen hits knocked the main door from its frame as the mob poured inside.

On the distillery's floor, its workers waited. Some were unarmed, though their brawny bodies and beefy fists looked intimidating enough. Others wielded broken absinthe bottles, lumber planks, crowbars, hatchets, or whatever they found at hand. Scattered among them, a dozen Hommes d' Leng waited.

Lucien stood on the catwalk above, protected by more of his servants. The distiller held a large object in one hand.

Initially, Drieu mistook it for a wizard's staff. Only after a minute did he recognize it as a massive spanner wrench.

The armies charged each other with savage cries. The Hommes d' Leng took flying leaps at the newcomers. Some of the Zut's toughs, students of the street fighting art of savate, responded with flights of their own. A hulking anarchist tossed several of his smaller fellows over the distillery's men to attack them from the rear.

As Drieu's forces gained ground, Lucien wrapped his spanner around a steam pipe feeding a distilling alembic. Turning the wrench, he unleashed a curtain of steam onto the attackers below. Screams rose as steam scalded and blistered. Moving forward to the next pipe, Lucien opened it, too, forcing his enemies back toward the entrance.

"Take the catwalk," Drieu shouted. "We've got to stop the distiller."

Drieu and Cara followed another group of Zut men up the ladder to the catwalk. Charging the Hommes d' Ling, the first of the toughs was knocked from the catwalk, falling to the concrete floor, never to move again. The exotic guardians made their way along the catwalk throwing down or incapacitating the gangsters and nearing Cara and Drieu.

Seeing one of his displaced allies desperately holding onto the catwalk's under-railing, Drieu knelt and wrapped both hands around his fellow's. Groaning under the weight, Drieu pulled him back onto the catwalk.

Standing, Drieu discovered a Homme d' Leng looming over him, impassive expression replaced by a wicked grin. Like the hare in the hunter's sights, Drieu froze. The Homme d' Leng had no such difficulties. Before his blow landed, Cara reached under her skirts and produced a roll of coins. Bones crunched as she drove the inconspicuous substitute for brass knuckles into his jaw. Reeling from the blow, her push sent him over the catwalk.

As the Zut's bravos and Hommes d' Leng wore each other down, Drieu and Cara found themselves face-to-face with Lucien. Focused on opening another steam pipe, the distiller was taken by surprise. Drieu's fists left him sprawled across the catwalk, unresponsive. Seizing the wrench, Drieu began shutting pipes, allowing his mob to again advance.

As gangsters and anarchists smashed the copper tanks, hot, white absinthe ran ankle-deep across the floor. Moving on to breaking the wooden storage bins, they tossed handfuls of aromatic herbs into the spilled liquor.

The remaining workers and Hommes d'Leng formed a line between the distilling room and bottling room. There, they appeared to hold off the attackers. Until their ranks began thinning from the back. One at a time, they were snatched into bottling room. Drieu's second group had forced entry through the rear door.

"We should get down there," Cara suggested.

Before he replied, the spanner was ripped from Drieu's grasp. Recovered, Lucien glared at the pair balefully and swung the wrench. Its arc stopped just shy of their heads. Launching into a frenzy of wild swings, the distiller advanced as Cara and Drieu dodged frantically.

Accidently connecting with a steam pipe, the blow's force separated the pipe at its joint. Steam blasting toward them, Cara raised her skirts in front of her and Drieu. The thick fabric turned away the steam, reflecting it at Lucien. His face and hands blistered and bloodied, becoming puffy and pink like boiled pig. Even as unseeing eyes looked for his opponents, he rushed forward bellowing with rage and pain.

Drieu caught the distiller's arms in his own and the two grappled desperately. At last, Lucien tumbled from the catwalk, plunging through a distilling tank and into boiling absinthe.

Perhaps it resulted from a distillery awash in superheated absinthe mixed with bushels of herbs, but green haze began filling the air with translucent tendrils of mantis, viridian, and lime. Through the vapors, shadows appeared on the far wall: lean, alien, and quadruped, moving predatorily through the distillery. Seeing the silhouettes, Drieu's mob panicked, retreating through whatever egress they could find.

As they fled along the street, a noise like ripping metal cut through the Montmartre evening. A geyser of steam and green-tinged flame roared into the sky. Amidst the chaos, the distillery's boiler had burst. Drieu and Cara held each other as they watched timbers, copper sheeting, and cart-sized chunks of drywall arc high into the air before crashing back to Earth.

"*Est-ce fini?*" she looked at him.

"I hope so…I think so." Arm in arm, they walked away.

Few questions were asked about the destruction of Absinthe la Reine's distillery or the disappearance of its owner and other persons. Paris accepted it with typical ennui and moved on as Montmartre's life returned to what passed for normal.

Drieu had no choice but to begin his article. It alleged the dead artists suffered a lethal reaction to one of the absinthe's unique ingredients. This was not, as Drieu understood it, entirely untrue. It displeased Vauxcelles, however. Ultimately, Drieu's story tarred the Cubists with nothing worse than being overfond of drink.

Happily, he remained in touch with Cara, seeing her a couple of times each week. She painted prolifically now, which pleased Drieu. She'd also begun to model for other artists again, which did not.

Bottles of Absinthe la Reine remained in circulation. Weeks, even months, might pass before all of them were gone. Drieu and Cara steeled themselves for more deaths. When they came, it was not as expected. It started, like before, with the Cubists. The Parisian, Huet. A Pole named Wawelski. But they weren't dead, not officially, only disappeared. So was Wawelski's model, Collette. Then it spread. Flower sellers. Gendarmes. Housewives. Musicians. Prostitutes. Rag pickers. Street cleaners. Even a nun. All told, nearly a hundred souls simply vanished from Montmartre.

Then came the vacancy. Number Six, Rue Cortot, was missing. Only a surgically clean space between Number Four and Number Eight remained. Clearly, something had been there. But no one remembered what. Records provided no answers. It was as if whatever once stood in the gap had been ripped from existence.

On a primal level, people understood something unnatural had transpired at Number Six. Quietly at first, undercurrents of panic swirled through Montmartre's streets and down into the rest of Paris.

"Something's wrong," Drieu came clean to Cara upon their next meeting. "It hasn't ended. This isn't the same, but it's connected somehow."

"I know. I feel it, too."

Of those with whom they had spoken, Poincaré seemed to possess the strongest grasp of what such strange events might mean. They would pay another call on the ailing mathematician.

Returning to the scholar's Sixth Arrondissement chambers, they encountered workmen carrying a dining table down the stairs. Two more followed, carrying fancy Second Empire chairs.

Reaching Poincaré's rooms, the fumagatory odors of camphor and sulfur greeted them ominously. Within, much of what had been there no longer was. White sheets covered much of what remained. Instead of the gregarious nurse, a small and nervous man approached them.

"We are looking for Monsieur Poincaré,' Cara began.

Awkwardly, the man cleaned his pince-nez. "I regret to inform you that Monsieur Poincaré lost his battle with illness. I am Lémery, the family's *avocet,* looking after the disposition of his affairs."

Disappointedly, Drieu and Cara excused themselves. Descending the stairs, Drieu contemplated how to proceed. Hearing a voice calling "Wait! Wait!" after them, they halted.

"Are you Monsieur Drieu and Mademoiselle Cara?" Lémery asked. "Monsieur Poincaré left something for you."

From his attaché case, the *avocet* produced a scrap of paper. The hand which wrote upon it had trembled, not the hand of a well man. Still, Drieu could read it.

B.N., Les Enfer, d'Erlette, re: Tindlos.

Deciphering the note was not difficult. "B.N." meant the Bibliothèque Nationale. And "Enfer," literally Hell, was the name of its restricted collection. Some volumes found their way there because of rarity or value; others because they were pornographic, obscene, or blasphemous. Some belonged in both categories. Posthumously, Poincaré instructed them to consult the entry for "Tindlos" in a book by d'Erlette, a name Drieu recalled him invoking.

At the Bibliothèque Nationale, *Les Enfer's* wizened and officious keeper expressed outrage at the idea of opening the collection to a beardless youth, even one of letters, and an artist's model. Displaying the note written in Poincaré's hand, however, secured his sullen cooperation.

He showed them to an ancient and uncomfortable desk before retrieving a large tome. Its black leather cover was blank and badly cracked. Inside, the title page named the book *Cultes des Goules*, by the Comte d'Erlette. On the following page, a printer's plate gave the time and place of printing: Paris, 1702.

If Drieu hadn't known the name Comte d'Erlette, he certainly knew *Cultes des Goules*. His great-grandmother whispered of this book, fearing it as much as the devil himself. It was a handbook of forbidden knowledge and black magic…acquired at the price of one's soul.

Seeking Poincaré's citation, they skimmed through the cyclopedia of necromantic cults across Europe, the Near East, and Asia with which d'Erlette claimed familiarity. The Ghoul

Cult of Paris received special attention. Drieu shuddered at evocative woodcuts resembling far too much the creatures he'd met in the *Cimetière de Montmartre*.

Toward the tome's end, they discovered a page beginning with the heading "*TINDLOS CULT.*"

> *An island in the Ionian Sea, Tindlos appears on no map. Only the oldest records of Alexandria's lost repository hinted at its existence. The island housed a cabal of wizards whose initiates, aided by a local drug, crossed vast distances and epochs.*
> *Their constant arcane travel weakened the Universe's architecture around the island. Eventually, the Hounds, guardians of Creation's remote corners, followed them back. Overrunning the island, they carried Tindlos in its entirety back to whence they come...inflicting eternal torment upon its inhabitants.*

Further on, d'Erlette's supposed history became an ominous warning.

> *Whenever Hounds scent an eroded state of Creation, as with Tindlos, they come not alone. Alhazred first questioned whether the Hounds were truly animals, like hounds, or more like bees. Given their region's unknowable geometries, are they even separate creatures as we understand it? One thing is certain: like bees, they have a Queen. Celtic and Norse legends of the Wild Hunt preserve a distant and mercifully clouded memory of the Queen and her Hounds. So, too, do myths of Hecate and her hellhounds.*
> *The disappearance of Tindlos is not unique. Several times have the Hounds and their Queen been drawn when local geometries grew weakened by frequent travel between realms. Each time, as punishment, they carried off some building, village, or domain.*

*Though Eudemus of Rhodes believed the
Pythagoreans preserved some of the cabal's
knowledge in extreme dilution, it is fortunate that the
Tindlos cult is no more and the supply of Lau
disappeared with it (Though I tremble at rumors
flowing from distant Thibet). For, with enough
damage to the numinous firmament surrounding and
protecting us, the Queen could carry off not just a
city, or country, but the whole world.*

One final note grabbed their attention.

*In another guise, the Queen of Tindlos is still
worshipped as the Green Muse. Though by a flock too
disordered to ever be called a cult. The painter,
Caravaggio, who knew far more than the Church
discovered, wrote "...though they are unaware, she is
the patron of painters. Every painting works in time
and space, and therefore woos the Queen of Tindlos.
Even trite portraiture dares to preserve its subject by
freezing time. Paintings are symbols knocking at the
door of time-space magic. Offering inspiration and
damnation in equal measure, the Green Muse is the
muse behind all muses."*

Departing the *Bibliothèque Nationale*, Drieu grew conscious
of being followed. The crone he first observed in Rue Chaptal
and, again, *en route* to his ill-fated dinner with Lucien, now
shadowed him once again. Though revolted by her, she
seemed to play some part in matters. Drieu could no longer
afford to turn away from any lead. Approaching with
trepidation, he noted her charred papers were clutched in
hands equally burned. He feared the black lace crossing her
face concealed similar horrors.

"Who are you? What do you want?" he challenged with false confidence.

"I…I am supposed to give this to you," she stammered, handing over papers blackened almost beyond recognition.

"What happened to these?"

"L'Opale Noir."

With her reference to Paris' most infamous opium den, destroyed with great loss of life in a terrible and deliberate conflagration, Drieu understood the document's condition. And the woman's. Scanning the charred papers, he deciphered on only a word here and there. But his eyes leapt to the still legible signature, "Toulouse-Lautrec."

"*The* Toulouse-Lautrec?" Cara asked, incredulous. The great post-impressionist. The habitué, chronicler, and champion of Montmartre's previous generation had been dead since the turn of the century.

Underneath her black lace masque, the crone nodded. "Before he died, Toulouse told me, if anything unnatural befell Paris, to find those investigating it and give them this."

"We can't read it," Drieu announced the obvious. "He didn't say what it concerned?'

"I didn't ask. And he didn't want to tell me. He said it wasn't good to know. I'm sorry," turning with a sob, she disappeared into the shadows.

"Useless," he said to Cara once they were alone, "her carelessness may doom Montmartre."

"Let it go, Drieu," Cara patted his hand as they walked, "she's suffered enough."

"If only we could ask Toulouse-Lautrec."

Cara stopped in her tracks. "We can."

"He's dead."

"We can travel back to when he lived." Seeing skepticism in his face, she continued. "I was there with you. I listened to Princet, read Jouffret, and heard Poincaré. And I've got a bottle of Absinthe la Reine remaining from Kasyanko."

"But the Hounds?"

"If we're quick. If we don't go too far. I think we'll be okay."

Drieu hated the idea but lacked a better one. "Can you really paint us there?"

"I can intuit what to do. But I think having something connected with Toulouse-Lautrec would help."

Next morning, Drieu returned to the offices of *Gil Blas,* enduring another meeting with Vauxcelles. For an hour, the editor thundered about Drieu's lack of progress and threatened to send him packing. Feigning contrition, Drieu departed with a promise to redouble his efforts. And more. Under his jacket, discretely removed from his editor's personal collection, Drieu concealed a self-portrait sketched by Toulouse-Lautrec.

That evening, they sat the sketch on Cara's easel. In post-impressionist pen strokes, it showed the artist: beard, mustache, pince-nez, and *fin de siècle* bohemian finery, casually reposed against the backdrop of his beloved Moulin Rouge.

Contemplating the sketch, they passed the bottle of Absinthe la Reine between them, forsaking ritual and taking big swallows. Feelings of energy, power, and insight surged through Drieu. His seat, the room, the world itself all grew disassociated from him. As if nothing was real yet everything became possible. Cara's face mirrored the pallet of sensations he felt.

Paintbrush in hand, Cara began isolating planes and angles hidden within Toulouse-Lautrec's sketch. She put into practice everything learned from Princet, Jouffret's text and, above all, Poincaré. Parts of the sketch not visible through linear space came into view. The back of Toulouse-Lautrec's head as well as the front. Torn upholstery under his chair. The face of a dancer who looked away from the artist.

The sketch grew huge, as if their faces pressed against the paper. Drieu wasn't sure when color and volume manifested.

But, as they had been promised, while Cara drew lines and angles, the fourth dimension crept into her work. The dancer lifted her leg, then lowered it again. Lautrec adjusted his pince-nez. As the dancer swung into full motion, Drieu had the sickening intuition that, twenty years later, she would become the burned woman handing them the charred manuscript leading them here. A green-edged whirlpool engulfed Drieu and Cara with motion and color until they stood in the Moulin Rouge.

"Who are you?" Toulouse-Lautrec asked, regarding them with an expression at once innocent, dissipated, and sad. Rubbing his dark beard, he added, "You don't belong here."

"How do you know that?" Drieu demanded, fascinated by the painter's distinctive proportions: the head, torso, and arms of an adult but the legs of child, the legacy of youthful accident.

"I don't know," Toulouse-Lautrec responded, baffled by his intuition. "I simply do."

"It doesn't matter," Cara stepped forward, "What can you tell us about this?"

Frowning, he scrutinized the charred pages. "I know my handwriting. But I've written no such thing."

"You will," Cara said.

With odd casualness, Toulouse-Lautrec accepted the truth of her statement. "What is it, then?"

"A warning. About someone or something intending great harm to Montmartre. Maybe all Paris. Not normal harm. Supernatural. Spiritual. Magical. I don't know what to call it," quickly, she and Drieu summarized their investigation.

"Apôtre, he called himself," Toulouse-Lautrec said after they'd finished. "Lucien Apôtre. He spoke and moved like a native Parisian. Though I never met anyone claiming him as kith or kin.

"He portrayed himself as the arch-decadent and sublime symbolist. He was Baudelaire to those who considered Baudelaire timid. Rops to those who thought Rops prudish. Huysmans to those believing Huysmans prosaic. Mallarmé for those judging Mallarmé too lucid. His disciples claimed he read *Cultes des Goules,* led ancient rites in the catacombs, haunted forgotten shrines in the wilderness, and conversed with things which should never answer.

"Most thought it mere posturing, after the fashion of the age. But genuine darkness dwelled within him. And power. I saw it. Verlaine saw it. Lautréamont saw it, too. His *Les Chants de Maldoror* was a parody of Apôtre…and a warning about him.

"But we moved in the same circles. Apôtre consorted with girls from Rue des Moulins brothels. Some went missing. To the gendarmes, a dead whore was a problem for sanitation, not law enforcement. Those girls were my friends. I determined to revenge myself upon Apôtre. Or at least ensure no others would disappear. Lautréamont had already found his nameless grave during the Commune. But Verlaine, who could never forgive Apôtre for putting Verlaine's beloved Rimbaud under his spell, stood with me. Together, painter and poet, we conspired to ruin Apôtre's reputation.

"And we did. His name became worse than mud in Paris. Indeed, one can barely find a soul who recalls it. He quit Paris in disgrace. Before departing, however, he swore he'd return and, calling upon fell powers, swore his vengeance. Not only against we bohemians, but the City of Lights itself.

"In my heart, I believed him. Hearing your story, Apôtre is who I think of. Make no mistake, killing a few artists will not sate him. If he's back, he means to destroy Paris. Depending on how black his heart has grown, perhaps the world."

Toulouse-Lautrec sniffed the air. Drieu noticed the acrid, evil smell, too. Green vapors rolled from where the Moulin Rouge's walls met its floor and ceiling. The dim light took on telescoping, verdant qualities. He heard scuffing sounds, as if creatures pawed at the Outside, thirsting to get In.

"We must go!" Drieu said, "Thank you."

"Don't forget to write your warning!" Cara reminded Toulouse-Lautrec. Instinctively, she returned them to her chamber.

Wild-eyed and edgy, exhilarated by her accomplishment and their narrow escape, Cara grabbed Drieu and kissed him.

Reluctantly, he pulled away. Cara had created a gate and the Hounds could follow through it. Her painting must be destroyed. As he attempted to do so, Cara clutched covetously at the paper. Drieu understood. What she'd executed atop Lautrec's sketch was magnificent. Proof she could hold her own in Montmartre.

"Cara, you did it once. You can do it again. But if the Hounds reach us, you'll never paint anything again."

That she nodded did not prevent her shedding bitter tears as Drieu soaked the paper in lamp oil and set it alight.

In the days after visiting Toulouse-Lautrec, Drieu obsessed over his kiss with Cara. He hated himself for halting it. Time had come to declare his affections. Inviting her to dine at the Grand Bouillon on Saturday, he interpreted her acceptance as a favorable omen. That evening, he supplemented a thorough wash and launder with new *eau d' cologne*, nacre studs for his shirt, and a bouquet of Grasse roses. Arriving outside of Montmartre's newest trendy eatery at a quarter to seven, he rehearsed his speech while waiting. Seven came. Then seven thirty. Eight. Nine. At ten o'clock, concerned and hurt, he walked rapidly to Cara's hôtel.

Knocking yielded no response. Trying the nob, finding it unlocked surprised and alarmed him. Inside, Cara sat at her easel, painting maniacally. He called her name several times before drawing her attention. Even then, she stared blankly.

"Cara. The Grand Bouillon. Seven o'clock?"

"I'm sorry," she blushed, "time got away from me."

Drieu saw what rested upon the easel. A Cubist masterpiece equal to Picasso or Braque. She painted its triangular and quadrilateral facets in subtle shades of black, steel blue, vermillion, and sunflower, all flecked with olive and fern. Though hurt to be forgotten and jealous of her talent, he was ecstatic for her…until he sighted the newly empty bottle of Absinthe la Reine at her feet.

"Cara, what the hell are you doing?"

"Don't you see?" she asked, eyes trumpeting her feverish obsession, "I'm better than any of them, Drieu! I have nothing to fear from the Hounds."

"I'm sure others have thought that, too. Stop. Destroy that canvas before it's too late."

"Destroy it? You're just like the rest of them. You want me to fail."

"Cara, you know that's not true. I know you're a master. And you must know I…" he halted. At first, he thought he'd misjudged the pallet she'd used on her canvas. Then, cadaverous green washed across the painting, obliterating all other color as *they* came through.

Like large greyhounds, emaciated to the point of mummification. They had neither eyes, nor ears, nor nose, nor mouth. Instead, the fore of their skulls writhed with masses of pink tentacles like nightcrawlers in newly turned sod. From heads as green as the absinthe-like ichor their tentacles oozed, the Hounds' color faded to gray-green near the haunches.

They stalked in silence. Cara's shrieking offered the only sound. Falling from her stool, she scrambled toward the wall. As their tentacles crawled over her body and bore into her flesh, her eyes rolled into her head while blood trickled from one ear. It seemed to Drieu that Cara screamed long after she was dead.

The Hounds turned their squirming, sightless faces toward Drieu. Le Canari showed they could not be outrun. Grabbing Cara's pallet, he smashed it against the canvas. Random paint splatters now obscured her work. As if catching a scent they disliked, the Hounds halted and reared back. Crushing tubes of paint directly on the painting, Drieu obliterated its sharp, angular Cubist features. The Hounds grew indistinct, fading rapidly as he defaced the mystic gateway through which they entered. Painting over the canvas entirely, the lingering fetidity dissipated instantly.

Even broken by Cara's death, Drieu understood the implications of what he'd done. Certain painting techniques brought the Hounds and their Queen. Perhaps others would bar their way. Maybe they could even strengthen local reality, removing the risk it presented. Had she lived, he would have relied on Cara for that. Acknowledging that her death opened other possibilities, Drieu felt as if his innocence died.

"Cut down on the opium or you'll end badly," Picasso chided Drieu. The master painter looked to Max Jacob. "Then again, things have been strange lately. Max, what do you think? What should I do?"

Drieu wondered how much rode upon the poet's reply. After wandering Montmartre's streets until dawn, coming to terms with Cara's loss and the menace facing Paris, he'd arrived at the Bateau Lavoir, Picasso's residence. Everything Drieu knew, and needed, poured out of his mouth in a half-crazed torrent to the painter and poet.

"My cards never lie," Max answered Picasso. "The danger is real."

"What do you want from me?" Picasso asked Drieu.

"Paint like you've never painted before."

He explained his need of the artist's skill to undo everything other painters had done to weaken reality's barriers. Repairing those barriers to prevent La Reine and her Hounds from breaking through required a master.

As Drieu expounded on the mathematics, Picasso waved him off. "I do not need the theory. I am Picasso," he said as if that explained everything. Hopefully, it did. As far as Picasso was concerned, his part in the conversation had ended. He returned to the still-life he painted, while Drieu and Max schemed throughout the night to ensure Montmartre's salvation.

In the pre-dawn hours, the trio stood in front of the Sacré-Cœur Basilica. The highest point in Montmartre and all Paris, it gave Picasso complete vantage over the damaged reality he would repair with pigment and brush on the enormous canvas before him.

Max had borrowed four gaslight spotlights from the Théâtre du Grand-Guignol. Affixed to tripods, he trained the quartet of lights upon the spot where Picasso prepared his canvass. Max hoped their hot, purifying white light would drown out the green hues that thinned the barrier between realities and empowered the Hounds.

To one side, still within the spotlights' protective glare, a second easel bore a smaller canvas. Drieu's own poor talents would, hopefully, hold the Hounds temporarily while Picasso repaired reality's firmament.

Drieu, Picasso, and Max had thrown down the gauntlet. Otherworldly forces accepted the challenge. For the first time, a green sun rose over Paris, hanging in the morning sky like leprous jade. Drieu marveled at the emptiness of normally teeming streets. Did some primordial awareness keep people home as the world ended? Or had the three of them slipped out of phase with local reality?

Silence, not noise, heralded the Queen of Tindlos. Sounds of the breeze and the birds ceased. Green vapor rolled from the Sacré-Cœur's doors like waves of absinthe. In the shifting realities, its sacred statuary transmuted into subtle blasphemies. The brief quiet shattered. From within the basilica, instead of the melodic Aristide Cavaillé-Coll organ, came voices piping and gibbering in minor octatonic scales.

The spotlights intended to keep terrible wavelengths at bay sputtered, sparked, and combusted. Scrambling, Max sought refuge behind his artists. From the Sacré-Cœur, Hounds poured forth. At their center stood a figure as tall as the basilica's grand doorway. Though on two legs, she was formed from the same substance as her Hounds. Desiccated as the most ancient cadaver. Green as decay itself. Face writhing with tentacular worms, La Reine spread covetous arms toward Montmartre. Toward Drieu's reality.

Through the green mist, another figure moved beside her. Only with difficulty did Drieu recognize what remained of Lucien, whom Toulouse-Lautrec called Apôtre. The corpse-thing shambled forward, chest ripped open, flesh flayed off by steaming absinthe.

Regarding the spectacle before him, the corpse-thing hissed triumphantly. "You fool! Bringing Picasso? Do you not understand? No true artist could resist destroying reality with their art. That is the ultimate proof of talent. In her heart, your Cara knew that."

As the remark freshened his pain over Cara's death, Drieu could say nothing. Resenting the interruption, the Spaniard answered. "There is no glory in painting something so magnificent that no one survives to envy you," Picasso grunted and continued painting.

Lucien's triumphant hiss melted into howls of frustration.

Flustered by the comment about Cara, Drieu's focused slipped. A Hound broke through Drieu's wards and charged them. Yelping, Max reached into Picasso's coat and produced Alfred Jarry's pistol. Firing at point blank range, he could hardly miss. Perhaps some lingering effect of Jarry's own cosmic struggle lent the bullets power. Vanishing, though the hound made no noise, a horrid high-pitched whine like a dynamo spinning out of control sounded in Drieu's head.

His painting, mostly, held the Outsiders. Max Jacob's totem-pistol dealt with any Hound slipping through the wards. Flinging pigment on canvas, Picasso repaired Montmartre's reality faster than La Reine could corrupt it. Stealing a glance, Drieu saw red, the opposite of green on the color wheel, as well as black and even colors Drieu could not name. Superimposing the canvas over Montmartre, he noted the locations corresponding with Picasso's first brushstrokes. Where the artists died. Sites of disappearances. The Moulin Rouge, tainted by Drieu and Cara's journey. The vacancy at Number Six, Rue Cortot. Most of all, the site of the vanished Absinthe la Reine distillery. Outward from there, gracefully curved brushstrokes, more Fauve than Cubist, wrapped Montmartre in a protective web.

Just as Drieu dared hope they were winning, the corpse-thing that had been Lucien walked through the verdant mists of space-time, out of the half-reality co-terminating with the Sacré-Cœur, and into the courtyard beyond. Into Paris. The real Paris.

Drieu cursed himself for not considering the possibility. Lucien was native to local reality. At least part of him was. Wards wouldn't hold back that part. Neither would Max's magic bullets. The corpse-thing had only to reach Picasso and strangle the life from him. Then Montmartre, and who knew how much more, would be lost.

Still, that in it which was not local slowed the corpse-thing's movement. Inspired by one of Princet's musings, Drieu made a desperate move. "Starting as the subject," the mathematician had said, "if you painted inward, you would pinch yourself off from the rest of the universe."

Putting fresh canvas on his easel, Drieu quickly daubed a Cubist self-portrait accompanied by the corpse-thing. Rather than expanding the portrait outward, he extended it inward. If Princet was correct about sealing oneself off in space-time and erasing oneself from existence, perhaps someone…something…could be trapped along with you.

With each brushstroke, reality choked Drieu tighter. Light and sound grew dimmer, warping inward toward a singularly. Too late Lucien grasped what Drieu intended. By the time the corpse-thing turned away from Picasso and shambled toward Drieu, only a few strokes remained. Drieu made one more, then the next. Waiting until Lucien was upon him, he executed the final stroke.

Cards had been a good idea, Max Jacob acknowledged. In the fortnight since the assassination of Austria-Hungary's archduke, even in blissfully self-absorbed Montmartre, days grew tense and sabers rattled. A night of cards restored the façade of normalcy.

Max examined the hand he'd dealt himself: Nine of Spades, Nine of Clubs, King of Clubs, Ten of Spades, and a well-worn joker. Hairs stood on the back of his neck. A memory fought to emerge as a name hung on his tongue's tip. "Do any of you recall the name Drieu Gaudin? A writer, perhaps?"

"Maybe I remember something like that," Apollinaire said, scrutinizing his cards, "I don't know."

About to speak, Modigliani's words were choked off in a consumptive fit. Instead, Picasso filled the silence. "Are you going to chat like a bunch of grandmothers? Or are you going to play some goddamn cards?"

The memory, or ghost of a memory, vanished as quickly as it came. Max tossed his chit into the pile and waited for the others to ante.

THE SONGS OF BURNING MEN

John Linwood Grant

Flanders
8th October, 1915

Private Carter failed to die tonight.

A dereliction of a soldier's duty, you might say. The sky cleared, briefly, around eight o'clock, with the barest fingernail of a moon above us. Despite being instructed in the use of a trench periscope, Carter tried to peer over the parapet towards the enemy lines. The firing step in that section is a broken ledge of smeared clay, as likely to precipitate a man into the filth at the bottom of the trench as to give him sight of the enemy. He rose, but as he tried to take position, his left foot lost traction on the clay. Had it not done so, the German bullet which ricocheted off his helmet would have taken him in the forehead.

Carter was spared to die elsewhere; I was spared the letter of empty words that I would owe his mother. "Your son showed the finest spirit of the British serviceman, and performed every duty with cheerful…" The usual lies. Carter was a draper's apprentice from Chelmsford—less than competent as a soldier, and too stupid to be afraid.

The boy ran his fingers along the mark where the bullet had scarred his helmet, barely sensible of his fortune. I wanted to scream at him, but I had the shakes again, and needed to get away.

In the early hours of this morning, some Hans or a Fritz had sighted his battery so well that it dropped twenty rounds of shells directly on the reserve trench, on the men who were there to support us. I had felt it necessary to go back, to see if there was anything I could do.

The men there had done their duty. Khaki rags, torsos and severed limbs lay everywhere, and the shelling was still bloody. I crouched in the muck and waited it out. Almost an hour later, I borrowed the whistle from their dead lieutenant. Bewcastle, he was called. I'd known him in training, but few would have recognised him from what was left.

When I blew the whistle to signal the all-clear, only one man managed to stand up in the section, and he was immediately hit in the head by a sniper's bullet. Killed like Carter should have been.

"Hell of a shot," said the corporal who'd accompanied me.

At dawn I sent two men and as many stretchers as I could spare. They could search the rubble for wounded. There must have been a functioning Aid Post somewhere. Or was this all there was, fields of wrecked trenches and moaning half-men, all the way back to the Channel? I was no longer sure.

Sergeant Graves was in the dugout, stretched out on one of the bunks meant for commissioned officers. At least the phonograph was silent.

"We need someone forward, in one of the listening posts before nightfall, sergeant."

He looked up, his face stubble and vinegar. "Probably do." He made no attempt to move.

I had imagined shooting Sergeant Graves. No one would have stopped me, and no one would have bothered to investigate. My Webley was somewhere under the barbed wire out there—an aborted assault—but the Luger I'd borrowed from a dead German officer would do the job nicely.

"See to it," I said. "Sergeant."

Graves stood up and left the dugout. He would get some corporal to choose a lucky man, a terrified eighteen year old who had to crawl along a shallow, badly-dug trench to the sap-head. That man's night would be filled with the laughter of the Germans, or the cries of the wounded, until he himself was heard and a grenade was lobbed into the sap-head to end all his fears. Or not. Maybe Carter would be sent, and he would miraculously survive again.

I took up pen and paper.

"Dearest Aggie, we are trapped in a Godforsaken bend in the forward line, with no relief for over a week. Command has forgotten us. The Germans (a company of Saxon infantry, I believe) are erratic and confused; my own men are tired, and of less use than geese. Tell the King we are dying here, for the sake of the mud on dead men's boots."

Then I tore up the note, and found the whisky. Graves hadn't touched it, which surprised me. More rain was coming, which would bring the dead rats and ordure above the duckboards. We would have to dig some sort of secondary sump.

The usual evening shelling began halfway down the bottle. Outside the dugout, Private Netherby was whistling. It was the tune from that damned record. Four or five times a day someone slips into the dugout and starts the phonograph up. If it wasn't the only music for the men to listen to, I would snap the record in half.

I cursed whichever officer had left the machine here. It wasn't British. Some of the dugouts and emplacements are French, from earlier in the war. Sappers and unhappy soldiers extended the trench system, clearing the dugouts and funk-holes as they went. Home-made grenades, a snapshot and a postcard or two—even once a half crate of a quite decent red. And the phonograph, with its single surviving record...

I left the whisky and went out to check on the men. Night had made its way through broken trees and settled over the corpse-strewn wire between the lines. Most of the bodies were from a German bombing party, caught clipping the wire when

169

a flare-shell blossomed crimson directly above them. Even Carter had managed to shoot one. I had virtually no sense of smell since my hospitalisation, but I was told that the wind brought a hellish stench.

"Useful," said Graves, one morning inspection. "If we can smell them, it means the wind's blowing this way. Ideal time for a Hun gas attack."

So the corpses became known as 'canaries.' Shattered limbs and bloated bellies, in a cage of rusting wire.

The night was monstrous with the noise of an artillery barrage from both sides, much as the night before. Inspection, and a check that everyone had their gas hoods ready.

"Canaries are quiet, sir," said Elliott, a beef-faced corporal from Guildford.

"Thank you."

Twenty seven men, stretched across a section of trench that would have better suited at least two platoons.

"Think we're in for a pounding, sir," added Elliott.

He was correct. Tonight's barrage was relentless. The spotter planes must have failed to find the batteries involved. The high-pitched scream and whistle of shells passing over our heads made conversation almost impossible. I had Graves set up a couple of the trench mortars.

"Lob a few over, sergeant."

If this bombardment was in advance of an assault, I wanted the Germans to know that we were still there and ready to fight. We had the range of their forward trench, whilst they seemed to have no mortars to hand. Half the bombs were duds, but it would make them think.

The dull crump of the trench mortars added to the racket, and as usual. the men began whistling. The first few nights I stopped them, but it seemed pointless. Low and discordant, the sound rose above the revetment and the sandbags. Even when our own guns opened up, far behind us, I could still hear it.

I had someone sent to get news from the listening post. In the darkness, a German shrieked. We hadn't fired a shot.

"They'll break soon, sir." Corporal Elliott grinned. "We

should go, up and over." He had one hand on the hilt of his bayonet.

"No." I didn't bother to explain further. We hadn't tested the German wire recently, and we had no idea of their strength.

I walked further along the trench, slipping on the wet duck boards as I made my way down a traverse.

"Careful there." Graves again, crouched with a couple of privates.

"Is the Vickers ready?" I ignored his refusal to acknowledge my rank.

He nodded, a furtive bob in the light of a lantern. Over the rear lip of the trench, I could see the gleam of the Vickers' muzzle, our only fully-working machine gun. There was another, nested twenty yards north, but it had a tendency to jam.

"Make sure it stays that way, sergeant. They could still make a push tonight."

A private ran down the trench towards us.

"Corporal Elliott's compliments, sir. Listening post's gone."

"Gone? How?"

The man—Coker—stepped back, as if I were going to hit him.

"Don't know, sir."

I cursed and followed him to where the shallow trench to the listening post began. Elliott was there, shading the lit stub of a candle. I flashed my torch at his uniform, which was smeared with a fine red ash.

"I went up there, lieutenant," said the corporal. "Wasn't a shell. The listening post was sort of flattened out, scorched."

"What about—"

"I think this is Private Netherby, sir."

He brushed his tunic with his free hand, and the red-brown ash scattered over the duckboards at his feet. Elliott didn't seem overly concerned about the affair.

"Flamethrowers." Coker pressed himself closer to one of the funk-holes in the side of the revetment. "Bloody hell."

"Easily dealt with." I kept my voice steady.

I'd seen the *flammenwerfer* teams in action, at Hooge. They were alarming at first, but it only took a shot to the tanks on the soldier's back, and they made themselves obvious enough once they began their work.

I passed the word that lookouts should be at every observation slit.

The enemy did not come. At four a.m. I went to get some sleep. That did not come, either.

9th October

At around nine in the morning, four frightened soldiers arrived with supplies for us. They had no news, no knowledge of when we might be relieved, and risked a crouching dash across open ground to get away from us as soon as their burdens were down. When I looked back at my platoon, I wondered. Unwashed, unshaved, and with the faces of prisoners.

Graves is sullen as usual—I preferred Jones, but he was sent back on the first day, a broken leg—and my two surviving corporals are erratic. Elliott is so eager to fight that he loses most of his reason; Senden seems to be one of those obsessed with the French record.

I can't say that I have a good ear for music. A little Mozart, maybe. Something light. This tune, a flute piece, is brooding and hard to describe. As if an old folk air had been messed with by one of these modernists—Schoenberg, is it? I can barely play the piano, and don't know if a melody can be tonal and atonal at the same time. I know this one sets my teeth on edge.

It was a shame about Georgie Bewcastle. He was a fine fellow. I had his whistle on my lanyard now, my own having been dented by a bullet a while back. He was musical—or had been. When he came to visit us on the second day of our turn in the forward trench, he listened to that record.

"All wrong, old chap."

He squinted at the handwritten label on the disc. It was a circle of brown paper, poorly glued down.

"'*Chanson d'Ocre*'? Never heard of it."

"My German's better than my French." I poured him a whisky. "The Brown Song?"

"Close enough."

He put it on again, and within a minute we heard the tune being picked up outside, Whitram on his tin whistle. Georgie frowned.

"Thought it was a flute, but I'm not sure now. Seems more like a recorder, sometimes. A peasant sort of thing. Minor chords, eh?" He hummed a fair imitation of the tune, and then gave the record a look of disgust. "It's all wrong, anyway."

I didn't see him again until I threw a blanket over his remains.

I stood some of the platoon down to get a late breakfast. I was no longer hungry. I remembered finding the burned bodies in the reserve trenches.

They were still eating when Graves came over to me. He had a cigarette hanging off his bottom lip, as usual.

"Private Collier's missing."

"Collier?" A fair-haired man, short, I seemed to remember. Another damned whistler, who I'd had to kick out of the dug-out. "Run, do you think?"

The sergeant scowled. "I'll have them check the nearest bomb craters and hidey-holes."

I am puzzled by how quiet the Germans are. Two of our Avros flew over in the afternoon, looking for signs of enemy artillery emplacements. The German guns, sensibly, held fire, not wishing to betray themselves by muzzle flashes or smoke. It's the same game most days.

At times I long to see a dog-fight between our airplanes and theirs, to break the monotony, but then I remember that there are men in those cockpits, men who bleed and die.

There was no sign of Collier.

10th October

The lookouts report that there was a blaze during the night. I wasn't called, because it happened near the German trenches. A flare of intense, red-brown flame, they said—I thought that a peculiar description—close to their wire. Faint cries in German, then silence.

"Looked like a man," said Corporal Senden, and he smiled. "Like a man on fire."

Hardly seemed something to smile about, even if had been a German.

Rain today, as expected. Our tenth day of a seven day turn on the front-line. Or perhaps not. This was called 'The Loop,' an extended bulge which seemed to serve little purpose. The heavy fighting was north of us, towards Ypres, as far as I knew.

Breakfast was a can of bully beef, and hardtack. There'd been some of that soft French cheese at the start, but the rats had taken the last rinds of it. At least we have plenty of tea. No milk, though.

There is a look in the men's eyes which reminds me of when I was in hospital. A deadness, which grows worse each day. Only Carter and Elliott don't seem to have it; the one because he seems too stupid to be affected; the other because, I suspect, he is obsessed with killing Germans.

The enemy are very quiet. I sent Private Chelmsley to the other listening post, the one further south. He came back around noon, filthy from the crawl.

"No movement, sir. I mean, they're there, but there's just muttering, the usual clank of gear."

"Did you hear anything about gas or flamethrowers?"

I'd sent Chelmsley because he was the only other man in the platoon who spoke German. He had an aunt in Dusseldorf, apparently.

"Yes, sir. Not gas, but they mentioned 'Britischer flammenwerfer' a few times. Couldn't catch everything, but they didn't sound happy.

"We don't have any flamethrowers." I stared at him. "You're sure, Chelmsley?"

"Yes, sir."

He picked up his rifle, wiping off the mud, and began to whistle.

"That damned tune," I murmured.

The private looked up.

"Sorry, sir. Heard it a lot this morning. The Boche seem to like it."

Why in God's name had the tune spread across these lines?

The rain clear later in the day. Parts of the trench were flooded, as I'd expected. I ordered Graves to pick a detail and dig more drainage. He looked at me with disinterest, but went off, calling out names for more 'volunteers.'

The telephone wires went when the reserve trenches were destroyed. After Bewcastle's death I sent a runner back, to find Command, but, like Collier, he hasn't been seen again. I can't spare anyone else. Surely Battalion will send word to me?

That night, the rain of fire continued.

11th October

As if my thoughts had made it so, an officer arrived the next afternoon. I was resting, as best I could, in the dugout. Senden knocked on the wooden post, and showed him in. The man was of middle height, in his thirties, I would have said. A captain, with a thin face and a neatly-trimmed moustache.

"No need to get up," he said, throwing his rifle and helmet onto the other bunk. "Are you B-b-bewcastle?"

"Milburn, sir. Bewcastle had the reserve trench…he's dead. Artillery fire, four days ago." I sat up and saluted. "Are you our relief, sir?"

"Passing through, M-m-milburn, passing through. How are things here?"

"Worrying, sir."

"Name's B-b-blake. Best fill me in."

I can't say that I took to him, or that he fitted my idea of a captain in the North Surreys, despite the uniform. Slowly I outlined the situation, our losses, the destruction of the reserve trench and so on. I mentioned the possibility of flamethrowers being in the area, and asked him about any news of recent gas attacks. He listened intently, and then saw the half-empty whisky bottle.

"Swop you a f-f-flask of cognac."

He produced a battered metal hip flask, tossing it onto my bunk. When I said nothing, he helped himself to a whisky. At a loss, I took a swig from the flask. It was very good cognac.

"Sir—Blake—we've been here eleven days. Our supplies are getting low—"

"Spot of fighting near Ypres. The Canadians are in trouble. Tried at Hill 60 again, bit of a d-d-disaster. Can't see them getting you relieved for a few d-d-days yet."

There had been plenty of stammerers on the ward at Christchurch Hospital, even a couple of mutes. Captain Blake wasn't like those men. He barely seemed to notice the impediment, his gaze moving from one corner of the bunker to another as he spoke. Assessing what he saw.

"We'll hold, I suppose." I washed the cognac around my gums.

"We'll see."

Before I could make a retort, he stood up.

"That tune, outside. Six or seven of your men—and a chap playing a tin whistle. Same thing. Where did it c-c-come from?"

I took a deep breath. The drink was helping.

"When we took over this section, we found stuff left behind by the French. Mostly rubbish, or badly-damaged gear, but this," I pointed to the phonograph, "This was untouched."

He eased the record off the turntable, and I noticed for the first time that he was wearing leather gloves.

"*Chanson d'Ocre.*" He passed me the record. "Peel the label off, there's a g-g-good chap."

I did as he asked, pulling away the handwritten circle of brown paper. Underneath was another label. Hand-written again, but neatly printed, with what looked like a series of times and co-ordinates. I showed him.

"Astronomy," he said.

"But what does it refer to?"

"A star." He considered the whisky bottle. "Did they tell you much about the Frenchies who were here?"

"Gas, and the rest. A German assault."

"Almost a year ago. There was g-g-gas, Milburn, but no assault. Something happened."

"What?"

"I don't know. Not all of it, anyway."

He eased the glove from his right hand, and took the record from me.

In the barracks back in England, I had seen two other officers take part in a dare, a simple one. Each was to hold his hand over a candle-flame, in the flame, for as long as he could stand it. Blake's face, holding the record, was the same as theirs had been. Concentration, determination—and pain.

When he placed it down on the rickety table, there was sweat on his forehead.

"Whisky."

I poured him another, and he took it with his gloved hand, downed it in one.

"You have a scar, by your l-l-left ear," he said.

"I...there was a bit of a set-to at Hooge. Back in May of this year. We were supporting the Cavalry Corps around there. Then the German artillery got our range...I was hit, had to go back home for a while."

He nodded. "Affect you much?" His clear eyes held me.

"They call it 'shell-shock' now, I think. Couldn't see properly, though they said my eyes were fine, physically. Still get blurred vision, sometimes. And I haven't been able to smell anything since."

177

"You may be better off, in that regard. This p-p-place stinks, old chap."

His smile was thin, a twitch of the moustache.

"You haven't said why you're here. Sir."

He put his glass down. "We should check on the m-m-men, I think, Milburn." A brisk dismissal of any further discussion.

It was fortunate that he was not an officer of engineering. Or any normal inspecting officer, perhaps. Sand-bags had burst; some of the parapet was sagging from the repeated rain, and I had failed to get anyone to repair broken duck-boards. A misstep and your boot went into ordure. Even attempt at strengthening the firing step had been botched.

"This is my sergeant, Graves."

Graves stared at Blake without acknowledgement of rank. A closed, sullen look.

Blake nodded, as if considering a parade. He turned slightly to look at the four or five soldiers crouched against the revetment, and then, somehow, he had the muzzle of his Webley an inch from the sergeant's forehead.

"Would you like me to pull the t-t-trigger, Graves?" From his voice, he might have been asking if anyone wanted a piece of toffee.

The sergeant closed his eyes.

"No. Sir."

"Hmm." He holstered his revolver. "Not a great enthusiast of rank, m-m-myself. But we keep up the show, eh? Can't fall apart just yet, sergeant."

He gestured to me, and wandered along the traverse. I trailed behind, aware that every man was watching us.

"He might not be well, Blake. The sergeant, I mean" I muttered.

"Or he might be the only one who is." He pointed to Whitram, who was perched on the firing step, playing his tin whistle as usual. "You hear that?"

"It's…somewhat irritating. Annoying."

The captain shook his head. "No, M-m-milburn. It's wrong. Utterly wrong."

"What were those figures, written on the record?"

"I'll show you later. How have the Germans been recently?"

We lowered our heads as someone fired a couple of exploratory shots in our direction. High enough over the trench—pointless, in fact.

"You seem very calm, sir." I abandoned calling him Blake. "Have you seen much action?"

"Action? I've k-k-killed a few people, if that's what you mean."

I decided not to ask more.

The trench should have bent on itself and continued towards the line held by the East Surreys, if they were still there. Instead, a failed attempt at supporting a charge had destroyed most of the northern section. Our artillery had fallen short, and almost wiped out a platoon of the Young Buffs. German machine guns had done for the rest.

A twisted set of craters made the area almost impassable, and a tangle of spikes and barbed wire, yards deep, made it truly a No Man's Land. There were corpses under the mounds of earth, from two months back, I'd been informed. Elliott said that he could smell them, much like the canaries, when the wind was right.

"The Germans? What have they been up to?" he asked again.

"I'm sorry. The occasional pot-shot, but surprisingly little, really. We think they have a flamethrower — "

"They d-d-don't. None in this part of the front-line."

"But — "

"They discovered that they had a problem with the supply of canisters. Sabotage." He smiled. "Why did you think they had f-f-lamethrowers, Milburn?"

I tried, badly, to explain the odd occurrences of the previous few days. He was particularly interested in the lost of the listening post, and the fact that the enemy were whistling the same tune as my men. We sat on the edge of a funk-hole, pushing abandoned, mould-covered webbing aside, and he listened intently.

179

"Dark soon," he said at last. "The Germans have gone to a lot of t-t-trouble recently to take out your reserve trenches. And communications."

"Do you know why, sir? Is there a push coming our way?" He shook his head.

"The real work is south of here. The North Midlands are g-g-going after the Hohenzollern Redoubt." He let out a long breath. "It won't cut the m-m-mustard, of course."

"You don't think they'll succeed?"

"Don't need to think, old boy." He stood up. "Dark enough, now."

Blake led me to a low, open section of trench, cupped by twilight. He seemed to know the area better than I did.

"Look south. See that f-f-fellow, not far above the horizon?"

At first I assumed he meant there was someone there, out in the open, but I realised that his gloved finger was aimed at a low star in the cloud-scudded night sky. The woods which might once have obscured our view were no more than broken trunks, none more than a man's height.

"Fomalhaut."

"I've never heard of it, sir."

"The numbers on the record label. You wanted to know what they were. They're the co-ordinates for that fellow." His hand dropped. "An amateur astronomy buff, with a thing for the flute, eh? You can never quite work out the French."

I knew that there was more, and at the same moment I realised that Blake wouldn't share whatever secrets he was holding.

"You're not from Battalion, are you, captain."

He smiled, looking down at his uniform.

"N-n-no. I dare say I'm not. But I serve the same King as you do—and for the moment, at least, I have your best interests at heart."

I nodded to the men waiting by the firing step.

"And theirs?"

He pulled at one corner of his neatly-trimmed moustache.

"D-d-do you have flares, maroons?"

"Yes, a few." Why was he asking this?

"There may be a moment, old chap, when you look at your men, when you listen to them, and you'll know. Light a m-m-maroon, and run, get the hell away from here."

"Pull the whole platoon out of the frontline?"

The captain sighed.

"Get yourself out. By then the rest won't follow you any more, and it won't matter a damn what you say, what you use to c-c-cajole or threaten them with."

It was hard to believe what I was hearing.

"How can you know that?"

In the traverse beyond, Whitram's whistle played notes which caused me to wince.

"One maroon will do, M-m-milburn. You'll realise when. Oh, and break that record, or melt it down. That's an order. Soon as you can."

Blake strapped on his tin helmet, pulled up his collar, and turned towards the remains of the nearest communication trench. I grabbed at his arm.

"You owe me an explanation!"

"Some d-d-debts are never paid."

He prised my fingers from his coat, and I stepped back. His eyes had met mine throughout without flinching, without any evident conscience as to what might come, and one hand had always stayed close to his Webley. I had the sudden feeling that if I tried to stop him, only he would leave this trench.

"It doesn't make sense." I sounded whipped, a beaten dog.

He tossed his cigarette stub into the foul water which had pooled in the bottom of the trench.

"No, it doesn't. But I know what I'm talking about, M-m-milburn."

"How?"

"B-b-because I saw what was left of the Frenchies. And I know who released the gas on them."

12th October

The men are worse. Private Crouch, who has been disturbed for some time, keeps to his position, rifle ready, but he mutters and whistles constantly. I would send him back, but how? I can't spare anyone to go with him, and Graves says the man can still fight.

Another flare-up in the night, and this time I witnessed it. It was beyond the wire again, on the German side. There seemed to be some scuffling out there, and I had the men make ready.

"Steady, now."

I expected another bombing party, but nothing came near us. Someone shouted, in German. It sounded like *Lieder* - and then a deep yellow glow could be seen, south and east of our line. It grew, a lantern point which took the form of a figure—limbs jerking with unimaginable pain. I tried to focus my field glasses, and even with blurred vision, there was no doubt that it was a man.

"For God's sake!" said Graves, and raised himself on the step to aim his rifle. He fired three times, but rather than fall, the shape of fire seemed only to dwindle, to fall apart.

"An accident with their munitions." My voice was unsteady.

Graves looked at me. "Of course. An accident." He spat, and went to check further down the trench. I rubbed my eyes. There, on the southern horizon, a star burned.

Fomalhaut.

Why had Captain Blake been here at all? He had no promise of relief, or reinforcements. He brought no new intelligence. And if he had come to see if we would hold our position, why? Our presence here seemed more pointless with every day. A token platoon, where we would not attack, where the Germans would not attack.

I no longer saw that earlier German bombing party as a real assault. I no longer knew what was happening in their trenches. There had been no follow-up to any of their actions. Private Chelmsley reported that the abominable tune could be heard from their line, and yet he said it with a dullness, as if he too were going the way of the rest of the platoon.

Blake was right. Graves seemed different. He never whistled the *Chanson d'Ocre*, or hummed it, never changed his attitude. He had been sullen and stubborn since we were first posted here.

My hands were shaking. I found Graves checking the faulty Vickers, and I clambered into the machine-gun nest next to him. The two men who should have been there were missing.

"Where's the crew, Graves?"

He tugged on an ammunition belt, trying to free a jammed part of the mechanism. "I put them on observation. They can get up here quick enough if they need to."

I wanted to argue, but it seemed pointless.

"Why are we here, sergeant?"

"You're the officer. Sir."

"Please, Graves."

That threw him. He wiped mud from his face, and his look was hooded, cautious.

"Permission to speak freely?" He had never bothered to ask before.

I nodded.

"Then I reckon that we're buggered. And Battalion knows all about it." He pointed to where the German corpses clung to the wire. "Canaries. If we make it, Battalion will carry on as normal. If we don't, they've lost nothing much."

"A platoon of men," I protested.

"The worst in the Company, led by a man who can't see straight and a sergeant with more disciplinaries than you can count. Half this lot can barely tie their own boot-laces." He laughed, an unpleasant sound. "I thought you'd got it, lieutenant. The best men were back in the reserve, with that mate of yours. That was Battalion's loss, when they got hit."

"But — "

"They were supposed to watch us. One of their sergeants told me, but he didn't know much more than that. They were to be ready, if we went down."

"They expected a German assault in this section?"

"No idea."

A burst of artillery made conversation impossible for a few minutes. Firing over us, as usual. We kept our heads down until it was over.

"What did that bastard Blake want?" Graves lit a cigarette.

"I don't know."

But he had been watching, observing us, as well.

"If...I don't know how to put this, Graves. He said I would know, that there might be a point when I looked at the platoon, and needed to get the hell out of here."

"You should have done that on the first day."

"No, he meant something different, something...strange, wrong."

"Hardly any shortage of that round here." He took a deep draw on his cigarette. "I tried to take that bloody tin whistle from Whitram yesterday. He started for his bayonet, and I backed off."

"It's that tune. It's in their heads."

Instead of scorning me, he nodded. "And in Fritz's."

"But it doesn't affect you."

He shrugged. "Tone-deaf. Can't carry any tune."

"Graves—what am I supposed to do?"

He rolled another cigarette, even though the old one was almost burning his lip.

"They'll shoot me if I run. You might get away with it. Sir." A bitter addition.

"Blake said to fire a flare—if it came to it."

"And what? We'll be rescued, relieved? Sent back to Blighty for a parade?"

It was fortunate that the artillery opened up again at that point. Graves and I both knew that there would be no parade.

13th October

Alone in the dug-out, I broke the record into pieces, and held the remains over a paraffin flame. It was fortunate that I had wet gloves on—the fragments flared, a sickly yellowish-red, and within seconds all that was left was a fine ash. Ochre, of course. *Chansons d'Ocre*, charred to the heart of whatever horror they represented.

I snapped the arm of the phonograph, and ripped out the mechanism. That was more for myself, a small attempt at catharsis, though I realised that it would make no difference. In the trench beyond, the sound of Whitram's tin whistle rose and fell, picked up by men's lips along the line.   The situation is worse. They neglect their duties, unless directly pushed. And they stare at candles and lanterns, watching the flames, even though Graves and I have warned them of the danger that they will make themselves targets.

Worse, at other times I have caught some of them staring towards the low star in the southern sky. That worries me more than anything.

German fire from the opposing trench has almost completely ceased. A couple of shots today, when one of my men laughed out loud (I don't know at what), but they didn't even seem to be aimed. The listening post can make no sense of what is happening over there. No mining, no sound of machinery or heavy activity of any sort. Little conversation, but more reports of that tune being hummed or whistled in their trenches.

We have a strange alliance, the sergeant and I. There is no liking between us, only the shared sensation of being the only two sane men in some terrible asylum. We make the men go through a show of their duties, but expect less and less.

This cannot go on. I shall have to be an officer, to take action. But what?

14th October

This morning I forced the men into a semblance of an
inspection, and set them to cleaning their weapons. One of
them—Bentley?—has found a harmonica, and now plays it as
a dreadful counterpoint to the *Chanson d'Ocre*. The Ochre
song. Nor is there any doubt that the Saxons are similarly
affected. We heard someone shouting around ten in the
morning, an officer from his tone and the words I could catch.
In mid-sentence there was a rifle crack, and he fell silent.
Moments later, that discordant tune was on the air, clearly
coming from their trenches. Some of my men looked at each
other, a vacant pleasure on their badly-washed faces.

I spoke only to Graves, and to Corporal Elliott. I think
Elliott is mad in another way, a sadist whose mind has been so
turned by this experience that he would kill any man on the
lightest pretext. I remembered his lack of concern over
Netherby's death in the listening post. The Germans are his
focus at the moment, but I would not have him at my back. I
explained that I planned a dusk assault, when the artillery
opened up.

"I have boards ready, sir—to throw down on the wire. And
cutters, sir." Elliott's smile was no more appealing than that
of the whistling men.

"Good, good. We'll take a squad each, broach the wire,
and charge them. Senden can watch your back, Elliott.
There's enough moon for us to see our way, but they won't be
expecting it."

"Neither will that lot," said Graves, tipping his head
towards the nearest two privates.

"Our only hope is action." I tried to sound firm, resolved.

"Damn right, sir," said Elliott. He sloped off to find
whatever equipment he'd been gathering.

The sergeant and I shared some tobacco. When he saw that

my fingers were shaking too badly, he rolled the cigarette for me.

"Didn't take you as the death-or-glory sort," he said as he lit my cigarette.

"I'm not. But we have nowhere else to go. We can't stay here."

"Amen to that." His glance flickered across my uniform. "Sir."

As the sun fell, I could have sworn that I heard the phonograph playing. It was not, of course. The sound came from both trenches, drifting across twenty yards of ruin and barbed wire, sharing the breeze which set the canaries fluttering, rags of uniforms moving in the last of the light.

Graves had gathered the platoon.

"We're going over, men. Time to turf the Hun out, and get ourselves a chance at relief. Hot baths, clean clothes, the lot."

Some semblance of understanding seemed to cling to most of them. I did everything by the book, hoping that military discipline would take hold when the shove happened. Weapons and equipment check, ordered off by number to their sections, mandatory—if hasty—meal. The sergeant and I had them adjust their tunics, straighten their helmets, anything which might remind them of basis drill and procedure.

It worked, after a fashion. Elliott and his squad went out first, and his dark oaths kept the tune from their lips, at least for a while. Thick gloves, boards and canvas sheets on frames. He had known what he was doing. Given that neither sides had maintained the wire barriers, and that shelling had torn it open in places, I had no doubt that he would clear us a path.

Whitram was still there behind the revetment, his tin whistle to his lips. I would have tried to shut him up, but Graves pointed out that this would be considered normal by now, if any Germans were listening. I let him be.

After half an hour, a man scrambled back into the trench.

"The corporal says it's clear, sir." It was Carter.

At Hooge I had blown my whistle, bringing my men up from shallow trenches to charge the chateau. Ten minutes later, I was being dragged back to an aid post, my uniform soaked with my own blood. This might end the same way, but I never wanted to hear a whistle again.

I gave the order, a murmur that was repeated along the trench, and we mounted ladders placed against the revetment. I turned to beckon my squad on, and saw Fomalhaut, that pale, malignant star, gazing down on me.

My hands were shaking, but I managed to unholster the Luger and set off in a crouching run for where the wire had been cleared or flattened, eight men behind me. A dozen yards down the line I could see Graves. Two of his men were carrying sacks of Mills Bombs.

The execution of our charge was according to the manual, except for the last ten yards. The Saxon Infantry were not in their trench, but around it. Some of them at least. I saw soldiers staring south, towards Fomalhaut, like spectators at a race, and I could already hear a muttering from the enemy, interspersed with fragment of *Chanson d'Ocre*. One caught sight of us and raised his rifle, a slow, unfocussed movement. He fell back, shot by someone in Graves' squad.

There was war, of a sort. Elliott began screaming in fury, the furthest away from me, and he seemed to be firing wildly. A German grenade fell near us, and Carter kicked it away, badly-the explosion almost killed some of Graves' squad.

"Come on, lads!" I charged, but only Carter followed me.

Both my men and Graves were faltering. One of his squad simply dropped his rifle and stood there. We had cleared the wire, and here were the enemy…but what were they? Not the Kaiser's picked men. These were almost shells of men, barely able to defend themselves. A German was sitting on sandbags, whistling that tune, his weapon forgotten at his feet; another, an older man with whiskers, only stared at us…

We were elsewhere, I felt, as if on a cratered world in which our war meant nothing. I saw Elliott die, bayoneted deep in the belly by one of the few functioning Germans, and I saw Graves in turn shoot the bayonet-man. There must have been paraffin lanterns or some other combustibles behind their parapet, because flame surged up in the aftermath of a Mills bomb, an orange flame which illuminated every ghastly element of the scene.

"Graves!" I called to him, hoping that between us we might make sense of it all. At that moment I reached the parapet. Machine-gun fire should have cut me down, but there was none. A German corporal crouched below, and we saw each other at the same moment. His face was white, his eyes sane.

"Hilf mir," he said, his voice hoarse.

I pointed the Webley at him, but couldn't pull the trigger.

"Was ist passiert?" I gestured at the aimless men, both his and ours, a struggle which seemed less and less to have any purpose.

"Lieder von Ocker." he moaned. "Bitte, der Stern. Der verrückte Stern."

The insane star.

"Kommen Sie mit, Korporal."

Terrified, suspicious, he clambered up to stand before me, my revolver still pointed at him. Graves came up, lifting his rifle.

"It's all right, sergeant."

"He's the enemy."

"I doubt that. Look around you."

Graves looked uncertain. He lowered his rifle an inch, two, and the three of us stood silent on what was less than a battlefield, more a wasteland occupied by shuffling strangers. A wounded man somewhere asked for *wasser*, and Carter was cursing as he fumbled with a sack of Mills bombs. For a moment, the only sound across the trenches was of ghastly, discordant whistling from the lips of British and German troops alike, and then Carter cried out...

I had little doubt, in that stark second, that Carter himself was the agent of his own end—a fumbled attempt at removing the pin, or failure to throw the grenade in time. The sack of munitions exploded with a deafening roar and a hail of shrapnel, tearing the private in half, ripping into the nearest soldiers and throwing them across No Man's Land. Graves and I fell backwards with the blast; the German corporal had taken a long sliver of metal to the head, with fatal effect. His

189

body lay a few feet from me, his eyes so very blue as the blood trickled down his face.

That was not the horror of the moment. The sight that transfixed us was that of the others, in their various grey and khaki uniforms, rising to their feet whether wounded or not. One man's uniform had caught fire, and he was burning, burning whilst still alive. I think it was Private Whitram. I had seen men burn, and they struggled, rolled, screamed. Whitram stood, arms jerking in spasm, and I swear he was still whistling that song as his lips blackened.

"They..." Graves shuddered. "Look at them."

Seventeen or eighteen soldiers from both sides, turned to the south, the mindless whistle of the Ochre Song on the air, all eyes on a low star as Whitram burned.

"Blake's moment," I said. "He told me there would be a time..."

I took the sergeant's arm, lifted him up, and we limped away, back towards our own trenches. The others paid no attention now, and Whitram—he was crumbling, like those flaring forms from the other nights, consumed. There was enough light from the fires to see the reddish ash as it lost human form and became one with the mud of Flanders.

Hooge had shaken me, damaged me. This night had blotted Hooge from my thoughts, brought clarity. I knew exactly what to do.

Back on our own trench, I drew Graves into the dugout, and offered him the remains of the whisky.

"I don't drink. Sir." No insolence, no tone to his voice.

Nodding, I finished the bottle in a gulp and began to write, as quickly as I could. I gave clear instruction that I had sent Sergeant Albert Graves, C Company, North Surreys, to find a functional Aid Post or Field Ambulance, on behalf of his platoon. He was to request immediate assistance for casualties at the front.

"You keep this safe," I said. "You take most of the night, even the morning. Get away from here as quickly as you can, but then rest, sleep, delay, before you present it."

Graves slipped the letter inside his tunic, and stood. He

190

understood that it was his ticket, a way to leave here legitimately and plead ignorance of what had happened.

"And you, Lieutenant Milburn?"

"Oh I'll be getting out of this hell-hole as quickly as I bloody can. I have one last task. Get going, Graves."

We didn't smile or shake hands. He ran down the trench; I made for the next dugout along, where some of our supplies were kept.

My unnatural calm was tested when I found that rats had eaten through the wax coating of some of the maroon rockets, but just behind them there was a brand-new Webley & Scott flare pistol, still boxed, with three flares. It would do.

I went up to the highest point behind the trench, one of the machine-gun nests. Perhaps nine or ten minutes had passed since the German corporal died, no longer. The remaining German and British soldiers—I could no longer say 'my men'—stood almost motionless between the trenches, lit by guttering fires. All faced south. The wind was shifting, and I could hardly hear the sound they made.

Lieder von Ocker.

Chansons d'Ocre.

The Ochre Song.

I stared one last time at Fomalhaut, and my shell-shocked brain provided two sights at once—a pale star low on the horizon, so far away as to be beyond comprehension, and at the same time, a monstrously huge, seething globe hung in blackness. A thing of fire, of pulsing, ochre fire, and of utter malignancy.

For once the shakes had left me completely. I held up the flare gun, and fired. The flare itself blossomed high above me, a bright, clean white light. I reloaded, and fired the rest of the cartridges. Each flare drove out the thought of Fomalhaut and its song.

I ran, careless of any enemy fire, across the open terrain towards free Flanders, to where, somewhere, there would be Battalion and a thousand questions. None of which I would be able to answer.

As I ran, the heavens opened with man-made fire, a

barrage of artillery fire that fell directly upon our old position. The ground shook, and as I paused to get my footing, I noticed the strangest thing. The artillery barrage was coming not only from behind our own lines, but from the German side as well, tearing open, obliterating the place where empty men had whistled and stared south.

I had no doubt that some artillery spotter, or Captain Blake himself, had been waiting in the darkness. Waiting for a signal, a judgement on the 'Loop.' And some Hans or Fritz had also been waiting.

And I thought that I knew then what Blake had not told me. In this place, a year before, a French officer had heard a discordant tune too many times, seen his soldiers look to one particular star too often on cold October nights. Perhaps that had been his phonograph, even his record. And in madness or in desperation, he had opened the taps of the gas cylinders, intent that a cloud of grey-green death should take his men before an ochre fire consumed them all…

CURSE OF THE WHITE INFERNO

Glynn Owen Barrass

Music filled the wall-speakers, a dramatic orchestral piece that Howard knew from the script was called *Omphale's Spinning Wheel*. As the violins reached a crescendo, the announcer, Sidney Fry, leant towards his microphone and began:

"Your local Black Diamond Coal dealer presents *The Red Hook Mystery Hour*, starring that menace of all crime and evil-doers and the scourge of the Underworld! This mysterious scarlet-clad figure of the night devotes his life to destroying evil, righting wrongs, and bringing justice to the unjust. Tonight's installment sees him in his continuing adventure across the wilds of Alaska, as he resumes his quest to save plucky reporter Helen Asher in...*The Curse of the White Inferno!*"

The music returned. The actress playing Asher, a beautiful young blonde named Joan Banks, smirked.

Howard tried catching her eye but failed.

Some sudden movements turned his attention to the sound booth to his left. The FX Man, Fred Williams, was darting frantically beyond the glass screen. He stopped, and the chaotic noise of a snowstorm replaced the music.

"Night, dark and windswept. When last we saw him, The Red Hook and his Mestizo-Indian tracker, Castro, encountered a terrible snowstorm while on the trail of Asher and her kidnapper, the escaped criminal Adolph Venke. We return now to our hero's plight as he battles the elements, in his mission to catch Venke and rescue his helpless victim."

Fry smirked, his pencil-thin moustache twisting with his lips. He bowed a head of slicked black hair, winked in Banks's direction, and pointed to Howard.

Fred Williams added crunching footsteps to the snowstorm.

Howard swallowed and got into character. "Castro," he said in a deep, resonating, tone, "I can't see anything in this blasted storm. Should we seek shelter?"

Redheaded Red Furlong, who had a number of roles on the show, replied in a deep but stilted voice: "No, Master, we must move on. This be heap big trouble, and dark forces wait ahead. We must push through."

Howard cringed at the dialogue as Red/Castro continued. "Look, Master, a shape in the snow."

He remained silent for a few moments, allowed the faux footfalls to fill the void, and said, "No! It could be Helen Asher!"

Faster footfalls followed, and Howard cried, "Helen, no!" Sounds of snow being uncovered filled the speakers, but to Howard, they more resembled scraping sandpaper. "Why, this is—"

"*Ro-owowll-owllllll.*"

Howard was quite impressed by the eeriness of Red's howl.

"Come back, Master, it is a thing of evil, a Snow Thing!" Red said, slipping from monster to Indian speech flawlessly.

"Why, what foul abomination is this?" Howard said. "The thing has drooping gray skin, hooves for feet!"

Red growled and hissed.

Howard saw Banks giggling in the corner of his eye.

"No matter," Howard said, and glancing at the Sound Booth, saw Fred lighting a blowtorch. The roaring flame joined the snowstorm, and Howard continued in a bold, commanding voice, "Foul beast! Face the justice of the Red Hook!"

The metallic din of slashing blades followed, and Red released a painful-sounding roar.

"Oh no, Master," he continued, shifting again from monster to man, "More Snow Things!" He roared again, and according to the script, it was the announcer's turn to speak. Silence followed, however, and Howard looked from his script to find Fry whispering to Banks.

The man looked up and quickly got into character.

"As the Red Hook and Castro are attacked, some distance away, in the dark woods, the evil Venke observes them. He is accompanied by his Medicine Man guide, and their unwilling prisoner, Helen Asher!"

"Why, you fiends!" Banks said, with a voice just as lovely as the woman herself.

"Ha ha ha ha ha ha! Foolish girl, did you really believe that red-clad buffoon would save you?" said Harold Trent in his trademark villainous tone. Blond-haired with a round, ruddy face, he looked far from villainous in reality. "Their plight is nothing compared to the coming wrath, the wrath of The Wind-Walker! Ha ha ha ha ha ha ha!"

Banks filled the studio with a high-pitched, ear-jarring scream, and the orchestral music reappeared.

It was time for an intermission, one that Howard sorely needed.

Two hours later, Howard was driving home through the soaked streets of Lower East Side under a continuous rainfall. The weather was growing torrential, and beat a merciless tune on his car roof and windows. He went to turn the radio on, and a hiss of static filled the car. Trying different stations didn't solve the problem, but added drifting, ghostly voices to the static. With an angry twist of the knob, he switched it off. The going was slow then, with jams to contend with as other drivers took their sweet time negotiating the lakes formed by blocked drains. The station's resident weatherman, Ted Cruise, had warned of snow before they had started the second act of *The Red Hook Mystery Theatre*.

The idea of worse weather made Howard wish he were home already, holding a warming alcoholic drink in his hand. But the journey was slow, leaving him trapped with his thoughts and the view from the car windows. The former just depressed him, and the latter? People, many soaking wet and without umbrellas, shuffled along the rain-drenched streets around him. Their faces appeared pale, slack and sickly-looking in the streetlamps bright glow. "Foul abominations," he whispered under his breath and, finding the street ahead clear, continued towards his apartment building.

After a further ten minutes of driving, he parked up outside his home of three years: the Fillmore Hotel. The doorman, Jake, rushed to his car with an open umbrella in hand and a smile on his brown face. This saved Howard from a soaking as he stepped across the sidewalk towards the building, and he handed the Negro a dime for his trouble. He headed through the packed foyer, taking the stairs to the second floor. Soon after, he was in his apartment, pouring a well-earned Highball, light on the soda.

The time, according to the wall clock in his lounge, was just after nine-thirty. With little to see but the neon lights filtering in through the rain-harried windows, Howard slouched in his well-stuffed easy chair and stretched his legs. He kicked off his shoes and wriggled his stockinged toes on the carpet. It was a pleasure to finally be off his feet for the night.

Howard sighed and took a large swig from his Highball. The room around him was a cave of memories, but also failures. Framed posters of his finest roles lined the walls, images of a younger him posing dynamically for such blockbusters as *The Black Pirate*, *Don Q Son of Zorro* and *The Blind Goddess*.

Hollywood could be a fickle beast—he knew this all too well. When Howard lost the lead in *Captain Blood* to that young upstart and rumored deviant, Errol Flynn, he had known his career was on the wane.

The only work he could secure now were roles in radio plays, a medium he could barely tolerate. The subject matter of *The Red Hook* especially was born from lurid dime novels: funny books aiming for higher than their dubious station.

Amongst the bottles lining the drinks cabinet facing Howard stood a promotional photograph of him wearing The Red Hook's costume. He couldn't see more than a shadowy silhouette of himself, spotted with the reflected lights from outside, but he could picture it in his mind's eye anyway: a foolish grin, a scarlet cowl, a mouth and jaw once rugged and square but now soft and sagging.

"Damn it to hell," he said, and resisted the urge to fling his drink at the photograph. His glass was still half-full anyway, and the alcohol was starting to warm him and lighten his mood, a little. Howard took a long gulp, stretched, and placed the glass on the table to his left. While his hand was there, he found and flicked on the lamp, the sudden yellow glow dispersing many of the room's shadows. The table held a dog-eared copy of the week's script, tucked between the lamp and the telephone. He retrieved the script, licked his finger, and lounged back in his chair.

He thought it would be good to catch up on tomorrow's script before bed, the grand finale of *The Curse of the White Inferno*. A few flips of paper taking him to the right section, Howard scanned the page, barely paying attention to the others' lines but memorizing his own.

"Tripe, utter—" A section of the script, not his part but one of Red Furlong's characters, made him pause and sit up.

What is this gibberish, some kind of typo?

The offending section was for the Ahltuno character—the villain's Medicine Man guide.

The words consisted of long rows of vowels, mixed in with random consonants. The letters were in such confusion that Howard attempted reading a word and failed. He considered the page for a moment, placed the script on his lap, and retrieved the telephone receiver from its cradle.

"Hello, Fillmore Hotel, Angie speaking. How may I direct your call?"

"Ahem, put me through to Orchard—3343," Howard said.

"Thank you, sir, putting you through."

"Thanks…" he said, but she had already connected him, the ringing signal filling his ear as he waited for the scriptwriter, Ralph Richards, to answer.

He counted the rings, reached twenty, and thought, *he must be out*. The connection then clicked, and a voice boomed, "Hellooo!"

"Hey, Ralphie, it's me."

Loud voices and jazz music filled the earpiece.

"Oh, Howard! Gimme a minute," the man sounded inebriated. A clatter followed, then it appeared the phone had been moved to a quieter area.

"Heh, just having a little shindig here," Richards said, the background noise having diminished considerably. "Got Fry and Banks here, plus a couple of the others. Hey, you'll have to come over one night…"

Howard's bland expression twisted into a scowl. *But you never invite me, do you, you little shit?*

"Ahum," he said, composed himself, and putting his rejected feelings aside, got to the matter at hand. "Ralphie, I've been going through this *White Inferno* thing, and I'm having trouble on page…" he looked down, squinting, the page number a little small without his reading glasses, "Page twenty-three," he continued, "All this mumbo jumbo stuff Furlong is supposed to spout."

"Oh, ha ha, the ritual, right. Hold on, I know it off by heart." A pause followed, then a rustle of paper.

Off by heart for sure, you phony. His sneer eased into a smirk.

"Ta-booooaaa hi goagh," Richards said, the words sounding deep and intense across the line. Win-te-ko-wa. Nu-daaaaaaaaaaaaaaaaaaah! Wza-y'ei! Wza-y'ei! Y'kaa haa bho-ii Win-te-ko-wa."

A female voice giggled in the background. Joan Banks? Possibly.

"Shhhh," Richards hissed at his companion. "Quite a mouthful, isn't it?"

"Just a bit," Howard answered. "I thought you'd taken a fit while typing." His tone was harsh: he didn't like this mystery woman eavesdropping in the background.

"Ah, well, they're authentic incantations, you see," Richards continued, "dug them out of some crumbling old book on tribal rituals. Those savages used to fill the sky with their chants, trying to summon up their gods. Ha ha. The monster at the end of the script, that's real legendry there. The Wendigo, the Windwalker."

A door opened in the background, briefly releasing loud party noises before it closed again.

"I guess we're the savages now, filling the airwaves with this tripe. Anyway, gotta scram, go wet my whistle."

Howard could hear Richards' hand, clenching and unclenching the receiver. He was obviously itching to follow whatever woman had exited the room.

"You take care, Ralphie," *Halfwit*. "Have a good one."

The connection severed, replaced by the dial tone's angry wasp buzz. Howard frowned at the receiver before placing it back into its cradle.

I guess I'm not the draw I used to be, he thought bitterly and finished off the Highball.

It was just a terrible place to be; the old man whose fame had dwindled, seated alone with his memories. This time, it took effort not to fling his glass at the picture. An unwanted vision appeared in his mind, that of Joan Banks, dancing and frolicking with all those young men. Three messy divorces had embittered him to 'romance,' but he still longed for the company of beautiful women.

Howard deposited his empty glass on the table and lifted the script from his lap. The first words to draw his eye were the Indian incantations.

"Ta-booooaaa hi goagh," he whispered, doing a passable facsimile of Ralphie's words.

We are the savages now, Howard thought, and wondered if those Indians would have had better luck broadcasting their chants through the radio.

A pattering sound turned his gaze to the window.

Snow. So Ted Cruise was right. Howard returned to the script and shivered, already feeling the cold in his aging joints.

The forecasted snow continued with abandon after those first few spatters, right through the night to blanket the city in white.

Howard had been pushing through it for some time now, huddled in a thick overcoat, still damp on the shoulders from his trek from the hotel to the car. To make matters worse, the heater was behaving erratically, switching from barely warm to non-existent. Clouds of breath plumed from his mouth as he breathed, his chilled hands white at the knuckles as he gripped the steering wheel. The UWNYC tower, an 86th Street building on the Upper West Side, was still some minutes away, at least at the rate he was driving. Night had fallen early and grayish black clouds covered the sky above. The snowfall had diminished some during his journey and the streets were thick with treacherous slush. Outside, through windows his wipers battled to keep clear, the dark shapes of other vehicles moved slowly around him.

"Might have been quicker if I'd walked," Howard said, but knew he was wrong. In good weather, the drive from his Third Avenue home would measure about fifteen minutes, three times that walking.

At the moment, he was making slow progress down the 85th Street Transverse, his car flanked on either side by Central Park. Trees and bushes leaned over the park's stone walls, their leaves thick with snow and frost.

The cars ahead slowed to a stop. Prepared for a wait, he glanced left, and something about the view stirred a memory. *No, a dream, that's it*, he confirmed, and puzzled over it as fragmented memories returned.

He recalled pine trees and frozen streams, snow crunching beneath his and Castro's heavy footfalls. No, not Castro, but Red Furlong, dressed in a brown leather powwow suit. The man sniffed the air like a dog as he guided them through eerily silent woods.

What brought the dream about? The combination of the script and the snow battering his bedroom windows, Howard supposed.

The loud *honk* of a car horn crushed his reverie. *Daydreaming, damn*. He put his foot on the gas and breached the gap between himself and the car ahead. Soon after, he left Central Park and headed down West 86th Street. The skyscrapers ahead were bright with lights, the sidewalks below filled with hurrying commuters hunched into their coats.

Damn the weather, and damn Ted Cruise. He was approaching the UWNYC building now, and with traffic moving faster, was soon pulling up before it. Some cast members used the lot behind the building, but not him: the street out front offered the quickest escape route from the studio. After parking up and killing the ignition, he left his car and entered what felt like a renewed snowstorm. The slush on the sidewalk was already gaining a fresh white glaze, the air thick with powdery flakes. He paused to examine the sky above the UWNYC: the building itself stood a grand twenty stories tall. Above it, the sky was dark purple, smeared with clouds the color of dirt-soaked cotton balls.

Howard shrugged and headed to the entrance, relieved to see the weather had deterred the odd autograph seeker that lurked out front on occasion. The building's doorman was well wrapped: his cap pulled down and his mouth swathed in a voluminous scarf. Howard gave the man a nod, entered, and blinked at the lights' intensity before stamping his feet on the already sodden mat. The foyer's bright red carpet was covered in footprints, many so damp he guessed some rude souls hadn't even wiped their feet.

"Hi, Mr. Hope!" the girl at the reception desk said and smiled at him prettily. He returned the smile and continued across the foyer towards the bank of six elevators flanking the back wall. As he approached, the second elevator from the right opened with a *ping*. Two men stepped out. Howard rushed past them before the operator had opportunity to close it.

"Good afternoon, sir," the elderly operator grinned with yellowed teeth, "Floor seventeen, yes?"

Howard nodded and turned to face the doors as they closed.

The operator didn't make small talk, *Thank God*, and the elevator ascended to the 17th floor without pause. This was good. Howard had just examined his wristwatch and found there were only ten minutes left till airtime.

The elevator stopped with a lurch and Howard received a second yellow smile before leaving to enter a lobby. He turned left here and stepped down a long corridor, pausing at a glass-panelled door a third of the way down. He took a deep breath and entered the studio reception.

Dolly, the receptionist, was sat behind a desk on the room's far side. She didn't look up; she pounded away on her typewriter. Large framed pictures lined the walls, *The Red Hook Mystery Hour* and other radio serials. To the right of the desk, next to the door to the Live Room, stood a mannequin wearing the Red Hook costume. Howard cringed at the sight of it before turning to add his hat and coat to the others on the wall-rack. As he passed the desk, Dolly sent him a reluctant smile he didn't bother returning.

The costume loomed in his vision as he approached the door: the gaudy red leather trenchcoat, the scarlet cowl, a ridiculous-looking iron hook hung from the left cuff. During a publicity event to promote the serial, another, younger man had donned the costume.

He gave the mannequin a glare. The mouth under its cowl smiled back with a permanent, frozen grin.

Once through the door, he headed down a short corridor towards the Live Room. As he approached it, voices issued from a doorway to his right, followed by two of his fellow actors.

"Hey, Howie," Red Furlong said as Harold Trent trailed behind him.

Silvery laughter issued through the doorway—Joan Banks, of course.

Howard glanced inside as he passed, saw her chatting away with Sidney Fry.

The sight invoked a sensation of envy. A following look at his wristwatch revealed they had just five minutes till airtime.

Howard scowled. *Banks and Fry had better get a move on.*

"Your local Black Diamond Coal dealer presents *The Red Hook Mystery Hour*, starring the menace of all crime and evil-doers and the scourge of the Underworld! This mysterious scarlet-clad figure of the night devotes his life to destroying evil, righting wrongs, and bringing justice to the unjust. In tonight's installment, he encounters the criminal Venke and his Medicine Man guide Ahltuno. Will he prevail and rescue Helen Asher from these vile villains? Find out tonight, in the concluding episode of...*The Curse of the White Inferno*!"

Sidney Fry bowed. The music followed, quickly replaced by a snowstorm.

"You fool," Trent/Venke began. "Traveling all this way just to perish in the icy wastes."

Howard waited a few seconds as Fred Williams cocked a pistol in the Sound Booth.

"You'll be the one to die, Venke, just as I dispatched your Snow Things. For Castro!" he cried.

The click of a trigger landing on an empty chamber followed.

Trent laughed like a madman, "Ha ha ha ha ha ha ha ha! Out of bullets and out of time, and Asher will watch you die."

Joan Banks whimpered into her microphone.

"Ahltuno," Trent continued, "show this hero just what your magic can do."

"Ta-booooaaa hi goagh," Red Furlong began, and continued the guttural words as crunching footfalls appeared and rose in volume.

"No. No…" Howard cried, "Castro!"

"Yes!" Trent goaded. "Your faithful companion is now one of my Snow Things."

Joan Banks screamed, and Red's chanting grew louder. Howard went to speak, and the studio lights flickered. *The storm, affecting the power, must be.* He looked around. The other players were all staring at Furlong. Cued for silence, Furling instead continued his incessant chat. Fry hissed, tried to grab the man's attention with a wave. Furlong's eyes appeared glazed. He wavered slightly where he stood.

Always the professional, Howard took the initiative, speaking boldly into the microphone.

"You think I need a mere gun to stop you, Venke? You forget that I am The Red—"

A fire door burst open, slamming loudly against the far wall. Everyone but Furlong jumped in surprise. A gust of snow entered the doorway, billowing into the Live Room.

"What the hell?" Harold Trent said, breaking character.

Howard stared dumbfounded as the snow continued to fill the room. Sidney Fry turned to the Sound Booth, signaling with a slicing gesture under his chin for Williams to cut to commercials.

"Well, this is unexpected." Trent looked around at his fellow players with a smirk. "Hey, Red—"

A shrieking maelstrom blasted through the doorway, the sudden snow-filled gust bowling everyone over but the still-chanting Red Furlong.

The unexpected loss of footing sent Howard to the floor face down. He saw a red carpet spotted with white, and then, darkness.

Shouts and a gunshot filled his ears as he came to, then the sounds of breaking glass and a woman's scream. An obscenely animal roar followed, something that belonged in a jungle, ancient and primal. The abrupt silence after was somehow worse.

Howard opened his eyes and climbed up unsteadily, gripping a carpet now thick with snow. His whole body shivered, plumes of moisture issued from his mouth as he breathed. Through blurred vision, he saw the snow below him turning pink as blood dripped from his nostrils. He wiped his nose against his sleeve and experienced a stab of pain for his trouble. Then, Howard looked around.

The studio was in shambles, bleached white with ice and snow. The microphones and stands were upturned, scripts were sodden and scattered. Harold Trent lay a few feet away, his limbs bent, his body a broken rag doll. His dead, rictus-faced expression looked awful, but worse was to come. Some feet beyond Harold, Fred Williams hung from his booth, impaled on the broken glass. His left hand held a revolver, dangling from fingers frozen in a grip of death. The blood, pooled on the floor beneath him, was a cherry red slush.

Of the others, of Banks, Furlong and Fry, Howard saw no sign.

"Damn, damn cold," he muttered, and painfully rose to his feet.

"Aiieeeeeeeeeeeeee!"

The sudden scream made him turn towards the stairwell. The scream was repeated, sounding more desperate this time. It was a voice he recognized, one he would know anywhere: Joan Banks, his leading lady.

Whatever lay beyond that doorway, whatever had taken her…Howard suffered a shiver far stronger than the cold.

I need to get away, call the fire service...just get the hell out.

Howard looked to the stairwell, then the exit. A wailing gust from the former snuffed out a third scream.

This decided him: Howard headed towards the exit.

Safe here, but not for long, he thought, walking unsteadily down the corridor. If he had any hopes of rescuing Banks, and the others, he at least needed something warm around him.

Howard pulled the reception's door open and expected to see Dolly, but no, she was missing. He was about to go retrieve his overcoat when a gaudy red costume caught his eye.

At least it's dry, he mused, and examined his own sodden suit.

A few seconds of reflection told him it was a ludicrous idea.

Howard reached for the mannequin with a smile on his bloodstained lips.

The costume felt tight around his midriff, the trenchcoat heavy, cumbersome. The cowl rested against his sore nose uncomfortably, but it was bearable. He raised his left hand, examining the hook in the light. "Huh," tiny holes spotted the curved steel, their purpose unknown to him. A handle, located within the trenchcoat's arm, required holding just to keep the hook stable. The handle felt like a gun grip: he could feel a trigger near his index finger.

Howard lowered the hook, took a deep breath, and headed back through the door. After entering the Live Room, he was halfway to the stairwell when a thought occurred to him. *I'm forgetting something...what? Oh yeah, the gun. Hah.*

He turned on his heels, avoiding Trent's corpse as he stepped towards the Sound Booth.

"I'm sorry, Fred," he said and knelt to retrieve the revolver. It was cold, ice cold, even through the costume's red leather glove. The dead hand released it with some resistance. A noise issued from the Sound Booth, a low, wavering static. *The studio's death throes*, he mused, *a final croak of mechanical life*. The gun felt unfamiliar in his hand, but wasn't as heavy as the ridiculous hook. Howard straightened himself up and asked, "What the hell am I doing?" The silent room held no answers, so he turned towards the fire exit.

"I'll do this." Howard spoke with a confidence he didn't quite feel. When he reached the open door, he paused, reluctant to go further. The wind had diminished but still echoed through the stairwell. He braced himself, and headed in.

The lights were dim, giving the snow-covered stairs a grayish hue. An unusual, acrid smell lurked in the stairwell, sweet and musky.

Howard steeled himself and ascended. His unfit legs were aching by the time he reached the first landing. Wheezing a little, he leant against the wall before looking to the next flight. The lights were out up there, nothing visible but the quietly moaning darkness.

Then, something drifted down with the wind, the sound of voices, twisted and echoing from the distance.

Is that a man's voice?

Howard recoiled as movements appeared on the staircase above. A strengthening of that curious, animal odor followed.

A man's silhouette stepped slowly down the stairs. Howard gritted his teeth and raised the revolver. The dark shape grew clearer to reveal a familiar yet distorted face.

"Howard, you look ridiculous," Sidney Fry rasped through blackened lips.

The gamy smell seemed to cling to him. Fry appeared hunched, crippled, his body coated in a layer of ice. His arms were frozen to his chest and, like his lips, his fingers were blackened with frostbite. His eyes, though…they glowed with feverish intensity.

207

"Not looking too good yourself, Sid," Howard reflected. He kept the gun trained on Fry, although in his condition, he surely couldn't be a threat. "Furlong and Banks, where are they?" he demanded.

Fry lurched painfully down a step, then halted. He smiled horribly and cleared his throat with a choking rasp.

"Can you hear the noise? The Windwalker always was more sound than flesh. Heh. He's been roaring through the static since the beginnings of time," Fry swallowed again and grimaced, his pained voice echoed through the stairwell. "Your local Black Diamond Coal dealer presents…The Red Hook, the menace of all crime and evil-doers, and, heh, the scourge of the Underworld!" Fry wavered, nearly toppled, then steadied himself. "Tonight's installment sees the has-been Howard Hope attempt to rescue Helen Asher from Ithaqua, The God of the White."

Fry giggled, the mocking noise following Howard as he rushed up the stairs.

As he approached the third landing, Fry screamed: "Win-te-ko-wa. He's coming!"

Another staircase put him a few steps away from the roof exit. The door stood open, beyond which hung a blizzard of snow-infused air. The ugly aroma seemed thicker outside.

Howard moved his leaden feet forward and headed into the maelstrom.

The moment he stepped outside, the wind pushed him backwards. In a panic, Howard pressed himself against an exterior wall. The wind subsided, the blizzard clearing to reveal a snow-smothered roof corner. Howard advanced cautiously. *They're not here, obviously.* The blizzard returned with a vengeance, tugging his clothes and sucking his breath away.

"Banks, where are you?" he yelled, and turned to face the structure behind him.

Up there, must be.

A smaller, three-story block squatted atop the UWNYC. An ascending iron stairway flanked its walls, leading to a secondary roof. The first stairway stood to the left.

Howard heard a drawn out moan, wavering in intensity as it drifted through the storm. *It must be them*, he realized, and made his trudging way towards the stairs. The steps felt treacherous beneath his feet, slick with snow and slippy. As such, he leant into the building, following the platform while avoiding thoughts of the terminal drop to his left. He passed the edge of the structure and began ascending a second stairway.

At the top, a strong gust nearly bowled him off the building. Howard hooked himself to a handrail for stability. *That was a close one*, he thought and laughed nervously. The wind subsided, so he pulled himself up as he clomped towards the next corner.

A guttural scream issued from above. *Furlong's voice*, he thought.

Howard paused at the corner, waiting out another gust before turning it. Ahead, through chaotic snow-filled air, stood the staircase to the roof. His whole body was numb now: he could hardly feel a thing. The gun seemed frozen to his hand.

"Nearly there," he whispered in an attempt to encourage himself forward. His lips, chapped and cracking, stung as he spoke.

"Ta-booooaaa hi goagh," boomed a voice from above. *Those words*, he thought, *the ones Ralphie put in the script, they're poison, we've filled the airwaves with poison!*

The building shuddered and the stairway followed suit. Instead of discouraging him, this spurred Howard to action. He used his final reserves to clamber the steps to the roof, and it took a lot out of him. His knees felt ready to buckle, forcing him to lean on a handrail for support.

The rooftop was draped in white. A small, one-story shed stood ahead and to his right—the generator room for the two radio masts. The masts themselves laid at the roof's far corners, their spindly metal points piecing the tumultuous cloud cover.

A human form stood between the two masts. A body lay slumped over its right shoulder, held there by a bent arm.

Banks! he realized with horror and moved cautiously forward.

Red Furlong, his free arm raised to the sky, continued his chant.

"Ta-booooaaa hi goagh, Win-te-ko-wa. Nu-daaaaaaaaaaaaaaaaaaaah! Wza-y'ei! Wza-y'ei! Y'kaa haa bho-ii Win-te-ko-wa."

The sky rumbled in response. The white-white clouds above Furlong were in a constant state of flux, teasing a nighted array of stars beyond.

Howard strode forward and paused beside the generator room.

"Put her down, Red," he said, raising his numb right arm.

The other man flinched in surprise. He released Banks and Howard gasped as she hit the roof.

"Red, you—"

Furlong twisted round, the sight of him snuffing Howard's words mid-sentence.

Red was no longer Red. His body appeared horribly emaciated; his suit clung to him with a coating of ice. Red's face was black, skull-like, his hair gone in large clumps. His eyes glowed like hot coals, the nose and lips beneath them shrivelled to nothing.

The flaming eyes met Howard's. Red's following, lipless smile was terrible to behold.

"Go, you fool," Red snarled. "Ithaqua is coming, coming for his bride."

A sickening stench accompanied the words, a tainted animal reek.

Howard felt his gorge rise. "Not tonight, Red," he replied, took aim, and pulled the trigger.

Five booming gunshots filled the air. Three found their mark, and three large holes blossomed upon Red's emaciated chest. Howard pulled the trigger on a half-dozen empty chambers before lowering the gun.

Red examined his wounds quizzically. No blood escaped them: they were black hollows, like the mouth now leering at Howard.

"Nu-daaaaaaaaaaaaaaaaaaah!" Red howled, "Win-te-ko-wa!" Then, he was gone, fallen into the snowy vortex.

Banks! Howard thought in panic. He discarded the gun and rushed towards the young woman.

"Joan! Joan, are you alright," he asked upon reaching her. He knelt and lifted her head, which lay dangerously close to the roof-edge.

The woman's face was deathly pale, her clothes crackling with ice as he moved her.

"Uh…what? Howie." Her eyes blinked and opened partially. They widened upon seeing his cowl and she smiled. "I think…I think I'm dreaming."

A piecing, inhuman shriek interrupted Howard's reply.

He looked up to see a man's body hovering in the sky, its arms and legs waving wildly.

The shrieks ended, followed by, "Oh! Oh! This fiery height! Oh, my feet of fire! My burning feet of fire…" The voice was Red Furlong's. As Howard watched, the man's floating form was crushed into a ball, as if squeezed by some mighty yet invisible force. It dropped from the sky and disappeared from view beyond the roof's edge.

Howard's horror didn't end here, but grew as he saw a cumulonimbus of distant clouds solidify to form a man-like shape. A malformed, bobbing head topped its massive white form. Two bright lights appeared on its featureless face, eyes that stared balefully towards him. Its shape wasn't completely solid, Howard realized, but wavered, fuzzy at the edges. It reminded him of radio static. Was this monstrosity radio waves made flesh?

Their gazes locked and Howard stood unsteadily.

"Howie, what's going on?" Banks's tone was confused, pitiful.

"This isn't finished," Howard replied. "Joan, you need to get away."

The cloud-thing was fast approaching, striding across the city with giant steps.

It's here for Banks. How can I possibly stop it? Howard considered in despair. *The Red Hook would*, he told himself,

211

and examined his left hand. A distant memory resurfaced: a bygone day of cameras and publicity. A young actor waved the hook to a small crowd's applause. Its curved shape glowed with flame and heat.

Howard found the trigger in the handgrip. A light touch induced a hissing sound. Pressing down harder, once, then twice, did nothing. "Ah, dammit!" He pushed down a third time and flames engulfed the hook. Howard grinned, feeling ridiculous.

The cloud-thing was almost atop them. The same reek that had dogged him since downstairs suffused the air mightily. The cloudy colossus appeared to kneel, lowering itself towards the roof.

Beneath him, Joan Banks had started crawling away.

A wide slit appeared on the cloud-thing's head. The opening puckered then expanded to become a crude, circular mouth.

You won't have her, he thought with determination, "You hear me? You won't have her!"

The head loomed forward, hungry, menacing.

Howard crouched in readiness. This was end of him, he knew that, but how long was it since he had really, truly, lived? He leapt forward and shouted, "Fear the justice of the Red Hook!"

Powerful winds seized him; the shrieking air tossed him towards the giant head.

Giddy with excitement, Howard swiped and slashed with the flaming weapon. The hook shredded into the cloudy face, the diaphanous matter coming apart with static, buzzing shrieks. He laughed as he attacked this goliath of a foe, and the heavens shook from its roars. Then, it inhaled, creating a powerful vacuum that threatened to suck him down into its dark, chasm-like maw.

A final, desperate attack burst the cloud-thing's face apart. The roar continued, too did Howard's laughter, now manic as the force of the explosion sent him tumbling through the sky. He twisted against the wind and gained a clear view of the UWNYC rooftop.

Human figures spotted it now, on their way to rescue Joan Banks.

I did it, she lives. Howard grinned widely, feeling little pain as the growing frostbite split his lips apart. *If this is death, let it be a good one*, he thought as he tumbled back towards the station roof. Howard closed his eyes, gritted his teeth in anticipation of the coming death. Suddenly, his fall ended, but not against a harsh, unforgiving surface. Instead he hung, swaying in the air.

He opened his eyes to find himself hanging a dozen feet above the roof. It appeared that a radio mast had snagged the Red Hook's trenchcoat, saving his life in the process.

"Ha, ha ha. I'm alive," he shouted to the people heading back inside the building. "ALIVE!"

THE BLUES OF THE ENDLESS SKY

Simon Bucher-Jones

"The introduction of novel fashions in music is a thing
to beware of as endangering the whole fabric of
society, whose most important conventions are
unsettled by any revolutions in that quarter."
Plato, *The Republic* (c.428 B.C. - c.347 B.C.)

Is music just an art or is it at the root of all arts? Music is after
all mathematics made audible, as much an expression of ratios
and proportions as anything in trigonometry.

It is, according to legend, Pythagoras to whom we owe the
insight that first devised the Octave scale on which all
Western music is based. In the seventeenth century, the
mathematician Liebnitz corresponded with the musician
Conrad Henfling about the application of Euclid's work in the
production of musical instruments and, in particular, in
respect of their tuning to specific pitches. And, for a time, the
classical world believed all was harmonious in nature above
the moon, and so outward through the singing of the eternal
spheres.

As early as Plato, writers were determined to limit and control music's supposed effects upon the human psyche. What is art, but the recording in another mode of stimuli intended to influence the human mind?

So I once naively thought, until I learned songs humans never sang.

My field of study was, and is, musical history, in particular that aspect called comparative musicology—the study of the different types of tonalities and their historical variations. I was, and had been from my youth, obsessed with the idea that the very earliest music might be recreated, by analogy with, and by observation of, the varied musical traditions of the current world. For, it seemed to me, not every cultures' music would have changed at the same rate, and here and there, a careful and sensitive ear might still detect the songs the sirens sang, or the drum-beats played by the earliest hunters to stir their blood to bring down the Mammoth or to drive the Smilodon from their caves.

In order to seek musical experiences from far and near, I pestered my fellow students throughout my time at university, and as we went our own ways in the wider world beyond its gates—I enjoined them to stay in touch with me and to advise me of any unusual or esoteric musical forms, whether old or new, which they might stumble across. As, I was relatively wealthy, at least at first—for the present stock market crash was then five years in the future—I was easily able to defray my friends' expenses in writing to me, and to arrange for the wax cylinder recording of any novel works of musical art. For a time, I amassed a great library of music and a grand collection of recordings.

Thus it was that, until 1929, I felt as secure as a musical spider, whose web reached out into the world and vibrated with sounds as diverse as the valve-less trumpets of Denmark—recorded for me in a tiny village by no less a person than an assistant to the US Ambassador to Copenhagen—and the drums and percussive music of the American Indians.

Alas, in that year, my great work of musical rediscovery still only half written, I found myself required by the necessities of sudden poverty to seek work. Instead of being the patron who purchased obscure recordings from my many acquaintances, I was reduced to the penning of begging letters, asking whether or not I might add my scholastic abilities to one of their endeavours. I believed at first I would be a benefit, as I was an avid note taker, an enquiring mind, and a reasonable mathematical logician. I was, in those days, possessed of the quality termed 'perfect pitch,' and although I had lived a quiet scholastic life, I was not unfit physically. Despite these qualities, however, I soon discovered that poor young men were not, in 1929, a rising commodity, and I began to contemplate eventual starvation, as my remaining funds would gradually be spent no matter what economies I might make.

It was in this condition that I was glad to receive a letter from a particular favorite of mine among my correspondents. Paul Mennens had been in the anthropology department of the University where we had both studied, and we had often argued late into the night as to whether or not Neanderthal men had a voice (the evidence of both Francis Turville-Petre's dig in Galille and Dorothy Garrod's discoveries on Gibraltor being maddeningly incomplete in respect of the hyoid bone in the larynx)—I said yes, Paul said nay—or exactly what it was about the Mixolydian Mode that Plato feared would effeminise the men of Greece. Paul had told me some shocking secrets of Greek history, which suggested that Plato was wrong to fear the arising of what already seemed so common a practise. It was he who had told me the whispered legend of the Chromatic Court, the δικαστήριο των χρωμάτων said to predate the Grecian Muses from whom all the arts including music had filtered down into the primal psyche of mankind.

Unlike many of my letter-friends, Paul had not dropped me when my fortunes ebbed, and he was quick to suggest I might visit him—and that he would be able to provide me with work upon his present project. He was engaged in research into the prehistoric cultures which preceded the incursion of European Man into the Americas, and he was carrying out an investigation based in the State of Texas.

He had enclosed with his letter a native musical instrument, which he asked me to examine and either return it by post at his expense with my advice, for which he would pay a fee, or return with it in person. He made it quite clear he would prefer the latter, and I own I was touched by his solicitude particularly when so many other of my friends had proved to be of the kind who desert a person in need, and are thus not friends in deed, only words.

The musical instrument was a form of rattle, or sistrum, apparently made to emulate the natural rattle of a snake, although it was very much larger than that of any snake with which I was familiar. Wrapped in blue and iridescent snakeskin, which had been affixed to the rattle itself by some kind of glue or lacquer, it ended in a carved bone handle. A label which Paul had attached read: Comanche work pre 1570? Skin perhaps akin to *Drymarchon melanurus erebennus*.

Most of my books had gone to the booksellers by this time, but as a gentleman I still retained my family bible and my Webster's American Dictionary in the 1841 edition; and as a Scholar, my copies of the Franklin Henry Hooper American 1910 edition of the Brittanica. I looked through the latter but could find no mention of the named creature. I attempted to find, from the article on snakes, which might have blue scales, but aside from the belly scales of the garter snake (too small and fine) and the Black Snake—colloquially but erroneously termed the 'blue racer' in some states, for reasons the article did not explain—(large enough, but neither blue nor iridescent), I could not confirm his reference.

I could however apply my musical expertise. The rattle was pleasantly balanced to the hand, and the grip of the carved bone felt moulded around my knuckles. It was not a true rattle by the sound, but must have functioned in the manner of a rainstick. That is, whereas, a rattle permits the beads or stones within free movement inside a cavity, a rainstick channels them in helical tubes within the stick, lined with thorns or pins pressed in from outside, so that their falling produces a sound like the hiss of rain. The mode of play was simple; the rattle was thrust upwards, impelling the stones or beans to rise. The sound would then built and reverberate as they fell back, spiralling around the helix.

The theory was the best I could devise, but the sound persisted beyond any possible elongation of tubes within the rattle's length. Consequently, I could not imagine how the sound was produced. The fundamental requirement for a rainstick is that it needs to be long enough to permit the sound to build up. The sticks can be four or five feet long. They are made in the Americas from dried cactus wood, and in Asia and Africa from bamboo. The rattle, though large, was no staff, and even the rainsticks I had examined did not produce so extended a sound. Was it possible that there were channels within the rattle wound around as the lengths of intestine are packed within an animal? Then gravity would not accelerate the grains within. It was a conundrum. I was strongly tempted to cut the rattle open to determine its construction, but of course I did not do so. Firstly, it was not mine to investigate through violence, and secondly, Paul's letter did not advise me how rare it might have been. I certainly could not risk anything unique.

Thirdly, I realised I had no need to. One of my other remaining friends from my university days, Tom Henty, was presently a post-graduate medical student with access to an X-ray machine. He was one of the first to follow up the work of Doctor Egaz Moniz in angiography—the new science by which the structure of the brain itself could be shown by X-rays. Surely a man who could discover the living fabric of the brain could find a way to illuminate the structure of this unusual musical instrument?

I decided I would take the rattle to my friend Doctor Henty, tomorrow as it was far too late now to find him at the university, so I made these notes and placed the rattle carefully between the pile of books and clothes that constituted my remaining possessions and the Euklisia Rugs ('sleeping bags' of the old Pryce-Jones' kind) that served me for a bed (the furniture, including my old four poster, having been sold) and fell into the uneasy sleep of the ill-fed poor.

That night, I dreamed of a desert under a boundless blue sky. A sky whose colour ranged from a pale robin's egg blue at the far horizon, to a deepening band of azure and darkening cobalt overhead. Above me was a band of darkened sky, not black but midnight blue. A blue more deep than black night, which can look flat and empty: a blue lit by cerulean shooting stars, and the rolling of electric blue aureoles around the shaded Egyptian blue heads of vast shadowed statues.

And the river of the sky was the body of a Maya blue serpent: and the sound of its hiss was the rain that never fell upon the desert's powderblue sands, and the beat of the hiss was the duke blue, steel blue, of tympani and cymbals.

In my dream, I fell forward on the blue-heat of the stone shattered sands and the blue prickling of St. Elmo's fire burned my hands. And I saw from my prone and supplicating position a figure walking towards me through the blue-grey haze.

It was a man—I thought—a tall man, with a hunched set to his shoulders and a cowled cloak around his face. His boots were indigo snakeskin, his trousers a faded workmanlike denim.

The snakeskin man reached down for me, and I saw that he did not wear a cloak, and he did not have a cowl about his face. He was cowled like a cobra, and his eyes were snakes' eyes and a snakes' tongue played around the ultramarine of his lips.

"You played the music of the snake, man. You have heard the song of Yig.

"It is an age since the people of Yig came forth out of the blue of the pacific, where the dragons twined under the ancient lands of Mu.

"It is twice an age since Yig dwelt in the land called K'nyan, which is also Cyan in the language of the Chromatic Court, the hidden abode of the muses.

220

"It is three time three the ages of mankind since Yig fell from the Blue Star: Zandanua, which mankind calls Archernar.

"In all that time, only a handful of men of the right coloured soul, and only a handful of woman with the spirit of the shade that pleases, have taken up the sacred sistrum—of which those of the Egyptians were the merest copies. Yig is strong to strike those who harm his children: but to those who exalt them, he is a God of gifts. What would you have, oh man, who dreams of the music of Yig?"

And I heard a music I had never heard, of all the musics I had collected and gathered, and I admitted to myself what I had never admitted when I was awake—that I had collected, classified, and sought out the primitive not with the cold dispassion I pretended, but in the desperate hope of finding, in the roots of all music, a form simple enough that my clumsy hands could make it, a song so fundamental that my tongue could not mangle: for I, the scholar and the aesthete, the man who could hear perfection in the pitch of the work of others, could never reproduce it myself. I had a corncrake's voice and hands like hams. I was as unmusical as a stone. A eunuch dreaming of erotic arts was as foolish as I had been, and it took this strange dream of the blues to teach me my folly.

The song I heard was the melancholy of the serpent in the blue-grass: the long low indigo mood of the burning midnight sky. The eyeless blue that goes on forever and has only the secret words of the heart engraved upon it.

Even in a dream, I knew then there was only one thing I wanted.

When Paul Mennen didn't hear from his friend, when the long blue days of summer ended, he came back to find out what had happened to him. His house was boarded up and for sale—his few books and goods seized by his creditors. Paul found his Comanche rattle, undamaged, with a 'what-the-heck-is-this?' price on it—a pittance for what it was archeologically. He paid it; it was far easier than trying to argue his priority. Sometime later, he would have the same idea his friend Michael had—and had the rattle X-rayed. He would find a strange whorl of passages within it, twining and joining like snakes—like a single snake with its tail in its mouth: an ouruboros. How it made the sound that seemed to want to go on forever no-one, musician nor X-ray technician, could say. Nor did Paul ever see his friend again.

If Paul had been a different man, following a different music than that of classical Greece, and a different road to that of anthropology, he might have one day (the world is only so large) stumbled upon a man, no longer easily recognisable as Michael Cranbourne. A man squatting at the roadside, with his cap laid down for coins—coins that always came. A man with eyes blinded by the blue of strange skies, but with a voice that spoke to the soul and made music not heard for thrice three ages. A man who sang the blues.

Tatterdemalion in Grey

Micah S. Harris

1.

I performed my marionettes beneath the ribbons and wreaths of smoke that had been my fellow Jews. The children on the grass before me did not understand that the ashes brushing their faces were kindly Mrs. Schwartz or perhaps gentle Malachi, the middle-aged half-wit. The children had given him the only friends he had ever known in the shadow of the Lethal Chamber which, in time, had come to embrace him as well.

Transformed into the ash that touched their cheeks, the atoms of their elders caressed the children in their passing. I hoped it gave the dear departed comfort, for the young ones had, thankfully, no comprehension of what was happening. They were concentrating on my marionettes who moved to the musical accompaniment of my friend Eli on guitar.

Perhaps you think me worse than a dybbuk to carry out such play in this grimmest of situations. But it was Purim, and all special merriment had gone out of the children's lives forever. Though, among those on the grass that day, only Eli and I knew that.

Then *they* came. I could see them at a distance, pausing, curious, pointing this way. A sheen of perspiration was now upon me and the breeze touching it made me shiver as I watched them coming closer.

But what was this?

The two Nazi soldiers appeared as mesmerized as the children by my puppet show.

They came silently until they stood within only a couple meters behind the children, who, so enrapt with the hanging of Haman the Agagite on his own gallows, had not noticed their approach. The men watched, exhibiting no desire to stop the show. But their presence alone did so anyway. I was perspiring now (Haman the Agagite had tripped on his way to the gallows accompanied by the off-noting of nervous Eli) and brought things to a hasty close.

Only then did the children notice the soldiers. They blanched and drew away like puppies threatened with a stick. They trembled on the grass, afraid to move, afraid to stay, until one of the Nazis barked "Go," and the children fled.

I was quickly packing up my marionettes when they came to stand over me, their shadows blocking the sun. I felt the chill from the dew on the grass. The soldier who had shouted at the children said, "Not you two. Puppeteer, you look familiar…Yes, I have seen you cleaning up in the latrine," he pointed at me. "You are *Herr Scheiss Meister.*"

"I am *Herr Scheiss Meister*, yes. You have spoken correctly, sir."

"How is it that you have been allowed to have your toys, Jews?" he asked, looking from me to Eli, who kept shifting his weight from one foot to another.

"I have a dispensation from *Kommandant* Heinz. He remembered me from bringing his children to the *Kinderhaus* in Frankfurt. I entertain them privately now on occasion at his estate. They like me…the children."

The truth was Heinz only had one child, one far more witless than poor Malachi had been. One that he kept secret from the rest of the master race. But, as hard as it is for me to say, that damned Nazi loved his boy, who had so little to

224

enjoy in this life. And my puppets made him laugh. And I was in no position to reveal the family secret.

"You have papers to support your story?"

"Yes," I said, fumbling them out and handing them to him. "And they include Eli. He makes the music for the puppets. For the children."

He looked them over, lingering, I think, just to unnerve us. There was no denying Heinz's signature and official seal.

He handed my papers back to me.

"Pray they don't grow up fast," he said.

Then their stern faces melted away.

"How do you do that? Make them walk like real people?"

"I, uhm, observe." I tapped my sweat beaded forehead. "I remember, and when I am creating a characterization, then I figure out how to convey it down the strings and into their limbs."

"That girl, she was like a real little nixie! Make her prance on the grass!"

"Very well," I looked at the trembling Eli. "'Sugar Plumb Fairy Waltz.'"

He played, managing to hold the tune together, as I timed, paced, and choreographed the Esther puppet's steps to it. Despite my nerves, I was able to make it through.

The Nazis brayed in laughter, shoving each other.

"Dat's good, eh, Hans?"

"Yah, yah!"

"My father," the one who was not Hans said, "is a clock maker. He made automatons for us kids. One Christmas, he made for me the robot from *The Sandman*."

Wasn't that robot a girl, I thought. *So, your father gave you a girl doll when you were a little boy? That would explain much, including your trousers, Herr Kommandant: do they make them for men, too?*

"I have an idea. You, *Herr Scheiss Meister*," he said, "will create a puppet play especially for me and my men."

"Sir, you are asking a lot of my talents…"

Their countenances fell and they frowned down in unison upon me.

225

"Do you feel you are being used too harshly, Jew?" the one who wasn't Hans asked.

A cloud's fleeting shadow passed over us, and I felt the presence of the smoke hanging in the air again. "No. No, *Kommandant*. Give me a month. And you will be much entertained."

"And you make it real, just like you did here. None of that..." he looked at his partner, "...Hans, whadaya call that decadent film we saw at the cinema, the one I couldn't sit through, but you did?"

"*The Cabinet of Dr. Caligari.*"

"Yah. Whadaya call that style?"

"Expressionism."

"Wawaz dat?"

"Expressionism."

He looked back at me. "No expressionism. You make it as natural with your puppets as *der Fuhrer* paints. And—you know the dance the Maria robot did in *Metropolis*! You know that sexy dance? Yes? You do something like that with this girl puppet here."

"Yes, *Kommandant*."

"Good," the one who wasn't Hans said. "We will be spreading the word. The men will be looking forward to Maria."

The two of them walked off cackling like school boys. I suppose in anticipation of salacious puppetry.

"It seems I have become Shahrazad," I said to myself.

"Brutes, are they not?"

My first thought was this questioner who had come from nowhere was another Jew observing Purim, for masquerade also was part of our ceremonies. But this was none of the historic personages involved in the story of Esther. This was no Mordecai, no Xerxes, not even a Haman. I had never seen any guise such as this.

The mask he wore was made of dented pewter and covered the entire head. Over this was a grey hood. The mask's expressionless features were Byzantine, offering only a suggestion of eyes and a mouth, conveying a sense of a lack of humanity in whoever wore it.

Around his tall, straight frame was a ratty robe the color of slate. His hands were wrapped in bindings the hue of ash. There was a scent about him, too, that I found disconcertingly unpleasant. That he would stand out to an olfactory sense dulled by my living among a people forced to dwell in filth stunned me as much as anything about him.

"Who are you supposed to be, friend?" I said rising, fearing that I was in the presence of a leper. Eli, too, was regarding the stranger with obvious discomfort.

"I am Abhoth, the Grey Eminence."

And I shuddered at that title. Yet he did not bear the Cendrée Sign, the tinctured constellation of the noose of the Hyaenas. Perhaps…

"That…is not a character from the scroll of *Esther*," I said with a small laugh.

"No. I am pestilence from the second scroll of Moses."

"That puts you out of place at Purim, but it explains much about your appearance. Who are you? I mean, behind the mask."

"I am as you: a marionettist."

"Are you one of the subversives who used marionette theater to spread propaganda against the Nazis?"

"I am one apt at subversive puppetry."

"I understand why you are here, then."

I was loath to have his perhaps unclean fingers take hold of my marionettes, but I felt obliged to offer a doll to him to demonstrate his art. He made no move to take it.

"I use no strings."

"You *don't* use strings?"

He turned his mask toward Eli, who took a step back as the man in grey walked toward him. Eli held his guitar like a shield. The stranger's wrapped forefinger reached out and plucked the top bass string. Suddenly, the E-note buzzed in the air.

"None with which you are familiar."

He pressed the top string against the third fret, plucked it with his other forefinger, and the same vibrating string became the G-note.

"Nor the way you use them."

He slid his finger down one fret. Plucked the same string again...

And the string became a grass snake stretched along the guitar neck.

Eli screamed and thrust his instrument away. It struck the ground with a discordant cacophony from all jarred six strings, the top one once again itself.

"Staff of Moses!" Eli shouted and fled.

I stared at the guitar. What Eli said made it clear that we had seen the same impossible thing. But where pious Eli had seen a miracle, my jaded eyes had seen but an illusion.

"You are a magician as well, I see."

"No. Merely a marionettist. Strings permeate everything. And often they are not necessary at all for my craft. Now, these Nazis want you to give them a puppet show," he said. "They think they pull *your* strings. But let us school them on the loss of category between puppet and puppeteer."

"Even given that such an effort as you propose sounds especially suicidal, how exactly would you go about doing that?"

"With a scenario which will cause their Prussian minds to collapse."

"You are talking of a play...that can drive people insane?" I looked at him in his costume and shuddered, for now there could be no doubt.

"They are already insane. The play will do for them what is far worse. It will grant them perfect lucidity."

"And...the title of this play?"

"It is called *Tatterdemalion in Grey*."

I felt myself pale.

"You...you wish for me to perform *that*? With *puppets*?"

"You are familiar with it then."

"You are supposed to be *that* Grey Eminence?"

"I *am* that Grey Eminence."

228

"I see," *I see how you lost your mind*, I thought, *if you were in a production of that play*. "Tell me: was…was it in Berlin? In the Weimar days?"

"I remember Berlin. Pestilence of the flesh; pestilence of the soul. Berlin's opulence was a diamond-studded bandage on a canker sore."

"But were you to be part of the Berlin cast of *Tatterdemalion in Grey*? Were you *there*?"

"I was."

"Then you understand why I will not be involved with that abomination."

"Why do you resist? You bear these Nazis no love—to say the least."

The way he had said that last. What all *did* he know about Berlin?

I looked at him. "It is not for them that I won't do it," I said and felt my lower eyelids begin to brim.

"Perhaps you fear what it will do to you. But is it worse than what they have *already* done?"

I looked at him.

And remembered Berlin.

"You are judged already."

I trembled at that blank, pitiless face.

"So," I said after a long pause, "why not have revenge while I still can?"

"If you will."

I will *have revenge on them,* I thought, *and if I discover exactly what you did that night, perhaps I will have revenge on* you *as well.*

2.

One afternoon in the days before the black Swastika first unfurled over Berlin's streets, I had awakened at Pris' side from a dream that the long dead Huguenots, who had fled to this city for religious sanctuary centuries earlier, rose up from its dust. They stood as silent wraiths on the streets of that decadent city, pointing at the girls in their bobbed helmet hair and leg baring skirts, carnally demonstrative with their young men in public. And on the silently moving lips of the revenants, I read their words: "It is a fearful thing to fall into the hands of the living God."

Pris stirred, turned her slim, pale body beneath the sheets, looked at me and smiled.

"Nightmare again, darling?"

"Yes."

"Your worrying about the child follows you into your sleep."

"Our sweet baby," I said, placing my hand against her bare abdomen.

She laughed and removed my hand. "You are so maudlin, Benjamin."

I ran my other hand over her forehead, pushing the bangs of her bobbed blond hair back. "You are too thin, Pris. You look malnourished."

She laughed again. "You have never complained about my figure before—just the opposite—and now you want me fat?"

"I want you healthy," I said, cupping her chin. "You and our child. Should you not be showing more by now?"

She kissed my palm, rolled over as she pulled away the sheet that covered us, and sat naked on the edge of the bed. She looked at me over her shoulder. "Not for a month yet."

"I do not want you to do this play."

She rose and gathered up the salmon-pink satin camisole that lay piled in a wicker chair by our bed. "Darling," she said, turning as she slipped it on, "I have told you this will be my last chance for a year or more. After the baby, I will be nursing, and then I will have to get my figure back. All that time lost. I don't want them to forget me. And there will be much publicity."

"Why? Why won't you tell me what it is about? Or even its title?"

"Oh—the title? *Tatterdemalion in Grey.*"

"And are you the titular tatterdemalion?"

"No," she said and there was that lilt of music in her voice which I loved so much as she went to make coffee. "I play a princess, I think, or some type of royalty. Her name is…Cassandra. I think."

"And what is the play about?"

"There is a masque that is part of it, I understand."

"You 'think?' You 'understand?' Have you even read it?"

"No."

"You haven't read it yet, but you are committed already?"

She turned and smiled at me. "I told you. It will mean instant notoriety."

"Why?"

"Well, this play has a reputation."

"*Why*?"

"It has been banned in England and France…and maybe the States?"

"I am liking this less and less, Pris."

"Darling, in Victorian England your little puppets would have been banned from performing Bible stories for children. *Bible* stories, Ben."

"We could be talking Grand Guignol here, for all you know, and that makes me worry about the stress on you and the baby. Can you not understand that?"

I was sitting now on the side of the bed in our small apartment. Having gotten the coffee going, she picked a cigarette from a serving dish. "You are overly protective," she said as she lit the cigarette.

"Must you smoke, Pris? Tobacco—"

"—took away your grandfather's lower jaw. You've only told me a hundred times before. How could just this once more hurt?"

"Once more and that leads to another and another…and it goes right into our baby!"

"As if I didn't know," she mumbled as she snuffed out the cigarette. "There. Are you happy now?"

"Pris, I don't wish to fight. But will you promise me you will back out after the read-through, if you see there is the slightest potential for danger?"

"Of course, my darling. Now let us have coffee...and then we shall screw. I *can* still do that, can't I?" She grinned. "Do I have your permission?"

I smiled and leaned back on the bed, naked as she. "My complete and unadulterated consent....well, my *adulterated* consent, I guess I should say."

"One good thing about pregnancy: it makes me want to screw."

It was sin, I knew, what we were doing. A violation of the seventh law of the second tablet.

Yet, for you, Pris, I have barred myself from the congregation of God. You knew my devoutness when we met, but your slender fingers immediately set to playing with my Hasidic curls. I was at university in Paris. And we found ourselves alone in my garret on that connecting lane between rue de Rennes and rue du Dragon.

"We are young," she was saying. "And we are in Berlin! The most wonderful place in the world to be young and an artist both! Stop your needless worrying, and let us enjoy our life together while it can still be good."

"But you *will* withdraw, after the read-through, if you see it will be too much for you?"

"Aarrgh," she exclaimed. "Impossible man! Haven't I told you so? Now, have your way with me."

I did. Knowing all the time that she was lying.

3.

Leaving Pris enjoying her second nap of the afternoon, I rode my bicycle to the *Cabaret Grabmal* to talk with Wilheim, the club's manager and the director of *Tatterdemalion in Grey*, as I had pried from Pris. I wanted to read this play myself.

I started to turn down an alley to take a shortcut and saw two men in Nazi uniforms, their grease-slicked hair hanging in their faces and their caps on the asphalt, kicking a young man who crouched in the fetal position with the remnants of pamphlets scattered about him. One had blown to the mouth of the alley, and I glimpsed the red fist and scythe on its cover. Last week, it was a Nazi I saw taking a beating from two Communists. I quickly turned my bike, pedaling hard down the long route.

As I crossed Alexanderplatz, I passed a Tram Station's billet board and glimpsed advertisements for *Café Dorian Grey* and its upcoming Wednesday night exhibition of dominatrixes with whips and asexual near-naked men in bondage being lashed by them for public delectation. There was also a bill featuring a hand colored image of what appeared to be, from the short skirt down, a woman's smooth sexy legs and kinky high heels and from the waistcoat up, a man with slick short hair, mustache, and monocle.

These were harbingers of the club and theater district that I now pedaled into, bringing my foot to the ground and the bicycle to a stop before *The Cabaret Grabmal*.

On the walls hung paintings in the cubist and Modernist styles. The art the Nazi party decried as decadent.

In the rear was the stage which as yet exhibited no set.

And on the stage was Wilheim von Zeffilin, a scoundrel, who, with nothing to back him up whatsoever, had for two years presented himself as the love child of Ferdinand Adolf Heinrich August Graf von Zeppelin and sued for his fair share of the family Zeppelin fortune. That Wilheim had migrated here is of no surprise. All things disreputable ended up in Berlin.

"Will!" I shouted.

"Ben! So good to see you, my friend." He leapt off the stage and strode over to me. "When will your Dorette the Doxy grace our stage again with her popular striptease?"

"I retired the act permanently when Dorette began to be propositioned as though I were not standing there, pulling the strings."

He laughed and led me to a painting I had not yet seen. "I believe I shall soon rival the collection of that lesbian in Paris. I have my own Picasso now," he said and nodded at a canvas: "*Woman in an Armchair*, 1913 version."

"She appears to have exploded," I said.

"More as though our vision has been opened to a fourth-dimensional perspective."

233

"I think I shall happily stick to three then, thanks."

"Oh, so you prefer the works of Adolph? Trees on the lawn, a barn in a field? A fundamentalist view of nature?"

"I am not here to discuss art; I want to know about this play of yours in which Pris is involved."

"Oh? And how much has Pris told you of our play?"

"Next to nothing. Will, I want to know the content before the mother of my child becomes involved. I know already that it is apparently outrageous enough that it has been banned internationally."

"Well, now, this is *not* that play. Not exactly."

"What do you mean?"

"The authorities are looking for a play entitled *The King in Yellow*. This *Tatterdemalion in Grey*, it is a pastiche. And no one is looking for it. Since the international lock down on *The King In Yellow*, its pastiche is the closest one can come to the forbidden experience of the original."

"But is it close enough that Pris will still be in danger by participating?"

Will momentarily clasped my shoulder. "Let us have a look, eh?"

"Have you read it yet?"

"Not through. This club demands my time employing management skills when I would rather be exercising artistic ones."

We went to his office behind the bar.

I noticed there was an unframed canvas, his latest acquisition I supposed, leaning against the wall, exhibiting its backside. He sat down behind his desk, pulled open a drawer, produced the book, and passed it across the desk to me.

I turned the slate-colored cover on which was embossed *Tatterdemalion in Grey*. On the title page was a stanza from a poem: "Oh Thou who burn'st in heart for those who burn / In Hell, whose fires thyself shall feed in turn; / How long be crying, — 'Mercy on them, God!' / Why, who art thou to teach and He to learn?"

Seeing my pause at this page, Will nodded toward me. "That is a tetrastich from *The Rubaiyat of Omar Khayyam*: a prefatory expostulating warning to those about to read the play."

"A warning? How many plays begin with a warning?"

Will grinned. "Good showmanship, isn't it? I think I shall take a few whores off the street the night of the performance, pay them more than they could make in a night, and have them in nurses' outfits stationed throughout the cabaret. There'll be a sign at the door saying they're there for the faint hearted in attendance. There is another epigraph, by the way, on the last page."

I flipped to the otherwise blank page and read, "'*Ne raillons pas les fous; leur folie dur plus longtemps que la notre. Voila toute la difference.*' 'Do not mock the madman; his madness lasts longer than ours. There is all the difference,'" I translated out loud. "Not a very encouraging parting word."

Will shrugged. "That did not originate with the original text of *The King in Yellow*. Its source could not be more mundane: a book on hunting, of all things. Adolphe d' Houdetot wrote that in *Ten Thorns for a Flower*.

"Now, flip back to Act One, Scene Three. Carmilla's brief meditation on the mystery of the interaction of physical bodies: 'There be three things that are too wonderful for me, yea four which I know not: the way of an eagle in the air; the way of the serpent upon the rock; the way of a ship in the midst of the sea; and the way of a man with a maid.'"

I frowned. "It is from the book of *Proverbs*," I said.

"Yes. Like the epigraphs, that is a later interpolation into the original text. Evidence that the writer of *Tatterdemalion In Grey* was working from a corrupted copy of *The King In Yellow*. And there is more as well. Go back a bit to Act One, Scene Two, where we have 'Cassandra's Song'…

Let the red dawn surmise
What we shall do,
When this blue starlight dies
And all is through
In Carcoso
If we have loved but well

Under the suns
Let the last morrow tell
What we have done
In Dead Carcaso."

"This replaces the longer 'Cassilda's Song' from *The King In Yellow* with a Bliss Carmon poem."

"Why use Carmon's poem?"

"Well, its cadence is similar to the original and loans itself to the interpolations into Bliss' verse of 'In Carcaso,' and 'In Dead Carcaso.' Note also Bliss' original singular 'sun' is *plural* here, an implicit sign to the intelligentsia that 'Carcaso' *is The King in Yellow*'s Carcosa with its twin solar orbs.

"But the main reason the stanzas are here is Carmen's poem with the additions of 'In *Carcosa*,' had already been interpolated as additional stanzas in 'Cassilda's Song' in *The King in Yellow*. The pastiche writer was drawing from the 1899 false folio."

"'False folio?'"

"The author of *The King In Yellow* knew better than to put his name on it. This had the effect of putting the play immediately in the public domain. When it became a cause celebre among fin de siècle decadent societies, a publisher named Nikolai Morello, an emigre of Bratislava, took advantage of there being no existence of an authorized or copyrighted edition to produce his own.

"What he did was interpolate into the original from an eclectic selection of preexisting texts to 'restore' *The King In Yellow*. Interestingly, Morello claimed that all the literary quotations that he had interpolated were from *The King In Yellow*'s author's personal commonplace book.

"Turn to the end of Act One and you'll find another. The Grey Eminence, when the character of Carmilla asks from where he comes, says: 'I have descended from the Darkness, that which Heraclitus says is the hidden *potentia* of nature.'"

"That is," I said, "a bit of a mistranslation from Rabelais' *Third Book of Pantagruel*."

"Correct! How did you know that?"

"I took a French literature course in Paris, long ago, before I was a disappointment to my parents."

"Ah, you were a student *bon vivant*?"

"Hardly. I had to live in a corner garret that overlooked the Court of the Dragon."

"So, learnt friend, what is the original context of this passage in Rabelais' book?"

"The character of Panurge here is referencing Heraclitus' fifteenth fragment: 'Nature prefers to hide.' Or, as our professor pointed out, one scholar paraphrases the ancient philosopher here: 'The particles defy analysis.'"

"Nature is basically 'unpredictable particles?' That sounds as though old Heraclitus is speaking the same language I hear when physicists talk *these* days," Will said.

"Perhaps the pasticher is more a physicist than a playwright," I said and started to read.

"Or a Sophist…like Heraclitus."

I remembered the canvas leaning against the wall, face away from me, and looked up from the book. "What is your latest acquisition?" I asked and nodded toward it.

Will looked over at the painting, then back at me and smiled. "I haven't put this up yet. I am waiting until opening night of *Tatterdemalion In Grey*."

"And why is that?"

"This painting," he said, rising from his chair and walking toward the canvas, "was the result of someone who read the play in its original form. It left him on the brink of madness, 'unable to love' he said."

He took up the canvas, pulled it away from the wall. "There are several versions, but this is one that captured the feeling while it was fresh."

He turned and revealed a self-portrait of insanity.

"This is *The Scream*."

I knew *The Scream*, of course; a visual record of one who has lost the ability to access the world as it is. What would the play that in Munch's head had produced this, even the pastiche of that play, do in Pris' brain? And how would that resonate into her womb and our baby?

I fled Will's office at the revelation of the painting, shouting at him, "You take her out of this play! Do not even allow her to read!" Then I raced on my bicycle, my head into the wind, to forbid Pris to participate in *Tatterdemalion in Grey*.

But my bicycle jarred to a sudden stop and I flew over the handlebars, landing on my stomach. I rolled over to see one of the Nazis from the alley earlier, with both hands tossing aside my bicycle. His friend stood beside him.

"We have been looking for you," he said. "Did you think we did not notice you earlier, or that we would just let you go?"

Then they were on me, half-dragging me by my shirt, half lifting me by my legs, off to the nearest side alley where they tossed me behind a dumpster. My head struck the alley's wall hard and my mouth opened, but I could not vocalize my pain as they began working on me...

4.

Opening night.

And closing.

I had assembled my set on the officers' mess hall's stage, a space that came with a small backstage area. The curtain presented a forest scene of sunlight slanting through the trees into undergrowth of ferns and clover while in the foreground, two nude Teutonic maidens washed in a stream.

Before this curtain pranced my Esther marionette, now redressed to be the character of Cassandra from *Tatterdemalion In Grey*. My audience, in their disciplined, rigid, perfect posture, shirts and pants crisp and creased, laughed and applauded.

How I kept my hands from shaking and spoiling her dainty steps, let alone giving her a seizure, I do not know. Nevertheless, I made her gracefully move to the oboe that lowed melodically at the mouth of a man who had been first chair in a Vienna orchestra before he and his wife and children were carried off in box cars to separate camps.

Then Cassandra stopped and addressed the audience. And a female voice spoke for her from backstage, that of a former character actress in radio ("the Austrian Mel Blanc") whom I had discovered in the camp. Her voice was lilting; her head shaven.

"When from Carcaso, the Hyaenas, Haitia, and Cynosura…" she began.

I am going to die, I thought. *When these curtains part, I am going to die.*

5.

The blow to my head had been a fortunate one. I was not long losing consciousness, and though I came to with one eye swollen shut, a pinched nerve in my lower back, and a nose pummeled flat, I am certain my suffering would have been more if I had been able to exhibit pain. Without that, there was little satisfaction that continuing with their fists had offered them.

Now it was dark and Berlin had come to nocturnal life. I limped to the road into the white glare of street lights, splotched by gaudy neon. My bicycle, of course, was nowhere to be found, not that my lower back would have allowed me to turn even one pedal.

I was abandoned to travel by foot (no one could be bothered to respond to the frantic waves for help of a severely pummeled man). By now, of course, Pris would have long ago reached the cabaret for the reading, but, fortunately enough, I had not gotten too far from *The Grabmal* before I was accosted.

I could not even run, my left leg catching with the pain radiating down my lower back, compelling me to heft it forward or drag it behind to make progress.

At last I came to *The Grabmal*. There was no one outside waiting, so I knew whatever time it was, it was not yet eleven when the cabaret opened. I entered, shouting for Pris, for Will, and received no answer.

What had happened here?

At my entrance, a grey mass on the stage separated into small shapes and fled with a rapid tapping over the floor. I winced. Rats. How had this pristine cabaret become so infested in the mere hours since I was here before?

I lugged myself onto the stage. Pages from the book I had held earlier were strewn about. All wooden chairs where the actors had sat were overturned but one. It was profusely wet, dripping still with a mixture of clear fluid and blood. And something else…something where the rats had been.

My hand went to my mouth, my stomach heaved, and I tasted bile.

A thudding sounded from inside Will's office.

"Will!" I shouted, forgetting my leg and leaping from the stage. I folded into a painful heap on contact with the floor and wailed. Grabbing onto a table I managed to draw myself up on wobbling arms, still weak from my beating and my exertions to get here.

On my good foot, grabbing onto tables to support my weight, I drug my numbing leg and made my way over the floor toward the office. "Will!" I shouted again.

I expected the office door to be locked, but it immediately opened inward on the dark room. I turned on the light.

The Scream now hung on the wall.

There was another thud, this from under the desk. I looked down.

"Will!"

Shifting himself around where he huddled in the space where the chair usually fit, Will looked up at me, his eyes narrowing until they were dark slits.

"Will, where is Pris? What happened here?"

"What happened? What *happened*? *He* came and declared the scion of the succession of the Imperial family should be born, a black star over the house of Carcaso, a sign and a ransom for the desolation of many!" I noticed as he spoke something quivering but refusing to drop from his lower lip.

"*My* baby? Will? *Tell me!*"

"Have you seen the Cendrée Sign? The tinctured constellation of the noose of the Hyaenas on his Escutcheon?

240

Tlao sounded the trumpet, Cynosura shouted, and the houses of Carcaso and Haitia cast down their spears and bowed the knee."

"What are you talking about?"

"He came down from the Hyaenas. And Cassandra brought forth the child…"

"*What*? You mean Pris? You bastard!" I lurched for him, and the pain that shot from my back down my leg sent me falling to my face on the floor. I looked at him, my face tear streaked. "You tell me you sent Pris with our child back home like I told you to, before you began to read this abomination! You tell me this or I will kill you!"

"Utai, and Thaele; Naos and the Eldones: the Lords in Oblivion."

"She miscarried on that stage, didn't she? *Didn't she*?"

His voice boomed as to an audience: "The exchange was made! Cassandra brought forth the child, a black star over the house of Carcaso, a sign and a ransom for the desolation of many!"

And then what had quivered on his lower lip fell to the floor.

Afterbirth.

What the rats had been eating when I disturbed them.

He grinned, put two fingers to his mouth, rolled his eyes from side to side and giggled. "We, who were but lowly handmaids and midwives, even we partook of the child's greatness," he said.

I lurched forward, the pain from the effort something distant now as my hands were grasping and crushing his throat. He gasped and wheezed and begged with his grunts before I shoved him back, his mouth gaping and his lungs heaving, trying to seize air to live. It was an ugly, grating sound, and I do not know if he survived or not and neither do I care.

I had to find Pris.

6.

The Cassandra puppet, her introductory speech done, exited to the applause of the Nazis with a pronounced wiggle of her buttocks that I had padded and rounded for this performance. She then disappeared behind the curtain.

After a pause, the curtain parted.

And the soldiers frowned.

The scene of nature at its most fundamentalist conception drew away to reveal, behind it, the miniature towers of Carcaso, and in *front* of them, twin suns. In the foreground, Cassandra now lay on a couch, her head tucked as she forlornly traced a hand back and forth over the floor. Before her, the shadow of her thoughts stretched, waiting for their subject to enter.

> (Enter the Carmilla puppet, Stage Left, dressed for a masque; she takes her mark to cast her waiting shadow).
> CASSANDRA
> You are come, Carmilla. Hail, she of the House of Haitia!
> CARMILLA
> Hail Cassandra, House Carcaso. What? You are not yet in dress for the masque?
> CASSANDRA
> I am troubled, dearest Carmilla, by strange dreams and visions. A darkling presence is at the threshold.
> CARMILLA
> Do not let such visions as you have cloud this day. Why should you fear? The covenants yet hold 'tween Carcaso and Haitia. What? Love you my brother no longer?
> CASSANDRA
> Oh, fie! Never have I loved him more.
> CARMILLA
> Then you shall be wed…
> CASSANDRA
> I wonder…
> CARMILLA

You shall be wed, I say. Then more secure shall be the peace between our two houses. War shall continue to be made no more, of a certainty, when doting age holds cherished scion on royal knee.

(Carmilla gently places her hand on Cassandra's stomach; Cassandra grasps it desperately.)

CASSANDRA

Shall peace then hold, Carmilla?

CARMILLA

You fear for your child?

CASSANDRA

Yes.

CARMILLA

You…dreamed of Yaotl?

CASSANDRA

I did.

CARMILLA

Mad Yaotl…

CASSANDRA

"The cloudy depths of Demme must conceal Yaotl forever." So spoke my granddame Cybil. So it was done.

CARMILLA

'Twas fit that it should have fallen upon Yaotl.

CASSANDRA

He talks with me in dreams now. He has spoken with the Lords in Oblivion.

CARMILLA

Do you not know a dream from waking? Up, cousin!

CASSANDRA

…from Utai, to Thaele to Naos and the Eldones. And they have told him…

CARMILLA

Up, I say!

CASSANDRA

…they have told him…

CARMILLA

Lay aside vain dreams!

243

CASSANDRA
Not upon us, oh, King! Not upon us!

7.

I once again lumbered into the Berlin night, my mind
struggling with the unthinkable. I stepped off the roadside into
traffic more than once, sending horns blowing as the vehicles
careened from me and nearly into each other. I did not know
how it was that I was not hit, so slow did I move, so incapable
of agility.

Then I saw her staggering aimlessly on a street meridian,
her gaunt figure sketched in passing auto lights. Her face was
pale and on a blue shift dress she wore, an inky blotch spread
over her belly.

Now my senses were sharp from fear that she would step
in front of one of the autos flying through the thoroughfares. I
could not step into the traffic to come to her aid because of
my own damaged body. I would succeed only in stepping
immediately in front of an automobile myself. I was forced to
watch as Pris absently weaved on staggering bare feet among
the automobiles bearing down on her, horns blaring, the
screech of rubber on asphalt....

"God of my fathers," I prayed. I prayed for the first time in
years. "*Please.*"

She stumbled at last onto the side of the street on which I
stood. I drug my leg behind me, a hot numbness shooting
down it and halting me before I had hardly moved forward.

But Pris had seen me and now trotted to where I stood.

"Pris," I said, sobbing as I put my hand against her slick
abdomen, the shift sticking to her skin.

"It's all right, darling. Don't you see it's all alright now?
The child is safe..."

"*Safe?*"

"...in oblivion."

"Pris!"

"He will have new friends, strange friends:
Utai...Thaele...Naos...the Eldones...safe..."

"How can you say such things?"

Her upper lip curled, and she looked me up and down. "*How*? You ask *how*? This *life* is mad! The Grey Eminence came from the Hyaenas, and we were in one accord. That I should give up the child as a ransom, to become a dark star over Carcaso, a sign and a cause of desolation for many!"

"No," I said and doubled over, beginning to sob again.

"Oh, no, my sweet. Do not cry. It's all right. Really. I know. When it was over, he lay still on the stage, even when I poked him with a stick to see if he would do anything. And then…" she began to titter, "…a greasy grey rat ran up and began dragging what there was of him away!"

"No!" I said and felt my face pale, my knees buckle.

"Yes!"

"*No*!" I said, rising suddenly.

"*Yes*. I watched him do it," she raised her hand and waved her slim little fingers. "I said, 'Bye, bye, baby!'"

My hand lashed out before I knew it, and in the next moment I was watching her face recoil from my slap.

"Pris!" I said as she tucked her head, hand alongside her jaw, "Pris, I'm so sorry. Forgive me! I know you are not in your right mind…"

But when she looked up, her eyes were clear, as though scales had fallen from them. The sudden transition into what surely appeared as lucidity made me take a halting step back.

"You are sorry?" she said. "You are *weak*! Weak to want to bind another life to this wretched world! We are only the progeny of viruses hurling in a void that is endless night, and it goes on forever! Forever! Why do…"

A tram trundled by then, the racket from it in my ears loud as that from a passing train…

…and then Pris was staggering backward, away from me, as though she would turn and run, like she could no longer bear to be in my presence; backward into the highway and in front of an auto…

The impact was instant. I watched her body hurl skyward, watched it fall into the midst of the traffic ahead to the shrieking of wheels on the asphalt. The autos quickly piled up, one upon the other, seemingly forever down the boulevard.

I turned and hobbled away.

8.

"Stop! Stop at once! This play is an abomination!"

The speaker was the one who was not Hans. He was mopping his brow, his fellow soldiers writhing in their chairs, all of their faces moist and grimacing, shirts clinging to them in dampness.

The puppets turned their heads in unison and looked at him.

"Come out and explain yourself! What is this place?" He pointed at the set of Carcaso.

My puppets have movement. You cannot know both movement and location.

"What does that mean? And who are you? Where is the *Scheiss Meister*? Bring him out!"

But I was already out, watching this unfold. As prearranged, I and the Jews who had participated in the performance had slipped outside between the first and second acts, before the madness was to be released. I had tarried outside the mess hall, safe from whatever was unfolding inside.

Still, it was apparent when all came to a jarring stop, with the one who was not Hans' booming command. I had looked into a window then and saw him on his feet, angrily addressing the stage.

"You bring me the *Scheiss Meister*, I say!"

You are in no position to make commands.

"What? You dare speak to me this way?"

I dare nothing less, fool.

"Filth! I am going to come up there and strangle you with your own puppet strings."

I use no strings.

The one who was not Hans' gaze involuntarily dropped to the puppets.

And they sprang from the stage, skittering across the floor with the rattle of bones, toward him and the others who were now leaping to their feet, drawing their Lugers. Some began to fire but the ammunition defied any trajectory of known physics. The bullets bent back—they did not ricochet—they *bent back* on the shooters, the impact hurling the soldiers to the floor, where the ones who did not die instantly writhed, bellowing. Defenseless in their pain, they were the ones on whose eyes the puppets set upon.

As I watched this, wondering if the madness of the play's second act had infected me after all, one of the Nazis, brandishing but not having fired his gun, rushed the stage. He trampled over the set, passed through the backstage curtains, then immediately was running *out* of them, a look of triumph on his face as he opened fire on his fellow soldiers, striking several down. The man on the stage halted, looked behind him, then forward again, his face pale.

He had been *entering* the backstage when he first began to pull on the trigger, but had discovered autonomy over the destined location of his body's arrival no longer his, as, without turning, he had found himself *exiting* the stage instead as his bullets spewed.

Behind the Nazi, frozen in his disorientation, appeared the Tatterdemalion in Grey. Hans started to shout a warning from the floor, but not before the solid stage beneath the soldier and the floor and the floor beneath it immediately became a swarming mass of gnats. His weight no longer supported, he immediately passed through uncertain molecules, dismissed into the bowels of the Earth. Then the stage and floor immediately reappeared. As solid and dependable as they had always appeared.

Hans turned and ran for the door.

Stop!

He did. And looked back....

—and remember Lot's wife.

What had been human was now a twisted slab of salt. In the next moment, it was no longer there.

"Monster!" the one who was not Hans said, training his Luger on the Grey Tatterdemalion. "What have you done with Hans?"

What is it you hold?

The one who was not Han's eyes darted down to see where there had been a gun he now clutched a scorpion. Its stinger lanced the soft flesh between thumb and forefinger. With a shriek, his hand went into a spasm to shake the venomous arthropod to the floor but he could not dislodge it.

As for your friend, Hans has been banished to a pasture in Geneva, where he shall serve as a salt lick, completely and always conscious, tenderly sensitive to the slow, worrying licking of the cows' tongues until he has dwindled to the last grain. Imagine a host of incessant worrying itches over your body and being unable to move to relieve even one.

"You are inhuman!"

Yes.

Now, you would do best to look to yourself; I suggest you do not attempt to turn and flee.

"You expect me to just stand here and die?" the one who was not Hans shouted, still trying to shake the scorpion from his hand, his face red and swelling.

Your death will be a tormented, lingering one if you do not *get medical aid, true. But you assume escape is possible. That would depend on the world still being where you left it.*

"That is insanity! The world is *always* there just as it *always* was."

You are not certain.

"There is no question!"

Then why do you not turn and open the door and look?

"I...."

Turn and look!

He turned. The door exploded open on its own.

Beyond it, the world had dissolved into a sea of roiling fog, its haze seeming to reach the orange moon that hovered in front of the spires of Carcaso on the far shore of the cloud lake of Demme.

248

The one who was not Hans again found his hand around the handle of a gun. He brought it to his temple and fired. Something flew from the other side of his head and struck the far wall as his body collapsed at the feet of the Tatterdemalion.

Stunned by the revelation of what lay beyond that door, only now did I notice from the stretching, boiling fog the screams of other unseen Nazi soldiers, the camp sirens, the reports of guns firing, searchlight beams sweeping through Demme's clouds…and a sound of great lamentation rising from distant Carcaso.

Then the Pewter Mask turned upon me.

I felt myself compelled to look up.

The stars had all extinguished. But an aperture of blackness deeper than the night hung in the sky. A voice of no human origin boomed: *Cassandra brought forth the child, a black star over the house of Carcaso, a sign and a ransom for the desolation of many!*

I felt myself pale. I turned and ran.

To find myself in the midst of the boiling grey clouds, my feet on nothing. Before me now he stood and brandished the shield that bore the noose of the Hyaenas. The trumpet of Tlao sounded.

Our partnership had ended, and, oh, how I felt the void between us.

All is now fulfilled.

"*You* brought all this about!"

I use no strings.

"I…I only wanted revenge for the loss of my baby, for *their* needless hatred, that stopped me from reaching Pris."

You are satisfied?

"How could any of this satisfy anyone? Anyone but you?"

But I am not. Not yet.

9.

I stood again with Pris on the side of the highway in Berlin, the deafening tram trundling by.

What did she say?

249

"I never knew. I couldn't hear…"

You knew. You heard.

Burning tears streaked my face now as they had done then. I knew. I heard.

"…you think I took a role in this play? *This* play? This way you could not hate me after it happened!"

"*Hate* you?"

"I went to the pharmacist days ago!"

"*What*?!"

"'A play that drives one mad?' Do you think I believed it could truly traumatize anyone? That I would trust a *play* to bring it off? But I could feign a breakdown afterwards."

I stared at her. "You…*staged* a miscarriage, Pris? You did away with our child?" I felt my fists clinching at my sides. "Our baby…and were ready to *lie* to me about it? For our *whole lives*, Pris? *Our baby, Pris*?"

Her eyes were swimming. She reached out to touch my face.

"I love you," she said.

But it was only one progeny of a virus speaking to another. And I shoved her…

And now I, too, was falling from the force of my own push, spinning into an eternal descent into brooding, boiling Demme. Endless screams of others drowning around me were a cacophony in my ears and, as the darkness enveloped me forever, only one voice, his voice, split what was a cataract's roaring as I was plunged into bottomless depths:

"It is a fearful thing to fall into the hands of the living God!"

THE FRIEZE OF HELMSLY AINSWORTH

David Bernard

Helmsley Somerset Ainsworth III was a patron of the arts, but strictly on his own terms. He thrived on creating minor scandals in the overly-dramatic world of the arts, so much so that he had his business card updated to list his occupation as "Arts Provocateur."

It was his personal opinion that, if one of the gallery showings he curated didn't evoke some sort of a tempest in a teapot, it was a failure. Of course, he didn't know when to leave well enough alone either. I have been his attorney since the previous firm chose to terminate the relationship in the wake of the riot in Seattle caused by his exhibit of the works of Enoch Coffin. In Helmsley's terms, that made the show a tremendous success. The Seattle Police Department was more inclined to use terms like "public menace."

My law practice was not sufficiently established to be refusing work from the deep pockets of Helmsley Ainsworth, so I carefully listened, dutifully pointed out the legal ramifications, and then spent copious amounts of my time and his money keeping him out of jail in the aftermath of his ignoring my counsel.

Helmsley's current idea was to create an exhibition of bizarre stone sculptures, built around a collection of carved rocks he had purchased at an estate sale in a town beyond Sacramento called Auburn. I thought he overpaid for them. He merely waved his hand dismissively and suggested if I didn't recognize the name of the sculptor (I didn't), my level of culture was beneath contempt. As long as his monthly retainer check cleared the bank, he could accuse me of anything he wanted. He planned to exhibit this "Smith Collection" in San Francisco, but his reputation preceded him, and the only available space he could find was ten miles down the coast in Pacifica.

I had been negotiating, in vain, to obtain the loan of some stone figurine from an obscure institute outside of Santiago. Whatever it was, the institute was not going to loan it out. Ainsworth seemed unconcerned.

"I'm not surprised, Douglas," he said, finishing off a bottle of white wine that cost more than two months' rent on my office. We were dining at the Gallomo Club in a section of Los Angeles, way above my comfort level, both financially and socially.

"The Sanbourne academics are so dry as to be positively desiccated. For years, I have nearly single-handedly underwritten their budget for acquiring obscure books on folklore and religion. I shall simply stop my annual donation to the institution. And when they ask why, I will tell them. Either I will get the figurine for the next show, or I will be looking for a new institution to donate funds. I understand there's a historical society up north of Boston that has some rather provocative gold jewelry."

"So, I was able to secure insurance for the exhibit in Pacifica," I said. "Apparently, there are still insurance agents who have not heard about the 'incident' at the Pickman exhibit last year."

I poked at my lunch, something called a "snezhanka." I had blindly ordered the cheapest thing on the menu, which turned out to be some sort of a cucumber salad covered in yogurt. It was still pricey enough to hope Helmsley was picking up the tab.

Helmsley sat back and motioned for the waiter. "Cancel that event, Douglas. I have something even more spectacular in mind," the waiter arrived and Helmsley ordered a dessert that was not on the menu, something that sounded very French and accordingly expensive.

I was a little surprised by Helmsley canceling a show of his own accord. Usually, it took a court order.

"Are you sure, Helmsley? You have invested a sizable amount of money in setting up this exhibit."

He waggled his hand at me dismissively. "What I have in mind is so bizarre and so unusual that even I have never even heard of anyone working in the medium. Douglas, my boy, I am talking about something so avant-garde that the so-called 'cutting edge' crowd might as well go back to finger painting mastodons on cave walls."

Helmsley looked positively giddy. That usually meant additional billable hours for me. His dessert arrived, something that looked like a stack of flapjacks covered in a thick white syrup and gold leaf.

"Douglas, I know you're terrified I'm going to make you cover the tab. Relax. I'm going to sit here and devour this mille-feuille and nurse a brandy of a vintage that would give your wallet a coronary. You can toddle back to your little office and pretend you're not secretly in love with that delightful little secretary of yours. I'll send you a list of requirement for the next venue. You can read it over and we'll talk over lunch—and yes, my treat. You can ask the questions I know you'll have. Remember, Douglas, we're on the verge of artistic history! Now shoo, and let me digest."

The packet from Helmsley arrived by courier later that afternoon. Stacy brought it into my office and looked at me questioningly. With more than a little trepidation, I started reading his requirements. Then I read them again. By the third time, I was sure I wasn't hallucinating. I looked up at Stacy.

253

"You might as well go home. There are potential liability issues here that I didn't think even existed. I'm going to have research this all night."

"Can I help? I could order in Chinese." Stacy looked at me. I would have preferred adoration, but merely saw sympathy.

I shook my head. "You'll have enough to do in the morning. Helmsley Ainsworth has outdone himself. He wants to rent a cold storage warehouse to renovate for an exhibition of ice sculptures."

Stacy cocked an eyebrow. "Ice sculptures? Seems a tad plebian for him."

I shook my head. "Far, far worse. The artist is also a physicist. His medium is some rare gas mix, cooled down to a solid. Like dry ice, only colder and more expensive."

"Of course," she said, the sarcasm dripping. "And I get to find the warehouse for them."

"Yes. But, on the bright side, the billable hours for that alone will cover your salary and the rent for the rest of the year."

She sighed and headed to the door. "I'll see you in the morning."

I kept reading the notes. Half of it was scientific mumbo jumbo and the rest was a massive class action suit waiting to happen. I decided to email an old college buddy and ask him about some of the technical jargon. He actually worked in water chemistry or some arcane thing that required dodging alligators while wearing hip boots, but I didn't have a lot of friends in the sciences. I went home. I had a feeling I would be sleeping in my office again soon enough.

I got to the office the next morning to find Stacy already on the phone. She did not look amused, so I assumed she was already looking for the warehouse. I just slipped into my office and spread out Helmsley's notes and then overlaid them with mine. Helmsley's new exhibit was a series of sculptures of people in historic costumes that he wanted to frame within a tableau made of ice. This frozen frieze (his term, not mine) was in a new medium never attempted before. Metal alloys were heated so hot that they melted, and then turned to gas. Then the gases were super-cooled into solid blocks of ice, which were then sculpted. This metallic gas-ice kept the colors properties of the metals, giving the work an iridescent, almost opal-like sheen.

The problem was keeping them cold. They needed to be kept so cold that the engineer that Helmsley had consulted was concerned that the building would be so frigid that it would make the support structure brittle—LA buildings were designed for earthquakes, not subzero temperatures. So, Helmsley's architects came up with a plan to build a smaller, freestanding structure to enclose the statues. This smaller structure would keep the air around the statues at the deadly cold temperatures they required, and use the warehouse refrigeration system to keep the rest of the building just cold enough to "alleviate the temperature variation strain on the containment structure." I barely understood anything other than it was really cold and insanely expensive. The interior design involved a lot of faux ice stalactites and manufactured snow. I didn't care for the design, but at least I understood all the words.

My email to Florida got a reply and Pete knew me well enough to use small words. He explained that for copper to get so hot that it turns into a gas, as one example, it has to be heated to 4600°F. Iron needs to hit over 5200°F, and even higher for other metals. Then, to freeze the gas, it would have to be brought down to nearly absolute zero almost immediately. The part of the email that stood out was: "That's not art, that's science fiction. It's a hoax of some sort. There are a handful of labs working in the absolute zero field and no one's reached it yet. None of them would have the funds, inclination, or capacity to create large blocks of frozen gas on that scale."

That made sense. I could easily see Helmsley's enthusiasm leaving him vulnerable to a con man. The thought was interrupted by the booming voice of Helmsley Ainsworth himself in my reception area, acclaiming Stacy was the

255

embodiment of Aphrodite. He burst into my office with a dramatic pose.

"Douglas McAvoy, why don't you admit you adore Anastacia and marry her? I warn you that, if you don't, I will steal her away from you and take her on a world tour of the most wicked and decadent places on Earth," as he stepped inside and closed the door, I heard her snort.

"Are you ready for lunch, Douglas? There's a new pop-up bistro in Beverly Hills I've been dying to try. They do traditional Italian cuisine in a wood-fired oven. They only burn cedar logs, imported from Lebanon, that have been cut by hand and then aged in hand-pressed, toasted sesame seed oil."

"Sit down, Helmsley. I want to talk about this project," I tried to sound professionally concerned, not bordering on panic.

"Let me guess, Douglas. You talked to some scientist who told you that the whole story is utter rubbish. I know."

"You know?" he seemed pleased by the look on my face.

"Of course I know," he scoffed. "The Ainsworth fortune was built in the steel industry. I know more than enough about smelting and alloys to make up nonsense when I need to. But Douglas, you have to see these statues. I've never seen anything like them. They're magnificent. They are so detailed that you'd think that, if you touched them, it would be real fabric. Of course, if you did touch them, you'd get third-degree frostbite."

"So," I said, "they're not really made of gas made of ice?" If Helmsley was pulling another extravagant backstory for the art crowd, I could deal with that.

"I have no idea what they are made of. I'm hoping that someone will challenge that tale and identify what they are. I might end up with egg on my face, but imagine the press when some egghead at Caltech calls me a liar. And if he can't identify it, it generates even more press."

He stood up. "Now, come along, Douglas. I would hate to see all that cedar being burned without my gustatory participation."

Per usual, I ordered the cheapest thing on the menu, which was a white pizza. It was an okay pizza, but not a great pizza. The only thing the special wood added to was the price. Helmsley had a baked pasta in a white truffle marina. I don't know what he paid for it, but they also sold the sauce at $1400 for a six-ounce jar.

I was beginning to suspect that Helmsley was dragging me to restaurants so he could be entertained by the look on my face when I saw the bill. I suspect the look was similar to the other tidbit he dropped on me on the drive back to my office. The engineering report was also total nonsense—the enclosure wasn't to protect the statues from the visitors, it was to protect the visitors from the statues. Whatever they were made of, they remained so cold that not only did touching them cause severe frostbite, the statues never warmed up, let alone melted. The refrigerated storage warehouse as an art gallery? More Ainsworth theatrical staging. He wasn't selling the art or charging admission, so it wasn't legally fraud. I returned to my office, toting a $90 pizza for Stacy. She eyed it suspiciously.

"I found a location for Helmsley," she said, gingerly picking up a slice. "It's an old warehouse in foreclosure on the San Pedro side of the port, near the main channel. No active warehouse wants to lease space for Helmsley to set up an exhibition—Helmsley's renovations and the crowds of art cognoscenti wandering around the facilities would just be too disruptive for their operations. I think he should just buy this one rather than rent it. The depreciation should cover the purchase in no time. And it's likely the Port Authority will want to buy it with the next expansion."

I looked at her. "You know, I keep forgetting you're studying to be a tax lawyer."

Very daintily, she dropped the half eaten slice in her waste can and handed me back the box. I didn't have the heart to tell her she just tossed a $15 slice of pizza in the trash.

"I'll call Helmsley," I said. "If he likes the idea, I'm sure he'll double the length of your decadent cruise."

"Everyone keeps offering to take me away, and yet, here I sit," she was still muttering as I closed the door. Helmsley was delighted with the idea and had me contact a realtor friend of his from his country club.

I kept researching fraud, to see if Helmsley was liable. Dinner was the rest of the pizza. Being cold did not improve the flavor. By the time I headed home, Stacy was long gone and I was developing heartburn. That night, undoubtedly thanks to my wise dinner choice, I had an odd dream.

I had no idea where I was, I stood at the base of a mountain of ice, gleaming white in the sun. There was nothing but a frigid wasteland in all directions as far as I could see. Suddenly the great ice mountain shuddered. A hissing voice echoed across the frozen peak.

"The worm awakens to the laughter of the Chromatic Court. Yikilth sets forth again and its journey is one of vengeance."

I woke up to the alarm clock radio. The morning team was having a grand old time making fun of a report out of Alaska that a fishing vessel had seen an iceberg south of the Aleutians, which a spokesman for NOAA said was "possible but highly unlikely." I couldn't care less about ice in Alaska, but that explained the dream.

The commute took twice as long as usual. There a steady cold drizzle and no one in South California knew how to drive when the roads weren't perfectly dry. The accidents were impressive, as was my irritation. Stacy lived downtown, so she was already there, and so was a stack of memos from

Helmsley. Apparently, my presence was requested at the warehouse.

Stacy looked me. The curse I had just uttered had not been made using my inside voice.

"So," I said, hoping to change the subject, "Want to go for a ride?"

Stacy looked out the window. "You want me to go with you in the rain to the commercial docks to visit an abandoned warehouse? You sure know how to show a girl a good time. How about I say no, and save you the trouble of apologizing later?" I nodded and headed down to the parking lot.

By the time I got there, the rain had stopped and fog had rolled in, creating whiteout conditions. The radio noted the accident rate had tripled accordingly. The warehouse looked like something out of a horror movie as it suddenly loomed into view out of the fog. The corrugated tin roof was bleeding rusty stains down the sides. The cement walls hadn't been painted in decades, what little paint that survived was fluttering in grimy strips peeling down the walls. Being nearly under the bridge out to Terminal Island, every surface was covered in road grime. Everything except for a gleaming white 1959 Rolls Royce Silver Cloud—Helmsley was already here.

I tried the office door—it was locked. I wasn't about to try to lift one of the dock doors, so I headed around to the back. As I walked along the building, a breeze came off the channel. It felt unseasonably cool. A side door was ajar, so I walked in. There was Helmsley, supervising what appeared to be the lower half of a man in oil-stained overalls sticking out of a piece of machinery. Helmsley looked up as I stepped in.

"Douglas, so good of you to pop by. This is Mr. Testabianca, a veritable Michelangelo of refrigeration," the overalls wriggled out of the equipment and stood up. He was a short man with a bad comb-over. Wordlessly, he walked over to a control panel and the machine roared to life. It was deafening and all three of us went outside.

"Well, Mr. Ainsworth," he said. "If you can keep the thermostat at forty or up, it'll run for a few weeks. But if you try to push it too hard, that compressor will not survive."

A look of concern flitted across Helmsley's face. "I only need it to run for a few weeks. I assume you can fix it if it breaks down."

The mechanic shook his head. "She's an antique, and they stopped making parts for it thirty years ago. And the harder you push it, the faster something will seize up, melt down, or just explode. I may be able to track down parts, but we're talking months. It'd be faster to replace the entire unit."

"Very well, Mr. Testabianca. Send me an estimate on the replacement with your bill, and I'll decide what to do later."

The mechanic nodded and then paused. "One more thing. Did you notice that white film on the insulation on the walls?" Helmsley nodded. "It's not my field of expertise, but I think that's vapor retardant. It keeps condensation from soaking into the fiberglass. I'd have that tested—some of the old stuff was pretty flammable. And you also have asbestos on the pipes. The building inspector will insist you have the asbestos encased or removed before you get an occupation permit. In the meantime, I wouldn't spend a lot of time breathing in there."

He drove off in a battered old white van that had been hidden in the fog bank. Helmsley looked at me. It was definitely a scowl. I had never seen anyone deliver bad new to Helmsley Ainsworth before. He was not happy—it was not a good look.

Of course, my news wasn't much better, so this should be a real treat for me. "I've been looking at requirements to open the building up as an art gallery. Because you're essentially changing a commercial building into a public facility, you're going to get all the inspectors—at least building, electrical, plumbing, and mechanical. If any of them find the building is in violation of the county codes, you'll get a list of violations. They'll give thirty days to resolve the problems before filing legal complaints."

Instead of exploding, Helmsley visibly relaxed. "The contractors arrive today to make the place look presentable and to build the viewing area. The inspectors can come when they like. In thirty days, the exhibit will be over and the premises will again be an abandoned warehouse."

A thought occurred to me. "Helmsley, I'm only asking as your attorney. Where did you acquire these statues?"

Helmsley gave a sly little grin. "I didn't acquire them. I borrowed them. Come with me."

He disappeared into the fog. I followed him. The fog was cold, and I could see my breath. We walked over to a shipping container coated in frost. Cold emanated from the metal. He fished a pair of gloves out of a pocket and unlocked the door. A wall of frigid air slammed into me.

He gestured me forward. I cautiously peeked inside. The container was filled with at least six statues of iridescent white ice. The nearest one looked like some sort of barbarian or Viking. The first thing I saw was a look of terror on the face, so accurate it looked like a three-dimensional photograph. Once I got past the look of the eyes, I studied the sculpture. The ice representation of his fur cloak was so realistic that looked like it should be rippling in the breeze. The skin had a slight bluish tint to the white, but every hair, mole, and scar was picture perfect. The sword in one hand was ice, but it was battle scarred. There was some sort of writing on the blade. I went to look closer at it, but Helmsley stopped me.

"Not without protective gear, Douglas. I can't afford the time to find a new attorney."

I was impressed. "The detail on these sculptures are incredible. I know you said they were detailed, but this is unbelievable. I can see freckles on that Viking's hand."

"That's not a Viking, Douglas. There is one in the back, but this a Hyperborean foot soldier. Seven statues in all— everything from an Elizabethan sailor to an Atlantean mage." He closed the door and locked it.

"They're remarkable," I said, ignoring the names I hadn't recognized, "but, borrowed? That's liability insurance, and lease contracts, and—" Helmsley raised his hand to cut me off.

"Douglas, if you stop thinking like a lawyer for five minutes," I paused, but I was overwhelmed with new legal concerns. "Douglas, it's a little more complicated than that. Let us depart this dreary place. I am positively chilled to the bone. There's charming little café just west of here. We can chat there."

I followed his Rolls to, wonder of wonders, a charming little café. I walked in the door and was transported back to the fifties—chrome everywhere, neon on the signs and Naugahyde on the booths. I followed Helmsley to a booth in the corner.

"Helmsley, how did you find this place?" I slid into the other side of the booth as he gestured to a white-haired little lady behind the counter.

"Douglas, I have my finger on the pulse of this city. Every gallery opening, every estate sale, and every restaurant."

"I know that. But this seems a little, err, beneath your level of sophistication?"

The white-haired waitress put down two mugs of coffee.

"Thank you, Blanche, need I ask how long?" Helmsley took her hand and kissed it.

Blanche smiled. "You know you can't rush some things, *mon cher*. It'll be ready in a minute."

Helmsley settled back in his seat with a boyish look of anticipation.

"To answer your question, Douglas, artistry is where you find it. I found it here, and I support it like any other art."

On cue, Blanche placed a steaming platter of a square pastry covered in powdered sugar.

Helmsley gleefully clapped his hands. "Douglas, prepare for a religious experience. Blanche is a refugee from Katrina and the foremost expert on the creation of the beignet. The French Quarter's loss is our gain."

He didn't wait for me. I tried one. It was tasty. Considering Helmsley was already on his third, I wasn't about to mention I wasn't particularly impressed—it was just fried dough, available at every carnival in New England. These were definitely fresher and better-tasting than the west coast version, something called "funnel cake."

After the fifth beignet, Helmsley finally stopped. His face was covered in powdered sugar and he looked like a cross between a cocaine addict and a snowman. With a contented sigh, he pushed the plate away.

"Now, then, Douglas, about my loaned statuary. It's a tad complicated, so I must insist you let me finish before you jump in with all your legal nonsense. Agreed?"

I nodded. I already knew I was not going to be happy. Helmsley motioned to his friend Blanche who refilled the coffee.

"Several months ago, I was in the Vasileostrovsky Harbor District of Russia, a dreadful place, even by Russian standards. I've been looking for folk art of an ancient Russian god that was prominent in the area before Stalin decided to wipe out any trace of the legend. I'm not even sure of the name of the god, just that it was some sort of horrible, giant humanoid squid."

He sipped his coffee. "The locals keep to themselves; they're close enough to St. Petersburg to assume any stranger is from the Secret Police. But word got out about the rich *Amerikanskiy* looking for old folk art. Eventually, I was introduced to Marek Raudsepp, the captain of an Estonian trawler. Captain Marek claimed that, decades before, as a young sailor, the ship he was on developed engine trouble and they were forced to anchor near a glacier to await a repair vessel. Being young and restless, he went ashore to explore. He claimed he had come across a castle made of ice, built into a glacier. Exploring the castle, he found a chamber filled with statues made of ice. About then, he lost his nerve and returned to the ship."

I said nothing, as promised, but so far, it sounded like a scam. Helmsley dipped his finger in his coffee and then traced it in the sugar left on the beignet plate. Licking his finger clean, he continued.

"It wasn't my giant squid-man, but the concept of ancient ice statuary was intriguing. I made a deal with Captain Marek. If he could find his glacier castle again, I would pay him for photographs of the statues. You know the rest. He eventually found the ice castle. I loved the pictures, so I paid Captain Marek to go back quietly and collect some of the statues. I had them shipped to me here."

I sat there, overwhelmed. Not by the story, but the implications—stolen art, disturbing an archaeology site, international smuggling. I couldn't afford to tell Helmsley to find another lawyer, but I could get disbarred for not doing something.

Helmsley looked at me as he sipped his coffee again. "I know you, Douglas. Your legal brain is spinning like a hamster on a wheel. It's even worse than you think. It turns out Captain Marek wasn't exactly sure where the glacier or the island were located. It's wasn't on any of his maps. He thought the ice temple was north of the Arctic Circle, but when he finally found it, he was correct. But it was also near enough to the Svalbard Islands that Norway might have a claim to the statues. That's why I made up the story about the physicist-artist."

I put my mug down and rubbed my temples. I didn't know where to start.

Helmsley looked at me. "That bad?"

I nodded. "Helmsley, as your friend, you need to get this art back where you got it as soon as possible. As your lawyer, I don't know if even an international law specialist could determine which countries are going to charge you with what crimes."

Helmsley folded his hands in his lap and looked like a guilty toddler. "I should probably mention the other complication. Captain Marek drowned earlier this week when his boat hit an iceberg. He was the only one who knew the location of the glacier, and even if he had notes, they went down with his ship. I have no way to return them. So, I'm going to continue with the exhibition—I don't know what else to do."

I stood up. "Helmsley, we're in trouble, but since I can claim lawyer-client confidentiality, I haven't heard a word you said. You do what you need to do. I need to take a crash course in several law specialties just to help hire the legal team if this blows up in your face."

Helmsley sat there. "Douglas, you're angry with me."

I leaned down so I didn't scream across the diner. "Yes. I am very angry. Helmsley Ainsworth, you are too reckless. I was able to convince Seattle not to press charges. The charges in San Francisco were dropped on a technicality, and the only reason you weren't sued in Providence was that the City Solicitor was an art aficionado. This time, you may have used up your luck. I can't see any way we're going to casually walk away from this mess. You paid to have antiquities stolen that may belong to Norway. And you paid an Estonian to steal them, and then smuggled them into the US out of Russia. The UN is probably going to end up determining who gets to extradite you first."

I turned and left. I need to go to the office, quietly sit down and figure out how to even start damage control. I was still fuming when I got back to the office.

Stacy looked at me. "You're taking me out for dinner tonight."

I was not expecting that. "Did Helmsley put you up to that?"

Stacy looked hurt. "No, it was my idea. Why would Helmsley be involved?"

"We just had a discussion. It did not end well."

She looked at me. "When you say 'not well,' are we talking 'former client' level of not well?"

I didn't answer, mostly because I didn't know. I went into my office wordlessly. I needed to clear my head and start contingency plans. There was a gentle rap on the door.

Stacy poked her head in. "I forgot to mention that you had a visitor. I'm not sure if he's a potential client or a salesman. He left his card and said he'd try again." She handed me his card. The card was an unremarkable white business card, with no logo. It simply read "Ormen Underordnet, Rlim Shaikorth Associates."

Stacy continued. "He said he had just arrived in the country and doesn't have a phone or office yet. Kind of a creepy-looking guy. He was a short albino, dressed in an all-white business suit with red sunglasses."

"Do we have any clue as to what he wants?" The fact he had just arrived in the country made me nervous in light of Helmsley's recent story.

Stacy shook her head. "He was very self-assured and was not going to chat to a mere secretary. Now, if you'll excuse me, I need to go home and slip into something inappropriately dressy before we go to dinner," she said and closed the door.

I jumped up and went into the lobby. "Stacy. I'm delighted to have dinner, but what brought this on?"

She opened the door to head out. "It was something the albino said as he was leaving. He turned and just said 'He'll never ask. You must take the lead.' So I did. The reservations are on my desk. I'll meet you there in an hour."

I walked back to into my office to grab my jacket. I had no idea who Mr. Ormen Underordnet was, but if he was looking to get on my good side, it was working. I straightened my tie and went out to Stacy's desk to see where I was meeting her.

Stacy met me in front of Café Bonhomme de Neige, a trendy bistro off of Sixth in the Arts District. The wind was picking up and it seemed to be getting even cooler.

"How on Earth did you score reservations here?" I was impressed. "I heard the waiting list to get in is six months."

She smiled as we went inside. "My brother is the owner."

She took off her coat. She was wearing a stunning white cocktail dress that shimmered as she moved. She was breathtaking. Helmsley's potential problems did not cross my mind again that evening.

I was standing on an iceberg. We seemed to be traveling at an unusually fast speed for a floating block of ice. I turned to see spires of ice glistening in the sky. I turned again and there was a pudgy little albino man in a white suit. Against the ice, he would have been all but invisible except for a pair of red sunglasses.

"Yikilth nears and even the Chromatic Court trembles. Only the most powerful of mages would have the hubris to steal from the all-powerful Rlim Shaikorth. Woe to those who anger the White Worm." He began moving toward me. I stepped backward and fell off the iceberg into the frigid water. As I sank, my last image was red eyes piercing through the water.

I woke up with a start. I was so cold my toes were numb, even though the room was stifling hot. The landlord must have turned the heat on overnight—for all the good it was doing me at the moment. I kicked off the covers and went to look out the window. The window wasn't where it was supposed to be. Then I remembered. I was at Stacy's apartment. That also explained the floral pattern on the sheets and Stacy sprawled across the other side of the bed. It was 6 AM according to my watch. I quietly gathered up my clothes and stepped out of the bedroom. I got dressed quietly and left her a note that I needed to get to work on saving Helmsley's ass and I would see at the office.

I stepped outside into another day of miserable weather. The car radio newscast was ninety percent traffic updates. Major traffic delays on all main roads because of accidents. The port and LAX were in white-out conditions. All because of a freak fog bank covering the coast from LA all the way up to Seattle.

I avoided the main roads but I switched stations. The morning jocks were having a field day with the iceberg reported off Alaska earlier in the week. Apparently, reports of the phantom iceberg were coming in up and down the Pacific Northwest coast. They talked to a guy at NOAA who said it was either pranksters or mass hysteria—if the iceberg even existed, it would have had to have drifted against the current to be where it was being spotted.

I started a pot of coffee and went into my office to change shirts and shave. I went out to get a cup of the coffee and there was someone in the waiting area.

To my horror, it was a short, pudgy man with white hair in a white suit wearing red sunglasses, despite it being a gray, cloudy day. Identical to my nightmare and exactly how Stacy had described her visitor. He must have seen the look on my face.

"I'm sorry, Mr. McAvoy. Did I startle you?" He had an odd accent and a bemused look.

I gathered my wits. "Mr. Underordnet, I presume?"

Mr. Underordnet brought his hands together in a steeple, then bowed his head to touch his forehead. "Mr. McAvoy, it is a pleasure to meet you." The gesture seemed Asian but his inflection seemed more Russian, but, then again, I wasn't very good at accents.

I gestured toward my office. "What can I do for you?"

His hands remained in a steeple. He nodded slightly. "I appreciate the hospitality, but I must not stay long. I find California to be unpleasantly warm."

I said nothing. Most people were complaining about how cold it was.

"Mr. McAvoy, I shall be brief. A client of yours possesses some statues that belong to my superior. They hold great sentimental value and he is anxious to rectify the wrong done to his estate as quickly and quietly as possible."

I fought down a moment of panic. "Are you an attorney, Mr. Underordnet?"

The albino smiled. It was not a good look. "You flatter me, Mr. McAvoy. I am but a humble servant. My master does not wish to involve such mundanities as the law."

That did not make me as happy as I had hoped. "Have you tried discussing the matter directly?"

Again, he smiled. It was more of a perfunctory gesture than an amused smile. "Mr. Ainsworth has been proven somewhat difficult to—how do you say—'pin down.'"

I could believe that. Helmsley had homes across the world, including three in Los Angeles, that I knew of.

The little man continued. "Mr. Ainsworth knows he is not the owner. The owner wishes the statues back. He belongs to a rather exclusive society and has been embarrassed by their theft. He has considerable resources to assure they are returned. We are asking you to act as an intermediary."

It might have been a threat, but it was said so matter-of-factly that I couldn't be sure. I decided to take the high road.

"Mr. Underordnet, I'll need to discuss this with my client to see how he responds to the allegations," it was an outright lie, but I needed time to think.

The little man nodded. "Thank you, Mr. McAvoy. I look forward to further discussions," he bowed again and backed out the door.

I turned toward the coffee and the door opened again. It was Stacy.

"Stacy? You're early. I assume you passed your little albino friend in the hall."

She looked back toward the door. "No, I didn't see anyone," she marched toward me and grabbed my tie, pulling me into a kiss.

"If you ever leave without saying goodbye again, you won't have the opportunity to say hello or goodbye again. The only reason I'm letting it slide this time is that I know how worried you are about Helmsley."

I nodded, finally got my coffee, and headed back into my office. I spent the day trying to get a better grasp of international law regarding the theft of antiquities. Every time I looked up, the sky outside looked worse. If I was in New England, I'd be thinking snow clouds. So, I finally closed the blinds. I had not been able to reach Helmsley and I knew him well enough not to bother leaving a message.

I took Stacy to lunch. She suggested dinner and a club, but I lied and said I had a meeting. I promised tomorrow we could head downtown. I'm not sure if she was disappointed or knew I was lying, but she left work promptly at four, for the first time I could remember. I started looking for international law experts. If things went as badly as I expected, I needed to know who to call. Helmsley could certainly afford the best. I ordered delivery and kept working into the night, listening to the howl of the wind.

I was standing near a building half buried in the snow. It seemed familiar but my attention went to an iceberg slowly sailing up to the dock. I recognized it because of the towers and spires on the top. Ormen Underordnet was suddenly standing next to me. His white suit had been replaced by a shimmering robe of pure white. That's when I realized the building was Helmsley's warehouse. I watched silently as the little man walked out of the building, lifting a statue of a Roman Centurion as if it weighed nothing. The cold didn't seem to bother him as his hands steamed where he touched the figure. As the iceberg gently touched the dock, Underordnet leaped nimbly onto the ice and carried the statue into a cave. He repeated the trip six more times. As he moved back toward the building, a sound echoed across the area.

I had heard that sound before, the whisper of the wind through the sleet, just before it turns into the howl of a nor'easter.

"Your task is complete. Yikilth departs for the Thule."

The albino paused and removed the sunglasses. His eyes were empty sockets and tears of blood rolled down his pasty white face. I suddenly realized he was not a man, but a man-sized maggot.

I woke up on my office couch in the morning, chilled to the bone. I had cracked the office window last night because the heat kicked on and the room was stuffy. But it was 70°F then. Now, I could see my breath.

I got up to shut the window and stopped in disbelief. It was snowing in downtown Los Angeles. I turned on the television—all programming had been preempted by the snow. Locals couldn't drive in the rain, so the snow was just a disaster. Snow had turned the Tenth into an apocalyptic nightmare of car crashes. A rescue chopper had gone down in Hollywood—no one winterized the helicopters, and the governor had grounded all airplanes as a part of a state of emergency.

It looked I wasn't going anywhere. Curious, I got online and researched the last time it snowed in Los Angeles. Aside from a couple of dustings that didn't last, the city had not seen significant snow since 1949.

I called Stacy to make sure she wasn't coming in, and as I hung up, I looked down on the desk—the business card of the albino was sitting on the pile of paper where I left it. I put a pot of coffee to brew and, like an idiot, I finally did what I should have done two days ago—I plugged "Ormen Underordnet" into a search engine. No results. I tried "Rlim Shaikorth Associates." No business with that name, current or past. I expanded the search to international firms—nothing. I tried again just using "Rlim Shaikorth." That got me some results but not anything I was expecting. I found a handful of scholarly citations referring to anthropological research journals I had never heard of. It did give me an idea though.

I pulled one of Helmsley's files and found the phone number for the Sanbourne Institute of Pacific Antiquities. They were far enough down the coast to be out of the

271

snowstorm. Of course, that didn't mean the director was thrilled to hear from me.

"Mr. McAvoy. I appreciate your persistence, but we have not changed our position on loaning the Ponape Figurine."

"Dr. Kester, that's not why I called. Mr. Ainsworth went in a different direction with his next exhibition and no longer needs the figurine. However, he is very disappointed and is considering canceling his annual donation. As I understand, it is a sizeable amount."

Dead silence. "T-that would be unfortunate," I think I could hear flop sweat forming through the phone.

"Dr. Kester," I lied, "I am arguing against ending the annual stipend. And I could use your help."

"Of course. What can I do?"

"Mr. Ainsworth is doing research for an upcoming exhibit on obscure folklore. If you could find some information on a topic he is finding particularly difficult to research, I am sure it would do wonders for mending bridges. Especially if the Sanbourne could find information using the collection he helps underwrite."

Not surprisingly, this seemed like a brilliant idea to the director. I gave him the name of Rlim Shaikorth, and though he was unfamiliar with the name, he assured me he would have a brief profile from their collection as quickly as possible.

I got up for more coffee. It was still snowing. There had to be four and six inches on the ground. It would be an inconvenience in New England, but they had plows and sanders. LA had nothing but construction equipment, ill-suited for this sort of work. The city was paralyzed.

I heard tapping on the door. I went out into reception. Through the glass door, I could see Ormen Underordnet. With a sigh, I unlocked the door.

"Mr. Underordnet, what a delight to see you," again with the lie. "What on Earth are you doing out in this dreadful weather?"

The little albino did the hands steeple and bowed head thing again. "Mr. McAvoy, you honor me with your expression of concern. The cold does not bother me, and travel in snow is a familiar experience."

"Well, I'm sorry you came here for no reason. I haven't been unable to contact Mr. Ainsworth. He forgets to bring his phone with him."

Underordnet frowned. "That is indeed unfortunate. You see, my superior will be arriving momentarily."

I went over to the window and looked. It was still snowing. "Mr. Underordnet, there are no planes or boats arriving in Los Angeles today. I don't even think trains are running."

I turned back to him. He was gone. I never heard the door and he never said goodbye. I stuck my head into the corridor. It was empty and I didn't hear the elevator. He either took the fire stairs of disappeared into thin air. The way this week had been going, I wouldn't discount either theory.

I needed to eat, but none of my usual delivery places were open. I went down the street to a twenty four-hour bodega. I guessed between six or seven inches of snow now— practically apocalyptic by LA standards. I grabbed a loaf of bread and a jar of peanut butter and headed back. Between the menu and the snow, it was like I was back in college in Massachusetts.

I had barely stamped the snow off my shoes when the phone rang. It was Dr. Kester at the Sanbourne. That was fast, and now I wondered exactly how large of a check they got from Helmsley.

"Mr. McAvoy, you can tell our dear friend Helmsley he picked a particularly obscure ancient deity. Fortunately, one of the former curators had put together some notes on the legend. Rlim Shaikorth was part of an ancient pantheon known collectively as 'The Great Old Ones.' It's more of a literary grouping than anthropological—there is a body of uncategorized godlore across the globe that seems connected only by its great age and a lack of known original sources."

"Fascinating," I lied. "So Rlim Shaikorth is just an old fairy tale."

"Oh no, the White Worm myth is far more complicated a myth than that," Dr. Kester said.

"White Worm?" I heard that phrase in my nightmare. It was either an odd coincidence or something very weird was happening.

Dr. Kester took that as encouragement. "Oh, yes. The myth states Rlim Shaikorth was a sorcerer who also happened to be a gigantic, white worm with hollow eyes made of globules of blood that dripped continually, making the charming fellow look like he was weeping blood. He traveled the oceans in a fortress made of ice on a gigantic iceberg called Yikilth, searching for other sorcerers, who he would devour, adding their magic to his. Those that angered the White Worm were frozen solid. Their white bodies so supernaturally cold that they couldn't melt."

Snippets of Helmsley's conversations, my nightmares, and the image of the albino Mr. Underordnet and his red sunglasses were all blurring together in my head. I was getting a bad feeling about where this was going.

Kester kept going. "The White Worm is really a fascinating tale. It only appears in one codex, an untitled manuscript known as the 'Commoriom Myth Cycle.' The only copy is in the *Biblioteca Nacional do Brasil*, supposedly found by Gaspar Corte Real in an ice cave in the Canadian Arctic."

I let him go on. I was trying to figure out how to delicately phrase a question so that it would sound like an art question and not like I was a lunatic.

Finally, I asked. "So, this is obviously a completely fictional story. Is Helmsley liable to stumble across any White Worm cults if he looks for art representing the worm?"

Kester laughed. "No, I think Mr. Ainsworth is safe. It's a very obscure codex, and there are even questions as to the validity. The author claimed to a high priest of Atlantis. He also claimed to have translated it from the original papyrus in ancient Hyperborean."

I vaguely recalled Helmsley saying that name. "I've heard of Atlantis, but Hyperborean is a new one."

Kester seemed to be more warming up to me. "Hyperborea is another myth. According to the ancient Greeks, it was a paradise of eternal spring, located in the far north. Imagine Iceland as a tropical land, and you'll get the idea. According to Klârkash-Tŏn's translation, the Arctic was formed when the Hyperboreans chose to battle the White Worm—and lost. As was his wont, Rlim Shaikorth smote the land, turning it into the arctic tundra it is today. Only one trace of Hyperborea has survived through the ages, only because the Worm kept one of the frozen warriors as a record of his victory, placing the warrior in his ice fortress where he kept a trophy room of such sub-zero monuments of his great victories."

I glanced down at the phone console. A blinking light told me I had a message. Without Stacy handling phones, it would just ring on her desk until it went to voicemail. I thanked Kester and assured him Helmsley would be very grateful.

I hit the button. It was a message from Helmsley. "Hello, Douglas, my boy. I know you're still annoyed with me, but the workmen placed the statues in their positions last night, and I've outdone myself, if I say so myself. Snow or not, I'm heading down there now. I need to look again in case I need any last minute tweaks. Apparently, there is also some sort of alarm going off. The thermostat is sending me an annoying alert telling me the room is getting too cold. I assume one of the workmen turned down the temperature on the refrigeration unit, which I certainly do not need. The statues make the room uncomfortably cold by themselves. Call me, or better yet, pop down for a preview."

I didn't believe in white worms or that bad dreams come true, but I knew one thing for certain—I needed to get Helmsley out there and fast. He wasn't answering his phone, meaning he had probably left it in his car again. I was going to have to drive down to the port. I looked out the window. The snow had stopped, but LA didn't own a snow plow. And like everyone else, I didn't have snow tires or chains. But I was too poor to buy snow tires back in college, so I had a pretty good idea how to deal with snow. The trick would be surviving any other idiots on the road.

I was fighting my way along the I-110, which was a snow-covered parking lot of disabled and abandoned cars, when the phone rang. The caller ID said it was the Los Angeles Fire Department.

"Mr. McAvoy? This is Lieutenant Griffith. Do you know the whereabouts of Mr. Helmsley Ainsworth?"

"I think he's at his warehouse. He left me a note that there was some sort of temperature alarm he needed to reset. It's next to the bridge across to Terminal Island. I'm on my way there now to meet with him."

There was a pause. "Mr. McAvoy, the building is on fire. Mr. Ainsworth's car is here but there's no sign of him. Could he have gone somewhere in another vehicle?" The tone in the fireman's voice suggested he already knew the answer.

I took a breath. "Helmsley would never leave that car behind. I'll be there as quickly as I can. And Lieutenant, be careful, the building is covered in a vapor retardant that's flammable. You know what that means," I didn't get an answer, but I could hear him yelling to someone to tell all teams to pull out.

As it turned out, "quickly" meant another twenty minutes. By the time I arrived, the fire crews weren't even trying to save the building—the dock had caught fire and it was all they could do to keep the fire from spreading along the wooden understructure. The building was fully engulfed in flames and I could feel the heat, yards away. Helmsley's mechanic was correct—the retardant was very flammable. With a screech of metal on metal, the building collapsed into itself and through the weakened dock, the murky harbor water dousing the flames.

The charred remain of his Rolls Royce was the only trace of Helmsley Ainsworth found after the fire was extinguished. The police assumed he died in the fire, trying to save the artwork. That made him a hero in the art community. Helmsley would have loved that irony, considering his low regard of most artists and art buyers. I saw no reason to correct the official report.

You see, the reason it took me twenty minutes to arrive was that I couldn't find a place to turn around. I had already left the warehouse and was heading back to LA. I had arrived just in time to see an iceberg slowly sailing away from the warehouse back toward the ocean. It was definitely being steered, there is no way an iceberg randomly meandered up the harbor main channel to Helmsley's warehouse. I fishtailed to a stop in the parking lot and ran to the building.

The doors were locked, so I went around the building looking for a way in. The side of the warehouse facing the harbor was gone. It wasn't torn open—it was gone. Piles of tiny metal fragments lay along the entrance. I realized as I crossed the threshold that the fragments were the wall. It had shattered like glass. I was standing in a cave of ice. At first, I thought it was Helmsley's exhibit staging, but the cold was much too bitter. I tapped an icicle hanging from the ceiling. It was real and unnaturally cold. My finger burned as if I had touched an open flame. There was only one statue left, in the corner. As soon as I saw it, I realized the legends were all true—the traveling iceberg fortress, the sorcerous White Worm—all of it.

I did what any man would do in such a case. I went a little mad. I ran into the machinery room and turned the refrigeration on full blast. Then I cranked the thermostat onto its lowest setting and ran to my car. The iceberg was all but invisible on the horizon. Rlim Shaikorth had reclaimed his trophies.

I heard the explosion as I drove out of the lot—Mr. Testabianca had been overly optimistic on how long the equipment would operate at maximum settings. By the time I reached the 110 ramp, I could see smoke beginning to billow out of the warehouse. Fortunately, because the city was shut down from the snow, it a while before the fire department was called, arrived, and they called me. By then, it was too late.

277

The building was fully involved. The rest of the details in the fire report are correct.

I got a lovely certificate from the county, claiming that my presence of mind to mention the vapor retardant had saved dozens of firemen. I hung it in the reception where it has remained for the last five years. I don't need to see it and don't need to be reminded of that day. Every night I'm already reminded when the nightmares start, and once again I am standing in the ice-blasted warehouse, viewing the one ice figure the White Worm deemed unworthy to take to his trophy room in his citadel—the one that now rests beneath the new dock that replaced the damaged one. The one I suspect will haunt my nightmares forever, that moment when I found the frozen alabaster image of a terrified Helmsley Ainsworth.

THE MATRON IN THE WOOD

Logan Noble

Nick loved it. Every square inch of it. Every patch of dirt. Every lake. Every fat mosquito buzzing at his ear. *Michigan.* He never thought he'd come back. It had been ten years since he'd last set foot in his home state, which, as far as he was concerned, was ten years too many.

The entire trip from Chicago to his brother Anthony's hunting cabin would take about seven hours. With his cruise set to 80, Nick was making good time. Before too long, the tree line on his left dropped away, revealing the dark body of Lake Michigan. Deep forest unfurled beside the road. A majority of the Upper Peninsula was made up of state forests like the one to his right, massive stretches of uninterrupted forestry, often extending for over fifty miles.

Nick peeked into the back seat. His hunting rifle was there, along with a bag of clothes for the long weekend. *Three days of hunting at his brother Anthony's cabin.* Though it had been a few years since they'd met up for their hunting trip, Nick couldn't wait. Bruce was flying in from upstate New York to meet up with them. Anthony had been in his cabin now for a couple of months, doing God knows what, in the rural area that served as their home town.

He hadn't seen Anthony since the funeral. Nick grimaced. Anthony had married a woman named Laura that worked with him at their architecture firm. They'd been married for about three years before she'd developed a bad case of cancer. He couldn't help but feel bad for his own behavior after that. Nick never drove up to visit. He'd never called. He'd created wild narratives to rationalize his behavior. That's why he'd been relieved (if not a bit apprehensive) when Anthony had called him up to invite him to the cabin.

The highway eventually bled into dirt. The road curved and Nick slowed. There, among the wilderness, was Anthony's hunting cabin. It was a true beauty. It was outfitted with an enormous porch and a back balcony, along with huge picture windows and a full kitchen. It was a far cry from the kind of hunting cabins they'd grown up in.

Nick shoved his car into park and grabbed his rifle and bag from the back seat. When he got out of the car, the thick forest air swallowed him up. He smelled pine and cedar. Crickets and other insects chittered. With his eyes set on the front porch light, he made his way across the yard. Parked off to the side were Anthony and Bruce's vehicles, a massive Chevy (Anthony) and a nondescript Subaru (Bruce). He gave the front door a knock before turning the knob and pressing in.

Just as he did, Bruce stepped out of the hallway. Bruce was an old family friend. He'd also grown up in their hometown of Carpenter's Landing and, much like the Maynard boys, had moved on to greener pastures when given the chance. He was a college professor at some microscopic liberal arts school just south of Buffalo. He was married and had three kids, each more ginger-haired and green-eyed than the last. When Bruce saw him, he threw up his hands.

"Nick! Glad to see you, man!" Bruce walked across the room and the two men gave each other a hug. "How was the drive?"

Nick shrugged. "Long. I'm worn out."

"I bet! Is it like 8 hours?"

"More or less," Nick looked around the lodge again. "Where's Anthony?"

Bruce adjusted his glasses. "That's a good question. He ran off into the woods somewhere. He keeps saying something about a big surprise that he can't wait to show us."

Nick raised an eyebrow. "I don't know if I like that."

Bruce chuckled. "Yeah. You want a beer?"

After they cracked open the cans, they settled in at the card table, quickly falling back into their easy rapport. They talked about the good old days. Getting drunk on cheap beer. Bonfires by the lake. A couple of brushes with the law. Then they talked about everything else. How Bruce's kids were doing (the older one is playing soccer, though she really isn't very good). How their jobs were getting along ('same old, same old' and 'they don't pay us enough, but we have to go anyway'). The two of them finished off three beers apiece before Bruce belched and trundled off down the hallway to turn in for the night.

Nick fetched his jacket off the back of one of the leather couches and stepped outside. He dug out his Marlboros and lit one up, leaning on the railing to look out into the forest. If he squinted, he could just make out the break in the trees where their hunting path began. That path wound for acres and acres into Anthony's dense land. He'd built stands in the trees for each of them, basically dividing their hunting area into three parts.

Nick took another deep puff from the cigarette just as he saw his brother's unmistakable shape emerge from the mouth of the trail. Anthony's wide frame solidified in the limited light as he got closer.

When Anthony reached the porch, Nick got a better look. He was dressed in a heavy jacket and blue jeans, his hair hidden beneath a wool cap. He looked older. Haggard.

"Well, hello, Nick," Anthony said, stomping up the stairs. "When did you get in?"

Nick flicked some ash off the end of his cigarette. "Few hours ago. I've just been hanging here with Bruce," Nick motioned at the forest with his cigarette. "What are you doing out there so late?"

Anthony flashed his trademark grin. "I'm working on something. A surprise. I think you and Bruce are going to be impressed."

"You building a big birdhouse?"

His brother shrugged and went to the door. "Something like that," with that, Anthony pushed open the front door and vanished into the darkness of the entranceway.

Well, Nick thought, *someone is being mysterious.* He took one last puff from his cigarette and dropped it off the porch.

Nick made his way back into the quiet cabin. Anthony, though he'd just went in, was nowhere to be found. Nick wandered down the hallway toward the bedrooms. Anthony always stayed in the final room at the end of the hall. His door was shut tight. Soft light spilled out beneath it. *Burning the midnight oil.* It always surprised him how little things actually change.

A knock at his door. Nick sat up in bed, the blanket a tangle around his legs. He looked around the room, his eyes heavy. His bag sat on the floor beside a small bedside table. A window, with the blinds drawn but slotted, showed that it was still dark outside. He didn't remember going to bed. He must have been exhausted. The knock came again.

"Hey, dummy. Wake up. We gotta' kill some stuff," Bruce's voice, muffled on the other side. Nick cleared his throat.

"Yeah. I'll be out in a minute."

Nick kicked the blankets off and rolled out of bed, stretching. His muscles felt taut and sore. He dug out a clean tee-shirt from his bag and shrugged it on. He finished getting dressed and stepped out into the hallway. Though they were just out of sight, Nick could hear Anthony and Bruce talking. Muffled laughter. The clink of silverware. And, above it all, the smell of eggs.

Anthony and Bruce turned to him when he entered. Bruce was at the stove, one hand on a large pan and the other around a coffee mug. Anthony grinned at him over his coffee.

"Look who decided to wake up."

"I figured I should probably get up to make sure you old men would be ready," Nick said.

Bruce snorted. "I'm still young enough to rearrange your teeth."

Nick waved his comment away and walked into the kitchen, grabbing a coffee mug from the nearest cabinet. He poured himself a cup and found his seat at the table.

"So what's the plan? Same positions as always?"

Anthony shook his head. "Slightly different this year."

Bruce brought two plates and set them in front of Nick and Anthony. "What do you mean? We can't buck tradition!"

Anthony glared at Bruce. "This year, we are. I don't want you two getting a peek at what I have planned."

Nick and Bruce shared a look. Bruce rolled his eyes and went back to fetch the scrambled eggs.

"Soon as we eat, we'll head out. We have to try and beat the sun."

The morning air was brisk. As they walked across the dead yard toward the forest path, Nick thought about the way his brother had emerged from the opening the night prior. *What the hell is he doing all the way out there?* Whatever it was, he was playing it close to the chest.

From his vantage point up on his tree stand, Nick watched the sun arrive, overexposing the forest in harsh light. A low mist had crept up on the forest floor below. Nick swept the woods with his eyes, squinting into the haze. Up here, mid-way up the tree, he could see quite a distance. He knew that, if he could sprout wings and take off of his stand, he'd be able to fly straight over the forest and into Carpenter's Creek. So many memories. Some good. Others, not so much.

Nick tugged his left hand out of his glove and picked up the binoculars he'd slung over his neck. He put them to his eyes, bringing the distant parts of the woods into stark view. He scanned the tree line, picking out all the oddities of the forest. A moss-covered stump. A felled pine absorbed into the undergrowth.

Movement.

Nick sat up, dropping the binoculars to his chest. He brought his gun to his shoulder and squinted down the scope. He saw antlers. *It's a buck!* But—

The figure stopped and the antlers swung up. Nick stared, his rifle dropping away from his eye.

It was a woman. There, maybe less than a mile away, standing among the ancient white pines and the amber shades of autumn leaves. The woman had to be over 6 feet tall. *No.* Taller than that. Completely naked, coarse hair hanging down past her breasts. At that distance, her face was an indistinct smudge. Nick blinked. Antlers pushed from the top of her head, brushing the tree beside her as she turned his way. Nick's mouth had gone dry. He was transfixed. He realized that he *had* to get a closer look. Every fiber of his being demanded it. He edged toward the ladder. The deer woman stared. An icy autumn wind made the leaves whisper, secrets of a winter to come. He would—

A gunshot cut through the forest, disrupting the deathly silence. Nick startled and gripped the tree behind him. He jerked his eyes toward the sound *(west, where Bruce was)* before looking back to the deer woman. She was gone. Nick cursed and brought the binoculars back up to his eyes. He frantically searched the forest floor, scanning from east to west, west to east. She had run off.

His walkie-talkie beside him chirped. Bruce's voice cleaved through a wall of static.

"I saw something! But I think—I think I missed it."

Nick pulled the radio from his belt and went to respond before pausing. What was he going to say? That he saw a naked woman with deer horns out in the woods? Bruce and Anthony would laugh him out of camp. He lowered the radio.

Anthony's voice crackled over the radio next.

"Let's meet up. I doubt we'll see any deer now. They won't be coming around."

Nick slid his walkie-talkie into his belt and gathered up his things. The leaves rustled and fell around him. The image of the deer woman replayed in his mind over and over. Nick began to climb down the makeshift ladder on the side of the tree, with his rifle, which hung from a strap around his shoulders, bouncing against his ribs.

When the two other men emerged from the dense tree line, they looked different than before. Anthony, with his grey hairs and wrinkles, looked older than ever. His face had been drawn tight. His hair, free of his wool cap, was messy and spiked with sweat. But he was still smiling. Bruce, on the other hand, looked completely exhausted. His glasses had fallen partway down his nose and his shoulders were slouched.

"What did you see, Bruce?" Nick called out.

Bruce picked up his head and his mouth worked itself into an uneasy smile. "A deer."

Something in his tone was wrong.

"A buck?"

"No. Looked like a doe," he paused. "I took a shot and I wasn't even close."

The three of them silently trudged back down the path, their boots crunching dead leaves. Something had changed among them. Bruce had lowered his head again, his thoughts elsewhere. Anthony led them, grinning that vile grin that he'd mastered in his concrete-jungle world. Nick smoked another cigarette, hoping that the shake in his hands would go away.

By the time they found themselves back in the cabin, Bruce's easy-going manner had returned. Things snapped back into place, back to how they were supposed to be. They settled in—per hunting tradition—at the card table. Bruce fetched a cold beer for each and Anthony dealt out the cards.

The game drew on. Then, at the end of a brutal hand, Anthony spoke up.

"Let's mix things about a bit."

Nick waved at Bruce, who took his turn. "What do you mean?"

"Either of you ever see a ghost?"

Both Nick and Bruce looked at Anthony. Anthony's face was stone calm. His eyes had taken on a steely cruelty.

"I assume you haven't. But I'm curious."

Bruce cleared his throat. When he spoke, his words were slurred. "Ghosts aren't real, Anthony."

"You don't think so?" Anthony turned his eyes on Nick. Nick felt his skin crawl. *He knows what you saw. And maybe what Bruce saw—*

"I don't see what this has to do with this hand, Anthony."

His brother ignored him. His tone, though still edged with a slight touch of malice, had become conversational. "You know, these woods are haunted."

Bruce squirmed. "Does anyone else need another beer? I think I do. I'm going to grab one—"

"These lands are stained with the blood of countless Native Americans. They were killed by the British. By the French before them," a dark weight was pulling at Anthony's face even as his strong, deep voice washed over them. "When the immigrants started coming north to work the mines, they used to tell them to steer clear of these woods. Said that there was something unnatural about them."

Bruce spoke up, his voice quiet. "We all know the history around here. Why the hell are we talking about this?"

Nick swallowed. He could feel his heart racing in his chest. He didn't believe in ghosts. Or monsters. Those kinds of things existed only in Stephen King books.

"I think it's important. I've been looking into it recently. It's very fascinating. This place is perfect for all kinds of bad things. It works better here. Maybe it's the soil? I don't know. But, of course, bad things happening around here is documented even further past the Native Americans. This region is older than that. *Much* older."

Bruce stood up suddenly, his eyes bulging. "Enough! I've had enough of this. If you're going to behave this way, I want no part of it," Bruce shoved his chair aside and stumbled into the hallway. Nick watched him go, wishing he was doing the same. Instead, he locked eyes with his brother. Anthony was back to grinning.

"Bruce scares easy."

"What's gotten into you? Some people don't like that kind of thing."

"What? History?"

Nick suppressed the urge to knock that smile right off Anthony's face. The night had taken a sudden turn into the nasty.

"No. Superstition."

"Just because something scares us doesn't mean it didn't happen," Anthony looked out the closest window. "The people up here used to worship all kinds of gods. Missionaries brought them among the uncivilized masses. French fur traders. Explorers. And gods…" Anthony sighed, "Gods remember. Even when people stop worshipping them, they remember. And they're always hungry."

Nick stood up, his hip smashing the table. A can tipped over and sent beer flying.

"I think you've spent too much time up here by yourself," Nick said, his voice hard. He was practically shaking with rage. "You've forgotten how to play nice."

With that, Nick turned and strode away, leaving the beer to soak into their cards. As he walked into the hallway, he felt Anthony's eyes on his back.

That night, he dreamed of empty darkness. It was a bare canvas, a blank page and a shapeless blueprint all at once. Nick gasped at the empty atmosphere around him. Then, as panic began to set in, the setting began to form.

First, the theater seats. Red velvet. Dusty and cobwebbed with disuse. Nick fell into the nearest one, his body gone rag-doll limp. The stage leaped into existence next, board by board, each gouged and scarred from the thousands of feet that had crossed over them. Stage lights sheered through the protuberant dark. At the back edge of the stage, the curtains loomed. The folds flowed, swaying and rippling, a fabric that closed in the stage before it. A building formed around Nick next, walls clicking into the ceiling with the great grind of tectonic plates. Nick swallowed a scream, pushing it down his windpipe and into his stomach.

The curtains pulled open. The motion, spasmodic and violent, made his gullet rise and shudder. A play was unfolding before him. A king in yellow tatters sat on a throne. He was a facade, pallid-faced and sullen. A court of partisans crowned out around him, a wrong-angled spread of scattered colors. Nick's eyes drug across them, every fiber of his being howling for him to look elsewhere, *anywhere.*

The court watched the action in the shadow of twin suns. A woman drifted out before them. She was dressed in amber robes, her head down, a curved bonnet hiding her face from view. The hot lights pinned her shadow to the swaying curtains. Though there was nothing to cast them, her shadow sported antlers, pressing into the rafters, bisecting into thousands and thousands of points, pushing into the outer dark beyond. *She was The Matron, a matriarch to all the unholy things that tear themselves into reality.*

She began to speak. Nick's ears *hummed.* Visions struck him. An alien forest below an alien sky. A child with too many appendages being born into the black dirt. Nick saw the wriggling horror his life pinpointed, shrinking and shrinking. The woman, The Matron, was there. *She was always there. As the Great Old Ones are born, The Matron is there to guide them on.* The court applauds. She is a servant to that ancient order. The squirming mass is growing. The cosmos ripples across its flesh. Its mouths wheeze into a Hyperborean eternity.

The Matron carries the squirming monstrosity to a cathedral. The grand cathedral sheers at reality, cracking at its porous edges. Every curve and beam holds her will. She sets the child aside. The Matron begins to strip, revealing amber wonders in every layer. Human flesh turns to fur. Her bones twist and change, the great snapping sound of bone breaking from bone consuming everything. A name is whispered into his ear. *Yhoundeh.* Nick tries to look away. But he can't. He knows that as much as he knows he's dreaming. But he knows so much more. There is something in the design of that cathedral, something that harkens out to the stars that have long burnt out.

Anthony is suddenly in the seat beside him.

"She spoke to me, Nick. So, I built it for her. No one will ever forget her again."

The curtains ripple. The lights burn. Nick gasps for air, his throat constricting.

Before him, the show is starting.

Nick jerked awake, his eyes flying open. He sat up, his heart pounding in his chest. *What the hell!?* The name, hissed in his nightmare, sticks with him. *Yhoundeh.*

His room had gone cold. Grey sunlight pushed through the bedroom's smudged glass. Nick went to the window, pulling aside the thin curtain. The entire yard was covered in snow. *It must have snowed through the night,* Nick thought. He let the curtain fall and went out into the hallway. Nick looked to Anthony's door. It was wide open, revealing the corner of his bed, the sheets balled up at the end. He went to Bruce's door next, knocking on it lightly.

"Hey, Bruce! Wake up!"

No answer. Nick sighed. A sense of unease crept over him. Where are they? Maybe after the awkwardness of last night, they'd set out hunting separately? He reached down and turned the knob, stepping into Bruce's room. His bed was also empty.

Nick walked down the hallway, his bare feet thudding on the hardwood floor. He paused at the gun rack, counting the rifles stashed there. There was only one gone. And it was Anthony's.

He didn't bother to put on socks. Nick tugged on his boots and grabbed a heavy jacket from the hook by the door. His unpleasant feeling had slipped straight into panic. He tried to contain himself. He was trying to rationalize this as something normal. But that didn't sit right with him. Anthony had a surprise for them. He'd said as much. Nick intended to see *exactly* what that meant.

Nick went to the gun rack and picked up his rifle. He hoped to God he wouldn't need it. He had no reason to believe Anthony had cracked. His brother's behavior had been strange but not unheard of. He was being strange and that was it. He checked to make sure the gun was loaded. *Strange. Yeah. Let's hope that's all it is.*

The winter air was violently frigid. Nick padded down the stairs, pulling up his hood. He looked to the ground, eyeing the snow for tracks. With the way the snow was falling now, heavy and fat, any tracks that Anthony and Bruce had left would be filled in before too long. After a second of scanning the ground, Nick found them. Two sets of boot prints, trampled together into the wet snow. With his rifle clenched in his gloved hands, he began to follow them.

As Nick walked, he kept his eyes peeled for movement. The forest had gone unnaturally silent. No squirrels chittered. No birds called. His boots crunched at snow and his breath steamed into the air. Nick half expected to see his deer woman, standing out among the bent pines, eyes fixed on him. *Yhoundeh.* A nonsense word uttered into the strange fabric of his dream.

When he reached the fork in the path, Nick looked to the tracks. The snow was falling harder now, the heavy flakes settling onto the old snowfall. It looked like the tracks led off to the left, but he couldn't be sure. Nick thought quickly, pushing his mind back to the day before. Anthony had switched up their positions. He'd wanted the farthest blind to stop them from seeing what he had been building out here. It was settled, then. The left path would take him into the depths of Anthony's property. Nick pressed on.

The path wove and eventually became narrower. The forest was beginning to change. Tufts of thick grass protruded from the blanket of snow. Thick roots had wormed onto the narrow path, curving from the snow like serpents from a black ocean. When the trees began to bend and twist, Nick somehow knew he was getting close.

He saw the building first. A wooden spire peeking out between the alien trees. The path was curving. Nick followed it, his gun at the ready. The wind tore at the trees around him, raking at the monstrous branches. Nick turned right. Left. The path opened.

A clearing. And, at the center of it, a structure unlike anything Nick had ever seen. 'Cathedral' was the word that came to mind, though that might not be accurate. He gaped at it, his mind drawn to all the symbols and designs before him. The front of the cathedral had no door. The front face's wood had been cut and shaped, creating ideograms that grew increasingly more elaborate and strange as Nick's eyes traced upward. The cathedral had to be over fifteen feet tall. Its roof, on one portion, curved down. Another portion curved up at an extreme angle. The more Nick stared, the more unsure he was of anything about it. It was an enigma made physical. The spire that rose from the top was serrated and etched. At its base, cut deep into dark wood, was a carved set of antlers.

"It's incredible, isn't it?"

Anthony's voice came from behind him. Nick turned, bringing his gun up. It didn't even make it halfway up before he saw that Anthony already had him in his crosshairs. One barrel. A round, oiled darkness.

"Put the gun down, Nick. We need to talk."

Nick did as he had been told, dropping the rifle into the snow beside his feet. Anthony was not dressed for the weather. He wore a long sleeve shirt and jeans, his hair wild and his eyes shining. Nick thought he looked insane. Except that wasn't quite right. There was something else behind Anthony's eyes. A shape. A knowledge.

"Where's Bruce?"

Anthony lowered his rifle lightly.

"He's fine."

Nick turned his head quickly to look at the makeshift cathedral. Though he was furious, he'd found a cold calm. *You might die here. Out among the snow. He's killed Bruce and you're next.*

"Put down the gun, Anthony. I can't talk if someone has a gun on me."

"I will. But first, I need to explain."

"Explain, then. What in the hell is happening? What is *this*?" Nick motioned one gloved hand toward the building.

"Do you remember Laura?" Anthony's voice cracked as he said her name. It was slight. But Nick heard it nevertheless.

"Of course I do."

"Good. Good! Do you remember her funeral? Every word the priest spoke as they lowered her down into the ground? Because I do. It wasn't fair. I knew it. Everyone knew it. The way cancer just crept up and just snuffed her out.

"I went crazy in my own house. I went crazy at work. I had a dozen buildings I was overseeing. I couldn't focus on a single one of them. I had to get out of New York. I sure as hell couldn't come back here. Laura loved these woods. Loved our little house. No. I had to go elsewhere.

"I traveled. I made a tour of it. I figured if I saw some of the world's most impressive architecture designs, it would snap me the hell out of it. Put all my pieces back together. I went everywhere to see buildings I've only ever seen in textbooks. The Sydney Opera House. The Shard in London. The Louvre. Nothing worked. So I went older. The Great Pyramids. The Saksaywaman in Peru. I saw carvings in caves and great murals dedicated to gods of every culture. Eventually, I found my way to Greenland. There is a dormant volcano there among the ice that houses temples unlike anything else the world has ever seen. I spent a lot of time in those temples, struggling to make sense of the history of such a place. I got most of my story from a holy man in the nearest village."

Anthony was rambling now. Every word thudded into the space between them, the barrel of his rifle bobbing as he spoke. Nick didn't take his eyes off it.

"The stories go like this: before Greenland was covered in ice, there was a civilization that lived there. They had a god they worshipped that watched over them. She was their matron. She protected them from dangers that could befall them. They loved her. They built temples to honor her. These ancient people believed that the best way to earn The Matron's favor was through what she whispered for them to build. She found great joy in these elaborate temples, and some of these early men thought she drew power from them."

"This god. What was her name?" Nick said, his voice wavering.

Anthony licked his lips. "Yhoundeh. But I think you already knew that."

Nick did. He thought he knew where this story was going to, as well. He thought he knew the purpose of the structure behind him.

"I found a new life there, among the carvings. Among the stories of those terrified people. They worshipped Yhoundeh until a greater force came along. A great frog god from some distant world. The fools dropped Yhoundeh and flocked to the new power among them. They demolished her temples and slandered her name. She died as they pulled the pillars down and smashed her statues across the tiles. She fell back to her world. Far away."

"And what," Nick said, "This is your offering to some fake pagan god?"

"No! Not at all! That's the wonderful thing about it! I learned what I could about Yhoundeh. I copied all those symbols that had been carved into the amber clays of those caves. She's been following me. Ever since then. Perhaps even before that."

Nick closed his eyes. His nightmare played out before him. Yhoundeh guiding a shapeless monstrosity into the world.

"This is nonsense, Anthony. Please stop this—"

"Every old god gets a chance to be young again. I've spent months with her in these woods. She's shown me everything that I need to bring her back. She has Gods that even she must serve. Much like those humans that once worshipped her, she has a duty to the great ones that live beside Lake Hali. And she has a duty to the great ones that she will help usher into the new world."

The wind had begun to pick up as Anthony was talking, stirring the alien forest around them. Nick could *feel* the cathedral pulling at his back, tugging him toward its foul radiance. Nick kept his hands up.

"What happens now? Now that you're finished? You worship her? Bring her burned offerings?" Nick gave what he hoped was a trustworthy smile.

"No. The door will open and Yhoundeh will come through. This forest will finish its transformation. Then she will take me away to old Carcosa to meet the court." Anthony turned his gaze upward toward the sky. Snow swirled. "Then we shall rule together. Because of what *I* did. Because of what I *made*. I'm in control. I'm—"

Nick lunged, catching ahold of the end of the rifle. Anthony snarled and tugged back at it. Nick held on and pointed the rifle away. They grappled in the wet snow. Nick threw an elbow and caught Anthony in the chest. Both men went down, thrashing over the rifle.

"Let GO!" Anthony howled, rolling onto Nick. His brother was too strong. Nick gasped for air as the hard metal edge of the gun dug into his throat, pushing him into the snow. He grabbed for purchase. Anthony shifted, pressing his weight down. His mouth was open wide, a high howl escaping his lips.

His world was fading. Behind Anthony's head, behind his mad visage, Nick saw the sky. The branches of the trees pressed out and up toward the blank canvas. The stone floor of a throne room began to form. Snow fell from the solid world onto the world of tattered yellow. Nick's hands were wandering. *Up.* Warm flesh. Darkness impeded. Yhoundeh's wards writhed in that space. The great elk-goddess laughed into the void. Her time was returning. Her prison was so cold. So *empty*. Carcosa called her. Earth called her. The court needed her as much as much as she needed them…

Nick's thumb caught something wet.

He pressed with everything he had.

His breath rushed back into his chest, the air slapping him back to reality. Anthony was screaming as Nick ripped his thumb from his eye socket. Anthony fell away, his massive hands clamped to his face. Blood ran into snow. Nick, still gasping for air, scrambled to his knees. He swept the ground for Anthony's rifle. Eventually he found it, pinned beneath Anthony's writhing body.

Nick grabbed it and tugged it out from beneath his brother. Anthony sat up suddenly, still howling. His hands dropped away, revealing a punctured red hole where most of his eye had been only seconds before. Nick stumbled to his feet. He gripped the rifle, the metal and wood slick with water and blood. As Anthony heaved himself up, Nick took a step forward and drove the butt of the rifle into his face.

Once he was sure that Anthony was unconscious, Nick stumbled toward the cathedral. He tried not to look directly at it. Instead, he kept his eyes glued to the ground, hoping to find tracks that would lead him to Bruce. Nick skirted the edge of the building, dismayed at the heat he felt baking off it. The heat stank of blood and dirt. As he found himself at one of the shifting corners, Nick spotted Bruce's prone figure there in the snow.

Nick gasped and rushed over to Bruce, dropping to his knees beside him. Though his eyes were closed, he appeared to be breathing. His hands were tied with twine. Nick grabbed at it, trying to unwind it. He needed to hurry. Nick found the knot and pulled it free.

"Come on, Bruce! Wake up!" Nick tossed the twine aside and shook Bruce's shoulders. Bruce's eyes slowly flickered open. "Can you walk? We need to get out of here, NOW."

Nick helped him to his feet. Bruce's eyes darted around wildly.

"We have to go before Anthony finds us! He's lost it!" Bruce mumbled.

"I know. We need to get out of here. This may sound crazy, but Anthony isn't alone. He's—"

"The deer woman," Bruce wavered on his feet. "I saw her when we were out hunting. I took a shot at her. And I saw her again as Anthony walked me out here. He was going to make us go inside this thing…"

Nick grabbed his shoulder and pulled him along. "He told me the whole thing. Now, let's go."

The wind whipped the snow into the air. The twisted trees bent wildly, lashing at the earth with its spread branches. Something was out among the trees. Massive. It pushed its way between them. *It's not Yhoundeh. At least not all of her. It's only one part...* Antlers towered among the trees. Pale flesh melded with matted amber fur. The deer woman had grown into something terrible.

"We need to run," Nick shoved Bruce. "GO!"

Nick leapt over Anthony's unconscious body and they raced down the path. The snowfall had whipped itself into a blizzard. Claw-like branches reached for them. They didn't slow down. Bruce was wheezing beside him. They ran and ran, sweat dripping. Nick's heart slammed into his ribcage, his vision wavering. The great deer-beast crashed onto the trail behind them. The earth shook. The sky spun. The alien trees began to thin as they reached the fork and the hunting cabin came into view. Neither men slowed down. They ran until they reached Nick's car. They both stopped, gasping for air. Nick hazarded a look backward. The path was clear. The deer-beast was nowhere to be seen.

"What...now?" Bruce gasped, his face burning red.

Nick didn't turn away from the path. He remembered the way the forest had changed. Yhoundeh's alien influence. *What would happen if she finds her way here? From whatever world she calls home?*

"We should leave, Nick! Call the police! Call the Army!" Bruce said, following Nick's gaze back toward the tree line.

"No," Nick said. He had one last thing he had to do before this could be settled. He walked away from Bruce and toward his car. He popped the trunk. Inside was a can of gasoline. He fetched it out, the heavy *slosh* sound a solid comfort after so much horror.

He was going to burn it down.

"You can't be heading back out there! That's insane! That...that monster will tear you apart!" Bruce stepped in front of him. "We should *leave*!"

Nick ignored him and went to Anthony's massive truck. He pulled the snowy handle and tore it open. There, in the cup holder, were the keys.

The cab smelled like sawdust, and now, with the gas can on the passenger seat, of gasoline. Nick started it up and slammed the truck into gear. He tore across the yard and onto the path, meeting Bruce's stare briefly before sweeping past him.

It was a rough ride. The truck rocked and groaned as Nick forced it faster and faster. Trees wiped by. The path forked. And, just like he had earlier, he went left. When he reached the changed trees, he peered out of the fogged-up windshield into the mess of forest around him. The situation was worsening. The trees, once thin and weak-looking, had thickened and grown. Nick, through the fogged glass, caught sight of animalistic figures moving amongst the trunks. *Yhoundeh's servants.* Nick kept his eyes forward and his foot nailed to the pedal. He wasn't stopping now. No matter the cost.

Eventually, the path closed in. Nick slammed on the brakes and leaned forward. He'd run out of space to drive on. The cathedral was straight ahead, through a mess of transforming forest. He had to continue by foot. He reached over and grabbed the gasoline and the rifle. He had his cigarette lighter tucked away his jeans pocket, ready to go.

Nick leapt out and didn't even bother to shut the truck door behind him. He rushed down the pathway. Nick could hear the creatures over his shoulder. He had to hurry.

The path opened up, spilling Yhoundeh's cathedral into view. The damned thing seemed to be *growing*. The edges had become more solid. The wood had transformed into some kind of ancient-looking amber stone. On the front face, where nothing had been minutes before, a door was forming. Just an outline now, the frame still hazy and indistinct. *You're running out of time.* As the blizzard pelted him, Nick sprinted at the church, the rifle stashed under his arm while working the plastic top of the gas can off. It came away with an audible *pop.* The sweetly acrid smell of gasoline wormed its way into the air.

The can was full, sloshing. Nick leaned forward and drenched the side of the church. The gasoline dribbled down the side, headed for the melted snow at the base. He worked his way around the church in that same way, splashing out gasoline as fast as he could. The woods groaned behind him. Something massive was headed his way. With sweat dripping from his face, he tossed the gas can aside, plucked his lighter from his pocket, and flicked the wheel.

A flame popped up, battling against the grey light and snow around it. Something grunted behind him. The sound was guttural. Nick smelled pain and despair, rotten flesh and maggots. Nature, nature of a faraway horror world, perverted.

Nick tossed the lighter at the building.

Time slowed. Nick followed the flame with his eyes, glinting, flickering. For that eternity caged in a second, he saw the world beyond. Anthony's skill had brought Yhoundeh's world into view. An alien world behind the incandescent door. Primordial trees, as black as oil. Great creatures that rushed past their swollen roots. Teeth. Blood. Yhoundeh among them. Towering. Godlike, eyes gone dark with rage. Antlers raked at her prison's sky. The court, just outside of view, screamed into the closing void.

The flame caught.

There was a great *WHOOSH.*

Nick stumbled backward, the heat nearly bowling him over. The cathedral, though wet with the violent snowfall, caught like kindling. The fire roared from the base upward, burning through whatever foul magic it contained. Black smoke billowed into the sky.

He turned away from it, ready to meet his fate. Instead of nightmarish creatures, he was greeted with a transformation. The alien trees were shrinking again, the swollen branches and bent trunks breaking back into their normal shape. All the creatures that had chased him were gone.

Nick blinked at it all as the heat radiated against his back. There in the snow lay Anthony, curled into the fetal position.

He walked slowly toward his brother. When he reached his brother's side, he collapsed in the snow beside him, facing the fire.

Anthony blinked at him with one good eye.

"You did it," he said, his voice nearly inaudible against the roar of the fire.

"I did."

They sat in silence. Fire rose up, higher and higher. All the symbols and intricate shapes burned away, reduced to nothing.

Anthony slowly uncurled and pushed himself into a seating position. From far off, drifting through the winter greyness and the forest below it, Nick could hear sirens. His brother spoke up again, this time a bit louder.

"Thank you, Nick. Thank you."

Nick nodded.

As distant red and blue lights bounced their way through the woods around them, Nick and Anthony watched the building burn.

THE DUKE OF RUST

MaTT Loughlin

"Dammit!" Cricket Simmons shouted. He'd missed his train. Out of breath, he stopped and let his roller-case fall to the ground. Ha—roller-case, indeed. The damn thing barely rolled, bucking and turning as he ran, like a stubborn bass fighting a line. He kicked the case and called it a bastard. Better to blame the shortcomings of his luggage than his own.

Still, he felt like a victim of circumstance. There was supposedly work being done on several of the main train lines, which had forced interruptions into normal service. As a result, he'd had to endure two frantic transfers just to get to this point. And this train (or, rather, *that* train—the train that he was now losing sight of around a bend) would have finally brought him to the airport. But his last train had been late, which forced him to have to run down the platform, up across an overpass, and down to the platform on the other side to catch his connection—which he'd missed.

He sighed. He hated running, especially when it got him nowhere.

Cricket had really like England up until this point. The trip to Bristol, where he'd attended a tattoo convention, went smooth enough. As did his trip down to Cornwall to visit a friend. But the journey home was gearing up to be a real bastard. At this point, Heathrow Airport seemed like a distant dream, some mythical place. El Dorado. Atlantis. Heathrow.

Huffing and sweating and still whispering abuse to his roller-case, Cricket looked up at a digital time display above him: an hour and a half. That was how long he was going to have to wait for the next train. *Dammit.*

He trudged over to a bench and plopped down on it. He looked around: It was the middle of the afternoon but both platforms were empty; they looked abandoned, a place the world forgot. He pulled out his phone, then put it back in his pocket, sick of looking at the damned thing. He wished he had a book to read, even though he never read. He thought about digging through his case for his headphones, but his will had left him.

He could do a bit of a drawing. He had a few tattoo commissions coming up, and it would be smart to get a jump on the artwork. But his pens and paper were in his case, too, so he wouldn't be doing that either. He felt like doing nothing, felt tired, fatigued, and hopeless that he'd ever make it on the plane back to LA. He still had four hours until his flight, plenty of time, but the way his day was going the next train would probably be late, too. He decided to push that chain of thought out of his mind for the time being; no sense in worrying about something you have no control over. He'd just wait for the next train, keep his fingers, toes, and testicles crossed that it wouldn't be late. After about fifteen minutes of sitting there, watching a bird pick at something dead between the tracks, Cricket decided to wander around a bit. He still had over an hour until the train came. What else was he going to do?

The station was surrounded by a quaint little village named Dingle Mockbridge, which made Cricket smile. The British and their quaint yet crazy names. He'd driven through a village called Buttsbear Cross in Cornwall, no lie. This place, like most of the places he'd been in the UK, looked old. *Really* old. The cobbled streets and stone cottages with their tilting slate roofs made you feel as though you had wandered onto the set of a costume drama. Cricket loved that about the UK, how it exuded deep history and almost brought you back and forth through time.

His first stop was the pub, which was just across the street from the train station. It was called The Purple Hen, and though he couldn't quite put his finger on why, he thought the place was well-named. He ordered a pint of whatever had the highest alcohol content and settled into a window booth next to the front door. As he sipped his beer—which tasted like a musty old dishcloth—he watched the empty street through a bleary stained-glass window.

Absolutely no one was around. In fact, since he'd stepped foot off the train, the bartender who served him was the only person he'd seen. It was weird, even for a little village in the middle of nowhere. The bar, like the town, was empty and lifeless; it didn't even have Wi-Fi.

Twenty minutes later, after fiddling on his phone and choking down the rest of his stale beer, Cricket found himself standing on the street again, wondering what to do next. He walked aimlessly up and down the main street, desperate for something interesting to jump out at him, but nothing did. He'd given up and decided to go back to the train station when he noticed a little sign tacked to the corner of a weather-beaten barn. It read: THIS WAY TO THE EMPORIUM. A blue, sun-cracked arrow pointed down a narrow path to the right of the barn. What the Hell, Cricket thought, at least the detour would burn up a few minutes. So, he turned right and followed the narrow, winding path lined with vines and fragrant honeysuckle. It led between the backs of houses to a ramshackle structure that Cricket realized was tacked onto the back end of the train station. It was long and lopsided, made of what looked like painted sheets of corrugated steel. Still, the place had a shabby sense of dignity to it. The building was freshly painted and there was not a spec of litter in the vicinity. Whoever ran this place took pride in their work and tried to wring every ounce of aesthetic pleasantness they could out of what might have once been a rough-shot utility shed or storage depot. He climbed the metal stairs and peered through a spotless Art Deco glass door: it was an antiques shop, and it was full from floor to ceiling. Deciding to err on the side of caution, he parked his roller-case outside and went in. He doubted someone would take it, and if they did, they wouldn't be able to run away with the damn thing. It wouldn't let them.

A tiny bell rung as he entered the shop. An ancient man reading a paper sat behind an equally ancient oak desk. The man nodded to Cricket but did not look up. The air was redolent of pipe tobacco and wood polish, as cool as a wine cellar. Antique lamps hung from the cheap drop-ceiling and dimly illuminated the cluttered interior, which seemed much larger and more cavernous than you would have believed from the outside. The aisles were crammed full of old chairs, tables, writing desks, and china cabinets which were, in turn, densely covered in all manner of lamps, vases, statues, and paintings. Stacks of books, dolls, bric-a-brac, and knick-knacks covered whatever scarce niches remained. The place was so full that Cricket was forced to walk sideways like a crippled crab through much of the place, his arms glued to his sides for fear of accidentally upsetting the precarious architecture. He was amazed at how expertly the place had been assembled, every inch of space utilized. Despite the cramped conditions, everything was dusted and spotless. The owner of this cluttered museum, this hoarder with OCD, ran a tight ship. Nothing had a price on it, and Cricket hoped the owner might be a haggler—not that he was planning on buying anything.

After a while of wandering through the store, the old man peeking at him over the top of his newspaper from time to time, Cricket found himself in front of a large, ornate bookshelf full of austere leather-bound books. He ran his eyes along the spines and beautifully rendered gold-leaf titles jumped out at him; they seemed to be old medical books with titles like *A Treatise on the Particulars of Hand Anatomy* and *Remedies For Digestion* and *The Testicle*. The bookcase itself was equally impressive. Standing over seven feet tall, it was covered in intricately carved geometric shapes, which did not speak to any specific era or period of creation. Evil-looking cherubs, whose eyes seemed to follow you, adorned the top edges of the bookcase, standing in defiant contrast from the rest of the piece. A white book, laying horizontally across the top row, caught Cricket's eye. He pulled it down and turned it over in his hands. It was bound in pearl-white leather and had no title on the spine or either cover. The bottom right corner was black and crispy from fire damage, as though it had been plucked from the pyre of some long-forgotten inquisition. With great care, Cricket cracked the book open somewhere in the middle, gently prying the pages apart, involuntarily holding his breath as he did. *You break it, you buy it* quietly ringing in his ears—despite the fact that almost half of the book looked like burned toast. He didn't think that would matter to the stern old bombardier behind the old desk, though.

From the moment his eyes caught the yellowing pages, Cricket was transfixed. Page after page was full of archaic diagrams, runes, and every sort of occult-oriented imagery and symbol you could imagine. He had always been obsessed with the occult, though not in a religious or ideological way. He loved the imagery that was involved. Skulls, crosses (both righted and inverted), sigils, ancient characters from lost alphabets—it all fascinated him. He loved the symbolism at work, even though he had no clue what anything meant beyond their superficial forms. Back home, in LA, he had a fairly substantial library of books filled with occult symbols and imagery, but there was stuff in this old, half-burned book that he'd never seen before, stuff that was more interesting and visually arresting than anything in his books at home. There were complex charts filled with what looked like zodiacal signs; there were beautifully rendered drawings of demons and monsters and witches and ghosts; and here— towards the back of the book—was an actual chapter about tattooing symbols on the body. *How cool.*

Simply put: The book fascinated him. It had everything he could ask for, and more. As he flipped from page to page, he thought about all of the cool tattoo designs he could make from the stuff in them. He attempted to read some of the text, but it was in Latin and he quickly lost interest. It was the pictures that mattered to him. He snapped the book shut, excited to have found such a treasure. Now all he had to do was buy the damned thing. Knowing his luck, the old man would probably look the book over and say it was not for sale after being struck by a pang of hoarder's remorse. But that was not the case. In fact, the old man seemed quite uninterested in the tome he was reading and barely looked at the thing before mumbling "That'll be ten pounds, please."

It took a moment for his eyes to adjust once Cricket was outside, as if he'd just emerged from a cave. In the distance, he heard the thrum of an oncoming train. He looked at his watch. His train was due in five minutes! He grabbed his roller-case by the handle and, for the second time that day, made a mad dash for his train.

Cricket made his train, though just barely. His flight was scheduled to be almost twelve hours long, and he'd planned to sleep for most of it. Instead, he found himself hunched over his new book, sketching tattoo designs. As he disembarked at LAX, he realized he'd filled half of his notebook with new designs. He closed the burned book, kissed it, and dropped it in his bag, excited at the prospect of mining more material from its brittle pages. As he stood, he cringed at the metallic taste the book left on his lips.

Cricket came home to find his girlfriend Bonnie sitting at the kitchen table reading a dog-eared Stephen King novel, absentmindedly gnawing on a carrot stick, her big toe compulsively tapping a table leg. She'd always been a fidget, especially in bed at night—which had very nearly driven him to smother her with a pillow on several occasions. But all of her faults were things like that: small, personable peccadilloes.

"Please, don't get up," Cricket said sarcastically, closing the front door.

"What do you want me to do?" she said, her eyes still on her book, "Run over to you? Kiss you all over?"

"That'd be nice," he said, parking his hated roller-case.

"Then get a fucking dog."

He hung up his coat, dropped his keys in the ugly bowl she'd made him while drunk in a pottery class on her 39th birthday, and sat down next to her at the table. She flicked her eyes over at him for a moment then smiled and continued reading. "How was your flight?"

"Fine. The seats were small as hell and I got a cramp in my left ass cheek, but I survived. How about you? Did you miss me?"

She lowered the book and gave him a long kiss, then said: "Fuck, no."

"Yeah. I thought so," he said, helping himself to a carrot stick. "What have you been up to today?"

"This," she said, waggling the book as she started to read again.

"All day?"

"All day."

"You didn't have any work to do?"

"Sure I did. But I did this instead."

As he chewed his carrot stick, he watched her read, scanning her face, taking in its familiar typography: the small birthmark to the left of her mouth (which she used to pencil in more, for added effect), her full lips and wide mouth that housed perfect rows of coffee-stained teeth, the lovely fans of laugh lines at the corners of her mouth, the crow's feet edging her large, green, feline eyes.

She was fifteen years older than Cricket, though he often forgot this fact. Bonnie had always looked younger but, at the same time, had always acted her age. And while he felt they were equals in their twenty-year partnership, there had always been the touch of a sage in Bonnie.

They met when he was twenty and she was thirty-five. Back then, you'd have never guessed there was an age difference. Not that it had mattered much to his mother. She'd always characterized Bonnie as a cradle-snatching opportunist whose sole purpose in life was to deprive her of her only son; and she'd gone out of her way to say as much on many occasions, albeit in more indefinite terms and with a saccharine smile. Bonnie—the saint—had always just nodded and smiled, too polite to say even a half-caustic word to his meddling mother. Though she'd made up for it in aggressive eye-rolling. Exposure to his mother was probably what had caused Bonnie's crow's feet—forced smiles etched into her face like battle scars.

If his mother were alive (she died four years earlier), she would still be needling Cricket to drop Bonnie and find a younger, more fertile woman so she could finally have the grandbabies she always wanted and deserved. He never wanted children, much less guaranteed them to his mother. He always joked that if she was so hell-bent on grandkids, she should have had more children herself. Diversified her portfolio in hopes of future asset maturation. But she hadn't because she couldn't. She'd been "stricken with sterility" after Cricket was born and more children weren't in her future. He guessed that's why she'd always ridden him so hard to have kids of his own. The fact that Bonnie couldn't have children naturally herself (and never wanted them either, thank you very much) neither won empathy or sympathy from his mother, nor made the topic of baby-bearing a moot point. His mother never cut her a break, and insisted until the day she died that Bonnie couldn't bear children because she was too old, past her prime, spoiled and out of date. He'd always hated his mother for that, and still did.

But now, twenty years later, he was forty and Bonnie was fifty-five, and the age difference was starting to show a bit more each day. It had started to bother him a little until he realized in another twenty years the age difference would again be unnoticeable, as it had been twenty years before—they'd both be old people, like when they were both young people. The circle complete, the state of affairs brought round to its equal but opposite pole. It was only this middle-age bit that broke the equilibrium. He loved her more than he ever had and thought she was as beautiful as the day he met her.

"What the Hell are you staring at, creep?" she said, momentarily distracted from her book.

"Nothing much," he said with a wink.

She sighed, rolling her eyes. "There's stuff for sandwiches, if you're hungry." Then her eyes flicked back to her book and stayed there.

"Dude, how are you?" Harry Pizmed said as he entered Cricket's tattoo parlor, aptly named Cricket's Tattoo Parlor.

A dead electric chime announced his arrival. (Cricket hated the chime; it reminded him of every corner store he'd ever stepped foot in. He'd always intended on changing the damned thing, maybe replacing it with a proper old-school ringing bell, but he just never found the time for it—another forgotten entry on the monumental to-do list he'd never get around to writing down.)

"How's Her Majesty doing, dude?" Harry asked, leaning against the waist-high partition that separated the red-walled, rustic waiting room from the white-walled, sterile tattooing stalls.

Cricket was sitting at a desk on the other side of the partition from Harry, bent over a light table, working on a tattoo design. Dropping his pencil, he removed his reading glasses and squinted up at Harry: "What?"

"How's Her Majesty? You know—the Queen? AKA, how the hell was England? Was it good?" Harry said, chuckling and shaking his head at Cricket's apparent ignorance.

"Oh. It was fine. Did a bunch of flash work, mostly sailor and old-school stuff. Visited a friend, missed a few trains—you know, the usual."

"Cool, dude. Cool," Harry said, nodding like a sycophant.

There was an awkward pause for a moment as Cricket looked expectantly at Harry, wondering what the twenty-something stoner wanted. Harry was a very apt name for this kid. With hip-length sandy hair and an equally substantial beard, he looked like a scrawny Wookie. The runt of Chewbacca's litter.

"So...I was wondering if you'd thought more about what we talked last time?" Harry said, suddenly serious.

Cricket knotted his brow in recall but came up empty. "And what was that, exactly?"

Harry started to nervously scratch a knot in the wood top of the partition, unable to make eye contact with Cricket. "Well...Remember I was asking if you needed an apprentice, and you said you'd think about it?"

Leaning back in his chair, Cricket rubbed his tired eyes. "No, what I said was that I didn't need an apprentice right now and didn't have the time to have one, even if I did. I believe you tacked on the 'thinking about it' part of conversation."

"So, it's still a 'no'?"

"Yup. Sorry, kiddo, it's just not in the cards."

For a minute or two, Harry didn't say anything and just sort of stared down at the floor, doing something with his feet. Then he nodded, as though he'd made a decision. "No problem, dude. I get you. Well, the offer still stands if, you know, you ever change your mind or anything."

"I'll keep you in mind if things change, okay?"

Harry was nodding again, a slight sparkle of hope reignited in his eyes. "Yeah, totally. Thanks."

Cricket nodded, put his reading glasses back on, and got back to work. Harry leaned over the partition to look at what he was drawing. On the page were two circular designs, both filled with branching geometric structures. Archaic symbols (some Harry had seen before and recognized as having occult connotations) ran around the outside of the circles.

"Those are cool. What are they for?" Harry asked.

"Ugh…Well, The Mrs. and I have our twenty-year anniversary coming up; I thought I'd draw us a pair of tattoos," Cricket said, not looking up at Harry, whose attention had now transferred from Cricket's drawing to the old book open on the table next to him.

"Dude, did you get the symbols out of this?' Harry said, picking it up and flipping through its pages.

Cricket sighed, took his glasses off again, rubbed his eyes and nodded in the affirmative, a strained, patient smile pulling his face awkwardly.

"This book is awesome, dude. Where'd you get it?"

"An antiques shop in England somewhere. While I was waiting for a train," Cricket said, gently taking the book from Harry and replacing it on the table.

"I got a friend—well, he's not actually a friend, more of an adversary, really—he's the dungeon master in one of my RPG clubs. He works at the State College, knows all about occult stuff. I bet he could he tell you all about this book, translate it and shit…"

"Nah—that's okay," Cricket said hastily, cutting Harry off. "I don't really care what it says, I just like the pictures. That's what I bought the book for, but thanks."

Harry, catching the drift, let the point drop and stood quietly for a moment, looking around the room. "So…You got any time free this week?" Harry said. "I kinda wouldn't mind getting something like that myself. Maybe you could design me one? I was thinking about getting something on my left shoulder, maybe."

Back to work, and determined not to let eyes his leave paper again, Cricket nodded and said: "Yeah, sure…Why don't you call me later and we'll set something up?"

Harry nodded and said that would be great and that he was totally psyched and that he would definitely give him a call later, definitely. Then he stood there for another twenty minutes, just watching Cricket draw.

Bonnie loved the matching anniversary tattoos. The idea of getting matching tattoos had never entered either of their minds, even after all these years in the business. To her, the sentiment was a sweet one, and novel, too. Novelty was a rare occurrence in a relationship as long as theirs, and she found it invigorating. "Where do you want to get them?" she asked, looking over the designs as they ate dinner.

"We don't have to get them in the same spot. That might be a bit too corny for my taste," Cricket said. "Besides, I'm running out of real estate," he lifted his arm and turned slightly in his chair, his densely tattooed torso on display, making Bonnie laugh and nod. "I was thinking I would get mine on the top of my left hand, that way I could do it myself," he said.

"I thought you were never going to tat your hands?" she said, lowering her broccoli-loaded fork in concern.

He waved the statement away. "I guess I'll have to make an exception for you, old dear. Besides, after fifteen years in my little tattooing hell-hole, I doubt a 'straight job' is in the cards."

"I think you're probably right. You're a lost cause. Oh, and—if you call me 'old dear' again, I'll stomp on your nuts while you're sleeping," she said, smiling. After a minute, she added: "I think I'd like to get mine on my leg," she reached under the table and touched a spot just above her right ankle. Cricket ducked his head under and nodded.

"That's a good spot."

"What do they mean? The signs?" she was looking over the designs again, this time with a squinted, more critical eye.

Cricket shrugged. "Found them in an old book I got. Thought they looked cool." Bonnie eyed him. "And…I thought the circles sort of signified…our relationship? Infinite and perfect."

She smiled at this, against her better judgment.

Later on, they both got drunk and Cricket did their tattoos, against his better judgment.

The room was as black as tar, the bitter tang of incense crept up his nostrils and coated his throat, making him cough uncontrollably. He covered his face with his hand and stumbled around, desperate to find a door or a window, but only found more darkness. He tried to talk, to yell for help, but the air was too thick with the horrible, ancient scent. All he did was cough more.

Flick—the strike of a match. Far-off ahead of him was the outline of a small door. In the center of the door sat the silhouette of a figure in profile, lighting what looked to be a long pipe. He staggered towards the doorway, eyes watering and lungs burning, desperate to escape the miasma. As he came closer to the door, the silhouetted figure turned its head and beckoned him to enter. He started to run. For a moment, the doorway seemed to stay the same distance away, hanging before him like a picture on a wall. Then, as though time had flashed forward to catch up with the present, he was at the door, then through the door. Falling to ground face-first into a rough circular carpet made of a densely coiled rope. His face burned as it scraped across the unforgiving fibers, centuries-old dust kicked up into his mouth. He spat and coughed as he struggled to get up onto all fours, then he vomited for what seemed like an hour.

When the heaving subsided, he wiped his mouth on his shirt sleeve and got to his feet, swaying slightly. Light-headed and heavy-hearted. A stream of smoke entered the bottom of his vision, spiraling upward like a distant jet in the sky, before billowing out into a cloud and evaporating. He followed the smoke's trajectory to the charred bowl of an ancient opium pipe, which sat in the mouth of a man with a chilling countenance: he was painfully thin, the sort of emaciated you only saw in the starving and the dying. His ginger hair had been roughly cut down to the scalp by something like sheep

313

shears. He wore a dirty red blazer with nothing underneath and candy-striped trousers. On the chest pocket of the blazer was a heraldic crest embroidered with gold thread. He looked as though he'd sailed away drunk from the yacht club only to be marooned in the seven depths of Hell. But what was most shocking were the red tattoos that covered every inch of this fellow: His face, neck, hands, fingers, chest—even the individual toes of his dirty feet. The thin man reached out with one of his skeletal hands and motioned for him to sit down next to him. As he did, he noticed a pair of bare legs laying on the opposite side of the thin man. They were the legs of a woman, a naked woman. She lay face down on the ground, covered from head to hips with a length of dirty black sackcloth; only her pale white buttocks and legs were visible. On her legs were the beginnings of a red tattoo—very much like the ones that covered the thin man. Something about the legs seemed familiar.

After taking a long drag off the odd pipe, the thin man placed it on the ground and took up two pieces of wood: one a darker color and shaped like a small baseball bat, the other a lighter color, thinner, with a large needle protruding from it at an angle. The thin man dipped the needle in a cracked porcelain tea cup full of what looked like blood and started to gently tap the needle into the flesh of the woman's leg. He was tattooing her, using old techniques from centuries past. He spoke as he worked:

"I wonder why you have lied yourself before me?" the thin man said, the hint of a knowing smile teasing the corners of his cracked lips, "I do not know you. You will give all, receive nothing. Why?"

For a long while, he sat and watched the thin man tattoo the woman. She didn't move. Yet the sackcloth slowly rose and fell with breathing, so she must've been alive. When the thin man was done, he once again took up his pipe. He tried to speak to the thin man, but every time he tried, the thin man would shake his head slightly and the air would be knocked out of his lungs, an invisible fist buried in his diaphragm. So, he stopped trying to speak. He could have been sitting there for hours or days. Time seemed unimportant in this place, forgotten and ignored like old sins. If you did not admit that it existed, then it did not. There was no light outside the grimy circular hatch windows of the squalid room, only eternal night. The smell of death and disease crept up through the dark spaces between the splintered floorboards. He realized for the first time that it was cold in the room and began to shiver.

"Do you know my name?" the thin man said. He had stopped his tattooing and was looking straight at him, his red eyes intense and barely human.

"No," he said, surprised at his ability to talk.

"I thought so. Otherwise, you wouldn't be here. She wouldn't be here," the thin man nodded towards the naked woman under the cloth next to him. "Do you want to know my name?"

"Yes," he said, curious but terrified of the answer.

"Then I shall tell you. It is a name that may mean nothing to you now but it has carried the weight of civilizations. It is a name that few know but all feel. I am an author, a shaper, of the narrative of life. I am the Keeper of the Dust. The Namer of Names. I am Quachil Uttaus."

The moment the name was said the man's skin began to shrivel and crack, like burning paper; his red hair turned grey, then white, then sprouted from his head and face before turning to dust. His laugh bellowed into a wheeze as his lungs dried and cracked like old plaster. His fingernails grew long and brittle, his fingers knotted and warped with a thousand years of arthritis until they looked like the claws of an apex predator. The thin man shrunk as he stood, the rust red tattoos fading from his wrinkling hide as though bleached by a thousand suns.

"To know my name is to know your fate, dear one," putrid dust spouted from his mouth as he spoke. He snapped his fingers—or, rather, his claws. Then there was nothing but the blackness between stars.

Cricket jolted up in bed, gasping and crying and covered in sweat. He looked around frantically: he was in his room; he recognized its shape and contours and the items silhouetted against the dim moonlight bleeding in through dusty windows. Bonnie was fast asleep next him, snoring softly. She'd have slept through Hiroshima.

He lied back down in bed, kicking off the blankets. Hot and sweaty and desperate to cool off. He thought he was still a little drunk. Probably why he was sweating so profusely. Next time, he promised himself, he'd lay off the tequila.

The sun was soft and not yet above the horizon when Bonnie awoke. Birds chirped cheerily outside an open window; the scent of jasmine rolled in on the cool morning air. What time was it? 6:14 AM. Smiling and yawning, she tried to remember the last time she had woken up this early, and couldn't. Bonnie was not a morning person, and wasn't much of a friend of the afternoon either. She liked her sleep and probably could have lied in bed all day, if not for the fact she had to get up and live her life. But she was up really early, and feeling great to boot. How weird. She'd indulged in some hard boozing the night before. She should be passed out now, covered in a sheen of oily sweat, snoring a sleep-apnea snore, not feeling chipper and ready to rule the world at six o'clock in the morning. But she'd take it. Better this than every other scenario that sprang to mind.

Cricket was still sleep. Of course, he was. He drank half a bottle of tequila last night. Then she remembered—*the tattoo*. Never ever, in all their years together, had she known Cricket to tattoo someone when he was drunk. In fact, he never even let drunk people within a hundred feet of his shop, unlike some of the more unscrupulous fucks in the tattoo business. She slid her right leg out from under the white sheet and rested it on top of the bedspread, the pink, cracking polish on her toes wriggling in contrast with the eggshell Egyptian cotton. He hadn't done a bad a job, thank God. All of the lines were crisp and straight, nothing looked crooked or unfinished. In fact, it was so perfect it looked like a machine had done it. Not bad for a drunk guy, even if he was a master of his craft. Odd thing was that he had done the tattoos in a dark red, almost a rust color; she could have sworn it was black ink he used. Oh, well. Still looked pretty good, if not slightly incongruent with all of the other black lines and shading that covered various areas of the same leg. Carefully, she reached over Cricket and grabbed his left hand by the middle and index fingers and picked it up, curious to see if his tattoo had come out as well as hers. It had. He'd done just as perfect a job on his, except there was something off: while the lines and design looked fine, the tattooed spot on his Cricket's hand looked infected. The tattoo lines raised up on a circuit of red, irritated flesh, as though it were branded on. If he bled ink all over their new sheets, she was going to have his ass over it.

Then something occurred to her, and she once again slid her leg out from under the covers and rested it on the bed. Hmm…her tattoo was completely healed. No infection, no scabbing, no discharge. Nothing. Completely healed, as though it had been there for years. She rubbed the tattoo again, just to make sure, but no—it was totally healed. *Weird.*

Getting out of bed, she decided to put it out of her mind. The sun was now over the horizon and it looked like it could be a beautiful day. Fuck it, she might even go for a quick run before breakfast. She hoped she could keep this up; she hoped this was her new self.

After two and a half weeks, Cricket's new tattoo still hadn't healed properly. Scabbed-over and discolored, antiseptic cream was almost constantly applied. Cricket had never known a tattoo to take this long to heal. Worst was the fact that the skin around the tattoo had started to wrinkle and sag. Running his other hand over the patch triggered sense memories of holding his Great-Grandma Winona's hands while saying prayers around the dinner table as a kid. She was a fixture at every family event when he was a kid, always sitting in the corners of rooms, watching people like an old piece of furniture that had come to life and didn't realize it.

Faced with a growing problem with no clear or simple solution, Cricket did what many stoic types do—he ignored it. Besides, he was booked up solid for a month, had a ton of work to do, he didn't have time to worry about some old-lady patch on his hand. It didn't even hurt. It would probably clear up in a week or two.

But it didn't.

Early one morning, Bonnie awoke to Cricket screaming in bed next her. "What the fuck is it!?" she screamed, frantically looking around the room for a burglar or a fire, something, anything.

"Look at my hand!" Cricket yelled, pointed to his left hand. It was grey and shriveled, almost down to the bone. The saggy skin was paper-thin, veins and sinew visibly writhing underneath as Cricket worked and flexed his fingers like a man with a new prosthetic.

Bonnie's alarm immediately turned into morbid fascination, as though all of the screaming and yelling and surprise were some sort of act. She grabbed his left wrist and pulled the hand closer to her, looking it over like an indistinguishable piece of roadkill.

"Well, that's weird."

"Yeah, I know that, thank you!"

"It looks like a creepy old man hand," she touched one of the overlong fingernails that had mysteriously appeared overnight and flinched with repulsion when the nail snapped off like a dry twig.

"Jesus! Just leave it be!" Cricket yanked his hand away, flustered and annoyed.

"Sorry. It's just so…weird."

Cricket nodded absently, assessing the state of his hand. "Yup."

"I don't care what you say, or what excuses you try to give, I'm taking you to see the doctor," with that, Bonnie hopped out of bed and disappeared into the bathroom. Cricket laid back down as the patter of the shower started a room away. He caught a glance of the Bonnie's naked backside through the half-open bathroom door as she hopped into the steaming cubicle. She was looking good. Really good. She must be spot-on with all the vitamins and yoga and meditation. He looked at his desiccated hand and wondered if he should be doing those things too.

Dr. Argelese, their regular GP, was completely baffled by the state of Cricket's hand, stating at least a dozen times that he'd "never seen a darned thing like it." Some blood was drawn; a biopsy was taken; a few Polaroids (*for purely education purposes, you understand*) were snapped; and, in the end, Cricket and Bonnie left Lyndon Medical Center just as baffled and freaked out as when they walked in.

All the tests came back negative, of course: no cancer, no flesh-eating virus, no bacterial infection, no disease, not nothing—leaving Cricket both relieved and annoyed.

The next week was a blur of waiting rooms, banal offices with certificates on walls, padded antiseptic tables covered in cheap medical paper. No one had any idea what was wrong with him. There was even talk of putting the case in a medical journal.

"Maybe there's another specialist we can see?" Bonnie said, stroking Cricket's salt and pepper hair as they sat on their terrace, watching tourists and surf bums and delivery people and dog walkers mill about on the street below. It was late morning. They always came out here to drink their coffee, if it wasn't raining—which it rarely did in LA. "Maybe we should think about some sort of alternative medicine?"

"What, like, Chinese herbs and magical crystals and shit? I don't think so," Cricket said, trying to not be annoyed with her, but failing. "I see your point," he continued, in a softer tone, "but a bunch of whacko hippy stuff ain't going to help the situation. It'll just be a waste of time and money."

Bonnie nodded sympathetically, letting the conversation taper off. She shifted in her seat and laid her long lithe legs across Cricket's lap. He ran his good hand across them, intermittently squeezing the supple muscles before coming to rest on her anniversary tattoo; he sat up suddenly, pulling her leg closer for inspection.

"What in the Hell are you doing?" she asked, still smiling in the sun with her eyes closed.

"It's your leg."

"What about my leg?"

"There's something weird…"

Bonnie opened her eyes and sat up fully, slightly annoyed. "Well? What's so weird about it?"

"This leg looks…I don't know how to explain it…Newer than the other?"

Bonnie furrowed her brow in concern. She opened her mouth to excoriate him and tell him he was being a weirdo, and that he should probably get his head checked along with his hand, when her eyes fell on her leg. *He's right.* She leaned forward and ran her own hands over her right leg, then along the left one, inspecting them like fruit in a supermarket. The skin on her right leg was smoother and lighter, devoid of the sorts of dermal inconsistencies she had on the opposite leg: moles, freckles, and blotches of darkened pigment. There was a definite difference in the muscle tone and flexibility. Even the accursed wrinkles that had started to form around her knee cap and in the bend of her leg were gone. Her toes looked different too. They looked a little less misshapen, as though forty years of high heels never happened. She straightened her legs and raised them up, side by side: they looked like a before and after picture. "What in the holy flying fuck is going on?" She left the terrace and padded into their bedroom and inspected herself in front of the full-length mirror on the closet door.

Cricket followed her inside and stood behind her in the mirror, scratching his chin, thinking. It was almost as though they were experiencing the same phenomena but in reverse. Then it hit him: "The tattoos..."

"What'd you say?"

"The tattoos. What if this," he motioned to her leg and his hand, "and this were somehow related to our anniversary tattoos? I mean, think about it: the hand where I got my tattoo went all weird; same thing with the leg you got yours on!" He knew he was on to something, but had no idea what. He was a dog stuck into an interesting scent, unsure if it would lead him off the edge of a cliff. "Let's shut the shop today. I've got some stuff to look into."

After calling to cancel the appointments he had that day, Cricket began searching the Internet for answers, knowing full well that searching symptoms online would inevitably lead down a rabbit hole of paranoia and imagined death, always making things worse than they actually were. That benign mole you've had all your life may, in fact, be a rare form of flesh-eating cancer. Just the tip of a malignant iceberg. Or that bump you have on the roof of your mouth could be this almost-unheard-of strain of herpes that only occurs in inhabitants of distant rain forests. Could it have come from that girl—what the hell was her name? Oh, yeah, Carla—that you hooked up with after that wedding a few years back? The one you went down on. Hadn't she mentioned doing missionary work?

Hopeless, and even more freaked out, Cricket left his computer and wandered downstairs to his shop, which was on the ground floor of the building that he owned and lived in. The shop was dark, lit only from the noon-time glare bouncing off the sidewalk outside, filling the space with a dim haze, everything chiaroscuro. Cricket wandered aimlessly around the space like a wayward zombie, trudging from one tattoo stall to another, his bad hand running over all the chairs and tables and shelves, infecting everything, nothing but a constant influx of gloom and doom cycling through his mind like dark electricity on a short circuit. He plopped down at his desk and switched on the light table. It clicked for a moment as the bulb found its life, then humming as soft yellow light radiated into the room, only to be absorbed by the shadows in the corners. *Not even light can escape a black hole.*

Cricket closed his eyes and leaned closer to the light table, feeling its feeble warmth, seeing the peachy color of his inner eyelids, pretending he was laying on the beach warming himself in the sun after a quick swim in the churning ocean, not worrying about anything except a potential sunburn. A car horn blared outside. He opened his eyes, pulled out of his daydream prematurely like a screaming baby from a womb. *Fuck those people*, he thought. *What a bunch of assholes.* They were ruining the environment, acting like feckless jackasses on reality shows and in public office. They murdered each other and fucked each other over, stole each other's money, and cut in front you at a bar during last call. And none of them—not the smartest or the richest or best educated—could help him and his weird hand. Fucking useless, all of them. Then he realized, if he got up and walked outside, he'd just be another face in the crowd. Just another aimless asshole flailing through life like everyone else.

But what did he have to complain about, really? Yeah, his hand was fucked up, but at least it wasn't his good hand. He could still work, still make money. How many people in this world were so hurt and fucked up and disabled they couldn't even get out of bed in the morning, much less make a good living like he did. Hell, he owned the building he was sitting

322

in. He was lucky and he knew it. For the moment, he was brought low, but his hand would recover; it had to, eventually. He realized that it was the mystery surrounding the condition of his hand that was weighing on him. If he had broken it or burned it or cut the damn thing off, he could deal with it because there would be a plan of action. Someone could explain what was happening. Doctors would know what to do; it was nothing they couldn't handle; they'd seen it a hundred times before, could do it in their sleep, blindfolded.

But that wasn't the case here. Something really weird was wrong with his hand, something that was not in a book or on a website. Something that maybe only existed in the far corners of the Earth, still waiting to be christened in archaic Latin.

Out of instinct, led by some subtle sense of dread, something pricked Cricket's attention, something out of the corner of his eye—it was the old book he bought in England, the one he found the anniversary symbols in. He snatched it up and ran upstairs to find the light of day.

Bonnie was gone, left for a yoga class, then to run some errands. Once again sitting on the terrace, he opened the rumbled little book and flipped through its pages, glimpsing a quick succession of glyphs and charts and illustrations of strange hybrid creatures. Soon, the book naturally opened to the pages with the two circular seals on them. They stared out at him like eyes; his bad hand began to itch. In that moment, he wished he'd never set eyes on the book. Putting on his reading glasses, he squinted at the bodies of small, tightly written cursive text that accompanied the pictures. His guess was that it was Latin. Some of the words seemed familiar to him: *exempli…vici…imperium…malefica.* In all the years he'd been tattooing—decades, in fact—he must have tattooed thousands of words or inscriptions in Latin (along with a slew of other languages) and never knew what ninety-nine percent of them actually meant. It never really mattered. Whatever the customer wanted. As long as it looked cool…

He turned the page, but as he did, he noticed the weight and thickness of the page was different—two pages were stuck together. Patiently, he fumbled at the corners, trying to work them apart, all the time cursing himself for biting his nails. Finally, there was a bit of separation, and he gently peeled the pages apart. He stared at the right-hand page, a page he'd never seen before: On it were two crudely drawn female figures, one with a rough crown drawn on her head, the other without; each had a circular seal placed between gestural breasts. They were the same circular symbols from the previous pages, the same symbols he'd tattooed on Bonnie and himself. A squiggly sort of arrow pointed from the woman without the crown to the one with. Written along the tail of the squiggly arrow was the word *vitae*. Cricket grabbed his tablet, opened the browser, and searched the word. It was Latin and meant life or vitality. His jaw tightened. He started punching in other words to translate:...to stay young...a drain of life...mark of the eternal young...mark of the damned...Devil's needle...

A cold sweat settled on his forehead. He fumbled for a cigarette and lit it with shaking hands. This was all fairy-tale bullshit. Must be. He didn't believe in magic, and that's exactly what it was—magic, of some sort. But magic wasn't real. People couldn't cast spells or steal souls. They didn't steal babies in the night and fuck the Devil. But he looked at his shriveled hand, saw the decay had climbed further up his arm, and knew that it was true. Whatever this book was saying was true. He searched the book for an author's name, or an inscription. Anything that would tell him who wrote it or who had owned it.

Nothing.

Eventually, he gave up—on the book and on worrying about his arm. He grabbed a bottle of homemade rum and decided to get drunk and smoke cigarettes instead. By the time Bonnie got home, he was plastered. He wanted to tell her about the book, wanted to warn her, but knew he'd just sound like a crazy asshole, especially now that he was drunk. He decided he would worry about it tomorrow. Or maybe not. Maybe he'd wake up tomorrow and realize he was being stupid and gullible and desperate. Realize that there was nothing magical about his shriveled hand or Bonnie's sexy legs. It would be some kind of bacterial thing or a genetic thing. A doctor would be able to figure it out, eventually. Right?

"Yes, hello. Emporium Antiques and Gifts. How can I help?"

"Oh, hi…My name is Cricket Simmons. I was in your store a few weeks back and I purchased a book from you."

"Yes."

"It was a small book, partially burned. Filled with a bunch of symbols."

"Righto."

"Do you remember it?"

"I'm very sorry, sir, but I can't say that I do."

"Hmm…Well, I really need to know where it came from. It's important."

"I see. Unfortunately, I run this establishment alone and don't quite have the time to keep a very detailed inventory, but if you were to give me the title of the volume I could see if I have a record of it."

"Yeah, see the book doesn't have a title. It's just a blank cover."

"Oh, that's unfortunate, sir. I'm not sure that there's much I could tell you then."

"I remember the book was tucked up into an old bookshelf. A large, ornate thing. Had angels around the top of it?"

"Ah, well that's quite a large item. I could look in my ledger and see where I obtained that, if it would help?"

"Yes, please."

"One moment then, sir…"

"Thanks…"

"It appears that particular bookshelf was purchased at auction, dear me, nearly ten years ago. If my memory serves me, that piece came from Briar Hall."

"Briar Hall?"

"Yes, sir. A local manor house. Once belonged to the Duke of Hammerstow. I believe the National Trust own and run it now. Lovely gardens."

"Okay…Well, thank you for your help…"

"It was no problem at all, sir. Glad to help….Sir?"

"Yes?"

"Is everything okay?"

"Fine. Just fine. Thanks again. Goodbye."

Cricket scanned the Internet for anything related to the Briar Hall or the Duke of Hammerstow, writing down anything he thought pertinent on a notepad:

> - Current Duke is Filton Whenmore (12th Duke of Hammerstow)
> - Briar Hall built in 1655 by Henry Whenmore, 1st Duke of Hammerstow.
> - Hall was damaged by fire in 1800s.
> - Now owned by National Trust. Tourist spot.
> - Hall is said to be haunted.
> - John Whenmore (2nd Duke of Hammerstow) was confined to an asylum for much of his life. His brother Richard became the 3rd Duke after his death.
> - Archibald Whenmore (8th Duke of Hammerstow) accused of witchcraft and crimes against God. Nickname was the Duke of Rust.

Tired and weary and feeling fairly hopeless, Cricket decided he'd investigate this 'Duke of Rust' and then call it day. He clicked the highlighted name and a new window opened: *The Weird Life of Archibald Whenmore, Duke of Hammerstow.* That was the heading of the page. Cricket slowly scrolled down and began to read:

> The life of Archibald Horatio Whenmore, Eighth Duke of Hammerstow (born on April 30th, 1815 at

Briar Hall in Essex) is a life filled with magic, mystery and violence. Many people, both aristocracy and peasantry alike, whispered of the Duke's connection to the occult and devil worship. He came to be known as the Duke of Rust, on account of the many rust-colored tattoos that covered his body from head to toe. Little is known of his life except that as a young man he traveled all over the world, disappearing for years at a time. He was later implicated in various crimes, including three murders and a case of incest, none were proven. It was said that he trafficked with the Devil and was possessed by a demon. He is thought to have died in a fire at Briar Hall, which also claimed the life of his father, Tyrion.

Cricket scrolled further down and stopped at a portrait of the infamous Archibald Whenmore. He stared at the screen, slack-jawed—it was the man from his dream.

"Hey, hun. What'ya up to?" Bonnie had come down the stairs and snuck up behind him, hanging her arms over his shoulders and propping her head against his. She kissed his ear and was about to ask him what he wanted for dinner when she noticed the portrait of the Duke of Rust.

"What the…" she said, leaning forward, squinting at the photo on the screen. "That guy. I know that guy. I had a fuckin' dream about that guy! Who is he?"

"What?" Cricket spun around to face her. "You had a dream about this man," he said, jamming his finger into the portrait on the computer screen. "You're sure?"

Bonnie was staring at the portrait, a sullen look now on her face, unaware of Cricket's mounting intensity. She nodded. "Yeah. It was a fucking weird dream, too. I was, like, in the dark and then all of a sudden, I'm in this smoky old room with this guy. And he's, like, sitting on the floor smoking a weird-ass pipe. Looking all skinny and gross."

"Was he tattooing a naked woman?"

327

"No…it was a man, I think. I wasn't sure, though. I could only see his hand. The rest of him was under a dirty old blanket. It was such a vivid dream. Really creeped me out."

"Did the man say anything to you in the dream? The guy doing the tattooing, I mean."

She shook her head. "Nope. Just smiled at me with these nasty yellow teeth, and nodded his head like we were both in on the same joke or something."

That was when Cricket started to cry. He'd never cried in front of her before, even after all these years—hadn't cried in decades, as a matter of fact. The last time being when he broke his leg playing football in high school, and even then, he grit his teeth while the tears ran. He'd been proud of that, not crying like a little bitch. But here he was, a grown-ass man, crying like he a baby who'd lost his mama. Bonnie immediately hugged him and whispered comfort in his ear, like the mama he'd lost. He hated himself for it, though he knew Bonnie was probably secretly relishing this a little. She'd always wanted to see him cry, and had made that point before every movie they'd ever watched together. *You can cry, if you want. I don't mind, really.* But if she was enjoying his tears she wasn't showing it, or making light of the situation as she usually did when things were shitty. She knew something was seriously wrong with Cricket and that it was getting to him.

"I…I…I…had the same dream as you," he said between sobs, unable to control himself, unable to prevent his stone-cold masculine facade from crumbling into baby powder.

"It'll be okay, hun. Really. We'll figure this all out," she said, trying to ignore what he was saying because it scared her too much. That dream had nearly sent her into a downward spiral of depression, and she'd had no idea why. The dream itself wasn't even that scary, just unsettling. Weird. Too real, too much like an untold prophecy.

After he'd calmed down and swallowed several fingers of scotch, Cricket told her about his dream, how it was similar to hers and how it was different. He told her his theory regarding the tattoos and showed her the diagrams in the book. And he told her about the Duke of Rust. He was surprised, and grateful, to hear that she didn't think he was crazy or delusional or just a little stressed out. She nodded solemnly as he spoke and seemed to take it all in with the utmost seriousness. When he was done, she sat quietly for some while, staring off into space, processing the wholly absurd yet seemingly plausible situation and how it might affect the other "situation" she was quietly grappling with. With everything that had been going on with Cricket's hand, she hadn't realized she was almost two weeks late.

She was told in no uncertain terms that the old baby-making system was permanently out of commission. She was completely barren, not even IVF would do the trick. And she'd taken it all in stride because she'd never really wanted children. Sure, she'd get the occasional maternal pang when holding one of her nieces or when she met a long-lost friend on the street pushing a stroller, but she always liked that she could hand the kids back when they started to smell or cry. There was also the added benefit of never having to use birth control pills or condoms with Cricket. So, pregnancy never even entered her mind. But now that the possibility was here, looming overhead like thundercloud, she wasn't sure how she felt about it. She was too old to have a baby, by all rights. Too old to get pregnant, she thought. Then again, the big M hadn't reared its ugly head yet, no hot flashes in sight, thank God. Still, the possible complications of late-life pregnancy spun through her mind like a poisonous top: Down's Syndrome, autism, birth defects. But all that could wait for now. Cricket's hand was withering like a discarded banana peel; there were more pressing matters to deal with.

She kissed Cricket's head and calmly left the room to make a pot of coffee. After, as she handed him a steaming mug, she asked: "What should we do, then?"

Cricket sipped his coffee and looked around the room for an answer. (This was something he often did whenever he was stumped or uninspired or losing an argument and in need of fresh inspiration.) His eyes landed on the torn, vintage Star Wars t-shirt Bonnie was wearing. Chewbacca was a part of the graphic ensemble; he was howling and preparing to shoot his bowcaster. *Bingo*.

By the next week, the blight had consumed more than half of Cricket's arm, spreading past his elbow, and his hair had gone from its familiar salt and pepper to just salt. Bonnie, meanwhile, looked better than ever. She looked years younger and joked that several people in her yoga class had asked her if she'd had Botox injections. Cricket was now convinced that the tattoos were draining him of life or vitality or youth, or whatever, and transferring it to Bonnie, who didn't want to believe it but couldn't deny how she felt and how she looked and all of the energy she had.

Cricket closed the tattoo parlor indefinitely, or at least until he could figure his arm out. In the last few days, he'd obtained the services of a voodoo witch doctor, a reiki specialist, a gothic Wiccan, and a lady with a crystal on the end of a chain. None proved effective. Whatever this magic was (if you could even call it that), it was the real deal, ancient and obviously known to very few people. He still couldn't believe what was happening. Every morning he'd wake up expecting his hand to be normal, as though it were all some strange dream, only to have his hopes crushed like grapes into sour wine.

After spending almost two weeks indoors, locked away from the world to slowly mummify in private, Bonnie had practically dragged him out to a beach-side café a few blocks from their house. He was wearing a black, long-sleeve shirt with a leather biker glove to cover his bad arm and hand, which were making him sweat in the bright clarity of the California sun. Despite feeling self-conscious and like some strange creature dragged out of its cave during hibernation, he had to admit it was nice to drink a proper coffee again. His cell phone began to ring. It was Harry Pizmed. He put it on speaker-phone and leaned closer to Bonnie so she could hear.

"Howdy, Harry," Cricket said, as sipped his coffee.

"Hey, Cricket. How'ya been, dude?"

"Good good. So, do you got some news for me?"

"Totally. That dude Angel I was talking about took a look at those scans you emailed me, out of that book. Dude, he was weirded out by it. Apparently, the pages you sent look like they're part of a journal or diary of black magic. He said he'd never seen anything like that it, and that's saying something—he has two PhD's in that shit! Anyway, he said the symbols on those pages you sent are part of a ritual called 'The Tether of Life.' It's supposed to, like, drain people of their life force, or something like that. Pretty cool, huh?"

Bonnie smiled and nudged Cricket on the arm, "See, you always said I was sucking the life outta you…" Cricket rolled his eyes.

"Oh, is that Bonnie? Hey, Bonnie!" Harry said, excitedly.

"Hey, Harry man!" she said.

"Anyway," Harry continued, "part of this spell is supposed to summon some kind of demon, and this demon is supposed to, like, make the thing work. I asked Angel whether there was a way to reverse the spell, like you ask about, and he said there wasn't anything in the book about how to do that. Except, it says something about appealing to the demon for mercy or forgiveness, or something. He found a spell that's supposed to summon the demon. It's all in this email I'm sending you."

"Thanks, Harry. I really appreciate it, brother," Cricket said, a tone of finality in his voice.

"Dude, no problem. It was my pleasure," Harry said, pausing for a moment before saying, "Maybe I could come hang out at the shop, when it's open and you're feeling better and stuff?"

"Sure, Harry. Sure."

That night, they tried to summon the Keeper of Dust. As per the directions given in Harry's email, a clipping of fingernail and a locket of hair were placed on a mound of dirt under each of their pillows. Bonnie joked that it felt like they were summoning the evil Tooth Fairy. Cricket tried to laugh but could only manage a smile. That's pretty much what they were doing. Neither of them were sure what would happen, but after finishing a bottle of wine, they both went to sleep wishing both nothing and something would happen.

There—a shooting star, faintly streaking across the sky. Instead of fading out, it continues on, arcing longer than usual before exploding against another pinpoint of light. The spry beauty of the scene instantly turned to cold despair, as if she were being pulled into the maw of a black hole. Had she just witnessed the destruction of a star thousands upon thousands of years ago? Had that star, along with a myriad of orbiting planets, been destroyed on impact? Milled into stardust, destined to spread throughout the dark universe like dead pollen? Then she was flung forward into the spaces between the stars, through a door, into a room. Once again, the thin tattooed man, the Duke of Rust, sat before her with his opium pipe, puffing ghost rings that seemed to hang in the air around him. He lowered his pipe and looked at her for a moment, staring through her eyes into the soft meat in the back of her head. He snapped his fingers. All of the hovering smoke rings dissipated at once. He held up a small bag: it was made of the same black sackcloth she'd seen in her previous dream. The top of the back was tied shut with a length of hemp and

332

something seemed to be struggling inside it, kicking and thrashing to escape. The Duke of Rust threw the small bag through the open door into the cosmic void, never taking his eyes off her.

"What do you want, bitch?" he said, grinning.

"I…I…I want his arm to be normal again. I want everything to be normal again."

"Why would you want that? He will crumble into dust—my dust—and you will be whole again. This is what has been set in motion, written in the dirt by a child's finger," the Duke laughed hysterically for a moment, then stopped suddenly, as if he had never laughed at all.

"I…I don't care. I want it to stop. Please."

"And what, pray, can halt the progress of cosmic machinations? You?"

"No, you. You can. That's why I…I just…I'll do anything."

The Duke smiled and nodded his head, "Yes, I think you would," he slowly got to his knees and pulled her closer to him. He lifted her shirt with his bony fingers. "Hmm? It seems there is something I want, after all."

"You mean…"

He nodded and nuzzled into her belly with his nose. "A life for a life. The scale is not tipped. What do you say?"

She wanted to cry, wanted to scream, wanted to descend on this man or beast or demon or God or whatever the Hell he was like a bird of prey and scratch his eyes out with her talons. But she knew this could never happen. All would be lost, obliterated in vain. Her talons would chip and break on the onyx eyes of an indifferent God, this God who gleefully wore the face of a man like a child wears a mask on Halloween night. She didn't think about it, didn't take a moment to consider. She would waiver if she did, chicken-out like the chicken-shit human being she was in the eyes of this serpent, so she closed her eyes tight and nodded. When she opened them she was laying in bed. It was morning. Cricket was screaming but she couldn't hear anything. It was all in slow motion. There was blood everywhere.

Bonnie awoke in Westwood Memorial Hospital. Cricket's old leather jacket hung on the back of a chair next to the bed. She guessed he was taking a piss or getting a cup of coffee. She couldn't remember how she got to the hospital. Her last memory was waking up in bed, sheets covered in blood. Then it all came crashing back. One moment she was feeling rested and hungry in a hospital bed, the next she was assaulted by memories of the dream and of the price she paid—under the water of a burst dam without even a single crack of warning. She bit her lip and forced her eyes shut, squeezing back the tears. She wasn't going to have Cricket walk in and find her in a state. She was fine; he'd be fine. Sure, maybe his arm would still be weird and his hair white, it was only a dream, after all. But deep in her viscera she knew it was all real. And if it was…She touched her belly, but it was under twelve layers of blankets. She dropped her hand to her side; she could deal with that later.

Cricket walked in five minutes later, a soggy sub sandwich hanging from his mouth. He practically spit the damned thing all over when he saw she was awake, the fool. He couldn't believe how good she looked. Radiant would've been the word to use. He sat next to her and held her hand and told her how lovely she looked. She scoffed and told him to stop being a kiss-ass. To her eyes, Cricket was looking much better himself. And while his arm and hand hadn't gone back to normal, it looked much better than before; and it hadn't gotten any worse or spread any further since she'd been asleep. She'd been in a coma since she was first rushed to the hospital two weeks before.

Cricket left the room to go find the doctor, so he could explain everything to her. A moment later, a tall, stern-looking man wearing circular gold-rimmed eyeglasses and a stethoscope entered the room with Cricket in tow. His name was Dr. Linneker and he was very glad to meet her and very very glad to see her awake. Sitting on the side of her bed, he told her that they weren't sure what had happened to her. They didn't couldn't find a lesion anywhere on or inside her body to account for all the blood she'd lost. They also couldn't tell her why she'd been in a coma for two weeks. The doctor joked that her condition was as odd and mysterious as Cricket's hand. She appeared to be in perfect health.

"And, best of all, I'm very happy to tell you that your baby is fine," Dr. Linneker said, his stone face cracking something like a smile.

"My baby?" She looked at the two men, not sure if she heard him correctly.

"That's right. I can book you in for a sonogram, if you'd like?" Dr. Linneker said.

Bonnie nodded excitedly and started to cry. The doctor excused himself and said he'd check in later.

"Did you know you were preggers?" Cricket asked Bonnie, after the doctor had left the room.

"Well, I thought I might be, but I wasn't sure. Hadn't gotten around to taking a test or anything. Thought it might have just been something else, like menopause?"

"Are you happy about this? Is it what you want?" he asked. She nodded almost immediately, more excited than she could have ever imagined. "Then so am I," he said before kissing her.

The next day, Cricket wheeled Bonnie down two floors to get a sonogram. She had put up quite a fight at the sight of the wheelchair, but he had insisted. Said it was doctor's orders, and also said it was finally his turn to push her around. What could she say to that?

The gel they rubbed on her belly was cold and incredibly gooey. It gave her goosebumps. The sonographer was large-set woman in her 50s who had very soft, delicate voice with a tinge of the Caribbean. Gently, she began to probe Bonnie's belly, which was a little larger than Bonnie remembered it being. She thought she must have put on some weight while she was a sleep. What had they been putting in the feeding tube? Cake frosting and bacon grease? Her stomach turned at the thought of that combo and wondered if it would affect the sonogram.

"And there's your baby," the sonographer said, smiling and pointing to a vague shape on a screen extending from the wall. "Looks like you're about three months along."

Three months? That couldn't be right. She'd only been a few weeks late before she went into the hospital.
"I...ugh...thought I was about a month along?" Bonnie said.

The soft-spoken nurse gave Bonnie a startled look, "A month? No no no, darling. That baby is much too big. I actually think it might be closer to four months..." The sonographer's face went still, her maternal smile gone forever.

"What is it?" Bonnie asked, sitting up in concern.

"Nothing, honey. Nothing. Just something looks a bit...odd..."

Bonnie grabbed the monitor and pulled it in front of her. "Oh, God," was all she could say when she saw the claws.

Sockhops & Seances

Seances

Curated by Nicole Petit

Preview
Nicole Petit's *Sockhops & Séances*
Featuring Jon Black's "Totmann's Curve"

PART I

September 10, 1955; Koenigsburg, Texas

It didn't start with the ghost. It started with Joe, Egg and me in my family's garage. Joe and I had just popped the hood on my '52 Pontiac Chieftain. Egg sat on the workbench, chewing gum as she read. Her legs, sticking out from under her plaid skirt, dangled over the edge as her feet kicked in time to the Chordettes pining for "Mr. Sandman" over the car radio.

Reaching into his shirt pocket, Joe pulled out a Lucky he'd filched from his old man. Then, striking a blue tip on the heel of his work boot, brought the blazing match to the cigarette. Dangling it from his lips, he peered under the hood. I had upgraded the factory straight-six engine to a more powerful straight-eight and wanted Joe to look it over.

"You finally got a real engine in this thing, Sam." Joe sounded less pleased than you would think. "But you've got to treat it right. A decent engine that's well maintained and properly adjusted will beat a good one that isn't. If you want to win more races, you need to fix the timing," he said, reaching into the engine bay.

"See where my finger is?" Johannes "Joe" Tegeler pronounced "finger" as if it rhymed with "stinger." Although it had been a century since immigrants from lands now split between East and West Germany had settled the Texas Hill County, some families still spoke German at home. The Tegelers were the only ones I knew personally. They'd moved to town from the deep hills to give their children a better shot in life. Joe spoke perfectly good English, but with an accent turning some sounds hard that should have been soft and other things soft that should have been hard.

Following Joe's finger, I loosening the bolt holding the distributor to the engine and started slowly turning the distributor. Every so often, I looked at Joe to see if we'd found the sweet spot.

"So, is everything set for new route?" Joe asked as we worked.

"Almost, I'm going to do one more drive through. Make sure I haven't missed anything dangerous. And Walter still needs to finalize everything with Old Man Daniels."

"I hate that we're working with that bastard."

"Walter? Or Daniels?"

Joe laughed. "Either. I meant Daniels, though."

"I don't like it either, but we need to keep Johnny Law away."

Everybody's got their thing. For Joe, me, and plenty of other kids, it was racing. Road racing. As you'd expect, a place called the Hill County has some pretty good driving. We used to race the backroads a couple of miles outside of town. Then, in June, two kids punched each other's tickets while racing there. The authorities came down on us like a gross of bricks. This being Texas, it didn't help that one of the dead kids had been the high school's star running back. Anyway, if we wanted to keep racing, we needed to do it someplace the law had trouble reaching.

"So, the new route, what's like?"

"You'll see," I teased Joe. "It follows the river most of the way. I made sure it was someplace that has good curves and a nice straightaway. And I packed in a few surprises. You'll like it. Oh, and it's a little longer than the last circuit, closer to six miles than five."

"So, say an average of seventy miles an hour, that's…"

"Five minutes, eight seconds," Egg volunteered before either of us did the math. We looked up at her. The top of Egg's glasses and her long black ponytail were barely visible above her comic book. *FREAKSHOW COMICS* it proclaimed in wild letters across the cover. Below, it pictured a rampaging doctor with wild eyes and green skin holding a butcher knife while chasing a busty nurse.

"Why does a smart girl like you read that crap, Egg?" Joe wanted to know.

"It's more interesting than anything around here," she replied. "And it beats reading *Silas Marner.*" Egg wasn't just smart, she was the kind of smart that prefers math and science to English and civics. "Egg," of course was short for "Egghead." *Marner,* her current assignment in Mrs. Stigler's English class, vexed Egg. "Besides, why do have to smoke that stuff?" Egg threw the question back with a disapproving look at Joe's cigarette.

He shrugged. "I guess it beats reading *Silas Marner*, too." We all laughed. I wasn't sure if Joe had any idea who or what *Silas Marner* was. But he knew a running gag when he heard one.

The door to the house opened and Mom came out, still wearing her apron. She carried a pitcher of milk, three glasses, and a plate of chocolate chip cookies on a tray.

I sprang from the Pontiac's side and intercepted Mom. Planting a kiss on her cheek, I took the tray. Yeah, I was happy to see her, and her cookies, but I was really running interference. I had to keep her attention while Joe crushed out his smoke and Egg stashed her comic.

"I thought you kids might want something to eat," mom said. "Your father has…gone to bed early…and I need to check on him." She turned her attention to Egg, "Eleanor, stay as late as you want. When you're ready, Sam will drive you home." That wasn't the kind of thing mothers said to a girl hanging out with two boys in 1955, so I should explain. Eleanor Eierkopf was my cousin; our moms were sisters.

I gave Mom another kiss on the cheek before she went back to the house. That was my way of keeping her spirits up, just the cookies were her way of doing the same for me. Once she was gone, Joe and I returned to the Pontiac and Egg resumed reading her comic book.

We all groan as the radio launched into Pat Boone's "Ain't That a Shame?"

"Don't they ever play anything cool?" Egg wanted to know. Joe and I had been to a record party where somebody played the Fats Domino's original, so we knew how big the difference was. Egg apparently had heard the original too…and shared our opinion.

"Not as long as Mr. Weidner's in charge," I answered. Sonny Weidner, station manager for KJZT-AM, wasn't a bad guy. He went to our church. Certainly he wasn't like some station managers I'd heard about who wouldn't allow records by black musicians. But he insisted on "family friendly" music. And that did not include Fats Domino's sultry drawl, a voice that made you want to dance *real* close with somebody.

Things were a little better on Friday and Saturday night. Friday, after the Junzt County Barn Dance, was Sheldon "Showboat" Smith's "Record Show." That late, even Mr. Weidner was willing to loosen the rules a bit. Showboat at least got into some real rock 'n' roll: Bill Halley, Chuck Berry, Elvis Presley. Still, anything smacking of s-e-x or, worse yet, hot-rodding was strictly verboten. Saturday night was a live set by *Jay Clay and His Cavaliers*.

That triggered a thought, "You want to hear some real rock 'n' roll, come out to first day of races at the new site," I told Egg.

"I know. Jay Clay and his Cavaliers are playing," she replied dreamily. "Did you know he's opening for Elvis when he comes through in October?"

We knew. "Jay's only told us about thousand times," Joe smiled.

After Joe and I worked on the engine a bit more, he walked across the street to his house and I drove Egg home in the Chieftain. Its engine purred. Joe's mechanical knack hadn't done me wrong yet.

"Sam, are you doing the right thing? After what happened to those boys in June?" Egg asked as we pulled up to her house.

I had been going over the same thing in my mind for months. I gave her the same rambling answer I kept giving myself. Nobody forced us to race, I told her. We did it because we wanted to. We knew the risks. Though every racer's reasons were different, we all came to the same conclusion: life with racing was more tolerable than life without. Yes, someone could get hurt, even killed, again. But we needed the thrill, the experience.

We sat in the Chieftain for a long time, both of us knowing that our homes, while occupied, were very lonely. Though cousins, our connection had become more like siblings. Once, both of us had been youngest children. But polio got Egg's sister. Six months later, a Soviet-made surface-to-air missile got my brother, Charlie, in the sky over some Korean town I couldn't even pronounce.

341

Egg's home life had been crap ever since. Her father hid in his work as a psychiatrist at Koenigsburg State Hospital and professor at Goethe College. Her mom pretty much just checked out of life. I got off a little easier. Mom was holding up okay. But Dad spent a lot of time sleeping. Even awake, he didn't do much else besides railing against the Commies. Egg and relied on each other because we didn't have anyone else.

Driving back to my house, I thought about the answer I'd given Egg. If Johnny Law just wanted to keep kids alive, did that make us the Bad Guys? Maybe. But even if we were Bad Guys, we weren't *bad guys*. Not all of us, anyway.

Saturday afternoon, an exodus began from Koenigsburg. A hundred cars. Maybe two hundred. It was a miracle the police didn't catch us after all. Traveling Highway 16 toward Kerrville, the drive put me in a good mood. Green farms lined the road for miles outside town, many farmhouses still with their original gingerbread trim. All of them had storm cellars and smokehouses. The approaching harvest was culling time for livestock as well as crops so many of the smokehouses were already busy. Smoke venting form their roofs sent aromas of beef and pork drifting through our rolled-down windows.

Beyond the farms, the land went wild. Thick stands of oak, cedar, and mesquite covered rolling hills. An occasional cluster of maples sheltered in shaded valleys. Most leaves remained emerald green. A few, mostly maples, had already changed; scattering reds, yellows, oranges, and purples. Beneath the trees, autumn wildflowers like sunflowers, asters, and goldeneyes carpeted the ground.

Along Highway 16 the trees formed a canopy over the road. It had always seemed a little magical to me. Not that I would ever have told anyone that. I cranked up the radio. KJZT was getting off some pretty good ones. Even Bill Haley's "Rock Around the Clock." I wondered if Mr. Weidner was out of the station.

As I drove, I reviewed the race route in my mind. Trying to remember every detail. Anything that could give me an edge.

Joe cruised behind us. His black 1952 Hudson Wasp had a thick white stripe running from grill to trunk. He called it

Stinkkatze, Hill County German for skunk. Joe must have realized how focused I was. Occasionally, he'd bumper-chase me to see how close he could get before I noticed. A couple times he got near enough he could have bumper-checked me. Though, between friends, that was bad form.

"That fool's gonna kill us all," I said to Egg, chuckling after Joe had gotten close again.

Egg either didn't hear or didn't care, absorbed in a comic book proclaiming *True Tales of Terror: New Orleans Issue*. Underneath the image of a wild gris-gris woman sending the living dead to do her bidding, the comic trumpeted its contents: *The Axeman Cometh—Marie LeVeau: Voo-Doo Queen—The Deaths of Gabriel Gibbs*.

If I thought it was weird, I could only imagine how Uncle Albert, the respected psychiatrist, and Aunt Eileen, star of the Sunday Social Circle, must feel.

"I can't believe your parents are okay with you reading those things."

She made a gagging noise. "Oh, God, they're not. If they found out, I'd be grounded until college. I hide them in my hope chest, wrapped up in a giant linen tablecloth Grandma Eierkopf left to me. And, Sam, if you want to live to eighteen, they better not find out from you."

We reached Switchbox. Most folks called it a "community," too small for a town but too large just to be a collection of houses. Late last century, its founders had expected the railroad to grow this part of the county. But people never came. Finally, the train stopped coming too. Today, Switchbox was just a couple hundred people, a handful of sad stores, a café, and a consolidated school. And the Yellow Rose Dancehall, of course.

Turning onto Jericho Road just before the dancehall, we crossed the tracks and drove a quarter mile before coming to a field buzzing with activity. Once, it held Switchbox's first, and only, church. In April of '46, a twister carried the entire thing away. Taking the event as a kind of divine editorial, locals never rebuilt it. But they still called the space Church Lot. It offered a perfect place to start and end our races.

Fifty or sixty cars already packed the lot. Some were models still displayed in dealership showrooms. Others were jalopies built closer to the Great War than Korea, and held together by spit and bailing wire.

Noticeable both for its tasteless extravagance and the wide berth other cars gave it was a white 1947 Mercury Town Sedan convertible. A chain of painted yellow roses ran from fender to fender along both sides. With a little work, it would have made a savage hot rod. But its owner had other passions. And other concerns. The Mercury was the calling card of the Yellow Rose's owner. And a relic of better days.

The crowd was young. High schoolers, mostly. Some older kids, usually somebody's brother or cousin. A few 20-somethings, racers themselves, curious about what the young folks were up to. With his thinning white hair, wrinkles, and liver spots, Old Man Daniels was a conspicuous exception. And yet, the man who drove that fancy Mercury strutted through the crowd, not doubt eager for his take.

The dancehall business wasn't so good these days. Rumor said the old man had taken to bringing in hoochie-coochie dancers and blue comics twice a month. If so, even that hadn't stopped his ledgers from bleeding red ink. When Walter had offered him $50 a week for allowing us to race in his patch, with the unspoken understanding he'd keep Johnny Law away, Old Man Daniels had accepted—after twisting Walter's arm up to $100 a week. Of course, that meant passing that hat. Anyone coming to church lot on race day, driver or fan, was expected to pony up a buck.

Someone had hauled a flatbed trailer to Church Lot's far side and hooked up a genny for electricity. Jay Clay and His Cavaliers used the flatbed for their stage. Jay Clay wasn't Junzt County's only rocker. But no one doubted he was its best. Kids flocked to the trailer to hear him play. Even the serious gearheads had to stop and watch admiringly as Jay put his Gretsch Duo Jet (not coincidently, the guitar favored by Chuck Berry and Bo Diddley) through its paces on "Hot Rod Lincoln."

To each side, the Cavaliers added their power to his. Loretta Dean, scarlet hair piled high into victory rolls, switched between backup vocals and tenor sax. C.C. Smith, a natural hothead, played standing bass while Luke Vogel provided a steady hand on drums.

From "Hot Rod Lincoln" the band moved into Roy Brown's "Cadillac Baby." Afterward, they took a quick break.

"Should we say hi?" I asked Egg.

Though Egg looked eager, Joe replied, "Nah, let's check out the competition." We wandered across Jericho Rode to where the other racers had their cars displayed.

Passing *Stinkkatze*, I wondered if my neighbor was going to race her today. Most of us had gotten into mechanics to make us better racer. Joe raced because it meant he'd always have some gearhead puzzle to work on. Even when he bothered to bring his Hudson Wasp out, half the time she just sat there. He was more interesting in showing off his mods, and seeing what others had done, than racing.

A few cars ahead, leaning against his glossy black 1952 Willys Aero, Jan Myska gave a casual nod in our direction as his lips curled into a half-smile around one of his fancy imported cigarettes. Jan looked like a coal-haired James Dean. That, combined with jazz records and ability to recite Beat poetry, ensured his popularity with a certain class of girl.

Several hovered around as we approached, including Denise Tarrant, I noticed with dismay. They scattered as Jan greeted Joe and me with low-fives before taking Egg's hand with a dramatic bow. My cousin rolled her eyes. Egg was not susceptible to Jan's charms.

"Denise Tarrant? Is that wise?" I asked him. Denise was fancy girl from Dallas who had a thing for bad boys. "Jockey doesn't like you as it is."

"Nobody does," Jan replied, "except you freaks."

"Maybe. But most people don't carry around a switchblade and pistol."

"It'll be fine. We're just going riding later on. Jockey won't find out about it. Besides, Denise is tired of his crap. She's going to dump him soon."

I sighed. Jan, of all people, should recognize bullshit when he heard it. "Just don't do anything dumb," I cautioned him.

"I dig, thanks."

Our group of four grew to five. With total silence, Denny Peta had joined us. He could disappear the same way, too. I still didn't know Denny's whole story. One day this kid from the

Tasiwu Reservation started showing up at our races. At first, he didn't talk to anyone and just stood around muttering to himself in Comanche. Neatly dressed, short hair parted down the middle, he looked like a major square.

One day, Denny stuck a potato up the tailpipe of a hot rodded Dodge B1 pickup belonging to Patten Randal, the biggest loudmouth blockhead in our set. He got his butt whipped by Patten for his trouble. But it made Joe and I take a shine to him. In his strange way, he'd taken to us, too. Denny could happily hang with us all day and only say a dozen words the whole time.

Before long, we walked past that very same Dodge truck. With its two-tone black and blue paint job, Patten called it "The Bruiser." We had another name for it. He and his gang of rednecks were busy roughing up some kid I didn't recognize. Joe looked at me as if asking *Should we get involved?* When I shrugged my shoulders, we moved on.

Beyond was another vehicle I was anxious to avoid. A two-tone red Oldsmobile 88 owned by the Jack "Jockey" Groce I had just cautioned Jan about.

Next in line was Denny's Model A roadster convertible. After hanging with us for months, never racing, never owning a car so far as we knew, he just showed up with it one day. The thing was a quarter-century old and had run like it. He lost his first race blowing his radiator cap, steam blasting from the overheated Ford as his opponent left him in the dust. Slowly, with some help from Joe, it got better. A lot better. Denny's shyness didn't apply to his wheels. The A's chassis was bumblebee yellow with red flames at the front. A foxtail hung from the antenna. The A had no radio, Denny stripped his rod for weight more completely than any other racer. Hell, he got rid of his door handles. But he liked how the antenna and foxtail looked.

Leaving the Model A behind, my eyes briefly locked with Marta Bauer's. Stretching her back, she wiped greasy hands onto denim coveralls as she took a break from working on her Ford Coup. Though her short hair had been out of style since flapper days, it showed off her strong features and green eyes so intense they seemed on fire.

Marta was friendly with our group, but not friends. She was a little too aloof and Look-Out-For-Number-One, leaving me uncertain where we stood. I didn't trust Marta to have my back. But I was pretty sure she wouldn't stuck a knife in it, either.

At the line's front was a Chevy Tri-Five. Today, of all the vehicles here, I had special eyes for it. And for its driver, Walter Horner. Always Walter, never Walt. Something it was healthy to remember. The oldest driver in our set, he'd come back from Korea. But I think part of him was still over there, if you get my drift.

Within the hour, I'd be racing him.

The drivers I've mentioned, myself included, weren't the only racers here. Not by a long shot. But we were the ones that mattered: the ones who always won. Unless we raced each other. We called the other drivers "also-rans." Not to their faces. Not usually.

Seeing a '54 Coronet hardtop cruising the other direction down Jericho Road, I tensed. Pulling even with Church Lot, Stevie Schreiber exited and gave me a "thumbs up." Stevie had been the best racer in our set. Still was, technically. But one night he and his girl got careless up on Knutschen Point. Walking to the Coronet's other side, Stevie picked up his son and piggybacked him into the crowd. Though Stevie had sworn off racing, he still helped out by driving the circuit before every race day, ensuring it was free of debris or other obstacles.

The time had come for a strange custom of the kind that probably made sense only to racers and other small, tight-knit communities devoted to something outsiders wouldn't or couldn't understand.

We called it the Social Lap, "The Social" for short, "The Circle," or, my favorite, "The Procession." One by one, the racers took to their cars. As the one who had laid out the rout, I led the Procession. Slowly, with no more than a car length between us, we cruised the whole course. The cars were filled to capacity, and sometimes beyond, with drivers, their buddies, their steadies, and sometimes just folks who happened to be standing around.

"Will you look at that?" Joe asked. A few cars behind us, Patten Randal had crammed dozen people in the Dodge's bed, half a dozen in the cab, and a half-dozen more hanging off the outside. They fell off as Patten sounded his thunder-like mufflers and dual horn, a look of idiotic joy on his face.

"Add them all together and you've probably got half a brain and a full set of teeth," Egg commented.

"Wonder if they know they're riding in a coffin?" I asked. We called Patten's truck "The Coffin" when he wasn't around. He'd loaded it with everything for speed and power and let the rest go to hell. We joked about Denny's car, but his reflexes gave him some cushion. The Dodge's driver couldn't say the same.

Putting Patten's deathtrap out of my mind, I again noticed what a perfect day it was. And felt very pleased with the excellent job I had done in choosing our racing route.

Why the Procession? It built solidarity between racers. Brought together by our shared obsession, we were competitors. But we were family, too. The Procession had a practical aspect as well. It ensured everybody knew that everybody else had driven the course. So no could say the race wasn't fair because they didn't know the route. Yeah, it sounds juvenile. But it happened sometimes.

But I think the practical aspects took a backseat, pardon the pun. The Procession was a ritual. Even more than we realized.

It took an hour for the cars to make a full circuit and return to Church Lot. And another quarter hour for the cars to disgorge their passengers, get everybody settled, and ready to race. Normally, racers got paired-up by a draw from the hat. But I had laid out the new route. Walter handled the other aspects of getting the races going again after what happened over the summer. Everyone felt it made sense for the very first race to be between us. In hindsight, that, too, feels like a kind of ritual.

I cruised the Pontiac Chieftain up to a checkered line somebody had spray-painted across Jericho Road. Walter's Tri-Five was already there. Waiting.

Nobody could say having Walter around hadn't been useful. Sometimes you needed an adult to deal with things. Even if "adult" meant "about 20." Still, it felt like cheating. He had adult money to spend on a car. Hell, he had GI money to spend. And it showed. His silver Chevy, which he called "Silver Streak," was the only current model year vehicle out there.

I wondered if, on some level, Walter knew it wasn't fair. The Chevy's mods weren't as aggressive as most of our rods. He'd shed some weight: lost the chrome, switched out the factory bumpers for lighter versions, got rid of the fender skirts, and changed the wheels. He had also louvered the hood, cutting rows of small vents into the metal that increased airflow to the 265 V8 engine, making it work better and less likely to overheating. If you're not a gearhead, that probably sounds like a lot. Trust me, it's not. On the other hand, a factory spec Tri-Five made a better rod than some of the also-ran's custom jobs.

Alma Hobson carried her green flag ahead of both cars. To have a chance against the Chevy, I had to get out in front of it in the straightway. For that, I need to be first to the accelerator. That was risky, jumping the flag meant disqualification. Fortunately, Alma had a tell. She always shut her eyes before waving the flag. I knew it. Hopefully, Walter didn't.

The instant her peepers closed, I dropped my foot onto the pedal.

It worked. As the Chieftain roared off, Walter was still registered the moving flag.

Even with my engine close to maxing out RPMs, it amazed me how smoothly it ran. Joe knew his stuff. I pulled a few lengths ahead of Walter. Aware the Tri-Five would soon eat into my lead, I nudged the Pontiac a foot or two toward the road's center; a gray area in terms of racing etiquette. Splitting lanes, driving down the middle of the road so your opponent couldn't catch or pass you was a no-no. But nudging your vehicle over a little, leaving enough room but testing the other guy's nerves, was totally acceptable.

Go figure, the guy who saw ground combat in Korea didn't scare easily. That Chevy blew past me like a missile. It struck me that the half-mile straightaway beginning and ending the circuit would make a damn fine drag strip.

Just before the first hill rose to left of Jericho Road, we came to a crossroad. Two-and-a-half lengths ahead of me, Walter skidded into a right turn, screeching onto Alton Bridge. Losing less momentum than Walter had, I turned onto the bridge barely a length behind. A solid chunk of WPA metal that would probably survive Doomsday, Alton Bridge could easy accommodate two cars side by side. I attempted to pass as we shot over the Klagewasser's dark gray-purple waters. Against the bridge's thick wooden ties, my tires made a furious tenor buzzing that continued until the far side…with me half a length behind.

Walter took a hard left onto Fischfalle Road and I followed. Looking like a tiny tank, an armadillo lazily crossing the road had to skitter the last few feet reach the underbrush's safety. A winding road, thickly wooded to the right and sloping down to the river on the left, Fischfalle Road could have been made to give my Pontiac the edge. A quarter mile along, I overtook the Chevy with a triumphant yell.

I pushed hard to expand my lead. The next part of the race was a wild card. I didn't know how it would work out. But, when laying down the route, it was too unusual an option to pass up.